THE RED WIND HOWLS

THE RED WIND HOWLS

A Novel

TSERING DÖNDRUP

Translated by Christopher Peacock

Columbia University Press

New York

Columbia University Press wishes to express its appreciation for assistance given by the Pushkin Fund in the publication of this book.

Columbia University Press
Publishers Since 1893
New York   Chichester, West Sussex

Translation copyright © 2025 Columbia University Press
All rights reserved

Library of Congress Cataloging-in-Publication Data
Names: Tshe-ring-don-grub, 1961– author. | Peacock, Christopher, 1986– translator.
Title: The red wind howls : a novel / Tsering Döndrup ; translated by Christopher Peacock.
Other titles: Rluṅ dmar 'ur 'ur. English
Description: New York : Columbia University Press, 2025.
Identifiers: LCCN 2024052308 (print) | LCCN 2024052309 (ebook) | ISBN 9780231213721 (hardback) | ISBN 9780231213738 (trade paperback) | ISBN 9780231559997 (ebook)
Subjects: LCSH: Amdo (China : Region)—History—20th century—Fiction. | China—History—Cultural Revolution, 1966–1976—Fiction. | Internment camps—China—Tibet Autonomous Region—Fiction. | Forced labor—China—Tibet Autonomous Region—Fiction. | LCGFT: Historical fiction. | Novels.
Classification: LCC PL3748.T776 R5813 2025 (print) | LCC PL3748.T776 (ebook) | DDC 895/.43—dc23/eng/20241231

Cover design: Chang Jae Lee
Cover image: *The Flowers of Dazhai Bloom on the Plateau*. Ca. 1972. Designer unknown. Publisher: Shanghai renmin meishu chubanshe. 53 × 77 cm. Collection of Stefan R. Landsberger, Amsterdam.

GPSR Authorized Representative: Easy Access System Europe, Mustamäe tee 50, 10621 Tallinn, Estonia, gpsr.requests@easproject.com

CONTENTS

Introduction: The Unspeakable History of
The Red Wind Howls   vii

THE RED WIND HOWLS

Part 1   3

Part 2   141

INTRODUCTION

THE UNSPEAKABLE HISTORY OF
THE RED WIND HOWLS

CHRISTOPHER PEACOCK

THE RED WIND HOWLS, the third novel by the Tibetan author Tsering Döndrup, is a work of incredible audacity. Spanning some thirty years and all of Mao's rule, it covers the early encounters between Tibetans and Communist China, the Great Leap Forward, the Cultural Revolution, and events more taboo than any of these: the Amdo uprising of 1958 and the brutal suppression that followed. Within China, it is a perilous undertaking to portray this history, the contents ranging from sensitive to entirely off-limits, but the novel translated here faces it all squarely, and from the rarest of perspectives. Written in the Tibetan language by an ethnically Mongolian author, it shows how this history unfolded in the unique context of the Tibetan plateau. If it is politically dangerous for a member of the Han majority to tackle the campaigns of Mao's China, then for Tibetans it is almost unthinkable. Considering that China's ethnic minorities face the strictest scrutiny and harshest repression in

INTRODUCTION

the country—a regime of control currently most visible in the Xinjiang "reeducation camps"—we begin to get a sense of just what an important work *The Red Wind Howls* is, and just what extraordinary courage it took to write it.

While hardly any aspect of Tibetan history could be described as household knowledge in the West, the events of 1959 are more well known than most. After the Lhasa uprising of that year, the Dalai Lama fled into exile in India, finally ending a decade of uneasy coexistence between the Chinese Communist Party (CCP) and the traditional Tibetan ruling elite. The area that had been under the Dalai Lama's jurisdiction, sometimes called Ü-Tsang or Central Tibet in the West and roughly equivalent to the present-day Tibet Autonomous Region (TAR), had been subject to some unique conditions. After the establishment of the People's Republic of China (PRC) in 1949, the CCP declared its intention to integrate Tibet, and military advances began the following year. The overwhelming superiority of the People's Liberation Army (PLA) was obvious, particularly after the one-sided Battle of Chamdo, and the government in Lhasa entered into negotiations, resulting in what the Chinese government still terms the "peaceful liberation" of Tibet. The two sides signed a treaty known as the Seventeen-Point Agreement. This guaranteed the protection of monasteries, religious beliefs, and the existing political system and promised that reforms would be carried out by the Tibetan government only when the Tibetan people demanded them.

However, Central Tibet is but one of the areas inhabited by Tibetans. Amdo and Kham, two other large and broadly

INTRODUCTION

defined regions that constitute what is sometimes called Eastern Tibet, were divided up among the provinces of Sichuan, Yunnan, Qinghai, Gansu, and later the TAR (established in 1965). Amdo is a territory roughly the size of France that overlaps largely with present-day Qinghai Province, with some parts falling into Gansu and Sichuan. A complex multiethnic and multilingual region, it is inhabited not only by Tibetans but also by Han Chinese, Hui Muslims, the Turkic Salar people, Mongols, and numerous others. There are plenty of farming communities in Amdo, but for many of the Tibetans and Mongols there it is a land of high altitudes, vast grasslands, and a pastoral way of life. Before the rise of the People's Republic, two broad power structures reigned over its pastoral communities: clans and monasteries, the former led by hereditary chieftains, the latter often by a *trülku* (a reincarnate lama). In the 1950s, when Amdo and Kham were absorbed into the PRC, no formal protections were accorded to their traditional systems, as in the TAR with the Seventeen-Point Agreement. Historians have often pointed to this as the cause of the subsequent unrest, particularly in Kham, where armed clashes with the PLA broke out in 1955, prompting thousands of Khampa refugees to flee to Lhasa, which in turn stoked the Lhasa rebellion in 1959.

What happened in Amdo in 1958 is much less well known—in the West, and within China, where public discussion of this history is essentially impossible. For many in Amdo, 1958 (not 1949) was the year that Communist China truly announced itself. Tibetans rose in armed revolt against their integration into the Chinese state, fearing the imminent destruction of their traditional ways of life under Mao's radical policies. The

▪ ix ▪

INTRODUCTION

rebellion and its merciless suppression remain one of the bloodiest and least known chapters of early PRC history. Few inside China have dared broach the subject, including in fiction, where it has only ever been referenced fleetingly. The renowned writer Döndrup Gyel, for example, touched upon 1958 in his short story "Tsultrim Jyamtso," but the allusions remain necessarily brief and oblique, the author seemingly relying on the shared knowledge of his audience to fill in the blanks. The prominent poet and political commentator Woeser, a rare outspoken critic of the Chinese government, offers this forthright assessment:

> Any discussion of history or the contemporary situation [in Amdo] must begin with the year 1958. It was in 1958 that the Chinese army and government perpetrated a human tragedy that affected nearly every family across Tibet, but especially here. This history is engraved deeply in the hearts and minds of the Tibetan people, so that some refer to the Cultural Revolution simply as "1958," despite the fact that the Cultural Revolution did not begin until 1966. The year 1958 has become shorthand for tragedy—a symbolic gathering point for all of the misfortunes that befell us after "liberation."

In a recent study of the events leading to the 1958 uprising, Benno Weiner challenges the conventional historical narrative of suspended reforms in the TAR versus revolutionary change in Amdo and Kham. He shows that despite the absence of a formal treaty, the CCP spent much of the 1950s trying to integrate Amdo's traditional lay and religious leadership into the new regime under the policy of a "patriotic United Front," a

INTRODUCTION

policy the Party was partly forced into due to its total lack of prior presence in the region. The first decade of PRC rule in Amdo was thus characterized by a tense balance between powers new and old; the unprecedented socioeconomic transformations taking place elsewhere in China came in fits and starts in Qinghai, with significant opposition to any initial attempts at reform. But as Mao Zedong's vision for an immediate transition to socialism took hold over the Party, what Weiner calls the "subimperial compact" between the CCP and the traditional power holders of Amdo gave way to a "revolutionary impatience," and soon Tibetans rose in mass revolt against the impending overhaul of their society. Weiner sees the 1958 rebellion not as an explosion of violence shattering a delicate peace but as a crescendo, the most intense and widespread act of opposition in almost ten years of resistance to CCP rule.

When rebellion broke out in the spring and summer of 1958, the Tibetan nomads, despite their familiarity with the terrain, never stood much chance. The conflict pitted a loose union of poorly outfitted, disparate, and disorganized clans against the might of the PLA—numerically superior, battle hardened, and heavily armed. After the resistance was quelled, ruthless retaliation began, with those who survived the initial military crackdown swiftly rounded up and taken away to labor camps. There, many more met their end through starvation, disease, suicide, or forced labor. The fact that so few survived or made it into exile to tell their stories is part of the reason this history has remained largely unknown beyond Amdo, but the existing eyewitness accounts surveyed by Weiner tell of "the widespread use of torture, extrajudicial killings, the emptying of population

■ xi ■

INTRODUCTION

centers, mass incarceration, and strategy-induced famine and epidemics."

For all its horror, 1958 was just the beginning. In an instant, Amdo's traditional clan and religious hierarchies had been wiped out and the region was launched headlong into the Great Leap Forward. Mao's plan to realize communism overnight entailed rapid collectivization and outlandish experiments with rural industrialization. The utter failure of these policies, exacerbated by natural disasters, resulted in the greatest famine in history, with estimates of the death toll in the tens of millions. For many Amdo Tibetans, incarceration and famine was thus their first experience of being fully governed by China. Then, in 1966, the Cultural Revolution began. For Tibetan regions, this meant intense campaigns against former monks, lamas, "herdlords," and other perceived enemies of society, as well as widespread destruction of the already emptied monasteries and their artifacts. This was yet another chapter of prolonged suffering that would last right through until Mao's death in 1976.

The statistics for the rebellion are astounding. Absolute reliability is hard to come by when dealing with suppressed history, but the figures available indicate the magnitude of what happened in Amdo. Chinese sources consulted by Weiner report that in Zeku County, the focus of his study, nearly a quarter of the population took part in what the Party labeled "counterrevolutionary armed rebellion." By the end of June 1958, 22,000 people across 24 counties of Qinghai had risen in open revolt. By the end of the year, 731 out of 859 Tibetan Buddhist monasteries in Qinghai had been closed, and nearly half the monks and nuns had been forcibly disrobed and returned to lay life.

INTRODUCTION

One report states that 121,752 "enemies" were killed in the pacification, and another that 52,000 people were reportedly arrested in Qinghai during 1958 and 1959. Weiner estimates that more than 10 percent of the province's Tibetan population could have been arrested or killed during and after the rebellion, which tallies with the estimates in the Panchen Lama's landmark report on the persecution Amdo Tibetans had endured since 1958 (his 1962 "70,000 Character Petition" was described by Mao as a "poisoned arrow aimed at the heart of the Party," and it earned him over a decade in prison). Popular memory in Amdo tells of numerous communities where only women, children, and the elderly were left alive, all the men having been either killed or arrested. Perhaps most shocking of all is that these figures are unrelated to those for the Great Leap Forward, which followed right on the heels of the rebellion, and during which almost 10 percent of the province's population is estimated to have perished.

But statistics alone cannot tell a story, and that is where Tsering Döndrup and his remarkable novel come in. Born in 1961 in Sogpo—an area of historically "Tibetanized" Mongols, now officially Malho (or Henan, in Chinese) Mongolian Autonomous County, Qinghai Province—he grew up in a world defined by 1958 and its aftermath. The Cultural Revolution had a direct impact on him, since he was only able to begin his schooling at the age of thirteen. Education was disrupted throughout China during that time, but Tibetans had yet more hurdles to overcome: their language itself was deemed a tool of "feudal" practices and religious "superstitions," meaning they were effectively prohibited from studying their mother tongue.

■ xiii ■

INTRODUCTION

Only the determination and quiet bravery of some teachers allowed clandestine Tibetan language instruction to carry on. When the Cultural Revolution came to an end, there was a renaissance of Tibetan culture both traditional and modern, which included the birth of novels, short fiction, and other new forms of literature. Tsering Döndrup was quick to contribute to this growing trend, publishing his first story in 1983. He has written nonstop ever since and is now established as one of the foremost authors of literary fiction in the Tibetan language. To date, he has published three collections of short stories, two collections of novellas, and four full-length novels. His fiction has been translated into several languages, and prior to the release of this novel, he had received numerous domestic literary prizes. *The Red Wind Howls*, arguably his landmark work, is also something of an exception, since it is the only one that remains unavailable to Tibetan readers in China.

Tsering Döndrup grew up tending his family's herds and listening to the tales told by his blacksmith father, an early exposure to the art of oral storytelling that would resonate throughout his writing. In *The Red Wind Howls*, this tradition plays a particularly important role. In addition to archival sources (sometimes referenced directly by the narrator), the content of the novel is based on countless oral narratives passed down from his community, which the author meticulously gathered and distilled into fictional form. It is not a historical account, but he is keen to stress the truth of the events relayed within. As he told the literary scholar Lama Jabb, "there are no lies in it, and I was prepared to tell them (the Chinese authorities) that if they questioned the historical veracity of my novel." Indeed,

■ xiv ■

INTRODUCTION

numerous details in the book corroborate and illuminate the historical record; thus, on one level it functions as testimony, a vital documentation of suppressed atrocities.

Few texts are comparable in this regard. In Chinese, a handful of sources have tackled the sensitive events of the late 1950s and early 1960s through interviews, for example *Farewell to Jiabiangou*, Yang Xianhui's semifictionalized account of a labor camp in Gansu, and *Tombstone*, Yang Jisheng's oral history of the Great Famine. Yan Lianke's *The Four Books* is one of the few novels to deal with the Great Leap Forward, a project the author described as "an attempt to write recklessly and without any concern for the prospect of getting published" (indeed, it never was published in the PRC). But of course, none of these is concerned with this history from a Tibetan perspective, or with the 1958 rebellion. In Tibetan, the closest comparable works to *The Red Wind Howls* are Naktsang Nulo's *My Tibetan Childhood* (likewise banned for its frank discussions of 1958), *Rinzang's Serial Notes*, and to some extent texts published in exile such as Tubten Khétsun's *Memories of Life in Lhasa Under Chinese Rule* and Pema Bhum's *Six Stars with a Crooked Neck*. All, however, are distinct from Tsering Döndrup's work in that they are memoirs. *The Red Wind Howls* not only recounts repressed historical events but also is an inventive work of literature—"rich, densely packed, and finely crafted," as Lama Jabb describes it, noteworthy for its "seamless fusion of literary and vernacular language, verisimilitude, dark humor, and meticulous research based on oral and written material."

One of the most striking features of the novel is its narrative structure. Unlike Tsering Döndrup's short fiction, which is

■ xv ■

INTRODUCTION

often divided into brief numbered chapters, this work has only a part 1, set largely in the punitive labor camps, and a part 2, set outside the camps during the same period. Together, they form a full picture of the tumultuous history of Tibet's forced incorporation into the PRC. Each section comprises a lengthy, unbroken flow of narrative—and flow it does, despite a fragmented chronology in which events are presented out of order, with sudden flashbacks and flashforwards that interweave the characters' contrasting fates before, during, and after the years of Mao's rule. There is minimal signposting for these time jumps. Even the year 1958, with its immediate and traumatic associations, is never mentioned; the events of the uprising are referred to simply as the "Harrowing Day" (for his fellow Amdo Tibetans, no further explanation is necessary). The novel begins at the end, with the protagonist, Alak Drong, restored to his position of authority in the early 1980s, before jumping back to his childhood, with the young reincarnate lama being enthroned at his monastery. This sets the tone for a narrative that moves ceaselessly back and forth among the events of the following years: beginning, in chronological order, with the arrival of the Chinese in the 1950s, the 1958 uprising, the labor camps, the famine of the Great Leap, the Cultural Revolution, and the limited revival of Tibetan traditions in the 1980s.

Why such a stark narrative choice? Lama Jabb points out that this style mimics the oral accounts on which the novel is based, a fealty to its sources that simultaneously lends it an avant-garde literary quality. At the same time, this fragmentary, nonsequential recollection is prevalent in trauma narratives in particular, in which harrowing events cannot be reconstituted in a

• xvi •

INTRODUCTION

simple linear fashion. *The Gate*, François Bizot's memoir of his experiences in Cambodia under the Khmer Rouge, begins in a similarly disorienting fashion, as the author jumps into the heat of events before trying to reorder his narrative: "I will come back to these moments later on . . . what is more urgent is to pin down where my thoughts lie; they leap about, pressed upon from all sides." *The Red Wind Howls* reads at times like a witness trying to relate something of the utmost importance but unsure where to begin. It pours out all at once but also comes in snatches. Unexpected associations lead in and out of memories that individually are lucid, but collectively constitute a blur of unpredictable political campaigns. The story is not only untellable for political reasons: the author also had to navigate the narration of unimaginable trauma.

Tsering Döndrup presents this harrowing subject matter in his own inimitable style, which has always been defined by black humor and sharp satire. Anyone who has encountered the author's work will find other familiar elements here, particularly the setting (the recurring fictional county of Tsezhung) and the unpalatable protagonist of part 1. Alak Drong, the reincarnate lama, is a constant presence in Tsering Döndrup's fictional world. "Alak" is an honorific title, and "Drong" the Tibetan word for a wild yak: a ludicrously unlikely name designed to insulate the author from potential accusations that he was lampooning a real-life lama (imagine something like a "Bishop Goat"). When reading Tsering Döndrup's fiction, it is not hard to see why: Alak Drong's many cameos paint a composite picture of a shallow, callous materialist, someone happy to abuse his revered status for personal gain, and in the

• xvii •

INTRODUCTION

The Red Wind Howls he plumbs yet worse depths. However, there are two major differences here: Alak Drong is now the main character, and we see his entire backstory, from childhood to his post-1980s restoration to religious authority (the guise in which he usually appears in the author's fiction). As Françoise Robin, the novel's French translator, has observed, it would have been easy for Tsering Döndrup to concoct a sympathetic protagonist, an innocent victim of the horrors perpetrated by the Chinese state, but the author "does not like the obvious or easy way out, in life or in literature." The choice to place his most infamous villain at the center of the historical stage is bold and brilliant: it denies readers the possibility of empathizing with the protagonist on the basis of his personal integrity (or even basic likeability), challenging them instead to weigh the morality of the events, not the man. *The Red Wind Howls* also allows us to see this otherwise odious character in a more forgiving light. He may be no less distasteful, but after learning all that he has been through, readers may find his later moral indifference more understandable.

As the character of Alak Drong suggests, Tsering Döndrup is known for his comical skewering of the Tibetan Buddhist establishment. Again, such predilections might have been put aside for the sake of this novel, but instead they are present in full force. The story takes us up to the post-Mao landscape of the early 1980s, a time that "saw an increase in people's quality of life, an increase in their freedom, and, at the same time, an increase in their avarice." Part 2 opens with the reconstruction of Tsezhung Monastery and the return of the faithful, and introduces the monk Lozang Tsültrim, Alak Drong's

• xviii •

INTRODUCTION

right-hand man. Both are now "enjoying the highest living standards in all of Tsezhung." It soon becomes apparent that this is not necessarily a cause for celebration when Lozang Tsültrim is revealed as one of the novel's primary antagonists. A petty, self-serving man, Lozang Tsültrim takes advantage of political campaigns to settle old scores, then returns to the monkhood when it suits him. Alak Drong's transgressions in prison pale in comparison to Lozang Tsültrim's actions on the outside, and the restoration of both men to positions of authority in the wake of the Cultural Revolution is hardly a flattering comment on Tibetan Buddhist institutions and their priorities.

In a sense, however, these critiques can be read as another form of resistance to the Party's domination of historical discourse in Tibet. The Chinese state continues to demonize pre-"liberation" Tibet as a feudalistic hell on earth run by slave-owning aristocrats and tyrannical lamas, drawing a clear line between the utopian "New Society" and the pre-Communist "Old Society" in a manner long since abandoned in most of the rest of China. Since the 1980s and the beginnings of what is considered modern Tibetan literature, writers critical of Buddhism have risked courting accusations that they have internalized such propaganda narratives. Tsering Döndrup's devastating portrayal of CCP policy in Tibet clearly absolves him of such charges. In fact, the novel frequently juxtaposes tired state propaganda about the "Old Society" with tangible examples of how much worse off Tibetans are under the new one. But at the same time, his view of traditional Tibet is far from rose-tinted, and its religious hierarchies are not spared his satire. In this way, *The Red Wind Howls* not only challenges the state's

■ xix ■

INTRODUCTION

discursive dominance over suppressed tragedies but also reclaims the right of Tibetans to critique their *own* society and culture, which has been usurped by the Party's attacks on religion and its self-appointment as sole arbiter of Tibetan history.

This is not to suggest that monks and lamas are simply targets of ridicule or criticism in the novel—on the contrary, some prove to be its most commendable characters. Part 2 tells the story of Lozang Gyatso and Tashi Lhamo, the former a monk trying to adhere to his faith, the latter a layperson who finds hers in the most unlikely circumstances. Lozang Gyatso is Lozang Tsültrim's cousin, and both were disciples of their uncle, the wise and noble lama Dranak Geshé, a rare source of steadfast morality in the story. Lozang Gyatso is almost a model Buddhist: he sticks doggedly to his principles through all the years of upheaval, refusing to kill his commune-allotted sheep when it would keep him from starvation and displaying boundless compassion even for his enemies. He is aided by a mysterious benefactor who one night tosses a copy of the *Sutra of Great Liberation* through his door—a sign of the community's adherence to its traditions, despite the odds. Lozang Tsültrim torments him for his refusal to renounce his religion, and most of all for the bond he forms with Tashi Lhamo, the object of Lozang Tsültrim's lust. Lozang Gyatso teaches Tashi Lhamo to read Tibetan and eventually introduces her to the basic teachings of Buddhism, and together they attempt to preserve their beliefs in the face of relentless persecution. Lozang Gyatso does undergo something of a crisis of faith, a recurring theme in other trauma narratives—Elie Wiesel's *Night*, for instance—but ironically, it comes *after* the traumatic events themselves, when

■ xx ■

INTRODUCTION

his cousin and other former tormentors resume their old roles as monks and devotees. By detailing Tibetan efforts to protect their language and culture from the onslaught of Mao's campaigns, the novel commemorates the everyday resistance of countless ordinary Tibetans, while nodding to famous figures such as the "Three Polymaths" (expertly studied in Nicole Willock's book *Lineages of the Literary*) who played instrumental roles in transmitting Buddhist traditions during this catastrophic period.

It is also significant that the author refuses to apportion blame along ethnic lines. In her groundbreaking work on the Cultural Revolution, the writer Woeser explores the sensitive question of Tibetan involvement in the movement—that is, the extent to which Tibetans themselves were responsible for carrying out political persecutions and acts of cultural destruction. Here, Tsering Döndrup does something similar in his fictional account, facing the uncomfortable truth that some Tibetans indeed did terrible things under the auspices of Mao's campaigns, whether it be Lozang Tsültrim, his fellow revolutionary Künga Huamo, or Rikden, the Party secretary. By the same token, *The Red Wind Howls* does not make villains of all its Han Chinese characters. There are those untethered from humanity and responsible for appalling crimes, particularly the cadre Wang Aiguo and the camp commander Song Jiantao. But there is also Song's predecessor, Yang Kai, a man described as intelligent and kind—the very qualities that ultimately lead to his downfall. Some of the most memorable and disturbing moments in part 2 concern the "Youth Shock Brigades," thousands of young Han Chinese from Henan Province who descend on

• xxi •

INTRODUCTION

Qinghai to help "open up the west of the Motherland." When the state's agricultural plans fail with devastating consequences, these "youths" end up roaming the countryside looking for food, until "they perished of cold or hunger or became food for the wolves, and every trace of them—their lives, bodies, and names, their joys and sorrows—was completely wiped out." The author displays great sympathy for these naïve idealists, and in the story, the very word "youth" becomes a local synonym for someone in the most pitiful and wretched of circumstances.

We must distinguish, however, between the novel's human sympathies and the reason all of this suffering is occurring in the first place. While characters are not relieved of personal responsibility, there is no doubt that the cruelty and violence of this period was unleashed entirely by the Party. Part I provides agonizing details of how the camps and campaigns warped minds, weaponized fear, and upended relationships. In prison, Alak Drong succumbs to the authorities' entreaties to inform on his fellow inmates and betrays Tsetra, his loyal disciple, a decision that leaves him socially isolated and mentally tormented. When Tsetra discovers this, he in turn reports on his former lama. Another inmate, Namgyel, escapes the Party's clutches after the Harrowing Day, only to be turned in by his own wife. These events confirm camp commander Song Jiantao's ominous warning that relationships such as teacher and disciple and husband and wife have ceased to exist under the new regime. The narrator puts it more starkly: "the power of reeducation and mass movements could annihilate the power of love and devotion. They could turn the sane into madmen, the wise into fools, the brave into cowards, the compassionate

■ xxii ■

INTRODUCTION

into devils." While treachery and paranoia take their mental toll, the prisoners are also broken down physically, turned into "labor machines" and worked, in many cases, to death. This process of remolding is almost literalized in the character of Chaktar Bum, an official sent to the camp for failing to meet his arrest quota, who loses his mind and becomes capable of nothing but relentless work, "a 'labor machine' truly worthy of the name."

If Part 1 demonstrates the psychological and physical toll wrought on those in the camps, part 2 shows that life was little better on the outside, where campaigns rewarded cruelty and promoted score settling that was more often personal than political. Lozang Tsültrim turns on Dranak Geshé largely because he was a poor student shown little favor by his teacher, while he jealously persecutes Lozang Gyatso for succeeding where he failed. The airing of his petty grievances is enabled by the state in vicious struggle sessions, during which he is encouraged by Wang Aiguo to torment his supposed class enemies. The most "revolutionary" usually turn out to be the most hypocritical. Lhalha, a "professional bitterness speaker" who tours the camps with her dubious tales of woe from the "Old Society," always has to be mindful of the shifting political winds, changing her tune rapidly after Lin Biao, Mao's second-in-command, is revealed to be a "counterrevolutionary" and performing her greatest volte-face in the post-Mao years, when she is seen once again prostrating at the feet of Alak Drong. The state's handiwork is particularly evident when it comes to the schoolchildren, "heirs of the revolution" who are molded into violent savages, "more reckless, vicious, pitiless, and downright

■ xxiii ■

INTRODUCTION

evil than even the most extreme of revolutionaries." And in true Orwellian fashion (Tsering Döndrup is an ardent admirer of Orwell, as well as Solzhenitsyn, the great chronicler of Soviet Russia's gulags), the revolution ultimately devours its own when even Wang Aiguo and Song Jiantao fall victim to the political upheavals, a testament to "a time when there was no distinction between friend and foe, no distinction between good and evil, and no recourse whatsoever for the unjustly accused."

Nor can there be any exoneration for policies that led to monumental human suffering and environmental destruction. Backyard furnaces, rapid collectivization, and other elements of the Great Leap Forward that proved so disastrous elsewhere in China were likewise present in Amdo, but the novel also describes schemes hatched for the unique environment of the Tibetan plateau that resulted in unique catastrophes. Most disastrous of all was the attempt to turn pastures into farmland, a mass movement aided by thousands of "youths" turning the earth upside down. As any of the nomads would have known (ironically, given the mass line policy of consulting the people), trying to cultivate the land thousands of feet above sea level "brought about as much benefit and did about as much damage as trying to graze your cattle in the ocean." Not only did the crops fail, the pastures—on which nomadic communities relied for survival—were ravaged, never to fully recover, and the result was unprecedented famine. The novel details several utopian plans to assert human mastery over nature, including a deforestation campaign described in military language and a farcical bid to crossbreed sheep. All of them fail dismally, with long-term consequences: 175-pound rams become "nothing but

▪ xxiv ▪

INTRODUCTION

a legend," thoroughbred mastiffs die out, rivers shrink, grasslands turn to deserts. Environmental degradation and the disappearance of the nomadic way of life in the modern world are notable themes elsewhere in the author's fiction, transformations often driven by a combination of state policies and the market economy (coal mining and nomad resettlement programs, for instance). In *The Red Wind Howls*, we discover the origins of these transformations in the ruinous economic policies of the Mao era.

It was not just that Mao's policies had specific local manifestations in Tibet—Tibetans experienced this entire history in a fundamentally different way from their Han Chinese counterparts. In its sweeping span of the Mao decades, *The Red Wind Howls* calls to mind several Chinese memoirs and novels with similar time frames (Yu Hua's *To Live*, for example), but for Tibetans, these catastrophes were imposed by an alien regime that was indifferent to and largely ignorant of their culture, religion, history, and language. In China, the old world order fell with the Xinhai Revolution of 1911 and 1949 represented the conclusion of a civil war between different factions, both recognizably "Chinese"—the "Red" and "White" Chinese, as they are referred to in the novel. The phrase is telling: the Communists represented cultural others first and a new political regime second. The novel reminds us of this time and again. When Alak Drong first encounters the CCP, he does not even grasp the concept of "China," let alone the "Communist Party," and this is just the first of many misunderstandings, because the imposed regime could only exist through an imposed language. Historian Tsering Shakya stresses the key role translation and

■ xxv ■

INTRODUCTION

neologisms played in the PRC's takeover of Tibet; the basic vocabulary of Communism—people, democracy, class, liberation, exploitation—had to be established before any political transformations could take place. This historical process is embedded in the text: in one scene, Dranak Geshé calmly thwarts a struggle session by failing to understand the word "exploit." Throughout, new Marxist terminology and imported Chinese loanwords are deliberately singled out with quotation marks, highlighting their strangeness. The politics of language in contemporary Tibet is another long-standing interest of the author's, and once again, this novel traces the origins of today's problems back to Tibet's first encounters with Maoism.

The personal cost the author has paid for this novel is further evidence (if it were needed) of just how taboo his tale is. Excerpts began to appear in the *Qinghai Tibetan News* in 2002, but when the final draft was complete, no publisher would risk taking it. In 2006, Tsering Döndrup was left with little choice but to print and release the novel himself. Enormous interest among Tibetan readers quickly drew the authorities' attention. On the pretext that the book did not have an ISBN, the remaining copies in the author's possession were confiscated and he was warned not to try to publish it again (today, copies continue to circulate privately, sometimes fetching high prices online, even though Tsering Döndrup has pleaded with readers not to profit off the book). In 2012, a Chinese translation of the novel was published in Hong Kong, featuring an introduction by the U.S.-based historian Li Jianglin. The publication of both the original and the translation resulted in lasting consequences. Tsering Döndrup was demoted from his post as head of the

■ xxvi ■

INTRODUCTION

county archives, had his salary and pension reduced, and was eventually forced into early retirement. His Party membership was revoked, and he was no longer permitted to receive literary prizes. Perhaps most serious of all, his passport was confiscated, and he has been unable to obtain one since, meaning that he is now a domestic prisoner. As Françoise Robin points out, he was not trying to gain the notoriety of a writer "banned in China," a label (sometimes of questionable veracity) that has been used to market Chinese authors in the West. Tsering Döndrup was well established before this novel, he has published prolifically since, and he remains one of the most prominent figures in the Tibetan literary world. In contrast to Yan Lianke's "reckless writing," Tsering Döndrup deliberately toned down some of the story's most horrific extremities, hoping that this and the fictional form of the book might make it politically permissible to publish within the PRC. Unfortunately, its contents were simply too sensitive, and the novel has since been consigned to the same fate of repression as the history it relates.

The Red Wind Howls concerns momentous events in Tibetan history, so it is fitting that its emergence coincided with the momentous events of 2008, protests that in some ways mirrored those described in these pages. Prior to the unrest of that year, a new climate of intellectual discussion had flourished in Tibetan university salons and magazines, where ideas of democracy and human rights were beginning to circulate. *The Red Wind Howls* emerged onto this scene in 2006, adding fuel to the fire with its vivid depictions of the glaring abuses Tibetans have suffered under the Chinese regime. In March 2008, as China was gearing up to host the Summer Olympics in

■ xxvii ■

INTRODUCTION

Beijing, a wave of antigovernment demonstrations spread across Tibetan regions, much of it led by monks, including monks from the major monastery of Labrang in Amdo. The unrest was quickly quelled by large-scale security operations, and reprisals began. Though nowhere near the scale of 1958, they followed a predictable pattern of ruthless state repression, with mass arrests and a clampdown on free expression. March was a significant month for Tibetans to protest, since it marked the Dalai Lama's flight from Lhasa in 1959; but in Amdo, the year itself was of major significance, as it marked fifty years since the tragedy of 1958. Half a century later, the recollection of that traumatic period spurred resistance all over again. The 2008 unrest was immediately followed by the onset of a long series of self-immolations, protests in which Tibetans have set themselves on fire in opposition to Chinese rule.

The Division of Heaven and Earth, a daring assessment of the 2008 protests by the writer Shokdung, drew heavily on their connection to 1958. *The Red Wind Howls* was among the few sources on 1958 that he cited—a testament to the novel's crucial function as a form of documentary evidence. Like Tsering Döndrup's novel, Shokdung's book was only ever circulated underground, and its distribution led to grave consequences for the author, who was subsequently arrested. Both texts were also similar in that they were meant solely for a community of fellow Tibetans—neither was an attempt to awaken Chinese readers or gain international attention. Tibetan texts are rarely read by non-Tibetan audiences in China, even when they are translated into Chinese, and Tibetan literature can hardly boast of a high-profile status in the West. But now the novel finds

■ xxviii ■

INTRODUCTION

itself in the new and unintended context of English translation. As the translator, I hope that readers will discover not only a repressed history of great significance but also a powerful work of literature by an exceptional author.

SELECTED FURTHER READING

Barnett, Robert, Benno Weiner, and Françoise Robin, eds. *Conflicting Memories: Tibetan History under Mao Retold.* Leiden: Brill, 2020.

Dondrup Gyal. "Tsultrim Jyamtso." Trans. Lowell Cook. *Journal of Tibetan Literature* 1, no. 1 (2022): 139–166.

Goldstein, Melvyn C. *The Snow Lion and the Dragon: China, Tibet, and the Dalai Lama.* Berkeley: University of California Press, 1999.

Lama Jabb. *Oral and Literary Continuities in Modern Tibetan Literature: The Inescapable Nation.* Lanham, MD: Lexington Books, 2015.

Makley, Charlene E. *The Violence of Liberation: Gender and Tibetan Buddhist Revival in Post-Mao China.* Berkeley: University of California Press, 2007.

Naktsang Nulo. *My Tibetan Childhood: When Ice Shattered Stone.* Trans. Angus Cargill and Sonam Lhamo. Durham, NC: Duke University Press, 2014.

Panchen Lama (the Tenth). *A Poisoned Arrow: The Secret Report of the 10th Panchen Lama.* London: Tibet Information Network, 1997.

Pema Bhum. *Six Stars with a Crooked Neck: Tibetan Memoirs of the Cultural Revolution.* Trans. Lauran R. Hartley. Dharamsala: Bod kyi dus bab, 2001.

Rohlf, Gregory. *Building New China, Colonizing Kokonor: Resettlement to Qinghai in the 1950s.* Lanham, MD: Lexington Books, 2016.

Shokdung. *The Division of Heaven and Earth: On Tibet's Peaceful Revolution.* Trans. Matthew Akester. London: Hurst & Company, 2016.

Tsering Döndrup. *The Handsome Monk and Other Stories.* Trans. Christopher Peacock. New York: Columbia University Press, 2019.

——. *Tempête Rouge.* Trans. Françoise Robin. Arles: Éditions Picquier, 2019.

Tsering Shakya. "The Development of Modern Tibetan Literature in the People's Republic of China in the 1980s." In *Modern Tibetan Literature and Social Change*, ed. Lauran R. Hartley and Patricia Schiaffini-Vedani, 61–85. Durham, NC: Duke University Press, 2008.

Tsering Woeser. *Forbidden Memory: Tibet During the Cultural Revolution.* Trans. Susan T. Chen. Lincoln, NE: Potomac Books, 2020.

INTRODUCTION

——. *Tibet on Fire: Self-Immolations Against Chinese Rule.* Trans. Kevin Carrico. London; New York: Verso, 2016.

Tubten Khétsun. *Memories of Life in Lhasa Under Chinese Rule.* Trans. Matthew Akester. New York: Columbia University Press, 2008.

Veg, Sebastian. "Testimony, History and Ethics: From the Memory of Jiabiangou Prison Camp to a Reappraisal of the Anti-Rightist Movement in Present-Day China." *The China Quarterly* 218 (2014): 514–539.

Weiner, Benno. *The Chinese Revolution on the Tibetan Frontier.* Ithaca, NY: Cornell University Press, 2020.

Willock, Nicole. *Lineages of the Literary: Tibetan Buddhist Polymaths of Socialist China.* New York: Columbia University Press, 2021.

Yan Lianke. *The Four Books.* Trans. Carlos Rojas. New York: Grove Press, 2015.

Yang Jisheng. *Tombstone: The Great Chinese Famine, 1958–1962.* Trans. Stacy Mosher and Guo Jian. New York: Farrar, Straus and Giroux, 2012.

THE RED WIND HOWLS

Part One

ALAK DRONG, the lama whose honorific prefix was paired with the rather unusual name "Drong"—Wild Yak—was sporting a pair of black crystal sunglasses on the bridge of his nose and a gold ring inlaid with an agate stone on his left ring finger. As usual, he was wearing a brown Chinese suit, which, in cold weather, was always complemented by a dark red fur coat with a lynx collar. At first glance, you might think he was a rich, uncouth businessman. But on closer inspection, the short-cropped hair, the collar of a yellow cotton undershirt poking out from his suit, and the simple rosary wrapped around his left wrist made clear to anyone with even a passing familiarity with Tibet that he belonged to the ranks of lamas and rein-carnations who, in those years, so terrifying when we look back on them, had come unstuck from their sacred vows like a snake unwinding its coils or a cap popping off a beer bottle.

Alak Drong was now in possession of one wife, two mistresses, three children (including one bastard), one monastery, 241 monks (including 52 who had given up their vows), and over 26,300 faithful followers. Many years before, he had, without quite knowing how, gone from being a snot-nosed shepherd with a rope for a belt to a dandy little monk decked out in the robes of the Buddhist order. Not long after that, he was conducted to Tsezhung Monastery, and amid the blaring of horns, the beating of drums, and the wafting of incense, he was installed upon the five-faced lion throne. When he thought back on that day, most of it was like a vague dream, but there were two details carved into his memory as though engraved in stone. The first was that a sudden violent storm, the kind Tibetans call a red wind, had swept through that afternoon, picking up several cotton tents belonging to attendees of the enthronement ceremony and the shawls of a number of Tsezhung Monastery's monks and tossing them into the sky like wind-horse prayer flags. His beloved copper chamber pot too, as red as the face of his teacher who had purchased it from a layman just a few days earlier for the price of two ewes, flew off into the air like a shooting star. At first, Old Red Features wasn't worried in the least; in fact he joked about it: "It's flown off into the big blue sky, but it's sure to land on the cold hard ground!" He commanded the devotees who'd come to pay their respects to Alak Drong to bring him the chamber pot as soon as it was found. And indeed, before long, an old one-eyed woman arrived bearing the lost treasure, but unfortunately it had been battered to a pulp, like an ancient helmet that had fallen into the midst of club-wielding bandits. *"Ah ho!* People in a degenerate age have a

THE RED WIND HOWLS

poor lot in life. Not even a chamber pot's worth of good karma,"
he said, completely deflated. "All composite phenomena are
impermanent," he added, in an effort to console himself. That
was around the beginning of autumn, and the red wind didn't
stop until the following spring. The people of the grasslands,
used to and fond of monitoring the omens, could find no auspi-
cious explanation for this unprecedented meteorological phenomenon. "It must be a sign that the venerable lama is angry,"
they ultimately concluded, which scared the wits out of Tsezhung Monastery's monks. The second thing he remembered
about that day was the huge spread of dishes that had been laid
out for him, each one giving off drool-inducing aromas, and all
within a hand's reach. But that day the old, gray-bearded monk
with a face as red as a baboon's butt stuck to him like a shadow
and fixed his terrifying eyes on him at all times, leaving Alak
Drong completely incapable of making a move.

Old Red Features strictly controlled his every move and
forced him to learn by heart all sorts of incredibly tedious
chants, beginning with the *Vows of Refuge*. He found the first
bit the hardest to remember, the part that went "I take refuge
in all the sublime and glorious root and lineage lamas who
have as their essence the body, speech, mind, precious qualities, and Buddha activity of all Tathagatas of the ten directions
and the three times and who are the originating source of
the 84,000 Dharmas and the benevolent lords of the noble
Sangha . . ."

It seemed like the old monk had limitless power, but it wasn't
long before Alak Drong realized that his own power was even
more limitless, at which point he found the courage to put Old

■ 5 ■

Red Features in his place: "What an old pain in the ass you are! Nothing good will come of us two being together in this life."

Old Red Features had also been the tutor of Alak Drong's previous incarnation, who had once said, "It would be best if the two of us go our separate ways in the next life." Recalling this now, the elderly teacher was left momentarily stunned. He slowly removed his shawl, then muttered an indistinct prayer as he prostrated thrice to the young Alak Drong, after which he vanished for good.

Alak Drong finally had his freedom, and he gorged on all the delicacies life had to offer until he felt sick and did whatever he wanted to the point that it became boring. Finally, he recalled his old favorite game: catching a pika and using it as a toy. Deciding there was nothing more enjoyable than this, he gathered some little monks of his own age and led them to the outskirts of the monastery. The young Alak Drong inspected each and every burrow like an experienced grave robber, then, tossing his robe up over his shoulder and winding his rosary around his wrist, he squatted on the ground and shoved his hand into a hole, meanwhile ordering the other children to take turns blowing as hard as they could into the other openings.

This land had been taken over by lay folk during the time of Alak Drong's previous incarnation. The pikas had accompanied them, and the land became their breeding ground. It looked as if there were still plenty around too. But the soil had become soft and the land was now more or less barren, and what's more, the little monks under the young Alak Drong's command were not very proficient at the task in hand—in fact they were wholly incompetent. No matter what method they used or how much they persevered, they didn't manage to catch a single pika. They ached with thirst, and their noses were so dry they practically caught fire. Fortunately, not far off, the pristine blue Tsechu River wound its meandering course. They ran to its banks, threw themselves on their bellies, and drank until they choked.

"*Eh ma*, such cool, clear water! If this isn't what they call the 'River of Eight Qualities,' I don't know what is!" Later, during the long years of hardship, this was the phrase Alak Drong would always utter every time he was plagued by thirst. He said it many times on that particular day, when, along with fifty others, he was loaded onto the back of a truck and carted off to the labor camp, and the blue Tsechu appeared before his eyes like a mirage and the sound of its flowing waters chimed in his ears.

Never before had he endured such mistreatment and torment. The truck bounced its way down a bumpy, pothole-filled road that could have shaken a person to death and jolted a corpse back to life. Tossed onto someone's head one moment and trampled under their feet the next, he found himself crushed left right front and back, to the point that his organs were nearly squeezed out of his body and his eyeballs almost popped out of his head. The nomads, who were riding in a vehicle for the first time, got so dizzy they threw up the entire contents of their stomachs, splattering everyone around them with vomit. The two soldiers perched on the cab of the truck, each with a rifle strapped around his chest and a leather whip clasped in his hand, barked "Shut up! Stand straight!" in Chinese as the tips of their whips lashed heads, faces, ears, necks, and shoulders, leaving some of the men with blood dripping from open wounds. Even more unbearable was the thirst that crept in with the onset of the afternoon. At that point, Alak Drong remembered with remorse the solitary bread bun and metal mug of boiled water that had been handed out to each of them that same morning, neither of which he had consumed on account of his despair.

In the midst of this nightmare, Alak Drong recalled his time at Tsezhung Monastery. After Old Red Features had gone, he became wild and unrestrained, doing whatever took his fancy. Once, when he was catching pikas as playthings, he saw some monks from the monastery engaged in a heated debate, as though they were plotting a great conspiracy, all the while taking copious amounts of snuff and using huge felt handkerchiefs to mop up boogers the size of sheep carcasses. One senior monk said, "He might be a lama, but we can't spoil him like this . . ." Alak Drong happened to overhear this, but he paid it no attention at the time. Nor did he listen to the rest of their conversation. Not long after, thirty or so monks and laymen came from various communities to pay homage and seek holy refuge with him. He knew nothing about these people except that they were going to Lhasa. Following the instructions of one of the monks, who was also one of his relatives, he gave each of them a blessing and a protective cord, after which he gathered up his band of little monks and went off to busy himself with the pikas as usual. Whenever he got thirsty, he just ran to the Tsechu and gulped down his fill of ice-cold water until he was heaving for breath.

As the afternoon got hotter the prisoners sweated more and more, and soon a thick, musty aroma was drifting in the air. The two guards on the cab up front grumbled angrily in Chinese and covered their noses with their hands. Ever since

THE RED WIND HOWLS

donning monk's robes and moving into a house, Alak Drong too had become gradually sensitive to this smell, and if a devotee came to prostrate before him in hot weather, he would cover his nose with his hand in just the same way. But on this occasion, there was nothing on his mind but water.

If I could just have a drink of cold water, I'd die happy, he thought. He couldn't take it anymore. Just like he did when he used to issue a command to his servants, he raised his voice and barked, "I'm dying of thirst. Bring some water!"

A fierce lash from the whip landed on his cheek, and a moment later black blood was trickling down his face, making it abundantly clear where he was and exactly where he stood. For a time he forgot the suffering of thirst, but it was replaced by a different kind of torment: recalling his now-past happiness.

When the first Red Chinese work unit arrived, they pitched their tents and set up camp in the vicinity of Tsezhung Monastery. Their leader was Wang Aiguo—"Patriot" Wang—and he was fluent in Tibetan. When he came to visit Alak Drong, accompanied by two bodyguards armed with strange rifles, he neither prostrated nor requested blessings; instead, he offered two bricks of tea and a *khata* and struck up various topics of conversation. The exchange ended with him indicating that the people of the Tsezhung grasslands—both lay and clergy—now had to accept their authority.

Before this, Alak Drong had only seen the "White Chinese." Their faces were indeed as white as snow, so in his mind he assumed that the "Red Chinese" must all have faces as red as baboons' butts, just like his first teacher. He was amazed to discover, therefore, that the faces of the people now before him

• 9 •

were actually whiter than the White Chinese. "Are you really the Red Chinese?" he asked.

"Haha! I suppose you could say that. But our actual name is the *Gongchandang*, the Communist Party. Hahaha . . ." replied the chuckling Wang Aiguo.

Alak Drong, prouder than an elephant, simply looked into the distance and laughed derisively. Eventually, in a most solemn tone, he said, "Let me explain something to you. Tsezhung encompasses the earth and Tsezhung encompasses the heavens. Is it I that must accept your authority, or is it you that must accept mine? That is, as yet, unclear."

Wang Aiguo responded with his own dismissive laugh. "Tsezhung is actually very small. So small, in fact, that you can't even find it on a map of *Zhongguo*," he said. Then, seemingly worried that Alak Drong might not understand the meaning of "map of *Zhongguo*," he held out his palm. "Imagine this is a map of *Zhongguo*—of our China. Tsezhung would just be this tiny little line here. Ha . . . not even that big."

"No no no." Alak Drong likewise held out his palm. "*This* is Tsezhung. This 'map of China' of yours is no more than this little line here. Not even that big!"

Wang Aiguo's derisive laugh turned into a hearty chuckle. "In that case, how about we take a trip out of Tsezhung, and by the time we come back, I guarantee our little problem will have solved itself. You can bring some of the community and clan leaders as well. I'll foot all the bills."

The young Alak Drong had long since grown tired of his dull life at the monastery, and as soon as he heard the words "out of Tsezhung," he made up his mind without a second thought. Upon his return, he proclaimed, "I, Alak Drong, have now traveled everywhere but the ends of the earth, and I have seen with my own eyes that the Communist Party encompasses heaven and earth alike! We therefore have no choice but to accept the leadership of the Communist Party—I, for one, will be accepting it." As a result, the work unit (in other words, Wang Aiguo) convened a meeting of local lay and religious leaders at which Alak Drong was praised profusely and conferred with the bizarre-sounding title of "Deputy *Zhuren* of the Committee" (what manner of authority this entailed was unclear), a position that also came with a regular stipend of several silver coins referred to as a "monthly salary."

One afternoon, when the red wind was blowing fiercely, Alak Drong dispatched a monk to fetch his teacher, to whom he put the questions: "What exactly is a deputy *zhuren* of the committee? And just how high a position is it?" His wise teacher, fully versed in a hundred treatises, fell deep into contemplation but ultimately shook his head in defeat. "I have no idea," he said.

This was the first time in ten years that Alak Drong had asked his teacher a question, and it was the first time that his teacher, renowned for his "comprehensive knowledge of affairs both religious and worldly," had been at a loss for words.

This monk, now known by the name Dranak Geshé— "Geshé Holder of the Black Tents"—Lozang Palden, whose fame resounded in those days like thunder in the blue sky, had once been one of the most ordinary of ordinary monks at Tse-zhung Monastery. When Alak Drong's previous incarnation had set off for Central Tibet on a pilgrimage, he followed along carrying his own little bundle, and not long after arriving in

Lhasa he had entered into the ranks of Drepung Monastery. The fact that he failed to return home from Lhasa aroused no more curiosity in his homeland than when he left in the first place. Some years later, however, he sent a letter to Jamyang Sherap, a friend of his at Tsezhung Monastery, which said, in essence, that although he was barely getting by on tsampa broth, he was willing to put everything on the line and study as hard as he could for the sake of the Buddha and all sentient beings, and he exhorted his friend to do the same. He also asked Jamyang Sherap to send a reply letting him know how his parents and his two sisters were doing. While this was all the letter said, his writing style was so obscured by ornate synonyms and poetic flourishes that the monks of Tsezhung Monastery could make neither heads nor tails of it—even the learned lama sent over from Labrang Monastery could only get the gist. "One day we'll have to think of a way to bring this venerable monk back to his monastery," the then Alak Drong had sighed. Unfortunately, this goal wasn't to be realized until the time of Alak Drong's next incarnation.

Even more unfortunately—for the new Alak Drong, at least—after Dranak Geshé did return to his homeland and take up a position as Alak Drong's personal tutor, he instituted a vigorous program of study for the young lama. Dranak Geshé felt that his own studies had suffered greatly in later life because he didn't have a good grasp of the fundamentals, and it was therefore absolutely imperative that a child have a firm grounding in the basics. *This one's lessons are even harder than Old Red Features'!* Alak Drong thought. *And this* Thirty Verses *is even harder to memorize than the* Vows of Refuge! Feeling hopelessly fed up,

THE RED WIND HOWLS

Alak Drong thought of any excuse he could (his favorite being a headache) to get out of his lessons. Eventually Dranak Geshé, thoroughly despairing of Alak Drong's laziness, gave up insisting and no longer forced the issue. *My family was never very well off,* he thought, *and I never had a teacher pushing me when I was young—that's why I never learned all that much. I'm getting on in years now and have no hope of becoming a scholar, but that doesn't mean I should just waste my life. Well, not much else to be done. I'll continue my recitations and my spiritual practice, and I'll take a few good students under my wing.*

It occurred to him that each of his sisters had a son. And another thing—after the great and good of Tsezhung had invited him to return home, the status of the Dranak clan had shot up. Their voices had boomed with a new authority, and they'd trekked all over Tsezhung collecting donations to build him a new residence. It couldn't compare to Alak Drong's mansion, but it was bigger than the quarters of other monks and lamas, and in fact it felt a little too big for him alone—a little unsettling, even—so getting a couple of disciples in seemed like a pressing necessity. Though Dranak Geshé had just turned fifty, his skinny frame and the four deep lines in his forehead made him look older than he actually was, but if you looked closely, his clear, starlike eyes still gleamed with wisdom, giving him the air of an accomplished scholar. If you looked even closer, you'd notice that his left eye was slightly smaller than his right, which made his face appear somewhat asymmetrical. Alak Drong felt an indescribable pain every time he saw this face, and it was amid that pain that he finally memorized the *Thirty Verses* and the *Guide to Signs* and grasped their basic

■ 13 ■

meanings, after which his teacher, just like Old Red Features before him, made Alak Drong memorize the *Vows of Refuge* and all those other dull chants, leaving him feeling thoroughly fed up again.

The truck broke down out of the blue right as they were crossing a large, bridge-less river, leaving them stuck midcurrent. Everyone took from their pockets the metal mugs, which the Chinese called *gangzi*, that they'd been given while at the county detention center, and after looping their belts through the handles, dunked them into the water. Some, not without skill, were able to scoop up a cold, refreshing mouthful or two. Unfortunately for Alak Drong, he'd been so dejected that morning he'd failed to stash his mug in his pocket, an oversight that left him even more dejected now. Just as he started to wallow in regret, a cup was extended before him.

"Venerable Rinpoché, my *gangzi* isn't very clean, but . . ."

"Not to worry, not to worry." Alak Drong downed the contents of the cup without even glancing up. The man retrieved some more water and presented the cup once again.

"Venerable Rinpoché, my *gangzi* isn't very clean, but . . ."

"Okay, enough of that now." Alak Drong seized the mug and again downed its contents, after which he finally took a look at the man. "Aren't you having any?" he asked. The face seemed extremely familiar to him, but he couldn't for the life of him recall a name or the man's clan.

"Please, have another drink first . . ." As the man lowered his mug into the water once more, the truck came to life with a violent splutter. Before they even knew it, they had surged onto the other bank, water spraying in every direction.

"Ah ho! You didn't get any water," exclaimed Alak Drong, trying to show his concern, but the man only looked rueful.

"It doesn't matter, really, Rinpoché. It's just that my *gangzi* isn't very clean . . ."

Well, it's cleaner than piss, Alak Drong thought. He was suddenly reminded of what had happened a few days ago when Lozang Tsültrim, a former monk from Tsezhung Monastery, had forced him to drink urine. That day, it had been as unbearably hot as it was today—maybe even hotter—and he and his tutor were standing, drenched in sweat, in the middle of a crowd that had come to carry out "class reprisals." Wang Aiguo, the chair of the meeting, had forbidden anyone from striking them, but still the scorching rays of the late-summer highlands sun were almost frying Alak Drong alive, and he was so thirsty he could barely speak. Finally, he managed to raise his voice and get a sentence out, enunciating each syllable: "Give me some water! Otherwise I can't confess my crimes."

"Ha! Look at this sly old wolf and his tricks. How about a nice glass of piss? Yeah! Didn't you used to make people drink your piss?" As he was speaking, Lozang Tsültrim glanced at Wang Aiguo to gauge his reaction. The latter took a drag on his cigarette and nodded, and Lozang Tsültrim continued with bolstered courage, rolling up his sleeves. "Yeah! Today, this old wolf will drink the piss of the proletariat!"

From somewhere in the crowd, the heads all covered from the sun's beating rays by jacket sleeves, there came a horrified cry: "May Drong Rinpoché have mercy!"

"Who said that? Who said that?" Forgetting about Alak Drong for the moment, Lozang Tsültrim dove into the crowd and started jabbing his finger into face after face. "Was it you? Was it you?"

"It wasn't me it wasn't me," blurted one terrified old man. "I swear on Drong Rinpoché!"

"What! What? Say that again!"

"It wasn't me . . ."

"Swear."

"I swear on Drong . . ."

Lozang Tsültrim dragged the old man to his feet and looked to Wang Aiguo for direction.

Alak Drong, thinking he might have earned a reprieve from drinking piss, was just starting to feel a little better when Wang Aiguo began to speak.

"Good folks, see here! Just look at how deeply these religious types—and Alak Drong most of all—have poisoned your minds. Alak Drong isn't going to save you—he can't even save himself! There's only one thing that can save you, and that's Mao Zedong and the Communist Party."

Wang joined his hands behind his back and began to pace back and forth. Typically, this habit was reserved for when he was pondering something important, and it was the most obvious marker of his difference from the local nomads. He was, as usual, wearing his khaki military uniform and a pair of black cloth shoes, the ones his Chinese wife with the bound feet had made for him, using as soles the gold-lettered copy of the *Great Treatise on the Stages of the Path to Enlightenment*, Tsezhung Monastery's most precious artifact.

That was back when several rows of blue-brick, blue-tiled Chinese buildings had been constructed in the vicinity of

Tsezhung Monastery, buildings that were referred to as "Tsezhung County." Most of the men from Tsezhung had lost their lives on the Harrowing Day, and after the few surviving men and the lamas and monks had been captured, Lozang Tsültrim and a handful of cadres began to seize Buddhist scriptures from Tsezhung Monastery and from the homes of the wealthier nomads and turn them into food for the hungry flames. It was then that Wang Aiguo's wife had recalled the precious texts that her mother or grandmother had long ago brought back from the Mogao Caves of Dunhuang and turned into shoe soles. She had beamed at the thought. "Such fine materials for such a sorry shithole!" she declared, commanding Lozang Tsültrim to bring her a few basketfuls of scriptures (including the gold-lettered *Stages of the Path to Enlightenment*), which she then set about making into shoe soles.

Having seen the pain and anger in people's eyes, Wang Aiguo decided not to make Alak Drong drink piss, and instead had someone bring him a bowl of cool tea.

Of late, Alak Drong had been forced to speak at countless gatherings, before every clan around and at struggle sessions large and small, and now he knew the script by heart: religion is opium; he had used religion to hoodwink and exploit the masses; there are no such things as the principle of consciousness and reincarnation in the next life; even if there were, he didn't possess the power to save people or help them transmigrate, etc. After running through this whole routine once again, he rejoiced inside at the fact that he would at least avoid having to drink piss.

From a personal point of view, Lozang Tsültrim had no bones to pick with Alak Drong and in fact didn't bear him any

THE RED WIND HOWLS

ill will at all; the only reason he was doing this was to demonstrate his revolutionary credentials and to ingratiate himself with Wang Aiguo. By contrast, he did have some grievances to air against Dranak Geshé, his uncle and erstwhile teacher.

"First you forced me to become a monk. Then you filled my brain with poison. And then you put me to work like I was a slave. And on top of that, whenever there was anything tasty to be had, it went to Lozang Gyatso, and all I got was the leftovers! Do you admit it?"

Dranak Geshé was so deeply disappointed in Lozang Tsültrim that he forgot the monastic code entirely and let fly with a stream of abuse. "Curved horns are a bane on the eyes, a wicked nephew is a bane on the uncle! What's the plan, you little bastard? You want to make me drink piss, is that it? Bring it over then, I won't disappoint you!"

"Haha! If you're thirsty, I won't disappoint *you*."

That put the fear into the crowd. It was well known that Lozang Tsültrim was capable of any evil imaginable. A short time before this, when all the monks and lamas had been made to attend a political study session in the monastery's assembly hall, he had been the first to draft a self-criticism, which ran thus: "Having fallen under the pernicious influence of Alak Drong, Dranak Geshé, and others, I did knowingly dupe and exploit the masses. I recognize this now and I regret it deeply. Henceforth I vow sincerely, in all my conduct, to aim my spear at religion. I ask that the authorities put me to the test." After presenting this letter to Wang Aiguo, he disrobed and donned the clothes of a layman, then ran straight to the Kelden Hermitage.

The Kelden Hermitage was an entirely ordinary little cave with barely enough room for two. However, in times past, this unassuming grotto had served as a meditation spot for numerous sages, Shar Kelden Gyatso and Zhapkar Tsokdruk Rangdröl among them, and since the tread of their venerable feet had turned it into hallowed ground, the locals treated it as a major pilgrimage site. In recent years, the cave had been occupied by a nun in her forties who was reputed to be a dakini. Every day at noon she came down with her alms bowl to collect her allotment of simple fare, and no matter how much her benefactors begged her, she wouldn't eat a mouthful more than was necessary. It was also said that one breath from her was more beneficial for a sick patient than seven days of medicine.

At first, people assumed that Lozang Tsültrim had gone to fetch the dakini and bring her to the political study session, so they didn't pay much attention to his disappearance, but he returned shortly thereafter with a repugnant, idiotic cackle. "I'm no monk anymore, and the so-called dakini ain't a nun anymore, either!" he announced. The people now realized that his vow to "aim his spear at religion" wasn't entirely metaphorical, and when they trekked up to the Kelden Hermitage, their hearts filled with fear, the dakini was nowhere to be found and the cave was bare—not a scrap of food or clothing in sight. "*Ai yo*," spouted Wang Aiguo, "incredible that she could live like this even in winter." Later, many people claimed to have seen the dakini fashion her robes into wings and fly off into the sky that day. Whatever the case, no one ever saw her again after that, dead or alive.

Wang Aiguo hauled Lozang Tsültrim off to one side and stuck his finger in his face. "Idiot! You absolute . . . it's against the law! If I handed you over, you'd get ten years at least!"

Lozang Tsültrim was terrified. "But Wang *Shuji*, ah— Secretary Wang, I was just doing revolution!"

"Shut your mouth. What the hell kind of revolutionary activity is that? Especially in broad daylight, with everyone watching! There'll be absolutely no more of this sort of thing. Not even with class enemies. It's the sort of thing the Jap devils would do. Ah, well . . . you're a revolutionary, so we'll let it go this time."

"Okay okay okay."

"But if it happens again I won't be able to protect you."

"Okay okay okay."

The sun was beating down ever more brutally, and in the blink of an eye the tips of the grass stalks had been roasted yellow and were beginning to curl. The bronze torsos of the nomads reflected the sunlight, and beads of sweat the size of peas were dripping from Dranak Geshé's short, ashen hair. Yet still he refused to renounce the laws of karma and reincarnation. "At the very least," said an exasperated Wang Aiguo, "you must admit that you exploited the masses."

"This term you're using, 'exploit,' it seems to mean something awful, like 'skinning' or 'flaying.' But I've never skinned an insect, let alone a man."

"It means to use deceptive or coercive means to take money and property from the hands of the masses."

"Oh. In that case, I've never used deceptive or coercive means to take money or property from anyone. I'm a monk, what would I do with money?"

THE RED WIND HOWLS

"Haha! Say no more. That fancy residence of yours—did it sprout up from the ground or fall out of the sky?"

"Oh. That was built for me when I came back from Lhasa. I said at the time that a solitary monk like me has no need for such a place, but everyone insisted. I didn't get it through coercion or deception. I didn't need the place then and I don't need it now. Whoever needs it can take it."

Wang Aiguo was growing increasingly exasperated with Dranak Geshé's stubbornness and realizing that he was no match for the geshé's calm, restrained reasoning. Suppressing his anger, he broke up the meeting. That night, Lozang Tsültrim made Alak Drong and Dranak Geshé each drink a bowl of piss. Thinking back on it now, Alak Drong had completely forgotten what it tasted like. That's how he was: a man who forgot things easily, good or bad, joy or sorrow.

The man who had just fetched a few gulps of cold water, indifferent to the threat of the whip, and who had freely offered them all to him, with no thought of a sip for himself—maybe he'd invited Alak Drong over to his house recently, or maybe he was one of those who'd lost a loved one on the Harrowing Day and offered him a horse in exchange for performing the last rites? Everyone in Tsezhung knew Alak Drong, from the white-haired elders to the white-toothed youngsters. If someone's mount got its hoof caught in a pika hole, it was his name they would invoke: "May Drong Rinpoché have mercy!" But it was impossible for him to know each and every one of them in this life. It was said that he would know them all in the next life, and what's more, he'd be able to save them.

One time, an aging bandit who'd spent his whole life killing men and stealing horses presented himself before Alak Drong with a sackful of silver. "Venerable Rinpoché, my name is Rapten Dorjé, from the Chumar clan. At a young age, poverty and hunger drove me out the door, and the wind and cold drove me from my home. I was left with no choice but to take up the life of a bandit. I've killed so many men and stolen so many mounts there's no chance an ordinary lama could save me. I'm an old man now, the time left to me as brief as the sun atop the pass and the shade at the bottom, and you, venerable lama, are my only hope of deliverance in the next life. I beg you, do not leave me without the protection of your spiritual practice!" After blurting all this out in one go, he prostrated three times, then left. Exactly one year later, the old man reappeared before Alak Drong, and said, "Venerable Rinpoché, do you recognize me?"

Alak Drong tilted his head to the side and stared at the man for some time, but he hadn't left a sesame seed's worth of impression on the lama. "No," he said eventually.

"Really?"

"Really."

"*Ah ho!*" cried the man in despair. "It was but a year ago, in this mortal realm of ours, that I brought before you a sackful of cash. That you don't recognize me now is a sign, either that I am lacking in good karma, or that you, venerable lama, are lacking in spiritual accomplishment. Either way, who knows whether you'll recognize me in the dark world to come? Give me back my money right now."

From then on, when Alak Drong received an offering, he made sure to take a long look at the donor's face, and over time this became a habit. And so, according to this habit, he inspected the face of the water donor and discovered that he was a young man of seventeen or so, whose most distinguishing feature was his huge body and his even huger face. Alak Drong thought that if the boy had a nickname, it must surely be something like "Muttonface" or "Balloonhead."

"Looks like they're taking us somewhere far away," he remarked to the young man as they crossed a relatively smooth section of road.

"They can take us as far as they like—to the next life, for all I care. As long as you're here, Rinpoché, I've got nothing to fear and no regrets," said the young man with unshakeable devotion. He stared out at the red dust swirling behind the truck and heaved a sigh. "What I can't stand is thinking about my grandma, and my mom, and my wife, and my girl, my little baby."

Alak Drong was delighted to still have such a faithful follower. He thought back on everything he had done recently in the hope of currying favor with Wang Aiguo, lessening his torment, and avoiding prison: breaking his vows, blaspheming against the saints and even the Buddha himself. He had sinned terribly, racking up a mountain of bad karma, and he felt ashamed and repentant.

The day was getting hotter, the grass sparser, and they were now passing through a deep, dusty red valley. Around each of the pale adobe houses, which looked just like the earthen stoves left behind when nomads moved camp, there were palm-sized patches of land where the scattered crops, barely the height of your forearm, had been scorched by the sun before even ripening. Occasionally men and women dressed in ragged goatskins who could only be described as hungry ghosts came and went, leading donkeys that were the spitting image of their masters.

THE RED WIND HOWLS

This sight was enough to confirm that they'd long since left behind the tiny line that constituted Tsezhung on Wang Aiguo's palm-map of China. If Alak Drong had had a good memory, he would have recalled that they'd passed through this very place the time Wang Aiguo had taken him "out of Tsezhung." The difference was that there hadn't been any road back then, and there certainly hadn't been any truck, and they'd traveled to Xining on horseback, a journey of seven days.

A yell shot out from somewhere in the group: "He's dead! Someone's died!" The two guards' first reaction was to dish out a few blows of the whip into the crowd and shout back in Chinese—"Shut your mouths! Stand straight!"—but, realizing that something was a bit different about the clamor this time, they brought the truck to a halt. After they had put away their whips, one of the guards mounted the cab of the truck and trained his rifle on the crowd while the other trampled over their heads and shoulders to go see what the commotion was all about. The latter shouted a few words back to the guard on the cab, who said a few words into the cab, and then a few words came out of the cab, at which point the guard standing on the prisoners' heads and shoulders signaled with the muzzle of his rifle for them to get rid of the body. The prisoners just stood there open mouthed, either because they hadn't understood the signal or because they didn't want to carry out the order, prompting the furious guard to start screaming and pointing his rifle in their faces one by one. He continued to make jabbing motions with his gun, commanding them to dispose of the body, and finally a couple of men hoisted it up, struggling for all they were worth, and threw it right over Alak Drong's head and out of the truck bed. It called to mind a shepherd coming home on his yak with a wolf-mangled sheep's carcass and dumping it on the ground outside his tent. The only difference was that this corpse didn't have a scratch on it.

The captain of the guards hopped out of the cab and briefly inspected the body, hands on his hips, then shook his head and mumbled something. Probably something like, "Shame. A good-looking worker!"

The guard standing on the prisoners' heads jumped down from the truck and motioned with his rifle for two of the men to get out. He fetched two shovels from the cab and tossed them on the ground in front of them, then scratched an outline in the dirt by the side of the road and signaled for them to dig.

The two nomads tied their sleeves around their waists, and with their bare chests dripping so much sweat it looked like they'd been plunged into water, set to digging. Neither of them, however, had any experience; in fact it was the first time they'd even held a shovel, on top of which at least 60 percent of the ground there was composed of rocks—it would be more accurate to say they were digging rocks than digging dirt. Even after a good while had passed, they'd still only managed to excavate an area some five feet long, a foot and a half wide, and six inches deep. The guard, growing impatient, barked at them nonstop until finally the two nomads, working themselves so hard they could barely breathe, managed to dig out a plot about twelve inches deep, into which they heaved the body, then piled the earth back on top.

THE RED WIND HOWLS

If that isn't "burying a body under the snow," I don't know what is, Alak Drong thought as the truck sped off in a cloud of red dust. At dusk the golden roofs of a handful of temple buildings appeared, shining through the foliage of a dense cluster of trees, and they arrived at a small town composed of various Chinese-style blue-tiled buildings, which had been built adjacent to the numerous whitewashed monks' quarters surrounding the monastery.

The truck barreled into a spacious courtyard where they were met by a large group of soldiers, identical in appearance to the two guards in the truck, who shouted ceaselessly and pointed their rifles left and right as they made the prisoners descend. The nomads moaned in agony as they tumbled out of the truck bed; some writhed about on the floor, while others fell face down and threw up. The forty-odd-year-old captain of the guards jumped down from the cab and accosted another man of a similar age, with whom he argued for a long time, gesticulating wildly, before entering one of the buildings, still gesticulating.

"Listen up!" The man of a similar age to the captain turned out to be a Tibetan. He addressed the nomads as he approached: "There are too many prisoners here right now, so there's no room for you. And since you're so late, there's nothing to eat either. But there's a decent place to stay nearby, so that's where you're going." He gave a signal to the soldiers.

The nomads weren't allowed back on the truck—they had to walk. Many of them genuinely no longer had the strength to get up, but for a people so averse to the smell of gasoline it made them want to throw up, walking wasn't all that bad. It was dark by now, and they couldn't see each other's faces. When, en route, they heard the trickling sound of a stream, every one of them charged madly toward it and threw themselves on the ground to gulp down their fill.

"You can't drink that!" yelled their Tibetan guide, "it's urine!" The guards struck at them indiscriminately with their rifle butts, but still no one raised their head. They didn't stop drinking until the liquid came dribbling back down their chins, at which point they registered a foul taste, something like rot or acid, and some of them immediately threw it all back up. Only the next morning, when they were being marched back to where the truck stopped, did they see the stream for what it was: a shallow strip of water topped by a murky, greenish-yellow scum that gave off an unbearably nauseating stench as soon you got anywhere near it.

"If you need to piss or shit, do it inside. Anyone who steps out the door will be shot." The Tibetan guide issued these instructions as he herded them all into a large room and closed the door. It was pitch black inside, but there was a powerful odor of butter and numerous soft, thick little objects beneath their feet, from which they deduced that they were in the assembly hall of a monastery. Everyone groped about in the dark and lay down on the monks' mats, and many of them fell asleep immediately.

The tubby man who had been following Alak Drong around like a dog sidled up to him again. "I don't think that man they buried by the side of the road was dead," he whispered.

"Impossible. How do you know?" Alak Drong whispered back.

"He was from the Arik clan. His name was Namgyel. I knew him. A man like that, young and healthy and strong, dying all of a sudden—impossible."

"Death and impermanence are matters of a moment. No one can be sure of such things."

"Yes, Your Holiness. But I've seen a dead body before. And I've seen a fresh corpse as well. There's a huge difference between the complexion of a dead body and someone who's still alive. He had the color of a living man, not a body."

"Completely impossible. I've seen a lot of dead bodies myself. I don't think you can tell the difference if they've only just died."

"Yes, Your Holiness. Ah . . . but if he wasn't dead, he must be on his way home by now."

"What? They buried him, didn't they? If he wasn't dead when they buried him, then he surely is now."

"Yes, Your Holiness. Ah . . . well, we all have to die anyway, so I wanted to try something . . ."

"What? Have you lost your mind?"

"May I ask you to do a divination for me?"

"Absolutely not."

His hopes dashed, the young man finally laid his head down. What the Tibetan who'd brought them here had said was true: it was indeed "a decent place to stay." The soft, thick cushion gave Alak Drong an indescribable feeling of bliss, and soon the messenger of sleep was on his way. In the past, he'd slept on a whole stack of cushions like these, but it had never felt as good as this one did now, and no rice with potentillas and ghee or yogurt or yak's milk had ever been as satisfying as the piss-water from the night before. After a brief spell of this blissful sleep, he was awakened by a sudden sharp pain in his stomach and felt the urgent need to void his bowels. As he lay there gritting his teeth, a chorus of tormented moans filled the air around him, along with a vile stench, and he knew this was the result of the sewage they had imbibed. Past caring, he emptied his bowels and lay back down. Unfortunately for him, that wasn't the end of it, and his aching stomach wouldn't let him sleep all night.

In his semiconscious state, the image of the man buried by the side of the road continued to haunt him. The mound of earth trembled, and bit by bit a head emerged; after gulping down several thick breaths, the man leaped up and began cackling madly and pointing his finger at Alak Drong. "You can go now," he said. Looking closely, Alak Drong discovered it was actually the captain of the guards. "You can go now," he kept saying.

Dubiously, Alak Drong looked closer still and saw that it wasn't the captain either, but Wang Aiguo. Wang Aiguo held complete power over Party and government affairs in the region, and if he pointed east and declared it was west there'd be no one to say otherwise. This was exactly as it had been before Wang's arrival, when Alak Drong had held complete power over religious and political affairs in the region, and if he had pointed west and declared it to be east, no one could have said otherwise. So if Wang Aiguo was saying he could leave, that really meant he could leave. How wonderful . . . amazing . . . a grinning Alak Drong was jolted out of his beautiful dreams by a loud commotion. The main door of the assembly hall was wide open and sunlight was streaming in from the small east-facing windows.

This hall was twice as big as the one at Tsezhung Monastery and could accommodate at least a thousand monks. *Thangkas* and religious texts were scattered across the floorboards and cushions like wind-horse prayer flags, and many of them were soiled with excrement from the night before. Alak Drong trembled involuntarily. An elderly monk fell to his knees and began beating his chest, snot and drool flowing down his chin as he wailed, "How can this be? How can this be? I'd rather be dead, I'd rather be dead . . . *Vajrasattva, Vajrasattva* . . ." This old monk was considered a member of the "proletariat" and had never "oppressed" or "exploited" anyone, but he stubbornly refused to accept that there was no such thing as karma and reincarnation, and trying to convince him otherwise was like throwing a stone into a lake. At each struggle session and each political study session, his "insufficient recognition of his errors" and "incorrect attitude" had infuriated Wang Aiguo, who had sent him down this path from which there was no return for a man of his age. The old monk's shock and confusion increased further still when he realized that the statues were all missing their heads, arms, and clothes; they looked like the sheep carcasses hanging in the cold storage of the Tsezhung County abattoir that would be built many years later. It was proof of the fact that here too there was a hero like Lozang Tsültrim—perhaps many. The heads and limbs had been tossed all over the place, but the precious jewels that had adorned the statues were nowhere to be seen, the severed heads and necks now like horse carcasses that had had their eyes pecked out by crows.

The sight was so unbearable that the nomads forgot their own wretched plight for a brief moment, but they were called back to reality by the piercing barks of the guards, who drove them straight back to the courtyard from the day before like wolves chasing a pack of sheep. There they distributed to each of the prisoners a hunk of bread and a ladle of rice gruel so thin you could see the bottom of the metal mug; then they herded them back onto the truck and set off without giving them so much as a sip of hot water. Unfortunately, after a short distance many of them began to throw up, and the vomit splattered all over the occupants of the truck bed. Unlike the day before, however, the road was a bit smoother, the truck didn't jolt so much, and it didn't seem as crowded, either.

The tubby man from before was at Alak Dong's side once again. "I dreamed of the man they buried by the roadside last night," he murmured.

"Me too," Alak Drong responded immediately.

"He crawled out of the dirt and went home, right?"

"I dreamed that it was me that went home."

The man, not understanding Alak Drong's meaning, looked at him with wide, questioning eyes.

"What clan are you from?" Alak Drong asked the man, not wanting to discuss his meaningless dream.

"I'm from the Tadzi clan. The year before last, in the autumn, you visited my family and conferred the Mahakarunika empowerment on our clan, do you remember? Ah, back then, my father and grandfather were still with us, before they went to the Pure Land . . ."

"Oh, yes, yes. You're the son of that wealthy Jikjé family from Tadzi, aren't you?"

"Yes, that's me, Rinpoché."

THE RED WIND HOWLS

"Yes, yes." Alak Drong cast his mind back to that episode two years before. The Communist Party was already in Tsezhung then, but you could still say that Alak Drong held power over religious and political affairs in the region, or at least that he could conduct religious activities and accept offerings from the faithful as he pleased. Alak Drong had already heard that there was a fabulously rich family—the Jikjés—in the Tadzi clan. Thinking back on it now, he had a vague recollection of a mutton-faced boy, but he couldn't form a clear picture of Jikjé senior or junior. What he hadn't forgotten, though, was the scene of his visit that day. The family had invited him over so many times that he eventually acceded to their request. He had donned his broad-rimmed *thangshu* hat, wrapped his monastic shawl over his shoulders, and tied two *khata* together as a sash. He rode a pure white horse, its head, mane, and hindquarters bedecked with finery, and was accompanied by a retinue of monks. They were met on the way by several men from the Tadzi clan shouting "*Ki!*" and "Victory to the gods!" and tossing wind horses in the air, then received in a tent so huge that it contained two large stoves. It was said that when they moved camp, they actually brought the yaks right inside to pack everything up. On top of one of the earthen stoves, a folded-up piece of felt a foot and a half thick topped with a bolt of yellow silk served as a throne. Before the throne there was a leather-lined wooden box, likewise draped in silk, on top of which was a plateful of sweets and fried pastries. To the right of the throne, a mat long enough for seven monks had been unfurled, in front of which were arranged plates atop a white cloth.

THE RED WIND HOWLS

A few monks from Tsezhung Monastery who were originally from the Tadzi clan had taken their leave three days prior in order to make preparations for the lama's visit to the Jikjé family. On the day itself, wearing triangular face masks made of brand-new cloth, they served the tea and an assortment of snacks in a prescribed order. As they served the tea, an elderly monk lifted his head and struck up the first notes of a chant, and was joined by the hoarse, melodious voices of Alak Drong and the seven monks:

> I make an offering to the supreme Shakyamuni
> Whose body is produced by abundant excellence
> Whose words fulfill the wishes of infinite beings
> Whose mind sees all with boundless wisdom

The last line was drawn out, and in the same way, a new chant was begun as the *droma* rice was served:

> I make an offering to the objects of refuge, the Three
> Jewels:
> Precious Buddha, the Unparalleled Teacher
> Precious Dharma, the Unparalleled Protector
> Precious Sangha, the Unparalleled Guide

When the meat was served, they chanted:

> To you, Vajrabhairava, I make an offering
> You whose wrath excels among the glorious bodies
> You whose deeds lie in the domain of heroes
> You who act to tame the difficult to tame

When the yogurt was served, they chanted:

To the gods of wealth and lords of treasure, I make an
  offering
To the great king Vaishravana, who guards the North
To the noble Jambhala, master of riches
To the goddess Vasudhara, who dispels poverty

After this final prayer, they enjoyed their meals.

Bestowing empowerments entailed a great deal of ritual, on top of which Alak Drong had some matters to attend to. As far as the Mahakarunika empowerment went, he contented himself with a quick read through of the scripture, after which he addressed some brief remarks to the clan (and the Jikjé family in particular): the cyclic existence of samsara is without essence, material possessions are impermanent, the only infallible objects of refuge are the Dharma, the lama, and the sangha, and so on. Finally he cut to the chase with a decisive conclusion: all worldly possessions should be offered to the lama and the monastery—only in this way could one remove obstacles in this life, be spared the terrors of the bardo, and avoid rebirth in the lower realms. This perfunctory sermon had an astounding impact. Not only did the Jikjé family give him a hundred horses and mares, two hundred yaks and *dzos*, and copious amounts of silk and silver, they also gave vast offerings to the monks, the likes of which they had never seen in their lives. As a result, the fame of the Jikjé family of Tadzi spread throughout the whole of Tsezhung.

Despite the impressive spread that had been laid out for him, it would have been unseemly for Alak Drong to eat his fill in front of all those people, so when dinnertime came around he was actually quite hungry. Happily, they had prepared his favorite dish, the one that none of his three meals a day could ever be without: boiled fatty mutton, served in a wooden tub. Alak Drong tucked in with relish, so much so that he had a bit of a stomachache that night, but thinking back on it now, he genuinely regretted not having polished off the whole thing.

Fortunately for them, Alak Drong and the tubby young man weren't suffering quite as much as the others from dizziness and nausea, so they were able to continue their hushed conversation. "What's your name?" asked Alak Drong.

"Tsering Tashi. They call me Tsetra."

"Oh yes, yes. How long's your sentence?"

Tsetra didn't understand. The tiny mouth in the middle of his huge face hung open like a question mark.

Alak Drong thought for a moment of how to rephrase the question in simpler terms. "Did they say how many years you have to be in prison for?"

"No, Rinpoché, they didn't say. At first, they wanted to put my mom or my grandma in prison instead, because I'm so young. But Uncle Rapgyé begged the official; he told him that my grandma was too old for manual labor, and if they took my mom the rest of the family would starve. In the end they let me take their place."

"How old are you?"

"I'm seventeen, but they said I'm actually sixteen."

At first Alak Drong was taken aback, but comparing his situation to Tsetra's, he thought that it must be true what Wang Aiguo had said: his own definitive sentence of ten years was down to his correct attitude. Either way, his case was clear as day, so all he had to do was accept it. It was a ray of hope, and feeling a sudden glimmer of optimism, he let his unfiltered thoughts slip out: "Ah! What a tough break. In that case, you'll probably spend your whole life in jail."

"Yes, Your Holiness. That's why I have to think of a way to escape."

"What? No one can escape. Even if you do, you'd have nowhere to go. The Communist Party runs heaven and earth now."

"But still, will you please do a divination for me?" Tsetra persisted, mustering his courage.

"Absolutely not. There's no need for a divination. I guarantee there's no escaping this."

"Yes . . . yes, Your Holiness." Tsetra, deflated, finally put his escape plans aside.

It was shaping up to be even hotter than the day before, and as midday approached everyone was groaning with thirst and swallowing their saliva. The two guards perched on the cab of the truck took out their dark-green water cans and drank. Watching them, Alak Drong thought, *Even if they extended my sentence by a year, it would be worth it to get my hands on one of them water bottles.* In the long years of hardship to come, every time he was tormented by the heat or the freezing cold, every time he suffered from hunger and thirst, and every time he collapsed from exhaustion, he'd ponder these hypothetical trade-offs. If every one of them had been granted, he never would have got out of prison, even if he had lived a thousand years.

One time, he actually did say to a cadre at the prison, "If you give me a day off, you can add a year to my sentence." The cadre replied: "I don't have the authority to give you a day off. If it's what you want, though, I do have the authority to prolong your sentence."

Another time, he told the prison cook that he could add a year to his sentence if he gave him another corn bun. The cook and the cadres had laughed so hard they cried. When they were done, one of them hollered, "Still trying to exploit people! This sly fox hasn't reformed his ways one bit. Throw him in solitary." Alak Drong was promptly sent to the isolation cell, now deprived of his "vegetable *tang*" broth and the one corn bun he did have. The cell was a tiny concrete room with an iron door, just big enough for one person to fit inside. The darkness was impenetrable, it was unbearably freezing in winter, and in summer it was so hot you could hardly breathe. Laboring outside, no matter how backbreaking, was enviable by comparison. That was noon on a midsummer's day; Alak Drong had cried and sweated so much he felt like he was in a food steamer. The heat and thirst on the back of this truck was a walk in the park by comparison. Before long, he had slipped into a daze, and in his semiconscious state he had visions of the cook and the cadres tossing piles of corn buns to each other, back and forth, back and forth, like they were playing basketball. When one of the buns landed in his hand, tens of thousands of prisoners surrounded him and pinned him to the floor, then piled on top one after another. Just as he was about to suffocate, the iron door emitted a sudden clang and he awoke with a jump. He was drenched in sweat and his heart was pounding.

He offered a prayer to the Dharma protectors and, gasping, thought, *They say you should never fall asleep in the freezing cold because you might not wake up. I think the same must be true of heat like this.* Steeling himself, he fought the temptation to drift off.

It was impossible to tell the time of day in that total darkness, but judging from the slight decrease in heat, he knew it must be nighttime, or at least dusk. Alak Drong's mind was much clearer now, and he realized how foolish his actions had been. At the same moment, he resolved to strive for an early release by heeding their call to atone for his crimes and prove himself. Plainly speaking, "proving himself" meant ratting out his fellow inmates, for example reporting on anyone who was carrying out reactionary activities like praying in secret, or anyone contemplating suicide. Many of the Tibetans prayed when they were alone, and what's more, a number of them had sought spiritual refuge with him. An even graver crime was planning to escape—or thinking about it. Stubborn types like Tsetra, for instance. Ah! So many opportunities to prove himself. But did they guarantee the anonymity of informants and offer them protection? And did they really reduce your sentence for "proving yourself"? It was worth a try, at any rate. It was worse than hell there; he'd be happy to get a couple of months' reprieve, a couple of days even, never mind a year or two. He didn't know if it was true or not that "one day in hell is like a year on earth," but one day in prison really was like a year compared to life at the monastery. Ten years of that—would it ever end? Even if it did, he'd be lucky to survive three years at this rate. That's why he had to do what they had demanded. Or at least give it a try . . .

THE RED WIND HOWLS

Though they encountered a few streams en route, their waters muddied with red dust, a tall bridge spanned every single one, dashing the hopes of the prisoners in the truck bed. Sometime in the afternoon they arrived at a small town, and someone began shouting gleefully, "Gandu! Gandu! This is Gandu!" The way he was acting, it was if they would be set free once they got there.

As the guard pelted the shouting man with blows from his whip, the truck pulled into a high-walled courtyard and creaked to a halt. The two guards hopped nimbly off and began yelling and pointing their rifles at the prisoners, motioning for them to get out.

The courtyard contained numerous rows of buildings with metal grilles covering their windows, as well as several rifle-toting sentries patrolling the entrance. From this, it was obvious that the place was a small prison—or a large detention center. A handful of peach, jujube, and pear trees grew haphazardly in the center of the yard, their foliage spreading out luxuriously. The prisoners were overjoyed to see a terra-cotta vat, so big that it would take two men to wrap their arms around it, filled with crystal-clear water and with a little wooden ladle bobbing on the surface. The sentries atop the walls could see everything in the courtyard as though it were in the palm of their hand, and now the other guards and the truck driver were nowhere to be seen.

The nomads, not holding back, drank their fill of the cool water, then gathered in groups of five or six beneath the shade of the trees, hiccupping. A short time later, they spread themselves out, some leaning against the tree trunks, some with their sleeves tucked under their heads, and fell asleep.

Alak Drong and Tsetra sat with their backs against either side of a pear tree. Alak Drong gradually drifted off, but Tsetra was staring at the blue sky between the leaves, lost in thought—pondering his escape plans, perhaps. The branches had long since been picked clean of their fruit and some of the yellowing leaves were drifting down with the faintest breath of cool breeze. Tsetra suddenly spotted a solitary pear, brilliantly yellow, hanging amid the leaves. For a moment, he didn't believe his eyes. Slowly he rose, holding his breath and not taking his eyes off it for even an instant, as though hunting an animal; then in one quick movement his hand shot out and snatched the pear. The ecstatic feeling of it, cool and soft, spread from his palm to every nerve. Tsetra peered about furtively. Seeing that everything was quiet and calm, he relaxed, then sat back down bursting with joy. Seeing the peacefully dozing Alak Drong, he became even happier, and gave him a gentle shake.

Alak Drong's treatment at the hands of Wang Aiguo, Lozang Tsültrim, and the guards over the last few months had made him as wary as a wounded animal, and he awoke with a panicked start. Happily, what greeted him this time wasn't a whip or the muzzle of a gun, but a beautiful yellow pear. Thinking that he must still be dreaming, he rubbed his eyes and looked at Tsetra.

Tsetra pointed to the branch with a grin, and whispered, "It's for you, Rinpoché."

Reassured, Alak Drong opened his mouth wide and took a bite. As a whole third of the pretty pear vanished like a rainbow from the sky, a fragrance so sweet filled the air that Tsetra couldn't help but close his eyes and drool. A second later, when

Tsetra opened his eyes, the holy lama had left no "venerable leftovers" apart from two trickles of juice running down the corners of his mouth—he'd even swallowed the core.

Two years earlier, when Tsetra's family had hosted Alak Drong, he had only sampled a mouthful or two of each dish—yogurt included—and had only taken a couple of sips of tea, leaving everything else untouched. The elders called these the "venerable leftovers," and everyone had fought to get their hands on them. It was said that lamas intentionally left some of these "venerable leftovers" for their hosts and that they held the power to vanquish a hundred maladies and to preserve one's health and well-being.

"Ah!" said Alak Drong, licking the juice from his lips, "this Gandu really is a great place."

"Yes, Rinpoché."

"Take a good look at each of the trees. With any luck, we might find a couple more," he said, as though issuing an order. These last two days, Tsetra had waited on the lama hand and foot, prompting Alak Drong's natural inclination to treat him as a servant to gradually reemerge.

"Yes, Rinpoché." Tsetra examined each and every tree but couldn't turn up even a trace of a piece of fruit. Alak Drong nevertheless remained upbeat. "Well anyway, this Gandu really is a great place. Maybe they'll even give us a good meal tonight."

Indeed, shortly thereafter a large door in one of the buildings swung open, and with it came a delightful smell that awoke all the sleepers. Large aluminum pots, each one wafting delicious aromas in their wake, were taken into each of the cells, and soon empty pots were brought back out. The nomads waited

THE RED WIND HOWLS

on tenterhooks for half an hour, swallowing their saliva, and finally an old Hui Muslim man who spoke impeccable Tibetan came over and asked gently, "Would you like to eat here or inside?"

"We can eat out here," the nomads replied in unison.

Two men arrived carrying a large pot. "Have your *gangzi*s ready!" one called out.

Fortunately, Alak Drong had learned his lesson from the day before: that morning, after finishing his gruel, he had secretly stuffed his *gangzi*—that is, his metal mug—in his pocket in case they came across any water on the journey. Though the pot only contained a few pieces of turnip and no meat, the noodles were delicious, and after devouring his whole *gangzi*-full in the blink of an eye, Alak Drong sat staring at the others' mouths.

"Would you like some more?" the old Hui man asked him.

"If it's allowed . . ." said Alak Drong deferentially, extending his *gangzi*.

"Of course it's allowed."

It seemed there was no limit to the food there, as long your stomach could take it. Alak Drong polished off four *gangzi*s of noodles in a row. Not since they had been detained had they been allowed to eat this much, and their faces flushed.

"Ah! This Gandu really is a great place!" Alak Drong couldn't help but exclaim once again.

"Yes, Rinpoché." Tsetra had, for the time being at least, forgotten about his escape plans. "It's just as you predicted. With food like this, the prison can't be all that bad."

At that moment, prisoners began streaming out from each of the buildings and strolling about in the yard. Another Hui

■ 42 ■

man with impeccable Tibetan, this one younger, approached each of the nomads in turn. "What have you got on you?" he hissed, flashing a couple of tiny penknives he kept hidden up his sleeve. "These can help you escape. They can also help you kill yourself."

The nomads were too terrified to look, but not Tsetra. "Let me see," he said, taking one of the knives and stashing it in his pocket.

"How about it? Looks like it was made just for us prisoners, right?"

"Not bad. Very useful. But what about when you're searched?"

"*Ai yaya*, nomads, nomads." The Hui shook his head. "You've got an asshole, don't you?"

Tsetra felt a sudden itch in his anus. "I'm sorry, I've got nothing to trade," he said, holding out the penknife.

The Hui stared at the bulge in Tsetra's clothes, declining to take back the knife. When Tsetra produced an empty *gangzi* from his pocket, the disappointed Hui snatched his knife back and took off.

Tsetra, feeling deflated again, watched the Hui walk off, thinking that it was true what Alak Drong had said in his sermon to his family: material possessions are like a dewdrop on a blade of grass; here today, gone tomorrow, here in the morning, gone by the afternoon . . . At the start of spring that year, his family had owned at least a thousand horses, five thousand yaks, ten thousand sheep, more money than they could fit in their trunks, and more trunks than they could fit in their tents. But that morning when the red wind began to howl, in the blink of an eye it had all been "confiscated"—brazenly plundered, to put it more accurately—and now he had nothing left but the hair on his head and the nails on his toes. He didn't even have the means to buy a penknife. Worse still, he had no idea how long he was in prison for, in fact he didn't even know if he'd ever get out. If it was a choice between suffering a bit and dying soon or suffering a lot and dying later, he'd prefer the former. All of a sudden, he was overcome by a wave of inexplicable courage and irrepressible rage, and he ran after the Hui man. "Hey! Stop there! I want to buy a knife."

"So what have you got for me?"

"Don't worry about it. I guarantee you'll be satisfied."

Hesitantly, the Hui handed him a knife. As soon as it was in his hands, Tsetra sneered and brandished the blade in his face. "To tell you the truth, I haven't got a thing on me. But if you don't give me one of these knives, not only will they confiscate all the rest, they'll double your time. Who knows, maybe you'll even get the death sentence. Go on, try me. See what happens."

The Hui glanced toward the guards, then back at the hulking nomad boy, who had suddenly become so angry his eyes had turned red. He shook his head and walked away, muttering to himself.

Tsetra put all his hopes into that little knife, but a long time passed without him finding an opportunity to use it. With the utmost secrecy, several of the prisoners had cut slender tamarisk branches into pieces with the sharp edge of a stone and then ground them down on the stone's flat surface until they resembled rosary beads. After boring a hole through each one with the tip of a needle, they strung ten or twenty of these beads

THE RED WIND HOWLS

together to fashion a makeshift rosary. Seeing this, Tsetra decided to finally put his knife to good use, and he discreetly carved a hundred-bead rosary, which he presented to Alak Drong. Compared to the ones made by the other prisoners with their stones, it was as finely crafted as if it had been made by a machine. A rosary isn't really strictly for prayer, because it's said that in the next life, the exact number of recitations you performed in this life will appear on the Lord of Death's mirror, as though it were engraved in stone. But because a rosary lets you keep track of how many you've done yourself, and moreover serves as a constant reminder to do more, for a person of faith—or anyone who does their recitations, at least—it's an indispensable accessory.

It came completely out of the blue, then, when Alak Drong handed the rosary over to the cadres. Worse still, the cadres realized that this rosary, knife marks clearly visible on every bead, was nothing like the crude stone-cut ones they usually confiscated, and as a result they knew the prisoners were concealing "weapons," a matter they immediately reported to Song Jiantao, the brigade commander. Song Jiantao was a very sharp man. He didn't conduct an immediate search or have Tsetra brought in for questioning; instead, he did two things: first, he ordered his brigade and unit leaders to closely scrutinize the actions of every prisoner under their watch, and second, he called Alak Drong straight to his office. "The time has come for you to prove yourself," he announced. "You must do everything in your power to track down that weapon, and you must also find out where it came from. From now on, you report to me directly."

■ 45 ■

"Yes sir, absolutely!" Alak Drong was overjoyed to be under his protection, but at the same time, something worried him. "Ah . . . but, you will keep my cover, won't you? Things don't end well for informants. If they find out I'm a snitch . . ."

"This isn't snitching, it's mutual cooperation. You could also say it's saving lives. Think about it: what if that weapon was pointed at you one day, or at me, hm? What if there are many such weapons, and those weapons get used against the guards, hm? What if those weapons are pointed at the great Communist Party, or at our beloved Chairman Mao, hm? This is a serious matter. An extremely serious matter!" As he spoke, Song Jiantao's voice rose in anger and he hammered his fist on the desk.

Alak Drong left Song's office absolutely terrified and discovered that he was drenched in sweat. He wasn't worried that the weapon would be used against him, much less that it would be used against Chairman Mao, but this time things seemed more serious than with previous incidents and it didn't look like Tsetra, or the man who was concealing the "weapons," would get off lightly. What's more, it would be hard to keep his name out of the whole thing. If they found out he had informed on them, the Tibetan prisoners would no longer have any respect for him or faith in him, in fact they wouldn't even say a word to him, and he'd be left completely alone. On the other hand, though, the more serious the incident, the more they would reduce his sentence. *Well, what's done is done,* he thought. *There's nothing for it but to keep doing what they want and see if I can at least shave some years off my sentence by reporting on the others.* Walking unsteadily, he arrived at the cells.

Seeing Alak Drong's shaken expression, Tsetra approached him meekly. "Rinpoché, did they make you do another criticism session?"

Alak Drong shook his head slightly. "They confiscated my rosary."

"Oh, no need to let that dampen your honorable mood. I can make you another, easy."

"They said it was made by a knife or something and they're treating it as a very serious matter. They said if I didn't tell them what it was made with or where it came from, they'd increase my sentence."

"*Ah ho!* I've done you a great wrong!"

"No, not at all. Let them increase it . . ."

"No, Rinpoché! I'll go to them right now and confess. It's true, I have a knife. I kept it all this time thinking it might come in handy if I ever got the chance to escape. But it's like you said all along—there's no escape. Even if they let me go right now, I could barely walk a thousand steps; what good's a penknife going to do? I don't even have a clearly defined sentence anyway, so there's nothing more they can do to me. I'm going to confess."

Tsetra set off resolutely, regretting just one thing: having robbed the Hui man from Gandu. He had always listened to his parents and his lama and had never gone against the laws of karma, but he had stolen that knife in a fit of anger and despair. He had regretted it ever since and had never been able to get the image of the poor Hui man walking away and shaking his head in disappointment out of his mind. But people are always shaped by their environment: in the great tide of backstabbing and informing that was to come, he too gradually became a man devoid of pity, a man who trampled the laws of karma and was all too happy to inform on his fellow inmates. He even settled scores with Alak Drong—who had had spiritual ties with his family for generations, who was seen as the embodiment of a buddha—informing on him, denouncing him on false charges, and getting him punished. Even more shocking was that he did all this without feeling an ounce of remorse and decided that he would simply keep on doing it. When he first found out that it was Alak Drong who had informed on him, Tsetra felt hurt and dejected, but slowly he became determined to get his payback. After fashioning a crude tamarisk rosary consisting of ten beads and hiding it under Alak Drong's pillow, he went to report to the authorities.

"You sly, two-faced wolf!" The cadre hit Alak Drong with a single savage blow that made his mouth and nose bleed, then without offering any explanation, threw him in the felons' cells.

Political prisoners like Alak Drong, or what they called "historical" prisoners, accounted for more than 90 percent of the convicts, while criminal offenders—murderers, arsonists, thieves, rapists—accounted for less than 10. The prison cadres would often take hopelessly stubborn political prisoners or those who had committed serious political errors and throw them in with the regular felons. The felons had many ways of "teaching" the political prisoners, one of which was stealing their bread and their "vegetable *tang.*"

When Alak Drong was brought back to the cellblock for the political prisoners after four days with the felons, he was visibly thinner and didn't have the strength to stand.

"Demons, the absolute demons . . ."

As Alak Drong wept, Tsetra, still not satisfied, went to report to the cadre that Alak Drong was spreading feudal superstitions in the prison, poisoning people's minds with talk of demons.

"Looks like you still haven't learned your lesson!" The cadre dealt Alak Drong a blow that knocked him head over heels, then had him sent back to the felons' cellblock. Two days later, when he was dragged back in by two men, limp arms slung around their necks, he could barely breathe, and for a moment Tsetra was anxious. But as soon as he recalled the torments he himself had endured in solitary and in the felons' cells, he was unable to let his grudge go. Alak Drong, by contrast, still felt some remorse, and he couldn't help but fall to prayer the moment Tsetra had left.

The brigade leader, Lugyel Bum, had taken Tsetra straight to Song Jiantao. Commander Song possessed a good deal of information on Tsetra—his plans to escape, his concealment of weapons, his incitement of religious practice through the manufacturing of rosaries—but since Tsetra had neither a file nor a definitive sentence, there was little he could do to increase his punishment. Regardless, in the end he sent Tsetra to solitary for a week, then to the felons' cells for another week, and only when Tsetra had reached the stage where he was almost beyond hope of recovery had Song's anger abated a little. As for Alak Drong, once he had been thoroughly brought to heel, he was given a one-year sentence reduction on the basis of his "good labor." This news encouraged Alak Drong to double down on his previous efforts, and he informed on his fellow inmates' every move like a madman. At the same time, Lugyel Bum and

Song Jiantao cleverly covered for him, meaning that in addition to their hard labor and meager rations, the prisoners now also had to pass their days in an atmosphere of terror and mutual suspicion. By this time, all they got to eat was a small corn bun and something called "vegetable *tang*," a thin broth containing nothing but a few greens that Alak Drong could polish off in three gulps, and even this meager ration was shrinking by the day.

The first time the nomads had seen this alleged food known as vegetable *tang* was in Xining. After eating a hearty breakfast in that lovely place called Gandu, they'd been taken to the city of Xining, where their heads had been shaved right down to the scalp. There, a cadre who liked to pace about with his hands behind his back just like Wang Aiguo yelled something at them, which, after it passed through the ears and out the mouth of an interpreter, became "Change your clothes!" As Tsetra was worrying about the penknife, each prisoner was handed a Mao suit, or in other words prison clothes, and the cadres marched straight off as if they couldn't bear the nomads' grimy appearance or their musty odor.

A tiny hat that only covered the crown of the head and looked like it had been made for comedic effect; a black padded jacket with only one pocket on the left breast; a pair of black padded trousers split from the waist to the crotch, and a pair of black cotton shoes with plastic soles: apparently these were the prisoners' winter clothes. The first problem the nomads encountered was that they didn't know whether the hole in the trousers should be in the front or the back. Some said the back, so it would be easier to take a crap, while others said the front, so

THE RED WIND HOWLS

it would be easier to take a piss. Since there was a lack of consensus on the issue, some wore the opening on the front and others wore it on their butts; others still decided that because Alak Drong was a man possessed of prophetic knowledge who had encountered both the Red and White Chinese he was sure to know, but when they looked to him for guidance, he too was at a loss.

At this moment the cadres reentered, accompanied by the interpreter. At first they were shocked, then they burst out laughing, and by the end of it they were crying. The assembled prisoners looked like a clown troupe: the prison uniforms were a mess to begin with, but on top of that, some were too big and some were too small, some people were wearing their right shoe on their left foot and their left shoe on their right foot, and some were wearing their trousers back to front. Eventually, the cadre who liked to pace with his hands behind his back like Wang Aiguo composed himself and commenced yelling, at which point the prisoners, stifling their laughter, began to rearrange their trousers and their shoes until everything was in the correct order.

The nomads, who had never queued up for anything in their lives except to see their lama, were lined up and marched into a room five or six times the size of the assembly hall at Tsezhung Monastery. There, several thousand men wearing shabby black prison uniforms like theirs were seated on the floor drinking something the Chinese called vegetable *tang* from metal mugs. It was nothing more than a thin broth with some sad greens, and the sight of it thoroughly disheartened the nomads. Since they'd recently eaten their fill in that lovely place called

Gandu, they weren't all that hungry. "Even if we're starving, we won't eat grass," they said.

What the nomads couldn't have imagined, even in their worst nightmares, was that in the years of hardship to come, even vegetable *tang*—which among themselves came to be called "grass"—would become rarer than gold. "If I could just get a good bowl of vegetable *tang*, I'd die happy," they would soon find themselves saying. A lot of prisoners had died by then, and the bodies were continuing to pile up. Those who were still living had no energy left to work, and dragging the corpses out of the prison and burying them had become their main task. Before too long, however, they didn't even have the strength to dig graves, so this task was reduced to simply throwing the bodies in the river at the foot of the mountain and returning with a bucketful of water.

With each passing day the prisoners grew thinner; their movements became slower, their breath shorter, their words fewer, and their eyes dimmer. Finally, without so much as a groan or a struggle, they slipped into a hallucinatory haze. When they lost consciousness entirely, some of the more recent arrivals would, with great difficulty, drag them outside for disposal, like bags of garbage.

In stark contrast to the prisoners' stillness, the red wind raged relentlessly. It would start to pick up just before noon, then gradually grow in strength. The whirlwinds came in from every direction, getting bigger and higher, sometimes looking like red columns planted in the sky, sometimes like living things that were chasing each other back and forth. The Mongolian prisoners called these whirlwinds "camel trains," and from afar they

THE RED WIND HOWLS

really did resemble a caravan of pack camels all walking head to tail. In the afternoon, the whirlwinds began to merge and the storm grew even fiercer, carrying the men forward a few steps before depositing them on the ground and whipping them with sand, dirt, and pebbles that would actually draw blood from their uncovered faces. There's a phrase in Chinese to describe a sandstorm: "flying sand, running rocks." Clearly, it's no exaggeration. Even more distressing and intimidating was the terrible howling. Sometimes it sounded like thousands of starving wolves all howling at once on the desolate plains, at other times like tens of thousands of Red Guards shouting slogans in unison on Tiananmen Square. Even on a clear, cloudless day, the red wind could obscure the sun's rays as though a great lid had been placed over the land. It was hard to make out others' faces even when indoors, and trucks could only drive with their high beams on. For prisoners in relatively good health, the red wind represented the best time to mount an escape attempt, but it also meant that the sentries and guards were extra vigilant. If a red wind blew in while the inmates were outside burying the dead, the guards would gather them up, make them lie face down on the ground, and keep their rifles trained on them until it passed.

Just as no day passed without a red wind, no day passed without a death. Every evening, the red wind died down slightly, and this was the signal for dinnertime. With weak, pained groans, the prisoners crawled stark naked out of their blankets and slowly donned their shabby black uniforms, which had been hung up to one side in an effort to save them from the lice. As soon as the clothes touched their bodies, thousands of lice all bit into them at once, making them feel as though they'd fallen naked into a pit of thorns. At first the prisoners tried to kill off the lice, which only left some of them with bloodstained thumbs. Next they tried laying out their clothes and beating the lice out with a broom, but this only served to increase their numbers. In the end, lacking the energy to fight them off anymore, the prisoners had no choice but to let the lice be. The only solution was to sleep naked under the blankets, which contained slightly fewer lice than their clothes. The blankets had also been given to them in Xining. Because they had refused to eat the thin vegetable broth they referred to as "grass," the cadre who liked to pace with his hands behind his back like Wang Aiguo was highly displeased. "Very well, very well," he snorted, "then would you gentlemen please follow me?" Taking them outside, he handed each man a mat and a blanket, then showed them all into an empty room, which he locked from the outside.

The sun was still high at the time, so it must have been at least two hours before dusk. The prisoners brought in from elsewhere were walking back and forth in the yard speaking various languages. If the nomads had eaten their vegetable *tang*, they too would be strolling freely in the yard. Trying to guess what their futures held in store was all that was left to them for the time being. How much food would they get? What kind of work would they have to do? Would they be able to see their families again? If so, when? What none of them could have predicted was that the next morning they would be loaded back onto the truck and driven farther northeast. Unlike the last few days, the road was wide and smooth, so they weren't jolted about so much, added to which they had

THE RED WIND HOWLS

swapped their big coats for prison uniforms, so the truck didn't seem quite so crowded. But their hearts continued to sink the farther they were taken from home. They had even more reason to be downhearted when, after a full day on the road, they were deposited in a vast landscape where forests covered the mountains and plains as far as the eye could see. "Listen up! This is your home now," they were told. As things turned out, for most of them it proved to be their grave.

For a free person, a forest might be a nice vacation spot, somewhere to get away from it all. But for someone deprived of their freedom it's the very opposite: it feels like a prison cell. In the mountains to the north, a thick blanket of cypress trees covered the sunny side of each of the valleys, while the shady side was all thousand-year-old verdant pines. A wide, clear river flowed at the foot of the mountains, forming a natural boundary between mountain and plain. Willows, poplars, birches, and azalea bushes were dotted among the tamarisk trees that covered the flat, boundless plain. An area of about half a square mile had been cleared in the forest near the river. There, inside a vast enclosure surrounded by a wall as high and solid as the Great Wall itself, numerous rows of buildings with tiny windows had already been constructed, and yet more were being added. In addition to these, there was an infirmary, a barber, an isolation cell, a shop, a dormitory for the cadres, a dormitory for the workers, an administrative office, an interrogation chamber, a dining hall for the cadres, a large canteen, a large meeting hall, and other facilities besides. This, then, was their "home."

Around six months later, when the boundless forest had been completely cut down and burned to ashes, there were at least ten of these "homes" on the plain. Each contained twenty or so brigades, with twenty-odd units to a brigade and twenty-odd prisoners to a unit, so it was no surprise that it had only taken them half a year to wipe out such an enormous forest.

The first difficulty the nomads encountered here was that they had to "report" in Chinese which brigade and which unit they belonged to. For example, Alak Drong, as a prisoner from Brigade 6, Unit 4, had to say, *Baogao! Wo shi diliu dui disi zu fanren Zhongcang!* (Reporting! I am prisoner Alak Drong, Sixth Brigade, Fourth Unit!). To Alak Drong, however, this was even harder to remember than the *Vows of Refuge*. After practicing it thousands of times, he had it down: "Reporting! I am prize nutter Alak Drong, Socks Brigade, Fourth Unit!" This always cracked the cadres up. "He really is a nutter!" they'd howl.

If this was the case for Alak Drong, who had "traveled everywhere but the ends of the earth" and had interacted with the Chinese (both Red and White), then it goes without saying how hard it was for those who had known little of the world beyond their cattle.

The tens of thousands of prisoners were like an overflowing anthill in a garden: some brigades were chopping down the trees with hatchets while others were arranging the logs into piles. The nomads assumed they must be felling all these trees to provide firewood for the city of Xining, but when they began to torch untouched sections of forest, they no longer understood the ultimate purpose of their work. When the weather got warmer, the brigades were set to work again. Some dug out the tree roots with pickaxes while others turned over the turf; some made piles of dry logs, topped them with the loose turf, then

THE RED WIND HOWLS

set fire to them; and others still were excavating irrigation ditches. It was then the nomads finally realized the plan was to cultivate this land.

The nomads knew how to ride animals, how to raise animals, how to slaughter animals and use them for food, and how to slaughter animals and use them for clothing. Other than this, they had no manual skills. They couldn't dig a straight ditch, let alone erect a building, so overturning the turf became their designated task. The first time they used the shovels and pick-axes, the nomads skinned their palms until they blistered and bled. Gradually they healed, and the skin became thick and callused. Since they had stubbornly refused to eat the vegetable *tang* for a month or two now and it wasn't in their nature to slack off when it came to hard work, they grew thinner much quicker than the others. At that point, they realized the vegetable *tang* wasn't as pointless as they had thought, and one after another they abandoned the oaths they had made in Xining and started eating the "grass."

It was at this time that another truckload of prisoners from Tsezhung arrived at the camp. When the inmates who had been there some two months already went to greet the new arrivals with a mixture of apprehension and expectation, both concerned for their fate and eager for news from home, Alak Drong caught sight of his old teacher, Dranak Geshé. His heart was filled with a joyous sense of hope, as if he had found a source of protection, but soon it was replaced by shame and remorse for the way he had acted two months before. As he stood there, wavering in doubt, someone cried out: "Drong Rinpoché! Hey, everyone, Drong Rinpoché is here!" The elation in his voice gave the

• 57 •

THE RED WIND HOWLS

impression that their suffering was now at an end, instead of having only just begun.

"Really? His Holiness is really here?" Dranak Geshé, clearly emotional, groped about in front of him, and judging from his reaction, he seemed to have long since forgotten about all the shameful things Alak Drong had done back home. Feeling as if a weight had been lifted off his shoulders, Alak Drong rushed to his teacher, but he was shocked to discover the geshé's face was horribly swollen and had become a patchwork of blue, black, and red. His eyes had swollen even worse, so much that he couldn't open them. Alak Drong, unable to utter a word, clutched his teacher's hand tightly and wept.

"Please don't weep, Your Holiness. I'm fine. The more torment we endure, the more we purge our sins and the closer we come to the path of liberation. This is a happy thing for us. So please don't weep, Your Holiness. I'm not suffering at all, really." These did not seem to be empty words; it really looked like Dranak Geshé did not consider all this pain to be a form of suffering. However, he followed this up with a long sigh and continued, "What frightens me, though, is that people are turning into savages. Mixing up black and white, not distinguishing vice from virtue, no regard for the laws of karma. And it's getting worse every day. Now they're ravaging the earth itself and turning the pristine Land of Snows into a barbaric wilderness. It's an utterly horrifying state of affairs. You must keep this in mind and make supplications to the Three Jewels! I am certain that if you do, saintly beings such as your noble self, as holy as Mount Sumeru, foremost among whom is the Omniscient Amitabha, will abide in great numbers, and all will be well." He closed his eyes—though he didn't need to close them—then clasped his hands together and muttered a long prayer.

We lay folk often say, "Don't listen to what a man says, watch what he does." Dranak Geshé, however, would say, "Don't watch what a lama does." This was because he believed that the actions of a holy being were unfathomable to ordinary people and it was therefore inappropriate for others to think or speak about them. Alak Drong's status as an authentic reincarnation was in no doubt, because it had been personally verified by an all-knowing lama, and he therefore felt it was not the place of ordinary people to speculate on the purpose of Alak Drong's recent "noble deeds." Later, when he was on his deathbed, Dranak Geshé called the prisoners from Tsezhung to his side to reiterate this point: "It's possible there's an informant in your ranks, but I believe the majority of you respect the laws of karma and know the difference between right and wrong. We common people cannot understand the deeds of a lama, and Drong Rinpoché's status as a reincarnation was determined by an all-knowing lama, so he is certainly no ordinary person. It might seem like there's no such thing as karma in this day and age, but karma will always be sure and true. I want each of you to remember this well; it will be beneficial to yourselves and to others, in both this life and the next." The next morning at sunrise, he passed away, sitting in the lotus position.

According to the newly arrived prisoners, demons like Lozang Tsültrim were multiplying back home, and among them was a corpulent, red-faced woman named Künga Huamo. She was related to Lozang Tsültrim on his mother's side, and she was even more reckless and cruel. If someone's child was misbehaving or wouldn't stop crying, all they had to say was, "Künga Huamo's coming!" and the child would wet themself in terror. The day before the prisoners were taken away from Tsezhung, a large struggle session had been held. As the revolutionaries were airing their grudges against class enemies for the last time, Künga Huamo hurled Dranak Geshé to the floor and began pounding him relentlessly. At one point she drove both fists into his eye sockets and twisted them back and forth like screwdrivers. After about fifteen minutes of this, blood was gushing from his eyes, and the leader of the session finally dragged Künga Huamo off him.

Though Lozang Tsültrim and Künga Huamo were equally firm in their class stand, they each had their unique way of expressing their class hatred. Lozang Tsültrim would punctuate every curse with a blow from his fist, while Künga Huamo, by contrast, would approach the "enemy" without a word, pace in front of them and circle them a few times, and then, unleashing a scream, suddenly grab the "enemy's" hair and drag them back and forth, or squeeze their throat until their eyeballs popped out, or claw at their face with her nails, or slap and punch them repeatedly, or plant her entire weight (all 160 pounds of it) on their chest and bounce up and down until it felt like their lungs would burst. At these times, mothers would hold their children to their breasts to prevent them from looking, because anything they saw would surely haunt their dreams and keep them awake at night. This wasn't just an ordeal for the children—it was equally so for the mothers, who had to get up in the middle of the night to milk the animals.

THE RED WIND HOWLS

"She's a demoness, no two ways about it," someone said, shaking their head, "and to think, I heard she's the geshé's niece as well."

"*Ah kha!* I feel so sorry for everyone back home. Better to be here in prison than have to face that. The food is pitiful and the work is hard, but at least there aren't so many struggle sessions here." This was said by one of the longtime prisoners.

One of the new arrivals agreed. "You're not wrong. The labor back home isn't easy either, and all you can think about is getting arrested. You live in constant fear, wondering if you'll be taken, and if so, when. They're arresting more and more people every day, and they only need the slightest excuse. Sometimes they don't even bother with an excuse."

A few days later, his observations were confirmed. A truckful of prisoners arrived from a farming region, one of whom was a man who heaved long sighs and muttered things to himself like "Oh, mother! Don't let this happen to me. Oh my wretched fate . . ." After four days and nights without eating, drinking, or sleeping, he suddenly began babbling. "Haha! Still so many to arrest! The regional quotas haven't been met yet! Still so many people to arrest, so many to arrest . . ." After this, he was taken to the sanatorium. The others who had come in with him later revealed that his name was Chaktar Bum and that he was a fanatic just like Lozang Tsültrim. The higher-ups had groomed him for the role of village head, and once he'd got it, Chaktar Bum's fervor only increased, and he ran around trumping up charges and fabricating evidence to his heart's content, imprisoning as many as he could. At some point he just started

THE RED WIND HOWLS

arresting people and taking them to the county seat without even bothering to fabricate evidence. Finally there was a time when he took nine prisoners to the county seat, and the official there clucked in disapproval. "What's this?" the official said. "Didn't you promise to bring in ten?"

"Yes, sir, I did, but all that's left now is women and children, the sick and the elderly . . ."

"Well, that's not your fault, I suppose. But since the quota hasn't been met, I can't let you leave."

"Haha! Very funny, *zhuren* . . ."

"I'm not joking. I hate jokes more than anything."

Indeed, the director—or the *zhuren*, rather—looked like he was deadly serious, and Chaktar Bum became flustered. "*Zhu . . . zhu . . . zhuren*, as you know, my . . . my forefathers, my forefathers' forefathers, every generation of my family has been proletarians. I . . . I . . ."

"Bad elements can be found even in the ranks of the proletariat."

"But . . . I . . . my . . ."

"Your crime? Your crime is that you harbored criminals and failed to meet the authorities' quotas. If I don't arrest you, these crimes will be on my head."

"Then let me go back, and I swear to you I'll bring one more. Two even, three!"

"Didn't you say the only ones left were women and children, the sick and the elderly?"

"There might still be one or two . . ."

"Time waits for no man. The truck leaves tomorrow morning, and it must be full."

THE RED WIND HOWLS

"Mother! It can't be done, it's impossible, I . . ."

"Hah!" One of the men Chaktar Bum had brought in interjected with a cold laugh. "Of course it's possible. You brought us here, didn't you?"

"Yes indeed, heaven has eyes! If we get to take a bastard like you with us, I'll have no regrets," said another, twisting Chaktar Bum's arm behind his back. Chaktar Bum turned to the *zhuren*, who by this point had already walked away, and was about to cry out when a hand closed over his mouth from behind.

On the way to prison, the others who had been arrested by Chaktar Bum subjected him to any and every form of torture they pleased. "This is just the beginning, you sorry piece of shit," they said. "Just wait till we get to the prison and all our brothers who you put there get their hands on you. Then you'll know the true meaning of hell."

"Well, we're all in the same boat now," concluded one of the farmers who had come in with Chaktar Bum. "I feel sorry for our poor families, but otherwise, better to be here where we know the score than to spend every day anxious and afraid."

It was true. There were no struggle sessions and beatings, no one had yet been placed in solitary, and above all, the high tide of informing was yet to arrive, so mutual distrust wasn't the rule. This all seemed to be thanks to the benevolent leadership of the old, bespectacled brigade commander, Yang Kai. When he saw what had happened to Dranak Geshé, there were tears in his eyes, and not only did he send the geshé for treatment, he pardoned him from labor duties until his wounds were fully healed. He also declared that he would send a report up the chain on those prisoners who had no record of a formal verdict or a definitive sentence, prompting even Tsetra to put aside his escape plans again and put all his faith in Yang Kai. Yang Kai furthermore announced that the prisoners would be allowed to write letters home to their families, on top of which he even tasked a handful of the Tibetan-speaking White Chinese (i.e., former Guomindang military officers) with helping them to write the names and addresses on the envelopes in Chinese. Dranak Geshé decided to write a letter to his nephew and disciple, Lozang Gyatso, with a few words of instruction: one, to hold on to his vows as tightly as he would a yak's tail; two, to dedicate himself to regular recitation and spiritual practice, distinguish right from wrong, and respect the laws of karma; and three, to keep his spirits up, because it was prophesied that the Buddha's light would one day shine again on the snowy mountains of Tibet. However, Yang Kai had made it clear that each letter had to be thoroughly inspected by the cadres before being put in an envelope, and that only plain language was permitted; innuendo and metaphor were strictly prohibited. Dranak Geshé, unconcerned with the joys and sorrows of this world, thus decided that sending letters wasn't necessary. He focused instead on internal prayer; no more could his melodious chanting be heard, and though his swollen eyes had finally healed, no more could that shining light of wisdom be seen. His scarlet monk's robes and volumes of scripture had long since been taken from him, leaving a clown hat, a shabby prison uniform, and a pickaxe as the companions of his twilight years. Just a few months before, hundreds of monks and lamas from Tsezhung Monastery—including Alak Drong—had all bowed

THE RED WIND HOWLS

to him in deference; now, just like the tens of thousands of other prisoners, he had to bow in deference to the brigade and unit leaders, the cadres, guards, foremen, and sentries. This confirmed to him the impermanence of the world, and his devotion to the doctrine became even more unshakeable.

At this time, Brigade Commander Yang Kai had ordered that each prisoner must work ten hours a day, but he hadn't assigned any specific labor duties, so there was no need for them to break their backs. Nevertheless, there was a world of difference between a book of scripture and a pickaxe. The prisoners got up at seven, donned their clown hats and prison uniforms, washed up with bone-chillingly cold water, and quickly ate a corn bun and drank a mug of boiled water, by which time it was eight o'clock. Shrill whistles arose from every direction all at once, and the prisoners would line up in groups of twenty and sound off in Chinese: "One, present! Two, present! . . . Seven, present! Eight, present! . . . Fourteen, present! Fifteen, present! . . . Nineteen, present! Twenty, present!" Next, the prisoner at the head of each row, who served as the unit leader and foreman, ran to his brigade leader and shouted, "Reporting to the brigade leader! All twenty prisoners of Unit X present and at attention!" After the brigade leader had given the order to march, each unit shouldered their respective tools—pickaxes, shovels, saws, axes—and set out for the worksite column by column, like black centipedes.

When Dranak Geshé, who was over fifty years old, arrived at the site having lugged a seven- or eight-pound pickaxe on his shoulder the whole way, he didn't even have the strength to lift his arms, never mind perform hard labor. Fortunately, most of the men in his unit were "nomads with no manual skills," and more importantly, at this point in time people still had some respect for their elders—or at least, there weren't yet that many who took pleasure in the suffering of others—so Dranak Geshé was able to do a bit of work then take a rest, take a rest then do a bit of work. Still, after he spent that morning pulling out three forearm-thick tamarisks by the roots, his hands were covered in blisters, which eventually burst and bled so much that the handle of the pickaxe was stained red, at which point the unit leader reported it to the brigade leader and he was given permission to take a break.

A multitude of wild animals roamed the deep reaches of the boundless forest, which was filled with reed-covered ponds and marshes. These scattered spots had become the happy homes of geese, cranes, and other waterfowl that sang and sported merrily, enjoying all that nature had to offer. But when they returned the following spring with their hearts full of hope, they circled in the sky for an age, eyes gaping and beaks wide open, issuing heart-piercing cries that brought tears to your eyes. When they descended in disbelief to the ravaged plain, where the howling red wind obscured everything from view, their cries became even more heart-wrenching. Something yet more terrible occurred at that instant: since the quality and quantity of the prison food had been declining by the day, the frenzied cadres and guards opened fire in every direction, filling the air with the sound of thousands of gunshots all at once. White feathers from the cranes and geese swirled about in the wind, and blood spattered the earth. More unfortunate still, as the remaining birds, caught completely off guard, stood there

THE RED WIND HOWLS

in a momentary confusion, another burst of rifle fire ripped the air like popping peas and yet more of their brethren fell to the ground. The survivors finally took to the sky, at which point they saw for themselves what it looks like when "a happy home is turned into a grim grave." The storm suddenly picked up, and the sound of the birds wailing in the sky and the men cheering down below could be heard amid the howl of the red wind. The bloodstains from the cranes and geese were as clear on the ground as red flags on a snowy plain. For the surviving birds, the image that had flitted across their eyes for but a moment would probably never fade.

From then on, there was not a goose or crane to be seen in the vast valley, whether in the sky or on the ground. You couldn't even find a duck or a cormorant or the tiniest unnameable waterfowl of any kind. It was for that reason that in the Great Famine soon to come, the cadres and guards from the prison camp would often say they regretted not having killed more of the birds and gorged themselves to death. But it goes without saying, of course, that the prisoners suffered twice as much as they did, and particularly the nomads, who had been the halest and heartiest of all when they arrived. When their strength first began to decline, they finally rued their lengthy refusal to eat the "grass" and their failure to slack off on the hard labor. The hunger tormented them for weeks and months until they couldn't even feel it anymore. At this point, their ration of half a corn bun and a serving of vegetable *tang* that was somewhere between a ladle and a spoonful would come out the other end as soon as they had eaten it. After several days of diarrhea came a horrible ringing sound in the ears, and after the ringing faded

• 67 •

THE RED WIND HOWLS

you went deaf and mute, your whole body swelled up, you couldn't open or close your eyes, you couldn't remember what your wife and kids looked like, you forgot your own name, you no longer worried about when you would die or even feared death at all, and you lay in a state between sleep and consciousness, between living and dying, for a day or two, or three or four, or five or six, and when you died, your body was likewise left there for a day or two, or three or four, or five or six; how long exactly depended mainly on how cold it was: in summer one or two days, in spring and autumn three or four, and in winter five or six or even more, because the deceased's half a corn bun and tiny ration of soup could extend the lives of the survivors for just a little longer.

An even worse kind of death was the one that befell Tsetra. After the arrival of Brigade Commander Song Jiantao, the prisoners didn't stay in the same units for long, switching places every week or month or season, but if he discovered that there was conflict between two prisoners, Commander Song kept them together on purpose. It was for that reason that Alak Drong and Tsetra remained together pretty much the entire time. One day, when Tsetra crawled naked out of bed, groaning in pain and on all fours, Alak Drong saw with horror that Tsetra's thighs were now as thin as his own arms had been when he was first brought to prison; the loose flesh hung down like an ox's dewlap, and you could almost see the sunlight shining through from the other side. Two elbow-like bones protruded from his rear end, looking like they were about to break the skin, and right between them sprouted a thumb-sized tail.

THE RED WIND HOWLS

There's an old saying on the grasslands of Tsezhung that if two relatives get married their child will have a tail. For that reason, it was taboo for men and women with even the slightest family connection to discuss such things, let alone actually get married. Thus, the term *mé*, which usually refers to the murder of a family or clan member, had another connotation in Tsezhung: intermarriage or sexual relations between family members. This was why, when he saw Tsetra's "tail," Alak Drong's first thought was, *Who'd have thought the bastard was an inbred mé boy!* Another man then crawled naked and groaning out of his bed, and he too had a thumb-sized tail, on top of which his penis looked unusually long. Amazed, Alak Drong glanced back at Tsetra and saw that his penis too seemed very long, at which point he involuntarily reached down to feel his own crotch, then reached a bit farther still and discovered something that scared the life out of him: a bump half the size of a thumb. More terrifying still, Tsetra's gums began to rot away and his teeth fell out one after another, his skin festered and came off in chunks, his hands and feet swelled, and his face turned black. His limbs could no longer support his body, and even before he took his last breath he looked cadaverous and smelled of death. On the Harrowing Day, when the prisoners from Tsezhung were at death's door, they had all cried out in unison, begging the Lord of Death not to take them yet, but now they all cried out for him to come as quickly as possible. They no longer hoped to gain their freedom or to see their families, and they didn't even hope for food—all they wanted now was the swift release of death. The cadres made their rounds in the morning, stopping at the doorway of each cell to bark, "Any bodies?" Feebly and in one voice, the surviving prisoners would reply "No" so that they could get the dead men's share of food. But the prisoners who met with Tsetra's fate smelled like decay before they even died, and after they did breathe their last the stench became truly unbearable, so in those cases, the feeble collective response from the surviving prisoners was "Yes."

The cadres ordered a few of the prisoners who hadn't yet lost all their strength—or the ones who could still walk on their own two feet, at least—to load the fetid corpse onto a small wooden cart. They set out from the camp and down a path by the river, and when they came to a high rocky outcrop bridging the water, they tipped up the cart and the body tumbled in, just like taking a rock from one worksite and moving it to another. This path had been formed by each unit taking it in turns to come down from the camp and fetch water. A few months before, Tsetra had been here himself, lowering a metal bucket tied to a rope down from the cliff edge to draw up water. Back then the water had been clean and clear, but now the sand and dirt blown in by the red wind had turned it a maroon color, and worse still, all the camps upstream had been throwing their own rotting corpses in the river. The bodies rolling and tumbling in the current reminded the prisoners from Tsezhung of the Harrowing Day.

On that day a few years before, the people of Tsezhung had fled, and after arriving at the banks of the Machu River, the women, the children, the elderly, and the monks had hidden beneath a cliff, while the men lined up on the cliff edge with their incredibly inaccurate, second-rate rifles to hold off the

THE RED WIND HOWLS

pursuing troops—or that had been the plan, at least. With each crackling burst of machine-gun fire from their pursuers, several men fell spiraling from the clifftop. Some of them simply jumped straight into the Machu and were carried off by the current, tumbling and thrashing. Some of them were able to get their heads above water just long enough to yell out an appeal to Alak Drong. When she saw her husband getting swept away, one of the women hiding under the cliff jumped up and shouted, "Venerable Jetsün Drölma! Merciful Alak Drong! Ah—Södor—wait! Your wife and child are coming!" She waded into the water clutching her one-year-old baby to her breast, and the child began to squirm and scream for all it was worth. Everyone knows just how terrifying it is to be dragged to the land of the dead. But this woman didn't want to live or raise their child without her husband. She squeezed the baby to her breast as hard as she could, and after taking eight or nine steps, gradually vanished out of sight. The corpses that day weren't all skin and bones, waxen faces, and rancid stenches like the ones now; they were as big as bears, black as frying pans, and they smelled like blood.

Since all the other streams had dried up, the river that ran red with silt and sand and wafted an odor of decay was the only remaining source of drinking water for all the cadres and prisoners from all the camps. This was why the surviving prisoners, after disposing of a body in the river, would each return to the camp with a bucketful of water.

Tsetra's death made Alak Drong neither happy nor sad. A few years earlier, after he had delivered his sermon and conferred empowerments to the Jikjés of Tadzi, old man Jikjé had been deeply moved and had come to kneel before Alak Drong along with Tsetra. "Venerable Rinpoché," he began, "since the time of my forefathers, my family has always maintained the illustrious golden bridge of our Dharma connection with your incarnation lineage, and as a result, generations of my family have been blessed with an abundance of grain, horses, cattle, and sheep. The time left to me now is as brief as the sun atop the pass and the shade at the bottom; these old eyes couldn't see a mountain move and these old ears couldn't hear a conch blow. The boy here will be inheriting everything. I implore you to always keep him under the protection of your meditations." Next, he issued some advice to Tsetra. "Listen up, boy. Drong Rinpoché is the object of refuge for all the people of Tsezhung, and more importantly, he is our family's root lama and crown jewel. You must put your unswerving faith in him. Make all the offerings you can. Give sacks of cash if you've got them and offer some flowers if you don't. This goes without saying for you, obviously, but your sons, your grandsons—every generation must do it. If you do, your descendants will have their wishes granted in this life, be spared the terrors of the bardo, and avoid rebirth in the lower realms." And indeed, the old man then proceeded to donate "sacks of cash" to Alak Drong. Tsetra, for his part, unstintingly offered his sip of water and his piece of fruit to Alak Drong, not daring to take any for himself, even in his time of greatest need. Back then, Alak Drong had concentrated his prayers on Tsetra's well-being, beseeching the Three Jewels and the Dharma protectors to look after him. When they first arrived at the prison, Tsetra had also given to Alak Drong the one-and-a-half-yuan monthly allowance distributed to each prisoner and begged him to pray for all his relatives who had been killed on the Harrowing Day—particularly his grandfather, Jikjé, and his father, Sangdak—and to guide their consciousnesses safely to the Pure Land. Alak Drong had quietly recited the *Prayer for the Dead*, but . . . well—but Song Jiantao had said that in the final analysis informing on fellow inmates was beneficial for both parties, it was a good thing, it was two birds with one stone: you could get your own sentence reduced and help stop others from taking an errant path. If, for example, a prisoner tried to escape, he would be doubling his crimes and might even lose his life. But if you knew of the escape plan beforehand, you could prevent him from adding to his transgressions and maybe even save his life. On reflection, this didn't seem unreasonable to Alak Drong. And more than anything, he wanted to escape this hell on earth as quickly as possible, so he decided to heed Song Jiantao's appeal to report on the crimes of his fellow prisoners.

At first he informed on people who had come from other areas, but their offenses consisted of nothing but discontented grumblings about the hardship of life in prison and the cruelty of Song Jiantao. Pretty much all the prisoners were guilty of that, and Commander Song soon lost patience with Alak Drong's worthless information. "The more people insult me, the more it shows my work is a success," he said. "And in the final analysis, the more it demonstrates our successful construction of the dictatorship of the proletariat. So don't bother me with these trifling matters. If you really want to prove yourself and get your sentence reduced, then keep your ears open for anyone who's opposing the Great Helmsman, opposing the Party, opposing the socialist system. Find out if anyone's planning to kill themselves or to escape. See if anyone's appropriating communal property for personal use, for example stealing an ear of grain from the wheat field, or a potato from the vegetable patch, or a bun from the canteen. Also, Tibetans and Mongolians are highly superstitious. See if anyone is engaging in reactionary activities—prayer, divination, that sort of thing."

After roughly six months at the prison, Brigade Commander Yang Kai had been arrested and sent to another camp on a charge of "treating reactionaries and class enemies with leniency, failing to meet production quotas, and thereby causing serious harm to the country," at which point Song Jiantao was promoted from plain old brigade leader to brigade commander. Song Jiantao was from Qinghai and was about forty years old. Since he knew a little Tibetan, it was possible that he had a Tibetan relative on his father's or mother's side. In his breast pocket he always carried a copy of the *Little Red Book* bound with a red plastic jacket. He must have memorized the whole thing cover to cover, because whenever he spoke, he was able to quote the words of Mao verbatim without ever having to consult the text. His favorite quote of all was "power grows from the barrel of a gun." It is said that clothes can express the mentality of a people or an era. The fact that Americans, for instance, can wear whatever colors or styles they like is a reflection of the freedom the people of that country enjoy as citizens. In the time of Mao Zedong's rule, the vast majority of people in China—with the exception of intellectuals, nomads, and prisoners—wore military garb. It's hard to say whether or not this constitutes proof that "power grows from the barrel of a gun," but as

THE RED WIND HOWLS

Song Jiantao was a proud military man on active duty, it goes without saying that he wore an army uniform and carried a pistol.

Song Jiantao studied Alak Drong for a moment as though he had just remembered something. He disappeared into another room and returned with a file, which he perused as he spoke.

"So you're a lama?"

"I used to be."

"And a lama in charge of a monastery."

"I used to be."

"After liberation you served as county head."

"Yes, sir."

"You duped and exploited the masses countless times."

". . ."

"And you only got ten years?"

"Yes, sir."

"A very light sentence indeed. Well, you confessed to your own crimes and helped reveal those of others. That's good. Look, the Communist Party is always correct. Even though you committed such a serious crime, you were given a lenient sentence due to your admission of guilt and your assistance with bringing to light the crimes of others." Song Jiantao closed Alak Drong's file. "Listen carefully. It's the same in prison. The more you report on the crimes of others, the more your sentence will be reduced."

"Okay, yes, sir."

"Well then, do you have any information of value for me?"

"Yes, I do."

• 75 •

THE RED WIND HOWLS

"Good."

Song Jiantao flashed a glance at his secretary cum translator, who immediately readied the still-blank paper on which he hadn't yet found reason to write a single word.

"There's someone who's planning an escape attempt . . ."

"Who? Give me his name."

"Tse . . . tse . . . Tsetra."

"Where, when, how? When exactly is this Tsetra planning to escape, and from where, and how will he do it? Be specific."

Alak Drong told him all about Tsetra's plan to escape and how he had advised against it. Song Jiantao rose, then clasped his hands behind his back and began to pace, just like Wang Aiguo. "With your special status, couldn't you gather more—and more useful—information?"

"Yes, I already did! He's also engaged in reactionary activities. A month after we got to prison, for example, he gave me his one-and-a-half yuan and asked me to pray for his father and his other dead relatives, to guide their consciousnesses to the Blissful Realm."

"And how did you resolve this matter?"

"I . . . at the time, no one had told me to report every single incident, so I didn't say anything."

"Fine. This is why your special status is an asset. You must put it to good use, and work to reduce your sentence by proving yourself."

"Yes, sir, very well."

"Now, what about this man Lozang Palden?"

"He used to be my teacher."

• 76 •

THE RED WIND HOWLS

"I'm talking about now. Has he made any reactionary statements to you, for instance?"

"Reactionary statements? I, uh, I don't think so . . ."

"Listen to me. Teacher and student, parent and child—these relationships don't exist anymore. The only relationships are class relationships: class brothers, class enemies. Nothing else. It seems to me this Lozang Palden is a stubborn reactionary and a dangerous element. At the very least, he does not endorse the leadership of the Communist Party and the socialist system. I saw as much in his eyes. You must keep a close watch on him; I want to know everything he says and does." Song Jiantao got so close to Alak Drong that their faces were almost touching. "If you can find out the crimes of people like him, that would be useful information indeed."

Alak Drong's mind swirled in confusion, just like the red wind outside. He didn't even realize when he got grit in his eyes on the way back from Song Jiantao's office, and by the time he arrived at his cell, dirty black tears had welled up at the corners of each eye. Shortly thereafter he registered a very uncomfortable sensation and began to cry profusely.

After becoming brigade commander, Song Jiantao had assigned each prisoner daily labor duties; only when they were finished were they allowed to return to the camp. If the prisoners hadn't finished their work by eight o'clock in the spring and summer, or by six o'clock in the autumn and winter, there would be no dinner by the time they got back. The quality and quantity of the food was declining by the day too. At some point the corn buns and coarse wheat buns were halved in size, and the potato and cabbage soup became a broth—or gruel—made of turnip and radish leaves. Their padded winter uniforms and quilts, originally issued once a year, were now issued only once every other year, on top of which the increasingly heavy labor meant the clothes wore out even faster. Now, white "flowers" bloomed all over the shabby black prison uniforms, as though in mourning for the departed inmates. One cause for relief was that the increasing death toll meant the surviving prisoners could get their hands on as many new uniforms and quilts and as much tamarisk and willow firewood as they wanted, so at least they didn't have to suffer in a cold hell back in their cells.

A young woman, no matter how beautiful, will always begin to lose her radiance when she sets off on the path to prostitution, and in much the same way, a prisoner, no matter how strong, no matter how innocent or guilty, will always get ground down once they're inside. The hard labor and the pitiful rations bowed every man's head down. They grew increasingly silent, and few people were now inclined to use the pack of playing cards that had been issued to each cell. Even if the occasional game did start up, it was a somber and lifeless affair with no noise, no laughter, and certainly no brandishing of cards in the air before a victorious hand was revealed with a slap.

Many of the prisoners were incapable of completing their assigned tasks on time, so they were deprived of rest for weeks in a row. On a Sunday when the men had been given a rare day off, four people were playing poker in the cell, with a few more watching. Alak Drong was usually one of the most avid poker players among the countless thousands of prisoners. It was a game he had learned from Wang Aiguo and some of the other cadres when he was county head of Tsezhung. He was no match for Wang, however, so he always ended up having to put his cards on his head when he lost, what they called "wearing the paper hat." He had no way of knowing that before long he would be dragged from clan to clan for struggle sessions wearing a real paper hat, long and pointed and covered with slogans, at which time he finally decided that this game was no fun at all. His teacher, Dranak Geshé Lozang Palden, had quietly taken him aside at one point and said, "You shouldn't be playing these card games. And wearing a paper hat is even worse. It's highly inauspicious." But as everyone knew, Alak Drong was a man who forgot his joys and sorrows all too easily, and as soon as the prison issued them with a set of cards, he was teaching all the nomads how to play, and so they whiled away their precious little free time with games of poker. That day, however, he went straight to his bunk without so much as a glance at the game underway. He leaned back against the wall, lost in thought, shedding bitter tears.

Tsetra was left momentarily stunned by Alak Drong's grim demeanor. Slowly he added a pinch of tobacco to the center of a rolling paper, rolled it up, and timidly handed it over to Alak Drong. From his breast pocket he took a box of matches with the words GREAT LEAP FORWARD printed on the cover in red Chinese characters, and even more timidly lit the cigarette.

For about a year after their arrival at the camp, they had been given fragrant, thread-like strands of tobacco completely free, so the nomads had taken up the habit of smoking. Though the tobacco no longer came gratis, they could use their one-and-a-half-yuan monthly allowance to buy it, along with toiletries and

THE RED WIND HOWLS

other such things. For the nomads, the hardest thing to come by wasn't tobacco, but "safe" rolling papers. They could get their hands on an old sheet of newspaper, but this was incredibly dangerous. If they used it as rolling paper and it contained an image of the Great Helmsman or other leaders or revolutionaries—even if it just contained their names—then the sentence of the "offender" would be increased by one to five years, depending on the identity and status of the "victim." Even more unfortunate for the nomad prisoners was that they didn't know Chinese, so if they did find a sheet of newspaper, they first had to ask one of the "White Chinese," or a "Red Chinese" intellectual, to check if it contained the names of any of the great leaders. The harder the times, the uglier the human spirit. Once, one of the nomads asked a White Chinese if his newspaper was safe, and when assured that it was, he rolled his smoke and lit up. With a cackle, the White Chinese immediately reported him to the cadres. The nomad got two years added to his sentence, and when he told the cadres that he'd checked with the White Chinese first, he was given an extra two years as well. After that, none of the nomads dared check with the Chinese—White or Red—to see if their rolling paper was safe. Even if one of them had dared to ask, none of the Chinese would have dared to look.

Alak Drong took a drag of the cigarette and let the smoke drift out through his mouth and nostrils. He turned toward Tsetra, and as their eyes met, his lip began to tremble and the tears fell even harder.

Each of the ethnic groups in the prison had their own private name for Song Jiantao. The happy coincidence that his

THE RED WIND HOWLS

name sounded just like the Tibetan word for the receptacle you do your business in made their nickname for him obvious. Tsetra, unsure of what had happened to Alak Drong, was initially at a loss, but he decided that Song Jiantao must have somehow mistreated and insulted the lama, which worked him up into a rage. "What has Pisspot Song done now . . .!" he began, but Alak Drong simply bit his upper lip and shook his head, bewildering Tsetra even more.

Alak Drong, now sobbing, looked into Tsetra's face a moment longer, then let loose a loud wail and beat his chest. *"Ah ho!* I'm not human, I'm not human! I'd be better off dead . . ." The poker players gathered around him, and a "rightist" who had been brought in several months prior began to bellow, his eyes red with rage, "He's right! This is contrary to the basic principles of humanism! They're fascists, pure and simple! We must protest!" The Red and White Chinese all voiced their agreement, and voices that had long been silent were now raised, fists that had long lain idle were pumped in the air. The nomads were petrified, and Alak Drong's brief moment of remorse was quickly erased by visions of all those struggle sessions he had endured back in Tsezhung.

The nomads had heard of the "the principles of the Dharma" but never the "principles of humanism," and they had no idea who they were calling "fat shits." Nevertheless, as the Red and White Chinese continued to align and the size of the crowd continued to grow, Alak Drong suddenly realized that this ruckus might well constitute "useful information indeed." While their attention was elsewhere, he slipped away to Song Jiantao's office, announced himself with a *"Baogao,"* and was

■ 81 ■

ushered inside. Much to his surprise, the office was already full of people—Red and White Chinese, nomads and farmers—all of whom had come to report on the incident. His confidential information had suddenly lost its value, and now his status as an informant had been revealed; he felt anxious, ashamed, and repentant all at once. Song Jiantao, however, praised the assembled group, declared them all to be allies, and said that they needn't mistrust one another. Before dismissing them, he announced that his door was always open and tasked them with reporting back to him on the ringleaders of the insurrection: Who were they? What was their plan? What was their objective?

As soon as he heard the word "insurrection," Alak Drong couldn't help but think of the Harrowing Day. One day, several furious clan leaders had come to him to report that the People's Liberation Army had committed a massacre against their people. After questioning them, Alak Drong learned that the previous morning, several "bandits" in open rebellion against the Communist Party had turned up at one of the Dranak clan camps from who knows where. As they were going from tent to tent begging for provisions, PLA soldiers suddenly surrounded the camp and called on the "bandits" to immediately throw down their weapons and surrender, otherwise they would use force. At that moment, the ultimatum-issuing interpreter was struck right in the chest by a reply from one of the bandits' rifles, and as soon he fell back on his horse, mortar and machine-gun fire erupted from every direction, mowing down people and animals alike. The "bandits" mounted their horses and rode resolutely into the gunfire, and only when their sacrifice was

THE RED WIND HOWLS

complete did the mortars and machine guns fall silent. Ninety-six people from the Dranak clan had been killed and forty-four wounded, and the clan heads said that if the matter wasn't resolved, they wouldn't let it lie, even if every man in Tsezhung ended up dead and only the women were left alive.

Alak Drong, outraged, took the matter to Wang Aiguo, but Wang was already well aware of it. "The Dranak clan harbored bandits, which is a serious crime," he said. "If they cease to stir up trouble, however, we can leave this in the past. And since this is a military matter, the local authorities have no jurisdiction here. Right now the situation is critical. As the foremost religious leader in Tsezhung, you have a responsibility toward the masses, and as a state cadre, you have a responsibility toward the Party and the government. Starting tomorrow, you must visit each of the clans and instruct them that it is forbidden to listen to reactionaries and to give succor to bandits."

Several members of the Dranak clan came to see Alak Drong the next day before his departure and asked him to perform the rites for the dead. His teacher Dranak Geshé was there, as was the elderly clan leader who had never worn an undershirt in his life. The latter, kneeling before him, said, "There are more and more Chinese troops these days, and they're getting more and more brutal. You've seen for yourself how they've turned our Tsezhung from still yogurt to boiling blood. What really gets me is that they slaughter all these innocent people and still they don't even dare show their faces—not a peep. And I heard that when Your Holiness went to talk to them yesterday, Wang Aiguo didn't so much as extend a hand in greeting. Our Dranak clan is no match for the Chinese army, but that doesn't mean

■ 83 ■

THE RED WIND HOWLS

we can just put up with them. We've no choice now but to turn our backs on the Tsechu River, head for the Machu, and lead a vagabond existence. This morning, the esteemed elders of the other clans came to pay their respects. They said that all the clans of Tsezhung are in this together. When things are going well, we ride our stallions side by side; when things are tough, we bear the burden as one. If you must cross the Machu and roam the land, then we roam together, they said. Venerable Drong Rinpoché, you are the spiritual and worldly leader for all of Tsezhung, you are our source of refuge in this life and the next. As our root lama, our crown jewel, I beg you to come with us."

As it turned out, performing rites for the dead was but a secondary goal, their primary aim being to persuade Alak Drong to accompany them across the Machu. Alak Drong's sympathies normally lay with his subjects and he resented Wang Aiguo's attitude, but there was no way he could ever be put on the same level as these shirt-less, pants-less clan leaders. Besides, he knew that if the map of China were the palm of your hand, then Tsezhung was only one tiny line—not even that big—and he also knew that the Communist Party ran heaven and earth now. He looked at Dranak Geshé, helplessly and hopefully. Unfortunately, the geshé was preoccupied with his chants for the dead, mumbling rhythmically and plying his rosary, giving no indication of his preference for one course of action or another. Left to decide for himself, Alak Drong issued a resolute "No!" then adopted his most commanding tone: "I will not go. And I forbid you from going either. There's nowhere we *could* go, to be perfectly honest. The Communist Party runs heaven and earth, so what good would it do to move to the other side of the Machu? There's nowhere to go. And I forbid you from going."

Much to Alak Drong's surprise, his people weren't as compliant as usual. Raising their voices and refusing to bow their heads, they replied, "Normally, anything a lama says is gospel and anywhere he points is east. But you can't say those things now. And it's no use anyway."

Alak Drong was stunned. Completely at a loss for words, he once more cast a hopeful look in the direction of his teacher. Dranak Geshé, unable to maintain his silence, said, "As I see it, there's no use in us quarreling about whether or not to cross the Machu. We should seek divine guidance from the Dharma protectors and the gods and spirits of the land."

"Precisely. If the prophecies decree that we must leave, then I, Alak Drong, will accompany you, my faithful subjects, to live and die by your side. If, however, they decree that we must stay, then not one person from Tsezhung will cross the Machu," he said, finding his courage again.

None of them questioned the wisdom of consulting the Dharma protectors and the local deities, but the wrath and resentment of the Dranak clan could not be so lightly assuaged. "If the prophecies say we must stay, are we supposed to just leave it at that?"

"And if we cross the Machu, will you be able to get your revenge then?" No one volunteered an answer to this question, so Alak Drong continued. "I, Alak Drong, have traveled everywhere but the ends of the earth, and I have seen with my own eyes that the Communist Party encompasses heaven and earth alike! Running away from the Communists is futile. And supposing we do cross the Machu and manage to escape them. Won't we have then lost our land on top of all those lives?" As before, the people of the Dranak clan couldn't muster a response to this. Nevertheless, the Dharma protectors and deities of the land still had to be consulted just as Dranak Geshé had decreed, and once the oracles had communed with the gods and the diviners had divined, the results left Alak Drong dumbfounded, for in one unanimous voice they had all answered: "Leave."

At once, the people began to burn their communal and private incense and make their offerings to the powers that be; then they gathered their belongings and prepared to set out for the Machu River. The community and clan leaders and all the power holders of note were even busier: day and night they held meetings, strategizing and making meticulous preparations for fording the Machu and holding off their pursuers. Alak Drong had become surplus to requirements: no one reported the plans to him, and in fact they seemed to have forgotten about his existence altogether.

Dranak Geshé Lozang Palden, who had also been left out of the planning, the strategizing, and every meeting big and small, considered the problem at great length and finally decided to call a meeting between Alak Drong and the clan and community leaders. "I don't know what your ultimate goal is, and I don't need to know," he began, "but it has come to my attention that you have not been paying the proper respect to Drong Rinpoché. This is truly appalling, and I fear the consequences will be even more so. It is my hope that you will not jump blindly into this, that you will heed the wise words of our benevolent lama. You must think before you act."

Alak Drong was in complete agreement. "He's right. I'm not bothered that you didn't pay me the proper respect, but this approach of yours is no good at all. We can report the incident to the higher ups. If Xining can't resolve it, we can take it to Beijing. The Jamyang Zhepa said the Communist Party crushes tyrants and protects the weak, I heard it with my own two ears."

"Please, we implore you both to stop this talk now." The people, sinking in an ocean of sorrow and burning in flames of rage, wouldn't even heed the nectar of their root lama's wise words. "We might be just a bunch of stupid nomads, but we know how things work. If the people fight among themselves, the king will step in to sort it out. But if the king oppresses the people, he's not going to punish himself, is he? The Dharma protectors, the gods of the land, and the common people are all in complete agreement on this one, so please, venerable lamas, stay out of it." Having said their piece, the nomads rose and returned to their business.

A few days later, with the red wind howling around their ears and machine-gun fire thundering at their backs, the people of Tsezhung came to a halt at the formidable Machu River. Many men had already fallen, and the bodies were continuing to pile up as the lamas and monks joined the women, children, and elderly in taking shelter beneath the cliffs by the river. The clan leaders' sorrow and rage had been overtaken by regret and terror, and now, amid all the chaos, they came willingly to seek the counsel of Alak Drong and Dranak Geshé. "Our plan was to get the monks, women, children, and all the animals and everything across the river, then we'd come back and find a chance to ambush the PLA troops. That way we could have our revenge, and eventually we could force the enemy to pull back, and then we could all go home to Tsezhung. We had no idea the pursuing forces would be so strong, so fast, and now we're almost out of bullets. What do we do?"

Alak Drong was even more furious with all the clan leaders and powerful community figures than the pursuing PLA troops. He bit his lip tightly and shook his head, saying nothing.

Dranak Geshé stopped reciting the *Protection from the Eight Fears*. *"Ah kha!* How can such dumb beasts exist in the world! What has Alak Drong said all along? The Communist Party encompasses heaven and earth, and there's nowhere to run. And what did I tell you? You were disrespecting Drong Rinpoché and the consequences would be terrible. Now you've got all these people killed. Are you satisfied? *Ah kha!* Fools! Oh, what's the point now? Blame is the lowest form of speech." Turning to Alak Drong, he said, *"Ya*, you're no ordinary lama, venerable Drong Rinpoché. If ever there were a time to perform a miracle, this is it—the lives of many sentient beings would be saved." Dranak Geshé closed his eyes and clasped his palms together.

Not too long before, Alak Drong had seen a film about the war between the White and Red Chinese, and that day scenes from it were playing over and over in his mind. In the film, the White Chinese had suffered one defeat after another until they were on their last legs. A hideously ugly White Chinese general had then tied a white cloth to the end of his rifle, and as soon as he held it aloft above their trench, the Red Chinese ceased firing. Alak Drong looked all around and saw that the young Alak Yak had tied his monk's shawl with a white *khata*. Without a word, he ran over and untied the sash from Alak

THE RED WIND HOWLS

Yak's shawl, then grabbed a rifle from one of the clan heads. "Get everyone to stop shooting!" he yelled at the clan leaders as he tied the *khata* to the muzzle. Cautiously, he stuck the rifle up above the cliff edge and waved it back and forth.

This was a wonderous "miracle" indeed: the PLA soldiers' guns fell silent instantly. Naturally, everyone's hair stood up on end in shivers of devotion, and they began prostrating to Alak Drong as though they had seen the Buddha himself. They wept tears of remorse, thinking the reason they had lost so many of their kin was not having heeded the words of the Buddha in the first place. Afterward, the people of Tsezhung referred to this as the Harrowing Day. The authorities classified it as an "armed insurrection," and most of the men involved—at least those who survived—were arrested. Alak Drong himself was labeled a "plotter and organizer of armed insurrection" and condemned to spend the prime of his life enduring struggle sessions, beatings, hunger, thirst, exhaustion, persecution, and fear.

It came as a big surprise to Alak Drong that the "plotters and organizers of insurrection" referred to by Song Jiantao had drawn up a list of distinguished and respected prisoners to front their uprising, and his name was on it. Absolutely petrified, he went to see Song Jiantao again. Even more to his surprise, Song Jiantao was so overjoyed with this news that he almost hugged him. He handed Alak Drong a cigarette and proceeded to pace up and down with hands behind his back. "The time has come for you to prove yourself and get your sentence reduced. As soon as you know the identities of the plotters and organizers of the insurrection, and how and when they plan to launch their revolt, I want you to come straight to me."

THE RED WIND HOWLS

Yet another thing that came as a surprise to Alak Drong was that the way the "insurrection" was instigated in the prison was completely different from the "insurrection" in Tsezhung. Without any recourse to divinations or prophecies, and without any offerings to the gods and spirits, each of the "plotters and organizers" was allowed to express their thoughts on how the prison administration ought to be reformed and how the lives of the prisoners could be improved. Alak Drong added that not being able to receive letters from their families was a notable grievance for the Tibetan prisoners, the nomads in particular. In the end, the "rightist" prisoners' representative summarized their demands as follows:

1. Immediate and significant improvement of living conditions at the prison. Cessation of forced labor for the sick and injured until such a time as they have fully recovered.
2. Hard labor not to exceed a maximum of eight hours per day and a mandatory rest day on Sundays. No hard labor for the sick and the elderly, or a lighter work allocation, circumstances permitting.
3. Equal treatment of political prisoners and felons. At the very least, equal treatment in terms of living conditions and labor duties. Political prisoners to be allocated work assignments in accordance with their skills, e.g., tractor driver, mechanic, cook, barber, etc.
4. Political prisoners not to be put in the same cells with felons, where they must endure beatings, persecution, and theft of food rations.

THE RED WIND HOWLS

5. Until it has been clearly determined that a political prisoner has committed a new error, he is not to be arbitrarily subjected to beatings, persecution, placement in solitary confinement, or placement in the felons' cells.
6. Reduction in the length of daily political study sessions.
7. Each unit head to be chosen by the unit members through democratic election. Felons to be barred from appointment as the head of a unit of political prisoners.
8. Written correspondence between family members not to be arbitrarily restricted when the contents of the letter are permissible.

All political prisoners will be on strike from hard labor until the above eight demands are met.

Since Alak Drong's task was to find out "the identities of the plotters and organizers of the insurrection, and how and when they plan to launch their revolt," he didn't pay much attention to the list of demands. Plus, they had only roughly translated the contents for the benefit of the non-Chinese minorities in the room. As a result, when he presented himself before Song Jiantao and mumbled his report, he could tell him nothing about the eight demands and their contents, and all he managed to provide was the surnames of a few men. *Idiot*, thought Song Jiantao. *Useless idiot. And you were the head of the district?* But his disappointment was assuaged by another thought: *Then again, it's not all bad. Idiots like these are the easiest to use.* After heaping praise on Alak Drong, he sent him off again to learn more.

Alak Drong went to great lengths to find out what each of the eight demands was all about, but by the time he returned

THE RED WIND HOWLS

to Song Jiantao, Song was already fully informed of the situation. The next morning, when the political prisoners downed tools and refused to work, Song Jiantao did not resort to force—in fact he spoke to them in a much softer tone than usual. "So, what are your demands?"

"We've got demands all right! But we intend to present them at a meeting of all the prisoners and cadres. You can have your say then whether you think they're reasonable or not."

"Very well. If I can't provide reasonable arguments against your demands in front of everyone, then they will be granted. If, however, my arguments prevail, then the present system will remain unchanged, and all the plotters and organizers of this incident will be punished." Commander Song spoke with all the confidence of an examinee who had stolen the exam paper in advance. He ordered the emergency bell to be rung—a meeting would be held immediately.

After all the units and brigades had filed into the assembly hall and taken their places, Song Jiantao, standing at the podium, invited the prisoners' representative to come to the front and state their demands. Without a hint of hesitation or fear, the "rightist" strode forward and began to read out the eight demands. When he reached the third, however, the felons started whistling in disapproval, and soon a chorus of cursing filled the auditorium, preventing the "rightist" from continuing. Though the felons only accounted for less than 10 percent of the prison population, their work was less punishing than the political prisoners', there was no one to steal their vegetable *tang*, and they were treated more favorably by the cadres, all of which meant that their strength hadn't been depleted entirely and their pride and brutality were even more intact, so the felons were always able to overpower the political prisoners, despite the latter constituting over 90 percent of the prison's population.

"We may have harmed a couple of people, but we've never had a bad thought about the Great Helmsman. We've never harmed the Party or the state!"

"We've still got the Motherland. You've got nothing!"

"You shit eaters have nothing. You are nothing!"

"Sure we've committed some crimes, but our class origins are proletarian through and through. You might not have any felonies to your name, but your class backgrounds are impure. You're natural-born enemies of the Party and state!"

"Down with class enemies!"

After the felons had had their fill of denouncing the political prisoners, Song Jiantao clasped his hands behind his back, paced up and down the stage a few times, then returned to the podium. "Listen carefully. There is obviously no merit to this nonsense—even your fellow prisoners refuse to back you—but I will allow you to continue nonetheless. Let us hear the rest of your demands."

No sooner had the "rightist" read out the fourth demand than the felons erupted in another chorus of abuse. He read out all eight demands regardless, then raised his voice over the clamor to issue his final ultimatum: "Until these eight demands are met, all political prisoners will be on strike from hard labor."

Commander Song rose with a hearty laugh. After pacing the stage a moment, he planted both hands on the podium. "Let me first ask you a question," he began solemnly. "Do you know what our beloved Chairman Mao is eating? Do you know what our working classes, the soldiers of the People's Liberation Army, and the poor and lower-middle peasants are eating? Let me tell you. Their living standards are identical to yours. In some cases, they're not even as good. Many people are starving to death on the outside too—in fact the death toll is even higher out there than in here. Now that Soviet revisionism has defied and double-crossed socialism, our country is facing a grave crisis. If you want to improve your living conditions as quickly as possible, then you must labor day and night, you must labor with unflagging ardor, you must labor with redoubled effort!" Repeatedly banging his fist on the table for emphasis, he continued.

"Let's see. 'Hard labor not to exceed a maximum of eight hours per day and a mandatory rest day on Sundays. No hard labor for the sick and the elderly, or a lighter work allocation, circumstances permitting.' Ha! Do you think this is a retirement home? Hmm? What else? 'Each unit head to be chosen by the unit members through democratic election.' Ha! Let me make this clear to you. China is a socialist state under the leadership of the Communist Party, not a capitalist country. You talk of 'democracy.' Where did you learn that? You demand a 'Reduction in the length of daily political study sessions.' A truly appalling expression! It seems as though labor has only trained your bodies; your thinking still hasn't turned toward Chairman Mao and the Communist Party. Don't forget—you're in here precisely *because* of your lack of political education. I could add five years to each of your sentences for that 'demand' alone. 'Written correspondence between family members not to be

THE RED WIND HOWLS

arbitrarily restricted when the contents of the letter are permissible.' Let me ask you this: Who here has had their correspondence restricted? Where is the proof? This is brazen slander against Party cadres! And the pick of the bunch: 'All political prisoners will be on strike from hard labor until the above eight demands are met.' Very good! Ha! Who do you think you are? Let me tell you. You are nothing. And if you are something, you are parasites, you are garbage, you are dog shit. You are prisoners of the dictatorship of the proletariat! You are reactionaries, you are oppressors, exploiters, and deceivers of the people! You are enemies of the people, crushed by the masses! You do not have the right to issue demands, nor to enter into negotiations!" He slammed his fist on the table like a madman, so hard that even the felons bowed their heads in terror.

Song Jiantao had been fully informed of the prisoners' plans in advance and had come prepared with an optimal strategy concocted the night before. Getting help from the felons was an unexpected bonus. It was clear that the "rightist," the representative of the political prisoners, had been utterly defeated. The "rightist," however, still refused to be cowed. "We still have some things to say," he announced boldly.

"Then you can say them in hell!" roared Song Jiantao, continuing to pound the table. "Take the insurgent ringleader to solitary." Two armed guards seized the "rightist," now also an "insurgent ringleader," twisted his arms behind his back, forced his head down, and marched him off without even letting him pick up the glasses that had fallen off his face. Given that he never came back, it was as though he really had gone to make his announcement in hell.

THE RED WIND HOWLS

Having seen their commander-in-chief defeated, his soldiers lost their courage one after another. "Anyone who doesn't want their sentence increased, get to work immediately," barked Commander Song, prompting roughly half of the prisoners to stand up. No matter how weak the enemy, if you see half your comrades-in-arms surrender, there's no way you can muster the courage to keep fighting. The rest of the prisoners, their spirits broken, rose to their feet.

When a young general earns their first victory, it naturally whets their appetite for the next battle. Song Jiantao's pride swelled to even greater proportions and he became determined to achieve even greater and more enduring victories by crushing the pitiful prisoners "until they couldn't stand and the stink filled the air." He recalled the groaning inmates from their labor and held study sessions for each brigade, at which the offenders had to confess their errors and denounce the "plotters and organizers of the insurrection."

The phrase "study session" sent another shiver of horror down Alak Drong's spine, and visions appeared before his eyes of the "political study sessions" held on the grasslands a few years before, which for the people of Tsezhung were the first steps to hell. After Alak Drong had fulfilled his teacher's appeal to perform a "miracle," the Harrowing Day finally came to an end at around five o'clock in the evening, and the fierce red wind, which had been roaring all day alongside the machine guns, finally subsided a little. With their hands bound behind their backs and all tied together in a long line, the surviving men of Tsezhung were marched to the county seat, which they reached at ten o'clock the next morning. Upon arrival they were

THE RED WIND HOWLS

taken straight to an enormous, high-walled jail, the construction of which had been completed just a few days before. Study sessions were held for each clan, with a separate session for the lamas, geshés, and other high-ranking clergy, and another two sessions for ordinary monks. The political study sessions took place in the nearby monastery, and what they called "political study" was in reality a political inquisition. First they released the old men and the thirteen- and fourteen-year-olds who were too weak to wield a blade, then the people who were too poor to even buy a blade, and finally, the middle peasants (or nomads, in this case) who hadn't wielded so much as a stick on the Harrowing Day and moreover could prove it.

The interrogation techniques they used on the lamas and monks were completely different from those they used on the laymen. Wang Aiguo was prepared to accept that the monastics hadn't taken up arms on the Harrowing Day, but he also believed that the older a monk was, the more time he had had to exploit the masses, and thus the more serious his crimes. As a result, he only released a handful of young monks who were still too little to blow their own noses. The rest were given a reeducation in atheism centered around various "no such things": there is no such thing as the eight classes of gods and demons, there is no such thing as consciousness after death, there is no such thing as reincarnation and the bardo, there is no such thing as the benefit of the Dharma, there is no such thing as karmic retribution, and so on. They furthermore subjected them to a bombardment of quotations and arguments to explain that the land of Tibet, led by its lamas and monks, had taken an errant course up until this point in history, but there

THE RED WIND HOWLS

was still a way forward for Tibet if those mistaken ways were abandoned, and that way forward would be illuminated by a shining path, etc. This tempted Lozang Tsültrim and a few other monks who had long since grown tired of monastic life to renounce their vows, and they decided to shed their monks' robes and don laymen's clothes to express their complete devotion to the Communist Party.

A contemporaneous report found some forty years later described this period thus:

After a month of studying and guidance, the majority of lamas and monks from Tsezhung Monastery have demonstrated a clear transformation in their thinking. Some have disrobed and adopted lay clothing. Some have also switched to Chinese civilian clothes. A matter for greater gratification still is that two lamas and thirty-six monks have abandoned their vows. Of these, seven have gone on to get married and establish happy socialist homes. One of the monks even took it upon himself to liberate a nun from her vows, a nun who was believed to be a "dakini" and who had long hoodwinked and exploited the masses. Several of the elderly monks have made comments along these lines: 'This is wonderful! We have been liberated from the darkness and led into the light. I'd love to find a wife and settle down to family life, but unfortunately there are no bullets left in the old gun.' Although we have achieved remarkable results, there are still many bad elements and stubborn reactionaries seeking to restore feudalism, so the burden on our shoulders remains heavy, and we must continue to raise our vigilance.

After further research, it became apparent that one of the lamas referred to in this report who had given up his vows was precisely our old friend Alak Drong. One night, in order to display his newfound loyalty to the Communist Party, he went out on the hunt for girls, accompanied by a cadre to act as his witness. When they came across a woman alone in a shabby tent, about five or six years older than he and who looked like she had "abundant experience," he had his witness wait outside to eavesdrop while he ducked in.

Now, while Alak Drong didn't know every single person in Tsezhung, not only did everyone in Tsezhung know him, they also obeyed his every command.

Alak Drong grunted lustfully and made a few lewd remarks, to which the "abundantly experienced" woman responded, "Yes, Your Holiness." Remembering the presence of his witness outside, Alak Drong felt rather embarrassed. "No need for all those formalities here," he said, to which the woman responded, "Yes, Your Holiness." The cadre, unable to take it anymore, burst out laughing.

The cadre's report also caused Wang Aiguo to crack up. "That bald old donkey," he muttered to himself with a chuckle, shaking his head. After a moment, he became serious. "That's all well and good, but it's not enough to wipe out the old donkey's crimes. Duping and exploiting the masses is not even his greatest crime; he is guilty of plotting and organizing an insurrection. So long and profoundly has he deceived the masses that they actually believe him to be a god, and no one will testify that he is guilty of fomenting the unrest. But I have a plan. He will soon admit to it himself without us having to produce any witnesses. Just you wait and see."

As it turned out, Wang Aiguo's "plan" was to gather up the class enemies like Alak Drong and the stubborn reactionaries like Dranak Geshé and parade them around all the clans and camps, where they were "struggled against until they couldn't stand and the stink filled the air."

After the time that Wang Aiguo took Alak Drong on a trip east to show him all the developments in China, they had returned to Tsezhung and Alak Drong had been given an official government post. "The future of this region is in your hands," Wang Aiguo had said. "My role is to help you in your work. You are the spiritual and worldly leader of Tsezhung, just as you were before. The difference is that we will now be working to gradually eliminate the differences between rich and poor, strong and weak. A goal that is entirely compatible with that of Buddhism, wouldn't you say?" And indeed, the people, lay and clergy alike, were given free medical care, and when contradictions arose among the masses, he helped Alak Drong to mediate them fairly and in accordance with the principles of karma. He was even more attentive and helpful when it came to the lives and work of the lamas and clan chiefs, prompting a deeply moved Alak Drong to think: *What a great man! I wish I'd met him sooner.* His relationship with Wang Aiguo grew ever closer, and they became frequent guests at each other's homes. It got to the point that it would have been an exaggeration to say they were one person, but it would have been an understatement to say they were two. There was one event, however, that came as a shock to Alak Drong. He happened to overhear a conversation between Wang Aiguo and his wife with the bound feet. The latter was in a temper,

THE RED WIND HOWLS

complaining to her husband that there was nowhere for her to have a bath in Tsezhung. Wang Aiguo said, "I've already picked out a lovely big bathtub for you. You just have to wait a little while longer."

"You're pulling my leg," his wife pouted. "Where would you find a bathtub in this shithole?"

"I found one, I swear. A huge bathtub, big enough for the both of us at once."

"Really? Where is it?"

"In the kitchen at Tsezhung Monastery."

"Are you talking about the big communal cooking pot?"

"That's the one. How about it? I'll send all the bald old donkeys off to fetch water from the Tsechu, and the two of us can have a bath in the cauldron."

Alak Drong didn't understand Chinese, but the peasant interpreter by his side suddenly dropped his jaw and turned pale. "Mama! Bad business . . ." he muttered involuntarily. From this Alak Drong surmised that Wang Aiguo and his wife must be discussing some important secret indeed, but when he asked the interpreter, he became flustered. "They're not saying anything important," he said. "Just husband and wife stuff."

"Husband and wife stuff? Why would you get so worked up about husband and wife stuff? Tell me what they're saying."

"Okay . . . but you can't tell anyone else."

"Don't worry about it. Just tell me."

The interpreter relayed the conversation between Wang Aiguo and his wife verbatim, and Alak Drong, still young, proud, and impetuous, threw open the door to Wang's house and marched straight inside.

THE RED WIND HOWLS

Wang Aiguo's wife was washing her feet in an iron basin. The sight left Alak Drong momentarily dumbfounded: at the end of her awl-shaped calves, thick at the top and thin at the bottom, were two tiny feet the size of a five- or six-year-old's. The woman, embarrassed, covered the basin with a cloth and mumbled irritably. Wang Aiguo arose without offering Alak Drong a seat as he usually did, highly displeased with this unwelcome intrusion. "What is it?" he snapped, his expression dark and stormy.

Alak Drong stared off into space. "It looks like that basin is too small for your charming wife. I think the cauldron at the monastery would be a much better fit. Wouldn't you agree, Secretary Wang?"

"So County Head Drong is a man who likes to eavesdrop, is that it?"

"I overheard by accident. I wasn't listening in on purpose."

"Well, if you heard it, let me tell you something. There's no reason we can't take a bath in the cauldron."

"You'd have to arrest me first."

"There's no reason we can't do that either."

"Very funny."

"Some people have been getting too big for their boots recently. But you Tibetans have a saying: 'The earth is big, but it's under the sky; the mouth is big, but it's under the nose.' Keep that in mind."

Their relationship began to deteriorate after that. The tension between them increased day after day, until one day, when Wang Aiguo was bathing in the cauldron and Alak Drong was out fetching water, Wang stamped the papers sentencing Alak

■ 102 ■

THE RED WIND HOWLS

Drong to ten years and had him thrown in prison. It was then that Alak Drong finally discovered that China was not only a big country but also a powerful one.

The study sessions, or political inquisitions, were capable of crushing a person's body and spirit even more thoroughly than hard labor. This was because everyone was forced to denounce each other, whether they were of the same ethnicity or from the same region, community, clan, camp, or family; even if they were father and son, brother and brother, teacher and student, lama and disciple. Everyone had to live in constant fear and uncertainty, wondering when they would be sent to solitary, thrown in with the felons, transferred to another camp, or even put in front of the firing squad. They only got two meals a day, which were forever getting smaller and more inedible. It was for these reasons that the ten days of study sessions were when the most suicides and natural deaths occurred, as well as the time that the foundations of death were most firmly laid for the surviving prisoners. It was during this time that most people turned into machines, their minds totally annihilated. It was during this time that Dranak Geshé strove to free himself from all joy and sorrow, all love and hate, and forever departed this hell on earth with a heart full of immutable faith and a mind full of boundless wisdom. It was during this time that most of the "plotters and organizers of insurrection" had their sentences increased or were taken to the firing squad. By contrast, Alak Drong and a handful of others had their sentences reduced, which naturally gave rise to suspicion among the prisoners who had had or were in the process of having their minds destroyed.

THE RED WIND HOWLS

When Tsetra found out that the "buddha" in whom his family had had unswerving faith for generations, who was their source of refuge in this life and the next, was nothing more than an ordinary human being, and moreover that it was due to Alak Drong's snitching that he had suffered so much, he was so despondent that he lost the will to live and ceased to care what would happen to him after death. He was furious, but he no longer had the strength to give Alak Drong the beating he deserved. Retrieving the hidden rosary he had made from ten beads of tamarisk wood, he plied it silently, not a syllable of prayer on his lips. Because there were no forests on the grasslands of Tsezhung, his homeland, wood was extremely hard to come by, and tamarisk even more so. It was said that it could purify defilements and ward off harm, and that "where the prized red tamarisk is found, child and horse are safe from evil spirits." If anyone ever got hold of a tamarisk branch, it would be cut into tiny pieces the size of the joint on your little finger and then hung around the necks of children or on the manes of horses. Tsetra had never before dared take a good long look at Alak Drong, but now that he did, he felt that his features, and his eyes above all, were full of deceit. *That Lozang Tsültrim was right to make him drink piss*, he thought. That night, Tsetra crawled naked out of bed and hid the rosary under Alak Drong's pillow. The next morning, he reported him to the cadres. That was the first time he had ever informed on anyone, and at first he felt shame and dread. But then he thought about how he had always cared for Alak Drong, helped him, even come to blows with the savage felons for him and earned himself a beating in the process, and how the bastard had sold him out again and again without a moment's hesitation, and how much he'd had to suffer because of it, and he felt that his actions were by no means excessive—if anything, Alak Drong deserved worse. What was that old saying they had in Tsezhung? "If you don't repay a kindness, the good dwindle; if you don't avenge a wrong, the bad multiply." He decided he would continue to exact his revenge, both openly and in secret. Unfortunately for Tsetra, the demons of sickness sank their claws into him and the Lord of Death called, and before long, escorted by suffering and hate and welcomed by the dusty red wind, he found himself standing before King Yama, telling him of the darkness of the human world.

The study sessions sapped the last vestiges of strength from the political prisoners, and now they could no longer lift a pickaxe or a shovel. Even worse, there was a drought of unprecedented proportions that year. The rivers dried up by half, the streams dried up completely, and the fields baked and cracked until they resembled the soles of the prisoners' feet in winter. The wheat shoots that had grown about six inches tall in the late spring all turned yellow and disintegrated. Yet another unprecedented phenomenon was that the red wind descended at the height of summer. Though the force of the wind abated from time to time, the red sand and dust that filled the sky increased the temperature still further and sucked every drop of moisture from every living thing on the ground. As a result, driving the "labor machines" to work every day became a task that was just as arduous for those doing the driving. Song Jiantao, left with little choice, decided to continue the study sessions, which were now, in reality, an excuse to take a break from the heat and the red wind.

No matter how many prisoners died, the number of new prisoners coming in was always higher, which seemed to have no adverse effect on the running of the camp itself. The new arrivals had undergone study sessions on the outside and eaten their share of vegetable *tang* so thin you could use it as a mirror, but unlike the "labor machines," they still possessed some of their own thoughts, as well as enough strength to wield a pick or a shovel; the problem was, there was no longer any arable land on which they could show off this strength. Nevertheless, as Song Jiantao had said, the camp was no retirement home. As soon as the heat abated slightly, the new arrivals were sent to do the heavy groundwork, and the old prisoners, hefting axes and saws instead of picks and shovels, marched on the great forest on the other side of the river, their heads bent, groaning in pain, sweeping the path with their exhausted bodies.

Before, the inmates had had only had a partial view of this forest from the prison and the fields, and all they could make out was a rough outline. Up close, they discovered that it was huge, dense, and ancient. Predators, game, and wild birds were surely to be found in abundance amid the lush pine and cypress trees, the tips of which pierced the sky, a realization that prompted the cadres to regret not having come here sooner to "improve their living conditions." A few guards were left behind to watch the "labor machines" while the rest set off hunting. Unfortunately, while they had been holding study sessions, thousands of cadres and tens of thousands of prisoners from the

THE RED WIND HOWLS

other camps had been plundering the forest, and now the hunting was nowhere near as easy as killing cranes and geese. Whether or not the cadres bagged any game was of no relevance to the prisoners, just like it was irrelevant whether they had a bumper harvest or a drought, because none of it made the slightest difference to their unchanging meal of thin vegetable *tang*. Their task was simply to grunt with each heave of the axe, pant with each stroke of the saw, and bring every tree to the ground.

By nightfall, the cadres had managed to kill a wild boar, seven hares, three snow grouse, a partridge, and a pheasant. If this haul were to be divided evenly among all the cadres, each person would be lucky to get a fingertip-sized piece of meat. The White Chinese thought the Red Chinese would end up quarreling over the food, maybe even coming to blows, but after plucking and gutting their catch, the Red Chinese cut everything to pieces, skin, bones, and all; threw it in their woks with some greens and seasoning; and boiled it all up as if they were making a pot of medicine. Soon clouds of steam began to rise from the woks, and with them came a mouth-watering aroma that the prisoners hadn't smelled for longer than they could remember. Even in the cellblocks farthest from the kitchens, where the doors and windows were closed, the prisoners found themselves sitting up in bed and sniffing the air. The aroma continued to grow more fragrant, more potent, and eventually even the "labor machines," who by now were all at death's door, opened their eyes too, and some crawled naked on all fours to their cellblock doors. The nomads were especially affected by the smell, just as they had been especially sensitive to the smell of petrol, and they were beset by visions of the past, when they

■ 107 ■

had sat by a clear stream on the flower-filled grasslands and sung merry folk songs while cooking meat and boiling tea in a pot perched atop three stones. Tightly scrunching their "clown hats" in despair, they wept.

By the time the morsels of meat in the woks were cooked through and the bones were boiled white, many of the "labor machines," some on two legs and some on all fours, had reached the cadres' canteen and surrounded it. Suddenly the alarm sounded, and the guards on the walls began firing warning shots into the air. The prisoners, however, were now indifferent to everything but the smell of meat; eyes closed and mouths hanging open, they had reached a state where it was hard to tell the difference between life and death. For them, this was an even more inhuman torment than being locked in solitary or thrown in with the felons. After this, whenever Song Jiantao wanted to extract a secret from someone or punish someone who had committed a serious error, he would conduct his interrogations while boiling a piece of offal and repeatedly swallowing his saliva. Once he used this technique on Alak Drong. "What is the current status of things among the prisoners?" he asked him.

"There have been no problems at all since we had the study sessions," Alak Drong replied, his gaze fixed steadily on the bubbling little pot.

"No problems at all?" Commander Song clasped his hands behind his back and began to pace. "And all these prisoners committing suicide, that isn't a problem?"

"Yes, it is," said Alak Drong, focusing on the pot with his eyes half closed.

THE RED WIND HOWLS

"So you had no idea that any of these people were planning to kill themselves?"

"Most people say they're going to kill themselves. I have no way of knowing who's actually going to do it, so I don't report it."

"Most people say they're going to kill themselves?"

"Yes."

"Have you ever said it?"

"No."

"You don't want to kill yourself then?"

"Buddhist scriptures say that taking your own life is wrong, just like it's wrong to take someone else's. That's why there are so few suicides among the Tibetans, and why I've never even considered it. Plus, you've already reduced my sentence, so I've got no reason to commit suicide." Alak Drong never for a moment took his eyes off the bubbling, aroma-wafting little pot.

"Ah, so you still have your religious faith, then?"

Alak Drong suddenly awoke from his daze. Pulling his attention away from the pot, he turned to Song Jiantao. "No, no, how could I?" he said in a fluster. "I gave up my faith a long time ago. Gave it up completely. If I were still a believer, would I have dared turn my teacher in?"

"Hmm. At first I thought Tsetra was just getting revenge when he informed on your crimes. That it was a false accusation. But now . . ."

"It *was* a false accusation!"

"No. It turns out you are a disgusting double-dealer. Maybe you falsely accused Lozang Palden, Tsetra, and all the others just to get your sentence reduced."

■ 109 ■

THE RED WIND HOWLS

"No, no, that's not true! Tsetra admitted that he was concealing weapons, didn't he? And . . ."

Song Jiantao brought his palm down on the table. "Listen here. I have the authority to reduce your sentence, and I also have the authority to increase it."

"Of course, of course, but I really . . ."

"So if you don't want your sentence to be increased, or if you still have hopes of it being reduced, then you must keep me fully informed of who is planning to commit suicide."

"Yes, yes, of course." With one last glance at the aroma-emitting pot, Alak Drong swallowed and left the office.

After they began their attack on the forest, the number of "labor machines" committing suicide increased. They didn't have the energy to mount an escape attempt, and even if they did, there was no way to tell the difference between north, south, east, and west in the dense, boundless forest, which essentially constituted a giant natural prison. Therefore, the prisoners who no longer had the will to bear the torment, who had lost all hope of ever gaining their freedom, would wait until the cadres had gone hunting and the guards and foremen weren't watching, then sneak off behind a large tree and use all their remaining strength to climb up. Once they had located a short length of vine and tied it into a loop, all they had to do was stick their neck through and it was all over.

Alak Drong had two roles: he was both a guard and a "labor machine." On the one hand, he had to keep a close eye on everything the other prisoners did, and on the other, he had to break his back doing hard labor. One day, a quick *swish* sang in his

THE RED WIND HOWLS

ears, he saw stars before his eyes, and the axe he was carrying dropped to the ground.

"Why are you creeping about like a thief instead of doing your work?" It was the unit leader and foreman, a felon who had been put inside after a prolonged spree of robberies. He had been scrutinizing Alak Drong's behavior for some time and had dealt him a blow on the head with a broken branch.

Alak Drong turned to look at the thief-foreman, rubbing his head. The foreman raised his branch again, frightening Alak Drong into blurting out an explanation. "Brigade Commander Song assigned me to keep watch on the other prisoners!"

The foreman lowered his stick. "What? Oh, you're a dirty little rat, are you? Hey, everybody, look! This bastard's a rat! Haha! Aren't you political prisoners always saying we felons have no shame? We might be shameless, but we don't get many informants. Look! The true nature of the political prisoner laid bare! Who's the shameless one now? Haha! Ahahaha . . ."

Tsetra had already told some of his fellow inmates to be on their guard because Alak Drong was a confirmed informant, but Alak Drong's status as a lama meant that hardly anyone believed him, while others still doubted Tsetra on the basis that there wasn't any reliable evidence. Now that Alak Drong's role as an informant had been confirmed beyond doubt, everyone's heads dropped in dismay. There was no one for Alak Drong to talk to after that, no one for him to play cards with, and he became completely isolated. If he was sawing down a tree with another prisoner, the man opposite would glare at him with hate in his eyes. What gave him reason to feel even more hopeless was that he had become worthless in the eyes of Song Jiantao. There were no words of encouragement or consolation when he saw him now; it was all "idiot" and "coward." And there were certainly no more cigarettes to be had.

Tortured by hunger, thirst, exhaustion, and isolation, Alak Drong was finally contemplating suicide when a new prisoner was brought in from his homeland of Tsezhung and placed in his very brigade and unit.

"Don't you recognize me? I'm the son of the Kelten family of the Arik clan. My name's Namgyel. We invited you over to perform a service when my father departed for the Pure Land, remember? We were taken in the same truck when we were first arrested, and I died and was buried on the way, remember?" Like Tsetra had done at first, Namgyel approached Alak Drong and got all this out in one breath. "As long as you're alive and well, Venerable Rinpoché, nothing bad can happen," he added solicitously, his heart filled with hope again.

Alak Drong couldn't recall a Kelten family, much less this Namgyel, but the man who died on the road when they were first arrested, the one who was buried, who Tsetra said was still alive—now that had left a big impression on him. "Oh yes, yes. So how did you escape back then?"

"Phew, that's a long story. It would take me nine days and nights to tell it. Tell me, Venerable Rinpoché, are you the only one left alive out of those fifty men with us on the truck?"

"There might still be one or two survivors in the other camps. In this one, probably only two or three. I'm the only one left in this brigade."

"Phew, Three Jewels have mercy!"

THE RED WIND HOWLS

"What are things like back home?"

"It's unspeakable, Rinpoché. No different from prison I'd say, except that people still have their families. *Eh*, but what use is it having your family anyway? Fathers informing on their sons, daughters denouncing their mothers, wives selling out their husbands. The world has turned upside down. And then there's the food shortages, the heavy labor—it's unspeakable. How could prison be any worse? At least here there won't be people informing on each other and denouncing each other."

Alak Drong felt a shiver run up his spine and his face turned bright red. He sat there silently, not knowing what to say.

Namgyel explained that he had felt dizzy in the truck that day and had fainted. He regained consciousness right after they threw him in the hole. Opening his eyes to take a peek, he saw that the hole wasn't deep, so he closed them again and prayed with all his heart to his lama, his guardian deity, and the Dharma protectors. He waited until he was on the verge of suffocating, then with a mighty effort he thrashed and struggled until his upper body broke through the earth. Following the main road was very risky, but he was so thirsty that he wouldn't have minded getting arrested again as long as he could have a good drink of water first. He set off back the way they had come, heading as fast as possible to the river where the truck had broken down. Despite the terrible condition of the road and the slowness of the truck, when compared to the speed of a thirsty man on his last legs walking beneath the blazing sun, it was like the hare versus the tortoise. They couldn't possibly have driven that far from the river, but he began to feel like he would never make it there on foot. Many times the thought occurred to him that the river might have been a mirage, and the chances of making it home alive seemed ever more remote. But then he thought that the mercy of the Three Jewels had brought him back from the next life and raised him up out of the ground, so maybe they would continue to protect him now. After praying fervently, he felt a clear sense of reinvigoration and proceeded full of courage, and before long, he found himself at the banks of the river. Water gives people energy just like petrol does a car, and Namgyel could draw on an even more bountiful motivating force besides: the intense desire to be reunited with his family, and above all his new bride. In this way, he arrived back in his homeland of Tsezhung without having to bear too much hardship. Of course, there's no need to describe the joy of his wife and relatives.

He had achieved this reunion with his family by hiding among the rocks during the day and creeping homeward at night. The time had arrived, however, when the "People's Communes" were established: the livestock of every household was collectivized and great communal canteens were set up. Every person was given a set ration for each meal, and each meal was smaller and more inedible than the last, until all they got was three and a half ounces of tsampa flour, an ounce of dried cheese, and a half ounce of butter. People became so hungry they felt dizzy. The ration wasn't enough to feed a single person, let alone enough to share around. Even so, through the power of love and devotion, his family saved from each of their rations a spoonful of tsampa and a fingernail-sized piece of butter, which they stored in a sheep's heart pouch and brought to him at night. Their actions in every way embodied the noble sentiment of that phrase, "If we have a scrap of food, we eat it together; if we have a stitch of clothing, we wear it together." Unfortunately, the power of reeducation and mass movements could annihilate the power of love and devotion. They could turn the sane into madmen, the wise into fools, the brave into cowards, the compassionate into devils. One day, Namgyel's wife asked him to turn himself in and go back to prison.

"What?" Namgyel was stunned. "Are you possessed?"

"I'll wait for you as long as it takes," said Namgyel's wife, seizing his hand with tears in her eyes. "I've applied to join the Communist Youth League. If they find out I've been harboring a criminal, I've got no chance. I'll probably be denounced."

"Harboring a criminal? Tell me, what crime have I committed, exactly?"

"If the Party says you're guilty, then you're guilty."

"What's this Communist Youth League?"

"Oh, it's a *glorious* organization. They're the right-hand men and women of the Party, its revolutionary successors."

"How could the wife of a criminal be accepted into an organization like that? Don't be ridiculous."

"If you're revolutionary enough, then maybe . . ."

Namgyel pulled his hand away. "I guess I can't really blame you. How can you feed someone else when you haven't even got enough for yourself? You don't need to save any tsampa for me from now on. I'll find a way to take care of myself. But I'm completely innocent, that's why the lamas and the Dharma protectors brought me back from death's door, and I'm sure they'll continue to protect me . . ."

"We're partners for life. Of course I'm going to share my tsampa, even if it means starving. But hiding you, that's a serious crime. So . . ."

"Fine, okay. You don't need to go on. I think you've completely lost it. I really had no idea until now how brainless you are. Three Jewels have mercy, what has the world come to?"

"You say I'm brainless, but I think *you're* the one who's lost his mind. Think about it: can you spend your whole life hiding like this? If you go to prison, at least you'll get out at some point. And if you turn yourself in voluntarily, they might lighten your sentence. Don't worry, I'll take really good care of your mother, you'll see. And . . ."

"Enough of this nonsense. I haven't killed anyone. I haven't stolen a horse. I haven't so much as harmed a lamb. I'm a good man, an honest man who was going about his business when I was arrested, convicted, and sent off to prison for no reason at all. And now that I'm actually guilty of escaping, they're going to lighten my sentence? Don't make me laugh."

"That . . ."

"Enough. I'm done with this." Namgyel had really lost his temper now. "Long of hair, short of sense. What do you know? If you don't want to feel the back of my hand, I'd stop talking."

"Hmph." Namgyel's wife, normally a gentle soul, had lost her temper too. "Men and women are equal now. Women hold up half the sky. And a husband doesn't have the right to hit his wife anymore."

"Men and women equal? Haha! Hahaha . . . when a mare mounts a stallion, then I'll believe men and women are equal."

THE RED WIND HOWLS

"What are you talking about? I think you're a stubborn conservative, just like that old monk Dranak Geshé."

"Well, I think you're going the way of that demoness Künga Huamo, and you're in danger of being infamous for generations to come."

"I think you'd best keep your opinions to yourself. Künga Huamo is a role model for young people, especially us young women."

"That is frightening. Truly frightening."

"Not in the least. You've been hiding in the rocks so long you don't have a clue what's happening out in the world. You've been left behind by the times. It's my hope that you'll surrender yourself voluntarily."

"If you hadn't shared your tsampa with me in such hard times, I swear I'd kill you right here on the spot. You listen to me: you'll have to sell me out and hand me over to them. I'll die before I surrender." Namgyel said these words in a moment of rage, never dreaming that his wife would actually sell him out. Shortly after he entered their shabby tent the next evening, it was quickly surrounded and he was arrested. He was first handed over to the crowd, where Lozang Tsültrim, Künga Huamo, and other heroes were allowed to carry out their courageous deeds, and then taken to Wang Aiguo. Wang, who had high hopes of turning this savage into an efficient "labor machine," sent him back to the prison camp.

In addition to news of the suffering and terror back home, Namgyel brought the surviving prisoners from Tsezhung yet more merry tidings: each of the clans had now become what the

Chinese called a "commune" (sometimes they were referred to as "townships," sometimes as "communes"), and each of the camps had become a "production brigade." The former Arik clan, for example, was now the "Red Flag Commune," the former Dranak clan was the "Unity Commune," and what was once the Lubum camp of the Dranak clan was now the "Unity Commune Forward Progress Production Brigade."

Suspecting that the reason they hadn't received any replies to their letters had nothing to do with Song Jiantao blocking them after all, the prisoners from Tsezhung decided to try writing to their families once again. About a month later, not only did they receive replies, they even got letters from prisoners in other camps and people long since presumed to be dead. Unfortunately, none of these letters contained any good news; each one was, on the contrary, a ladleful of ice water poured over the prisoner's hearts. The letter that Alak Drong received, for instance, informed him that both of his parents had died and his only sister had gone crazy.

This news plunged Alak Drong into prolonged contemplation. He began to feel profound regret for having informed on his fellow inmates—his own teacher, even—and he resolved not to engage in such acts again, even if it cost him his life. He showed sincere kindness and concern for Namgyel, giving him extensive advice on how to navigate life in the prison. Namgyel, meanwhile, felt that he must have accumulated an enormous amount of good karma in his past lives to have the company of Alak Drong, a man renowned as a buddha in the flesh, in this hellish place. Thinking himself the fortunate among the unfortunate, he served Alak Drong in every way he could, and the two became like father and son. Sadly, as soon as Song Jiantao learned of this special relationship, he transferred Namgyel to another brigade, casting Alak Drong back into isolation and leaving him contemplating suicide once more. Such thoughts were, however, quickly dismissed by the terrible spectacle of another man's suicide. As they were cutting down trees one day, one of the prisoners cried out in sudden horror, "Another one's killed himself!" In the forest, suicide by hanging was extremely common, so no one paid him any mind at first. But when someone shouted, "It looks like Brigade Commander Yang Kai!," the old "labor machines" dropped what they were doing and went to look.

Yang Kai, the first brigade commander of the prison camp, had always been skinny, but now his cheekbones protruded alarmingly and his eye sockets were so sunken that his two huge eyeballs had almost completely come out of his head. More shocking still was his tongue, which hung so far out of his wide-open mouth that it went past his chin. If it weren't for the black plastic glasses that had slipped to the tip of his nose, it would have been hard to tell that it was Yang Kai. The three thin strips of wet bark that he had braided into a noose cut so deep into his flesh that they touched the bone, and from the deep maroon of his neck, it was clear that simply donning a rope had failed to end things instantly, and instead he'd been forced for one last time to relive the pain and terror of his life in concentrated form. You couldn't help but feel that his big, lifeless eyes were boring hatefully into a world filled with darkness, that his gaping mouth and long, stretched tongue were violently cursing a time turned upside down.

THE RED WIND HOWLS

The prisoners had seen countless corpses of men who had died from starvation or committed suicide—sometimes as many as ten a day—but never one this hideous. No one dared go near the body, let alone untie the rope and bring him down, so he was left there to gaze upon that world ravaged by the red wind, to decry the horror of those unfathomably turbulent times.

The dense forest provided prisoners who no longer wanted to live with the opportunity to end their lives, and it provided those who didn't want to die with wild herbs, frogs, and earthworms. And so, the "labor machines" foraged just like their ancestors hundreds of thousands of years before them, eating any fruits they found on the spot and using twigs to tie their trouser legs closed so they could stuff them with mushrooms and frogs and anything else they found. These they would boil in a washbasin when they got back to the prison, then mix in with the salty vegetable *tang* they got from the canteen.

Taking another life is the most grievous of the ten nonvirtues of Buddhism. To Alak Drong, killing a frog or a worm was an even worse sin than selling out his friends and his teacher, and he refused to consider taking the life of a sentient being even if it meant starving to death. He had heard that most of the mushrooms in the forest were poisonous. Sadly for him, he couldn't tell which were poisonous and which were safe; in fact he couldn't even tell the difference between edible plants and weeds. Staring enviously at the mouths of the others and swallowing his saliva, he raged inwardly at how Dranak Geshé, famed for his knowledge of a hundred treatises, had forced him to waste his youth on the *Thirty Verses*, the *Great Treatise on the Stages of the Path to Enlightenment*, and other things entirely useless in a crisis, instead of teaching him how to fend for himself when survival was on the line. Alak Drong stealthily inspected the wild spoils gathered by the others, and just when he had learned to identify a handful of edible herbs and nonpoisonous mushrooms, the fierce autumn wind blew in and all the little plants yellowed, withered, and finally blew away, completely uprooted. Before the prisoners could even lay eyes on the golden hues of autumn, there was a sudden and noticeable drop in temperature, quickly followed by freezing blizzards, and their hopes of foraging for flora and fauna completely evaporated.

Since they didn't have to work when it was snowing, the "labor machines" finally earned a few days of rest. The prison was an empty, desolate place: there was no food, no laughter—no trash, even. There was, however, one thing that they never ran out of, and that was firewood. Each work unit had its own cell that accommodated its twenty members, and each cell contained two large stoves. Every day, the prisoners were able to burn three or four logs as thick as human thighs in each of the stoves.

When the snowstorms finally eased a little and the "labor machines" were sent out into the sludge to resume their attack on the forest, a new prisoner arrived in Alak Drong's unit who seemed very familiar to him, but he couldn't put his finger on where and when he knew him from. As they were cutting through the bogs, Alak Drong approached the man and whispered, "I feel like I know you. What's your name?"

The man stopped in his tracks, stood at attention, and bellowed, "Reporting to the brigade leader! The name of the criminal is Chaktar Bum!" Everyone turned to look at him, utterly astonished, a flustered Alak Drong most of all.

"Oh, of course!" said one of the long-serving prisoners. "Isn't he the farmer who was brought to our unit a while back? The one who lost his mind right after and was taken to the nuthouse."

Chaktar Bum turned to the man immediately and stood at attention. "Reporting to the brigade leader! The criminal is indeed the farmer Chaktar Bum who was brought to your unit a while back, the one who lost his mind right after and was taken to the nuthouse."

"So tell us, have you been in the sanatorium this whole time, or were you at another camp?"

"Reporting to the brigade leader! The criminal does not dare speak about things that he shouldn't."

Not only did Chaktar Bum refer to everyone as "brigade leader," he also spoke to them with the utmost seriousness, even during the course of normal conversations, as if he really were making a report to a brigade leader or cadre. Seeing that he hadn't recovered from his mental illness, everyone decided to ignore him. When they got to the woods and commenced their labor, however, there was a stunning scene: Chaktar Bum instantly set about a tree trunk with his axe, attacking it tirelessly until he lost consciousness and collapsed. When he came around and recovered the strength to pick up his axe, he went right back at it, not letting the axe out of his grip until he had passed out again. After repeating this process several times, not only had he failed to fell a single tree, he had also lost the ability to stand. When the shift was done, the others had to carry

THE RED WIND HOWLS

him back on a makeshift stretcher. Despite this, the cadres declared that "everyone should learn from Chaktar Bum."

This little comedy routine wasn't performed just once or twice—he did it every time. The "labor machines" realized that Chaktar Bum had been transformed into a "labor machine" truly worthy of the name.

It was around this time that people stopped going to the infirmary, even if they were so sick they were knocking on death's door. The sick actually accounted for the majority of prisoners, and there was no doubt that they were all dying or soon to be dead. Whenever the prison doctor came to do his daily inspections, he would simply glance at the prisoners, shake his head, and leave. If a sick man came to ask him for medicine, the doctor feigned surprise and said, "Medicine? Ha! The best medicine for your condition isn't in the infirmary, it's in the canteen. Go ask Brigade Commander Song for help with that." There was no chance he would give them any treatment, and there was certainly no chance he would admit them to the infirmary.

The next time Alak Drong saw Yang Kai's corpse, his tongue and eyeballs had been pecked out by the crows, leaving big black holes in place of his mouth and eye sockets. It was an even more sad and horrifying sight than before. The Buddhist principle of "emptiness" that Dranak Geshé always used to talk about didn't seem to have any real connection to the gaping cavities in Yang Kai's face, but for some reason Alak Drong couldn't get the term out of his mind. If only the man hanging from the tree was Pisspot Song, the prisoners thought. Not wanting to let the snow, the birds, and the beasts continue to molest Yang Kai's body, the prisoners cut him down and were going to bury him, but the bitter cold had arrived especially early that year and the ground was frozen solid, giving them no choice but to leave him where he was for the day. When the shift was over, one group of prisoners carted off the unconscious Chaktar Bum on a stretcher made of several branches while another group brought Yang Kai's body, which they dropped into a hole in the ice while crossing the bridge over the river.

From the next day onward, the snow came again, and except for the odd morning and afternoon or a day here and there, it fell incessantly for over a month, burying everything under a blanket of white. The daily trek from the cells to the canteen required the paths to be swept first, and soon piles of snow taller than a man had formed on either side. The piles of firewood stacked in front of each row of cells, as tall as the buildings themselves, were likewise covered in snow, and it took two "labor machines" all their strength and a whole hour to dig out the amount they needed for a day. The convoy of trucks that had shuttled ceaselessly back and forth, transporting the endless amounts of pinewood chopped up by the prisoners back to the east of China, was nowhere to be seen. The road had been cut off by the snow, or so they had heard. According to later arrivals at the camp, the snowstorms had resulted in a disaster of unprecedented proportions in the nomadic areas, killing livestock by the hundreds of thousands. At the same time, this horror had managed to save the lives of tens of thousands of humans, for although the meat of the animals that had starved to death was tasteless and contained no fat, it was a nourishing, delicious feast compared to the coarse tsampa they had been surviving on. Moreover, since so many of the livestock had died, it was impossible to skin them all, meaning that anyone who skinned a dead sheep and handed in the pelt not only got to keep the meat for themselves but also earned high praise. For a time, the nomads regained their vigor and a healthy glow returned to their cheeks. Even the old folks and children lying in their beds, awaiting death with their eyes closed, would open them the second they were given a taste of that mincemeat porridge, as though they had drunk the nectar of the gods.

Such a windfall was unthinkable at the prison camp, where the lives of the "labor machines," hanging by a horsehair, were ever drawn out by meager rations of thin vegetable *tang* and coarse buns. A month or so of rest in their warm cells had, however, given the majority a reprieve from death, and some of them had even seen their "tails" shrink and their bodies recover slightly, compared with a month before.

If this novel were divided into chapters, then this would be the chapter about the Eight Cold Hells. Donning their filthy plastic-soled shoes and filthy padded jackets bursting with cotton flowers, the "labor machines," axes on shoulders, hands stuffed in sleeves, were sent back out into the bone-chilling cold to wade through knee-high snow and resume their attack on the forest. From afar, they looked like line after line of black text scrawled clumsily on a white page. By the time they reached the woods, their hands were so numb they couldn't grip the handles of their axes. They kept breathing on their hands and rubbing them together, and some even stuck their hands right in their mouths—the worst kind of solution, just like drinking salt water to stave off thirst. It was especially bad for the nomads, who had no socks or underwear and had to wear the padded uniforms and plastic-soled shoes on their bare skin. Freezing wind blew in through their sleeves, collars, and the bottoms of their jackets and trousers, making them shiver so hard their teeth clacked. The guards and foremen weren't immune either, having to stamp their feet constantly to ward off the cold. Chaktar Bum, the "labor machine" worthy of the name, got down to business without a second thought, heaving his axe relentlessly into the base of a tree until his face was glistening with sweat and white steam began to curl around his head. Seeing this, the prisoners gritted their teeth, raised their axes, and set about the trees. Though the repeated blows caused snow to fall from the branches onto their heads and into their collars, their bodies were soon suffused with warmth, and steam began to rise from their heads, prompting the guards to pull their hands out of their sleeves, stop stomping their feet, and seize some axes from the prisoners so that they too could warm themselves up with some tree felling. By this point, Chaktar Bum had already collapsed in the snow. He woke up frozen stiff, clenched his jaw, and resumed swinging his axe.

Thanks to their mad teacher, the bona fide "labor machine," the other "labor machines" had learned how to stave off the cold. But swinging an axe for all they were worth sapped their strength even faster than the cold, and they quickly came to the realization that this was not a viable long-term solution. Within just a day or two of having resumed their assault on the forest, everyone's ears, hands, and feet were frozen and covered in blisters that soon burst with water, pus, and blood, rendering them completely incapable of holding anything in their hands or even

THE RED WIND HOWLS

standing on their own two feet. This was followed by an intense fever that confined them to their beds, from which many never rose again. Even when they weren't completely paralyzed by the cold, the skin of their hands, feet, and faces cracked open and bled. Alak Drong's wise tutor Dranak Geshé had once told him about the cold hell where the bodies of sentient beings split open like lotuses, which seemed to him a very apt description of his present circumstances. It didn't look like there was any hope of returning to the grasslands alive now. Then he thought that he hadn't died on the Harrowing Day; he hadn't died after the beating and torment of the struggle sessions; he hadn't died of thirst, or hunger, or heat, so if he could just survive the cold, what else could they possibly do to him? Besides, it had already been three years, minus another two for his sentence reduction, and that left him with only five more. The quality and quantity of the buns and vegetable *tang* seemed to have been slowly improving of late and the number of deaths among the prisoners was dropping slightly. So perhaps it was true what they were always saying about how the country was going through a tough time right now, how it was temporary, how it would soon pass. And now that nearly all the old prisoners were dead and had been replaced by new arrivals, he wasn't as isolated as before. All in all, he felt hopeful; he felt that things were looking up for him and he just had to stay the course and get through the next five years. In fact, his life did indeed continue to get better, so much so that his "tail" eventually vanished.

He had no way of knowing then that when he finally did gain his "freedom" five years later, he wouldn't be allowed to return to the grasslands but rather would be made to stay on at the prison as a "worker" under the camp system of forced job placement.

When he learned of this, Alak Drong neither wept nor wailed, nor did he do anything crazy like slap himself or tear at his clothes or curse the cadres. He simply returned to his cell and leaned against the wall, sighing now and then. There he remained, his eyes half closed, neither eating nor drinking, staring into the distance and contemplating the many ways he could kill himself.

The door banged open and a man appeared in the doorway clutching a net bag containing a basin, a *gangzi*, a towel, a woolen sweater, and two copies of the *Little Red Book*. Before anyone had had the chance to get a good look at him, the guard gave him a fierce kick in the rear, and after staggering forward a few steps, he collapsed face first right in front of Alak Drong, scattering the contents of his bag all over the floor. He slowly lifted his head with a groan, revealing a bleeding nose, and looked up imploringly at the man before him. In contrast to his past track record, this time Alak Drong recognized him right away: it was Wang Aiguo.

"Secretary Wang? Wang Aiguo?" stammered Alak Drong as he snapped upright.

"Yes, the criminal's name is Wang Aiguo. Wait . . . you . . . you're . . . Alak Drong, County Head Drong!" A smile spread across Wang Aiguo's miserable face, and he was about to get to his feet when Alak Drong pounced. He kicked him in the chest, threw him onto his back, then straddled him and rained down punches until Wang's face was such a bloody, pulpy mess that Alak Drong's fists were slipping off their target. A simple beating, however, was not enough to dispel all the pain in Alak Drong's heart. He began to cry even before Wang Aiguo did, then ran to the stove and retrieved a calf-sized log, at which point the others finally intervened and demanded an explanation.

"He's the dog that put me in prison for no reason at all," Alak Drong said between heaving sobs. "And not just me. Thousands of innocent people from Tsezhung, all jailed and sent on the road to death by this piece of shit. I'm going to settle the score with you. I'm going to settle the score for all the people from Tsezhung you murdered, you can count on that. I'm sure you remember my kind and wise teacher, Dranak Geshé Lozang Palden, and Tsetra, the boy from the Tadzi clan—maybe you don't know him—and then there's . . . well, I can't remember all of them right now, but I'm going to settle the score for every widow and orphan in Tsezhung, you can count on that, and then I can die happy. Hah! Heaven has eyes and karma exists. Liar, beast, murderer! If I don't butcher you with a needle, I'm no man! If I don't make your bound-foot Chinese wife a widow, I'm no man! We'll settle the score—one day." When he was finished, he continued to weep.

This was the first time since he was a child that Alak Drong had raised his hands against someone in anger. His grief and rage had made him forget everything: religious laws, community laws, state laws. Only after cursing Wang Aiguo with every superstitious, reactionary, filthy, and foul insult he could think of did he feel like his pain and suffering had abated somewhat. Happily, there weren't many informants around anymore, and most of the political prisoners had suffered at the hands of cheats and savages like Wang Aiguo just as Alak Drong had, so their sympathies were with him and their animosity was directed squarely at Wang.

"I don't blame you, any of you, I don't blame you at all. I was under such pressure from above, I had no choice." Wang Aiguo pulled himself upright and sat on the floor in a stupor, as if his soul had left his body, not even wiping the blood from his face. Wang became thoroughly isolated, just as Alak Drong had been, and when he hanged himself a few months later just like Yang Kai, thereby realizing Alak Drong's threat to make his bound-foot Chinese wife a widow, Alak Drong regretted having given the former secretary such a brutal "welcome." Alak Drong offered a prayer for the deceptive lowlife so that Wang might be spared the terrors of the bardo and avoid rebirth in the lower realms. Since almost all the trees had been cut down and the once dense forest had been largely reduced to a few scattered saplings, Wang Aiguo's body was discovered immediately. His corpse wasn't nearly as horrifying as Yang Kai's, but it was disgusting: his face was covered in snot, drool, and tears, and he had urinated and defecated all over himself. No one would go anywhere near it.

The forced laborers at the camp were classified as one of the "three types of personnel." Unlike the prisoners, they didn't have to wear the shabby black uniforms or the clown hats, they didn't have to refer to themselves as "criminals," they received a monthly payment of forty-eight yuan for their labor, and on Sundays they were permitted to go on outings to the county seat that lay some nine miles away from the prison. In this town, Alak Drong saw women up close for the first time since he'd been put in prison, and it made him think back on the woman from eight years ago who had replied "Yes, Your Holiness" to anything that came out of his mouth. This memory suffused his entire body with a strange and indescribable feeling, and he found himself trailing after a woman in a trance, his eyes fixed on her behind. She was a middle-aged woman "ample of buttock," as it says in the *Mirror of Poetry*, and it looked like she hadn't been through the "Three Years of Hardship" at all: as she strolled down the street, her butt bounced up and down with every step, barely held in by pants that were almost splitting at the seams. The image called to mind a goose-down pillow. Alak Drong, feeling hot all over, his palms sweating, was still trailing along with his eyes fixed on the woman when someone suddenly bellowed, "Down with X!" Like a teacher making his students recite the alphabet, the call was quickly followed by a thousand simultaneous cries of "Down with X!" renting the air like thunder, instantly snapping Alak Drong out of his trance. There appeared before him a crowd bearing a horizontal banner that read "Long Live the Great Proletarian Cultural Revolution!" and driving before them like an animal an old man in his sixties, his head covered with a pointed paper hat and his hands tied behind his back by a hemp rope that wound around his chest and neck. The procession made its way imposingly down the street, men and women with sleeves rolled up to their elbows, belts tied tightly around their waists, calling out one slogan after another: "Long Live the Great Leader Chairman Mao!," "Down with Ox Demons and Snake Spirits!" At one point, "The East Is Red" blared from the loudspeakers on the street, and everyone stopped to listen to the announcer reading out "the latest directives, the latest directives . . ." When the directives were over, the crowd marched on, driving the old man with the pointy hat off into the distance as they sang: "Sailing the seas depends on the helmsman / Life and growth depend on the sun / Rain and dewdrops nourish the crops / Making revolution depends on Mao Zedong Thought!"

Alak Drong watched the marchers recede into the distance, and in his mind there appeared a crystal-clear vision of the county seat back in Tsezhung, the grasslands in the background. By that time, the Tsezhung county seat abounded with gray buildings erected by the Chinese, and a wide road stretched through the town. It was on this road that another crowd, sleeves rolled up to their elbows, belts tied tightly around their waists, had tied Wang Aiguo's hands behind his back and put a long pointy paper hat on his head. The crowd had shoved him around and shouted, "Down with Wang Aiguo!," after which he had been taken to the same detention center that had housed Alak Drong and Dranak Geshé over eight years before, and the morning after that, he was put on a truck and taken off to prison. It seemed that Wang Aiguo went through just as much suffering as Alak Drong had eight years prior. That had been the "Harrowing Day"; this time, it was the "Cultural Revolution," a truly terrifying movement that turned people into machines and led to countless murders, beatings, imprisonments, and suicides.

Over the last few months, not only had the number of "historical" prisoners—that is, political prisoners—greatly increased, the majority of the new arrivals were leading experts, university professors, high-ranking officials, writers, artists—in short, the cream of society. The running of the prison changed overnight too. Study sessions now took up more time than manual labor and regulations of all kinds became stricter, leading to even more suicides than there had been during the "Three Years of Hardship."

By the time the marchers wound their way back to where Alak Drong was standing, the old man with the pointy paper hat had lost his shoes, he was foaming at the mouth, and his eyeballs had rolled back in his head. The crowd was basically dragging him along, and Alak Drong couldn't help but shudder in horror. Forgetting all about the woman with the rear end like a goose-down pillow, he hurried back toward the prison camp.

What had been a boundless tamarisk forest dotted with muddy ponds some eight years before was now a wasteland. In winter and spring, it was nothing more than a stage for the sandy red wind, which blew so hard you couldn't open your eyes. But in the summer, green buds poked up through the ground, which in the autumn became undulating golden waves, and the "labor machines" couldn't help but feel hopeful and happy, even though it made no difference to them whether there was a bumper harvest or a drought. After Yang Kai's arrest, Song Jiantao reported to his superiors that the prison was producing one thousand three hundred pounds of wheat per *mu* of land, and as a result, the prison became a model for the northwest region and Song Jiantao was granted an audience with the Great Helmsman himself. The nomads knew that such a high figure was impossible, but even so, it was undeniable that this was among the most productive pieces of farmland on the Tibetan plateau.

■ 133 ■

THE RED WIND HOWLS

The autumn harvest was approaching. Instead of going straight back to the prison, Alak Drong lingered for a while in the vast "golden ocean," soaking up its beauty. He was gradually able to put those terrible things he had just witnessed out of his mind, and his thoughts returned to the woman with the rear end like a goose-down pillow. When the wives of the forced laborers came to see their husbands, didn't the prison let them have conjugal visits? And didn't that mean that forced laborers were allowed to get married? Since there was no hope of him ever returning to the grasslands, wouldn't it be best if he could get married? But where was he going to find a woman in such an unfamiliar place? And even if he could, who would marry one of the "three types of personnel"? If he were still on the grasslands of Tsezhung, and if he were still a lama, taking a hundred beautiful women as his consorts wouldn't have been a problem at all. Ah—a little tryst in a tranquil field like this, or out on the empty grasslands, that must be the most beautiful thing in the whole world . . .

As the nomads say, "an autumn day is but a fingerspan long." The days were getting shorter and the nights longer, and Alak Drong had accomplished nothing in town aside from stalking that woman and watching the spectacle of the marchers. He hadn't even managed to have a bite to eat. Seeing that it was nearly dinnertime, he made his way back to the prison. When he was at the monastery, he had had to do his recitations for one or two hours every day without fail, and now, in much the same way, he had to attend one to two hours of political study sessions after dinner. During this period, the sessions weren't about domestic and international affairs or how to increase grain production, but rather how to raise up and propagate wave after wave of the Great Proletarian Cultural Revolution. Alak Drong was reminded again of the old man, his mouth foaming and his eyes rolling back in his head.

Something that came as a complete surprise to everyone was the fate of Brigade Commander Song Jiantao, a man whose every other word was "revolution." The morning after Alak Drong's trip to the county seat, Song Jiantao arose to find several cadres from the prison at his office door bearing a big-character poster. This they made him read aloud; then without letting him say a word in his defense, they planted a pointy paper hat on his head and made him bend to his knees and stick his arms out behind him in the "airplane position," after which he was dragged to a mass meeting of all the cadres and forced laborers, where he was proclaimed a "counterrevolutionary" and struggled against until he couldn't stand and the stink filled the air. It had long been said that there was serious discord in the ranks of the prison leadership, so the whole affair was obviously a calculated plot. However, it also stood as clear testament to the nature of a time when there was no distinction between friend and foe, no distinction between good and evil, and no recourse whatsoever for the unjustly accused. They heard later that the cadres interrogated Song Jiantao that night and presented him with a prepared confession detailing his crimes. They said that if he didn't sign it, he would be handed over to the political prisoners, who would be allowed to have their way with him for eight days straight, one for every year of their grievances. Song Jiantao, terrified, signed the document and added his fingerprints without even looking at it, after which he was taken away. Needless to say, the faces of the political prisoners lit up with a joy that hadn't been seen in eight years. "Heaven has eyes!" cried Alak Drong. "It was about time. Pisspot Song had it coming, and I pray he never comes back."

While the political study classes were still ongoing, the autumn harvest wrapped up successfully. After every last sack of grain had been handed over to the state, the first red wind of the year blew in and the temperature dropped by half. It was discovered then that every room in the prison—the cells, the cadres' dorms, the offices, the kitchens—was short of firewood, and the "labor machines" were sent up into the mountains lugging their saws and axes. Unfortunately, with the exception of a few trees on hard-to-reach ridges, there wasn't so much as a twig left to be found; the whole place had been razed as thoroughly as a prisoner's freshly shaved head. Worse still, up on the hills, shorn of the cover of foliage, the red wind was twice as fierce and biting as it was on the plains, and the "labor machines" had to endure cold and suffering even worse than when they were working in the depths of winter. A month or so later, when every remaining tree on either side of the vast mountain had been tracked down and felled, they finally had just enough firewood to get them through the three months of winter—if they used it sparingly.

Believers repent their sins and seek forgiveness before the images of their gods. Christians, for instance, offer their prayers before a representation of Jesus Christ on the cross: "O Merciful Lord Jesus, forgive me for I have sinned . . ." Materialists call this "superstition." Every morning, the prisoners (including the forced laborers categorized as one of the "three types of personnel") had to stand before a portrait of Mao Zedong and recite, "Esteemed and beloved Chairman Mao, Great Leader and Great Teacher, we confess our faults to you. We are criminals. We accept our lawful and just punishment. We will root out the cause of our crimes. We will reform ourselves through labor, sincerely and obediently." One day, a cadre overheard Alak Drong's response to this: "Hehe, if this isn't superstition, I don't know what is." Without delay, he was struggled against until he couldn't stand and the stink filled the air, then he was sentenced to another year and found himself once again wearing that shabby black uniform and the "clown hat."

A year later, when he once more returned to the local town with his forty-eight yuan in hand, the shops were all empty and the restaurants were out of food. The one thing that could be found in abundance was colorful and tattered big-character posters, which the red wind blew up and down every street and alley. Quotations from Chairman Mao were painted on the walls of every house and yard. Not only that: every door, tree, vehicle, and cart—in short, everything that could move and everything that couldn't—was plastered with slogans, denunciations, big-character posters, and political caricatures. The one that left the biggest impression on Alak Drong was a sketch of Liu Shaoqi, his nose bigger than his head, a huge fist in the form of an "East Is Red" tractor on his spine, pinning him to the floor like a sheet of paper. Alak Drong only knew a few of the Chinese characters from the caption underneath: "Chairman Mao," "enemy," "our," "down with." He surmised that it said something like: ANYONE WHO OPPOSES CHAIRMAN MAO IS OUR ENEMY. DOWN WITH ALL ENEMIES!

The red flags flapping in the wind and the endless piercing slogans blaring from the loudspeakers gave the place an even more fearful atmosphere than the prison camp. Alak Drong returned to the camp without having had so much as a bite to eat. The prison food was still awful in those days and there was no way it could fill you up, but it was nothing compared to eight or nine years before, when the prisoners went to bed starving and woke up starving. The labor was lighter too. All you really had to do was make it seem like you loved Chairman Mao. More than ten years passed in the blink of an eye, and before you knew it, the Party had pinned responsibility for all past mistakes on Lin Biao and the Gang of Four. All the political prisoners and forced laborers were released, sent on their way with two bricks of tea per person and a flowery speech about the glorious shining future that lay ahead of them.

"*Ah ho!* More than twenty years of hunger, thirst, exhaustion, torture, and abuse. And we get two bricks of tea." For many of them, twenty years of lament and twenty years of tears were let out all at once, and they tossed away the bricks of tea like a stone you'd used to wipe your ass.

Alak Drong didn't know whether to feel happy or sad, but either way he didn't dare throw away his bricks of tea. He was about to set out when he was greeted by an unexpected visitor bearing a *khata*: it was Lozang Tsültrim, who some twenty years ago had struggled against him until he couldn't stand and the stink filled the air—and had made him drink piss. In addition to the *khata*, Lozang Tsültrim had brought a burgundy lambskin coat, a yellow undershirt, and a pair of shoes. Alak Drong

THE RED WIND HOWLS

was touched, and he set off for home, feeling no desire at all to reflect on all that had happened over the last twenty years.

As he crossed the bridge near the prison, he saw that the river, which had once been as blue as turquoise and clear as glass, which had once slaked the thirst of countless thousands of prisoners and swallowed the corpses of countless thousands more, had almost completely dried up, and the remaining current had turned a deep crimson, as though stained by the blood of all those dead men.

Alak Drong shouted at the top of his voice: "Cadres and felons, carry on eating human flesh, carry on drinking human blood!"

Part Two

THE LARGE assembly hall and Alak Drong's mansion, both of which had been rebuilt after repeated donation drives spanning the whole of Tsezhung, and a handful of tiny, shoddy monks' quarters—that's all there was. Every other hall, temple, and residence had been reduced to rubble, the ruined walls facing up toward the sky as though demanding the repayment of a debt. This was how Tsezhung Monastery looked ten years after Alak Drong came home from prison. Alak Drong was now the Deputy Chairman of the Tsezhung County Regional Committee of the Chinese People's Political Consultative Conference, and Lozang Tsültrim had become his faithful right-hand man, who followed him everywhere like a shadow and was devoting all his energy and brainpower to the lofty undertaking of rebuilding the monastery so that the bell of the Dharma could sound once more. At the same time, like Alak Drong, Lozang Tsültrim was enjoying the highest living standards in all of

Tsezhung. But every time he saw those ruined walls demanding their debts, and every time he noticed the locals gazing at him in shock, he became extremely uncomfortable and turned to look at something else.

It was a late autumn day, the twenty-second of the ninth month in the Tibetan lunar calendar, when Alak Drong reentered the newly reconstructed assembly hall and was installed upon the five-faced lion throne, just like forty years before when he had first taken his place as the head of Tsezhung Monastery. The people shed profuse tears of devotion and performed breathless prostrations and circumambulations.

This was the day Lozang Gyatso had been waiting for for thirty years, and he had arrived at the monastery the previous afternoon carrying his complete monk's attire. But when he saw amid the throngs of frantic prostrators and circumambulators all the people who had been unabashed revolutionaries during those terrifying years, especially Lozang Tsültrim, now refitted in robes and buzzing obsequiously about Alak Drong, he couldn't help but feel disgusted. He found himself contemplating that question again: was cladding yourself in Buddhist garments and reciting scriptures the true way of the Dharma, or was it better to adopt layman's clothing and lead a good, moral life in accordance with the laws of karma? This was a problem that had been bothering him for some time now.

The morning before, he had finally decided to return to lay life and marry Tashi Lhamo. Tashi Lhamo, however, was aghast at this news and let loose a desperate prayer. When she calmed down, she adopted a serious tone and said, "You've been waiting thirty years for this day, and now that it's finally here and

THE RED WIND HOWLS

your dreams are about to come true, you start with all this nonsense. If this isn't an obstacle to the Dharma, I don't know what is. Get those ideas out of your head and get yourself off to the monastery right now. Tomorrow is a joyous day, and you'll be wearing your robes for it!" She busied herself preparing his outfit and gathering his things.

"But what will you do when I'm gone? You've wasted your youth on me. We've got no kids, and there's no way you'll find a good husband now. And then there's the trouble you've been having with your joints. I think that . . ."

"Come on now, stop all that. You don't need to worry about me. I've got my own plans in life. You just get going now."

"It's easy for me to leave. But you . . ."

"Have you forgotten your teacher's last words? I'm begging you, please go! The monastery's waiting." Tashi Lhamo virtually pushed Lozang Gyatso out the door.

Tashi Lhamo hadn't been out of Lozang Gyatso's thoughts for a single moment since he had left home the previous day. He even dreamed about her all night long, his mind filled with visions of the two of them getting married and having a kid, right through till dawn.

When it gets warmer next spring, I can build myself a nice little monk's hut and devote the rest of my life to recitations and spiritual practice, and I'll have nothing to worry about in this life or the next. But what about Tashi Lhamo, who gave up her youth for me, who doesn't have any family in the world she can call her own? Leaving her all alone like this, isn't that just despicable, heartless selfishness? Lozang Gyatso clambered to his feet and stood in the middle of the madly prostrating crowd, racked by doubts.

THE RED WIND HOWLS

A young man accosted an elderly monk and handed him one yuan. "Akhu, would you please recite the *Spontaneous Fulfillment of Wishes* for me?" he said.

The old monk didn't seem too thrilled with the request. Ignoring the one yuan note, he gave the young man a disparaging look. "Boy, if that's all it cost for a chant that made your wishes come true, why would I do it for one yuan when I could just recite it for myself?"

The elderly monk walked off, leaving the young man stunned. As Lozang Gyatso stood there, even more shocked by this exchange, the young man rushed after the monk, producing a ten yuan note. The old man stuffed it begrudgingly into his vest and continued on his way.

Lozang Gyatso, growing tired of the anthill of activity in the assembly hall, went and climbed the hill behind the monastery and looked down on the scene below. Spotting the ruins of Dranak Geshé's former residence, he recalled his erstwhile teacher's appearance—those clear, starlike eyes that gleamed with wisdom—and heard his words in his head: "Hold on to your vows as tightly as you would a yak's tail. The Buddha's light will one day shine again on the snowy mountains of Tibet." He jumped up in a hurry and was about to head back to the monastery, but Tashi Lhamo's pure, white face reappeared in his mind and he sat back down. Lozang Gyatso gazed out over the grasslands of Tsezhung, now a wilderness occasionally lashed by the red wind, a desolate place where nothing grew anymore. Gradually his gaze shifted to the county seat, which some years ago had sprung up at the foot of the monastery, and he became lost in thought.

■ 144 ■

Alak Drong, Dranak Geshé, and all the others had been taken off to prison. Not long after, the remaining inhabitants of Tsezhung received official notice: all of them, without exception, were to report to the "county seat."

This "county seat" was an area a little less than a mile square that had been cleared at the foot of Tsezhung Monastery. It was divided by a main road fifty yards wide, on either side of which lay enclosures of differing sizes surrounded by walls of adobe and clay. Inside them, several rows of buildings with white-washed bricks and blue-tiled roofs were in various stages of construction. If you looked closely, you would discover that these buildings included the county Party committee, the county government, a military garrison, a courthouse, a public security bureau, a civil affairs bureau, a school, a clinic, a grain and oil co-op, a general store, a bank, and a post office. Of these, the most popular addition among the nomads was the clinic, which employed a gentle, skilled doctor and gave out medicine that was both free and highly efficacious. A large multiuse building was being constructed with wood from the ruins of Tsezhung Monastery and trees cut down from the banks of the Machu, which could serve as a movie theater, a meeting hall, and a place for public sentencings and struggle sessions (some twenty years later, this hall would host a major meeting at which Alak Drong and a handful of other survivors, as well as Dranak Geshé, Wang Aiguo, and the many who had lost their lives on the Harrowing Day or in the prison camps, were all formally rehabilitated. The living and the dead alike were offered two bricks of tea, a felt mat, and a small aluminum pot by way of consolation and compensation. At the same time, it was announced that the people would be free to practice their religion and that the monasteries could be rebuilt. Alak Drong magnanimously donated his four bricks of tea to the monastery's coffers, an act that was seen as a major contribution to Buddhism and to which more than three thousand words of detailed description were devoted in the *Chronicles of Tsezhung Monastery)*.

Lozang Gyatso arrived in this new "county seat" with his mother, Dekyi. By that point in time, he had already shed his monk's robes. The old fur-lined coat he was wearing had belonged to his father, who died on the Harrowing Day and whose body was never found. Like most people who have just given up their vows, Lozang Gyatso felt that the clothing didn't sit right on him, that it looked ridiculous, even. This didn't just apply to fallen monks, though: if Chinese people or even Tibetans from farming families donned one of the big fur coats worn by the nomads, they suddenly looked absurd and clownish. There was a deputy county governor several years later, a Tibetan from a farming community, who commissioned the best tanner and the best seamstress in Tsezhung to make him a first-rate fur-lined coat. When it was done, he wore it about town, feeling very pleased with himself, but much to his dismay, everyone who saw him burst out laughing. Thinking that it must be to do with his shoes, he switched to a pair of long boots, but that just made the damned nomads laugh even harder. As we all know, it took something genuinely side-splitting to make people laugh back in those difficult days. In the end, the forlorn deputy governor never wore his big fur coat again.

Like most of the women in Tsezhung at that time, Lozang Gyatso's mother, Dekyi, didn't have a shirt to her name, and she walked down the streets of the county seat with breasts that drooped almost to her navel swinging to and fro. She wasn't yet fifty, but she had lost her husband on the Harrowing Day; Dranak Geshé, her older brother, had been imprisoned; and all the family property had been confiscated, all of which had aged her overnight. Now, if you told someone she was sixty years old, they wouldn't bat an eyelid.

The walls on either side of the main road were plastered with red, green, and yellow banners bearing slogans in Chinese and Tibetan: WARMLY WELCOME THE YOUTH SHOCK BRIGADE! LEARN FROM THE YOUTH SHOCK BRIGADE! SALUTE THE YOUTH SHOCK BRIGADE! RAISE HIGH THE FLAG OF SOCIALISM, DEVELOP THE NORTHWEST OF THE MOTHERLAND!

Lozang Gyatso had been a disciple of Dranak Geshé Lozang Palden, one of the most learned and widely respected men in all of Amdo, which in turn made Lozang Gyatso just about the most learned of all the hundreds of monks from Tsezhung Monastery. And yet, the banners before him were filled with words and phrases that he had never encountered in all the thousands of tomes and scriptures he had read, to the point that he couldn't even really understand what they meant. Not only did he look ridiculous—his brain had become a joke too.

A large group of cadres was arranging the nomads into two lines on either side of the road. Each of the nomads was given a red paper flower the size of a wooden cup. "Everybody listen up!" shouted a cadre. "When the youths pass by, I want everyone to lift up their flowers and wave them, and give our guests a big warm welcome in Chinese by shouting as loud as you can, '*Relie huanying, relie huanying!*'"

Waving the flowers was a piece of cake, but for the nomads, it was as hard to remember "*relie huanying*" as it had been for Alak Drong to memorize the *Thirty Verses*, and pronouncing it correctly was completely out of the question. After practicing as much as possible in the time they had, the majority had finally managed to nail down the troublesome phrase: "really bam bing!" It was hard to say whether or not this was a language of earth, and it was even harder to tell what it was supposed to mean.

The cadres were far from satisfied with "really bam bing," but even Wang Aiguo, the local representative of the triumvirate of Party, government, and military authority, was powerless to do anything about it for now, so "really bam bing" it was.

The nomads had been standing on either side of the road shouting "really bam bing" for about four hours. It was almost five o'clock by the time they heard the distant rumbling of truck engines. The roar got gradually closer and louder until it sounded like a thousand thunderclaps at once, making the nomads' hearts hammer in their chests. In a panic, they began mumbling desperate prayers to Alak Drong, who at that moment was suffering in a prison camp miles away, exhausted, hungry, terrified, and tormented, unable to save even himself. As the children at their mothers' breasts began to wail and wet themselves, a cloud of red dust loomed up from the east, from which there emerged a huge fleet of trucks driving bumper to bumper.

THE RED WIND HOWLS

The county cadres, with Wang Aiguo at their head, rushed to gather at the east end of the street, but to the nomads' surprise, the fleet of trucks came to a halt. About forty people descended from each truck, and after wiping the dirt off their faces with their handkerchiefs, they arranged themselves into neat rows and began to march forward in even strides, faces beaming with smiles. When they reached the eastern end of the street, a man of a similar age to Wang Aiguo gave a signal with his hand; the cadres briefly exchanged some words, and then all of a sudden erupted in a loud cry of *"Relie huanying!"*

Unfortunately, the nomads had been scared so senseless by the roar of the truck engines that the red flowers and the "really bam bing" they had been practicing all afternoon were completely forgotten, leaving just the measly voices of a handful of cadres. A rather crestfallen Wang Aiguo continued to shout by himself, and gradually he was joined by more, and more confident, renditions of the phrase, until eventually the whole town shook with a mighty chorus of "really bam bing."

As they continued to produce sounds that may or may not have belonged to a language of earth, the nomads saw to their amazement that what had been described as "youths" was in fact a brigade composed of thousands of fresh-faced young men and women, all of the same age and height, with skin as white as milk, their faces wreathed in smiles and their bodies adorned with clean, colorful uniforms that were as red and green as the summer flowers on the Tsezhung grasslands. Was this some kind of illusion? It was hard to believe that such beautiful people existed in the world—these must be gods and goddesses in the flesh! The fame of the "youths" swept immediately across

Tsezhung. If someone saw a particularly good-looking person or someone wearing fetching clothes, they would cry enviously, "*Ah tsi ah tsi!* You look just like a youth!" Sadly for the youths, within two years they completely lost their luster and transformed into real-life hungry ghosts: the skin on their feet, faces, and hands was cracked and bleeding, their clothes were in tatters, their hair was a mess, and they were covered head to toe in lice. Afraid of getting caught by the cadres in the windswept farmlands, they instead roamed like hungry ghosts around the pastures, the county seat, and the mountains, valleys, and riverbanks, devouring anything they could get their hands on: the carcasses of horses and dogs, frogs, baby birds, pikas, mice, dried-up bones, old boots, animal hides, grass, herbs, bark—basically anything that wasn't metal, stone, or dirt went in their mouths. This went on until they perished of cold or hunger or became food for the wolves, and every trace of them—their lives, bodies, and names, their joys and sorrows—was completely wiped out.

In Tsezhung, the term "youth" thus morphed into a synonym for someone dirty, ugly, pitiful, loathsome, disgusting, or wretched. If you saw someone looking worn out or disheveled, you might say, "Hey, you look just like a youth!" Crazy people, simpletons, and beggars were also referred to as "youths." Almost half a century later, this is still the case.

One memory emblazoned on Lozang Gyato's mind was the snowy day on which a female "youth" suddenly came barging into his home around dusk. At her breast she clutched a squirming newborn baby, wrapped up in a tattered old piece of sheepskin she had surely torn off someone's dead body. This must have been the fruit of lips touching and bodies intertwining, a lover's tryst held not long after her arrival with a young man from back home, someone of the same age, who spoke the same language, who felt the same way as her, conducted in a barley field where the crops would never ripen or amid an array of blooming flowers in a secluded meadow. It was also likely that the young father had already given up the ghost or, like her, had been driven to destitute wandering by the hunger and cold.

The woman looked imploringly at Lozang Gyatso's mother and mimed with her hands to indicate that the baby needed food. But the nomadic areas had also been collectivized by this point, and all the food was distributed at set times and in set amounts at the canteen of the People's Commune, meaning they didn't have so much as a morsel at home for themselves, let alone anyone else. People were so hungry they felt dizzy and staggered around unsteadily. Children, the elderly, even healthy adults were starving to death one after the other, and the death toll was climbing by the day.

Not only were they unable to give her anything to eat, Lozang Gyatso and his mother were terrified at the mere prospect of having her in the house, because it had been made clear that anyone harboring a runaway youth faced severe punishment. In recent days, cadres from the commune and supervisors from the farms had made repeated trips to the nomads' homes to check if they were sheltering any escapees. But as they were faced with the wretched sight of the young mother and child trembling with cold and on the verge of starvation, empathy quickly won out over apprehension. Sitting her down by the stove, they stoked up the fire so she could at least get warm.

THE RED WIND HOWLS

The mother extracted her baby from the lambskin swaddling so it could feel the warmth of the fire. The poor little thing could only gasp for air, lacking the energy to even cry. Lozang Gyatso and his mother both felt a sting in their nostrils and began to weep. If tears had any nutritional value, they would have at least had something they could use to save the baby's life.

The young woman clearly knew the nomads' homes were bereft of food, but she nevertheless scanned every corner of the tent, refusing to give up hope. Eventually her lifeless, drooping gaze alighted on something in particular, and she held out her right hand limply, pointing at it. Lozang Gyatso followed her gesture and saw the old, dry shoulder bone of a yak with not even enough meat left on it for a mouse to nibble at. His mother used it as a spade to collect dung, and there were still a few flecks of dried excrement sticking to it. He pointed at the bone in surprise, and the woman nodded. Lozang Gyatso retrieved the bone and handed it to her, dubiously, and the young woman put it straight on the fire without a second glance. When the bone began to smoke and turn black, the woman, clutching her baby in one arm, removed it from the fire with her free hand and flipped it a few times until it had cooled slightly. She took a big bite of the bone and began crunching and chewing and sucking; then she extracted a little piece and gently pressed it to her baby's mouth. To Lozang Gyatso's amazement, the baby, without even opening its eyes, accepted the piece of bone with a slight parting of its lips, then swallowed it.

A tiny smile of hope flickered across the young mother's grimy face, and she held her baby's face to her cheek. Returning her attention to the burnt bone, she started to bite into it madly

THE RED WIND HOWLS

and swallowed as much as she could without even chewing, occasionally pausing to produce another soft, sucked little piece for the baby.

Snowflakes the size of the nail on your little finger continued to drift in through the skylight of the old tent. Slowly the flakes became smaller and more numerous—a sign that a medium- to large-scale snowstorm was on the way. The young mother had stopped shivering and was focused intently on her burnt bone. Dekyi, on the other hand, was now quivering and sobbing as she shoveled more dung into the flames, and she spoke her prayers out loud for all the world to hear: "Three Jewels have mercy! These poor children. Don't they have homes? Don't they have families? Lord of Compassion protect them, Drong Rinpoché have mercy . . ."

At that moment, they heard the dog barking and the horse snorting outside, quickly followed by footsteps in the snow. The flap of the tent flew open.

The sight of the visitor struck fear into the hearts of Lozang Gyatso and his mother: it was Rikden, Secretary of the Party Committee. He was a Tibetan farmer from the east of Qinghai. Because the Tibetans there had had many years of contact with the Chinese and Hui Muslims and could speak some poorly pronounced Mandarin, they were the first to be appointed as cadres and the quickest to be promoted to positions of leadership. Rikden had been nothing more than an ordinary interpreter when he first arrived in Tsezhung, but he was handed rapid and successive promotions and within two years had become the secretary of the Party Committee for the commune.

▪ 153 ▪

Rikden wore a short black lambskin coat over his dark blue Mao suit, carried a rifle over his shoulder, and had a pistol holstered at his waist. He was known as a straight shooter, defined by his words, which were more direct than the barrel of a gun, and his hands, which were more ruthless than bullets. Today was no different from usual: without a word, he began lashing the young woman with his horsewhip, driving her out the door. Turning to point his whip at Lozang Gyatso and his mother, he said, "I'll deal with you two later."

If one of the supervisors or cadres from the farms found a runaway youth, they sent them back to the fields, which at least gave them some small measure of security. But if a cadre from the People's Commune found a youth hiding in a nomad's home, they simply drove them out into the wilderness, not caring where they went or if they lived or died. The young mother and her child were sure to freeze to death outside on a snowy night like this—if the wolves didn't get them first. Lozang Gyatso and his mother fell to their knees in prostration, begging Rikden to let her go, but it was no use. Dekyi grabbed his leg to stop him from leaving, sending Rikden into a flying rage. He dealt her a kick so savage it knocked her out cold; then he mounted his horse and disappeared into the snow, driving the woman before him.

Dekyi regained consciousness just after midnight. "Go out and look for the youth," she said to Lozang Gyatso. "If she isn't dead yet, bring her back."

"How can I leave you on your own in this condition?"

"I'm fine. Besides, it's a mother's good fortune if she dies before her son. Go on now, no time to waste."

THE RED WIND HOWLS

"But it's past midnight already. She'll be long since dead by now."

"No she won't. It takes a long time for people to stop breathing. Don't you remember what your uncle said? 'Saving a life is the highest expression of the Dharma.' Go, hurry!"

"Mother, don't be ridiculous. Even if we can save their lives for tonight, what about tomorrow? I think it's best if . . ."

"What? Since when did saving a life mean you have to look after someone forever? Looks to me like you've been a monk for ten years, reciting all those scriptures, but you've . . ." Dekyi was interrupted by a fit of coughing. "If you won't go, I will," she said, shaking her head in despair. She tried to get to her feet, struggling and coughing, sending Lozang Gyatso into a panic. "Mother, stop! I'll go, I'll go," he said, rushing straight out the door.

Lozang Gyatso felt there was no hope of finding the young mother and her child. You couldn't tell north from south and east from west on a snowy night like this, and his mother getting knocked out had sent him into such a state he'd had no time to pay attention to which direction Rikden had ridden off in. After tromping aimlessly through the snow for some thirty minutes, he came to a halt and yelled out, "Hey—! Youth—!"

Apart from the muffled howl of a wolf somewhere up ahead, the world was completely silent.

He called out for the youth again and was answered by the howl of a wolf coming from another direction, followed in short order by the ferocious barking of a mastiff from a nomad household somewhere behind him. Gathering all his strength, he made a big circuit around the nomad camp, accompanied by

■ 155 ■

THE RED WIND HOWLS

howls and barks, at the end of which he barely had the energy to move.

After the establishment of the People's Communes, a large communal canteen was established in each nomad camp—or what they now called a "production brigade." At the same time, half of the people from every brigade were sent to the slightly warmer, lower-altitude areas on the banks of the Machu and the lower reaches of the Tsechu to begin cultivating the land and turning it into barley fields, while the other half continued to raise their livestock and store up butter and cheese. Before too long, people began to waste away, and starvation and death soon followed. Unlike the people in the fields planting barley that would never grow, the majority of the people working with livestock were able to put off a meeting with the Lord of Death, but even their fate could change in the blink of an eye. If, for example, one of the workers in the fields died or got so exhausted they could no longer stand, then one of the livestock herders or someone from their family had to replace them, which, frankly put, meant shaking hands with the Lord of Death, or at the very least having to live like a hungry ghost.

There was a simple reason for this disparity. Although the farmers and herders were equal in the communal canteen, the barley simply would not grow on fields more than eleven thousand feet above sea level. This meant that there was nothing the farmers could steal to supplement their meager diet beyond a handful of seeds here and there, which only the bravest and cleverest among them would do. It was the opposite for the livestock herders. When they were milking the animals before dawn, the women could sneak a few mouthfuls of milk, which

■ 156 ■

could pretty much keep them going for a whole day. It wasn't bad for the men either. If one of the ewes miscarried, they had a free meal, and if they found the carcass of an old yak killed by the wolves but with some meat still on it, then they could feed their whole family. Later, when they were hit by unprecedented snowstorms that buried all the pastures in three feet of snow and killed off half the livestock in the county, those who skinned an animal and donated the pelt to the community received a commendation and got to keep the meat for themselves. The livestock herders of Tsezhung referred to this disaster as a "life-saving snowstorm." Not long after, the authorities were forced to admit that—in the high-altitude nomadic pastures, at least—the communal canteens and the attempt to reclaim wastelands for farming had been a huge mistake and a dismal failure, and the people were finally given a reprieve from starvation. It was too late, however, for the pastures on the banks of the Machu and Tsechu Rivers, which were the biggest, flattest, and finest pieces of land in Tsezhung. These grasslands never recovered from the wounds that had been inflicted on them, and they slowly deteriorated into deserts of black earth, blasted by winds so fierce you couldn't open your eyes or catch your breath.

According to the Chinese-language *Annals of Tsezhung County*, that year over six thousand young men and women were sent from the villages of Henan Province to Tsezhung County in Qinghai to help the border regions, and all of them were members of the Communist Youth League or generally "Outstanding Youths." When they first laid eyes on the beautiful landscape of Tsezhung and the simple, authentic lives of the nomads, they vowed to put down lifelong roots in the grasslands and to "open up the west of the Motherland."

The six thousand-odd youths were organized into a large production brigade, the Victorious Youths of Agriculture, which was further subdivided into several branches: Red Flag, Forward Progress, The East Is Red, and so on. They descended on the banks of the Machu and the Tsechu, where they constructed little huts for themselves made of earthen bricks and trees cut down from the nearby mountainside. They planted red flags all over the place; then the county boiled and burned with activity as the youths set to work while whistling, shouting slogans, and singing revolutionary songs, and by the time spring was over, most of the best grazing pastures in Tsezhung had been dug up and turned into barley fields. They also used the space around their huts to plant potatoes, cabbage, and radishes, then sat back and waited expectantly.

The buds grew rapidly amid the plentiful rains that year, and the ears of barley looked full and ripe when autumn came around, but after they had been harvested and dried in the sun it was discovered that pretty much every ear was empty, leaving the youths feeling even emptier. And yet, astonishingly, when the autumn harvest was over, cadres and reporters were brought in from the provincial, prefectural, county, and commune levels and a grand meeting was held on the banks of the Machu to celebrate the bumper harvest with pounding drums and fluttering flags. A summary of the production levels was read out in which it was announced that each *mu* of land had yielded six hundred fifty pounds of barley, and next year they were planning to plant wheat and white mustard. The cadres and reporters were also shown the leftover seeds from the spring sowing, which they were told were new grains from this year's harvest.

Tsezhung became famous overnight, both in the province and beyond, and the county and the young farm leaders became models for all of Qinghai. At the start of the next spring, cadres and workers were sent from the departments of animal husbandry, agriculture, and transport, as well as from the universities and schools. At the same time, half of the laborers from each livestock brigade were sent up to the hills with their animals, while the rest were given shovels and put to work in the pastures. People flooded onto the grasslands of Tsezhung and turned every inch upside down, planting endless truckloads of seeds in the newly dug-up ground. But when the autumn harvest came, every single crop was as shriveled and empty as the tit of an eighty-year-old grandma. Refusing to accept the laws of nature, the fever-brained cadres blamed it all on the lack of rain, and the following year they called in even more people and planted even more seeds. With the death toll climbing ever higher, they were finally forced to go back home, shaking their heads in tragicomic bewilderment.

One of the Victorious Youths of Agriculture who ended up aimlessly roaming the grasslands like a sheep in a flood was the young, baby-clutching mother. That night, by the time Lozang Gyatso had plowed his way home, chin tucked into his chest, his mother was already dead and cold, the blood she had thrown up still on the floor.

At that moment, what pained Lozang Gyatso even more than his mother's death was the fact that there was no lama to perform the last rites, and he couldn't even muster a butter lamp to light in her memory. By this point, nearly all the tears in Tsezhung had long since dried up, and if something did make you cry, it was proof that you hadn't yet hit rock bottom. As Lozang Gyatso chanted *manis*, his face pressed to his mother's cold cheek, dawn gradually broke. Covering her face with the collar of her fur coat, he stumbled out the door and headed for Lozang Tsültrim's place.

Ever since "aiming his spear" at the dakini, making Alak Drong drink piss, denouncing and abusing his teacher and uncle Dranak Geshé, and setting fire to the religious artifacts and scriptures of Tsezhung Monastery, Lozang Tsültrim had been seen by the people of the Dranak clan as a demon in the flesh. Even though Lozang Gyatso felt the same, Lozang Tsültrim's mother, Lhamo Drölma, was still his aunt and his only surviving close relative, so he felt he had to go let her know what had happened.

Much to his surprise, Lozang Tsültrim seemed even more upset than Lhamo Drölma, and he pulled up his sleeves, vowing to kill the old farmer, Rikden. His aunt, by contrast, took the news like a saintly yogini. After closing her eyes and sitting in silence for some time, she gently caressed Lozang Gyatso's head and said, "She is blessed to have passed before her son. And I think we still have many horrors in store, so she is lucky she won't have to live through those either. There is no need for you to feel sorrow. Go back with your cousin, take her to the charnel ground, and dismantle the tent; then you can come live with your aunty."

"What are you saying, Aunty? How can she be blessed when I can't even light a butter lamp for her or bring a lama to make the final offerings?" Lozang Gyatso suddenly seized Lhamo Drölma's hand. "Oh, Aunty! My poor, sweet mother. Just the thought of her down in the netherworld . . ." He began to choke up, and the sight of him made Lozang Tsültrim well up too. Not knowing what to do, he tried to pull his cousin away, but Lozang Gyatso clung to his aunt and wouldn't budge.

"Just look around you," said Lhamo Drölma. "All these people dying, and who's lighting any lamps for the dead? Who's bringing in a lama for the last rites? I'm saying that if you died first and then she went after you, that would really be a miserable fate. I need you to keep it together and bear the pain. If we don't take her to the charnel ground when we've got two stout young men like you in the family, others will ridicule us. So off you go. I'll speak to the cadres." This calmed Lozang Gyatso down somewhat. After some quick calculations in his head, he realized that today would in fact be an appropriate and favorable day for a funeral, and he headed back home accompanied by Lozang Tsültrim.

The two cousins cleaved through the dense snow, panting heavily as they took it in turns to carry Dekyi's body. All of a sudden, Lozang Gyatso came to a halt. "This must be her," he said.

The "her" he was referring to was the young woman Rikden had driven out of his home the previous evening. She was already covered by a couple of inches of snow, making it hard to tell there was a human body lying there. Lozang Gyatso transferred his mother's body to Lozang Tsültrim's back, then used his sleeve to wipe off the snow. Her top button was undone and she was holding her baby to her breast with one hand; in the other, she still clutched the burnt shoulder bone.

"That's her. The youth Rikden forced out of our home last night." Lozang Gyatso began to tremble. "The poor thing. We have to take her and the baby to the charnel ground too."

"What? There are thousands of youths dying all over the place. If we took all of them to the charnel ground, we'd end up there ourselves!" Lozang Tsültrim was panting now. "And it's this tramp who . . . it's because of her that your mother . . . come on, let's go." He set off by himself.

It was midday by the time they got back. A whistle came from the doorway of the communal canteen at the center of the camp, signaling lunchtime. People immediately poured out of every tent, clutching children and leading the elderly, and descended on the canteen like vultures on a charnel ground. Lozang Tsültrim said a few words of comfort to his cousin, then went to join the line.

That night, someone tossed something through the doorway of Lozang Gyatso's tent. He went outside and looked around, but there was no trace of the person. When he went back inside and picked up the object, he discovered that it was a copy of the *Sutra of Great Liberation*, wrapped in a piece of felt.

Lozang Gyatso was afraid at first, but his fear soon turned to amazement. He'd known this entire sutra by heart a couple of years ago, but not having had access to the text for some time, had felt it start to slip from his memory. It was extremely dangerous to read books like that in those days, but reciting the

Sutra of Great Liberation for his dear mother would be such a noble deed. Without considering it further, he heaped more dung into the fire while quietly reciting the text twice through, after which he had it down again. He got faster with every recitation and by dawn had managed to go through it seven times, which finally gave him a sense of relief, the feeling that he had repaid some of his mother's kindness. Later that morning, when Lozang Gyatso took the herd up to the slopes of Amnye Lhari, he smuggled the book with him and hid it in a cave. The cave was on the shady side of the mountain and the narrow entrance was flanked on both sides by dense azalea bushes the height of a man, making it virtually invisible even close up. Inside, however, the cave opened into a room-sized space with a smooth floor and ceiling. In one corner, several thick cypress planks had been laid down, on top of which were numerous volumes of scripture wrapped up in quality yellow cloth.

When Lozang Gyatso had first discovered this cave and poked his head inside he was a little scared, but as soon as he saw all those scriptures, he was overcome with faith and joy. Scanning the titles, he discovered that not only did they include the *Heart Sutra*, the *Sitatapatra Practice*, and the *Praises to the Twenty-One Taras*—the kind of texts that even an illiterate nomad family wouldn't be without—but also copies of the *Great Treatise on the Stages of the Path to Enlightenment* and the *Great Treatise on the Stages of Mantra* by Tsongkhapa, the *Wish-Fulfilling Vine*, the *Garland of Birth Stories*, the *Sutra of the Wise and the Foolish*, Setsang's *Collected Topics*, and the hagiographies of the first and second Jamyang Zhepas. They must have been stashed there before the Harrowing Day by some great master like his teacher Dranak Geshé, or at least a keen student of religious texts. In addition to the scriptures, there were bronze statues of the Buddha and Tsongkhapa, *thangkas* of Amnye Machen, Palden Lhamo, and Tara, and a silver mandala inlaid with turquoise and coral. The place felt like a small chapel or a meditation retreat.

What was called the "communal canteen" was in fact a large tent, spacious enough for a yak to be brought inside to load and unload goods. Needless to say, it had been the home of a wealthy nomad family before the arrival of the Harrowing Day. Four large stoves had been arranged in a line directly beneath the skylight, atop each of which was a pot big enough to hold an entire yak carcass. Sadly, the stoves contained nothing but ashes, and the pots were even emptier. The sight of them alone was enough to make people feel cold and desolate inside.

When the People's Communes were first established, many of the camps were gathered together into one big group, and the livestock, grain, and possessions of every family, rich and poor alike, were put under collective control. It was decreed that they must "municipalize their tents, militarize their conduct, and collectivize their lives." The elderly were taken to old people's homes, the children to nurseries, and the adults labored together and ate together. The communal canteens became like oceans of milk and yogurt, mountains of butter and cheese; there was meat and bread on every plate, and tsampa for all. In the past, they hadn't enjoyed such an abundance of delicious food even on the first day of Losar, and for a while the nomads forgot about the horrors of the Harrowing Day and rejoiced at what they felt must be the true meaning of communism. Even

THE RED WIND HOWLS

the formerly wealthy families thought this New Society wasn't half bad if this was what it consisted of. Within a few days, however, problems cropped up one after another. For example, since so many camps had been gathered together, the animals quickly devoured all the nearby grass, and they had no choice but to take them farther and farther out to graze. With the smooth grasslands being churned up for agriculture and the nomads forced to split their time between farming and live-stock herding, they were ultimately forced to abandon the "municipalization of the tents," and each of the camps split up and relocated to their own valleys, along with a communal canteen each.

Things got worse each day, and soon all the people of the Dranak clan received for each meal was three and a half ounces of tsampa flour, an ounce of cheese, and an amount of butter that the nomads described as "a broken fingernail's worth." And the worst was yet to come. Lhamo Drölma, Lozang Tsültrim's mother, managed to save up her broken fingernail's worth of butter for three days; then she mixed it with some tsampa and fashioned it into an offering lamp to light for her sister. She didn't feel that this had had a noticeably adverse effect on her health, but shortly after, the tsampa ration declined still further and the butter and cheese provisions stopped entirely. The nomads began to steal, and those who weren't able had to emulate the youths and eat whatever they could get their hands on. One day, Wang Aiguo and Rikden marched into the Dranak camp and convened a meeting of the masses. They brought with them a forty-something-year-old nomad woman who held in one hand a tattered fur coat that looked like it had been peeled

■ 165 ■

THE RED WIND HOWLS

off someone's corpse or shredded by a pack of wolves and in the other hand a whip as thick as a forearm. At the meeting, Wang Aiguo launched into a lengthy speech.

"Comrades! Under the leadership of the great and correct Communist Party of China and the beloved and esteemed Chairman Mao, we have thoroughly smashed the evils of the Old Society and are in the process of building a blissful New Society. In the Great Family of Nations that constitute the Motherland, which bloom like the glorious flowers of spring, all are equal. There is no more oppression or exploitation, and the masses of all races alike enjoy an abundance of happiness. However, due to the tampering of Soviet revisionism from without and capitalist roaders from within, compounded by this damn freak weather we've been having for the last two years, our living standards have deteriorated slightly. But this is only a temporary setback, and compared to how things were in the Old Society, it's like night and day. Despite all this, some people are starting to forget just how bad the Old Society really was. This is an extremely dangerous tendency, which is why the Central Committee and Chairman Mao have issued an important directive specifically addressing this matter. Today, we cadres will join the masses for a bittersweet meal, one that will help us recall our suffering under the Old Society and give us fresh impetus to build the New Society."

The nomads applauded half-heartedly as they swallowed repeatedly and wondered what exactly this "bittersweet meal" would taste like and how much of it they would get.

The "bittersweet meal" was being prepared in the large tent known as the communal canteen, so everyone flocked to it and

■ 166 ■

lay down on the ground holding their bowls. People enduring a famine are especially sensitive to smell, and the smell that filled their noses now was particularly unappetizing, one that resembled no food they had ever eaten before. Nevertheless, they continued to wait expectantly.

The tent flap was finally pulled back, and two people emerged carrying a large, steaming pot between them. The nomads immediately stretched out their long, thin necks to look, and discovered that the "bittersweet meal" was in fact a green liquid that resembled the mixture used to dye cloth. As they stared in amazement, the cook gave the green liquid a quick stir with his ladle, causing a flurry of leaves to float to the surface, and before they knew it he had scooped a serving into everyone's bowl. The nomads were looking from one cadre to the next, utterly baffled, when Wang Aiguo took a big, reluctant draft from his bowl. He held the concoction in his mouth, returning the gazes of the assembled nomads, then closed his eyes and swallowed with a grimace. He set his bowl down on the ground, shuddering slightly, then got to his feet and began to pace back and forth with his hands behind his back. "I admit this is a very unpleasant meal, but this was the food that we impoverished masses had to eat in the Old Society. It is vital, therefore, that we all eat it, and finish every last drop. Only in this way can we recall the suffering of the evil Old Society; only when we recall the suffering of the Old Society can we recognize the joy of the New Society; only when we recognize the joy of the New Society can we have the belief to construct socialism; and only when we have constructed socialism can we realize communism, when we will never be short of food or clothes again. And another thing—the People's Liberation Army never got food like this on the Long March. So you must eat it, comrades, eat it now!" Having concluded his speech, he recommenced his pacing, supervising the crowd.

In truth, this was a meal that not even the dogs of Tsezhung would have eaten in the evil Old Society, let alone the people. But because Rikden also finished off the entire bowl with a grimace and a shudder, none of the nomads had the courage to refuse.

Wang Aiguo told the woman he had brought with him to stand up. "I think some of you have seen this woman before. Her name is Lhalha, and she was a servant girl who belonged to the Lodrö herdlords of the Lhadé clan. She will now speak her class bitterness and tell us of how the merciless and brutal herdlord Lodrö subjected her to unimaginable torments in the dark times of the Old Society." The woman picked up her tattered fur coat and held it out for all to see, then explained that it had been handed down from her grandmother to her mother and now to her, and that for three generations they had worn it spring, summer, autumn, and winter, never taking it off. Next she picked up the thick whip, which she told them was what the ruthless herdlord Lodrö had used to beat his servants. She said that one blow from this whip was enough to knock a person out cold, and that Lodrö would beat his servants with it at least once a day. Bursting into tears, she went on to describe how hard their work was, how they had to sleep in their clothes year round, how they worked their fingers to the bone until many of them died at an all too tender age—her mother included. She spoke of their hunger, how the servants were only fed the leftovers the Lodrös' dog wouldn't eat, and because there were so many servants, by the time they had shared it all out, more often than not it wasn't enough for a mouthful each. She wailed bitterly until finally she passed out, and many in the audience were moved to tears by her testimony.

For more than ten years Lhalha's only job had been to cross the rivers and mountains of Tsezhung, visiting each and every camp to tell her tale of woe over and over. She had even been provided with a horse, and she ate for free anywhere she went. Before long, she had her tone of voice, her facial expressions, and every other aspect of the performance down to a fine art, just like a professional actor. Even some of the people from the Lhadé clan who knew what really happened found themselves helplessly tearing up at her version of events. Over time, however, pretty much everyone came to know her story by heart, and as soon as she began speaking her bitterness, her audience would drift off one after the other and start snoring loudly. Nevertheless, wherever she turned up, the whole camp abandoned its work and a meeting was called.

The only effect of eating the "bittersweet meal" was to loosen everyone's bowels. Almost as soon as they had swallowed the liquid, they were struck with diarrhea that wouldn't stop. This was even more unpleasant than having to put up with hunger and thirst—and even more dangerous. After being made to eat more successive rounds of the "bittersweet meal," and more successive rounds of diarrhea, many of them began to experience swelling, weakness, deafness, and faintness, and in the end, with their bodies emitting a nasty odor, they followed the youths into the next life.

THE RED WIND HOWLS

The appalling living conditions and the debilitating labor also took their toll on people's reproductive capacities: only five children were born in the whole of Tsezhung that year, and only one of them survived. The child had a strange, inauspicious, and particularly horrible-sounding name: Duktruk, "Misery Boy." Aside from the fact that they were too drained to think of a proper name, the parents had decided there was no point in giving him one anyway because they didn't think he would actually survive. But the child had an iron will to live, and far from dying, he grew stronger by the day. One day, a neighbor asked what they had named their baby. "Misery Boy," the father replied without thinking.

Misery Boy grew older, and life improved a little bit—or at least, people stopped starving to death—and everyone began to mock him for his name. Only at this point did his father feel that it had been a mistake to be so offhanded when choosing a name for the boy. "My son's name isn't Duktruk," he announced. "It's Dotruk—Boulder Boy."

It was perfectly understandable that those working in the fields were bitterly envious of the livestock herders. Their labor was back-breaking, there was no meat or milk to be had, and the crops they planted never ripened. After enduring the exhaustion of beasts of burden and the starvation of hungry ghosts, they finally collapsed, and many never got up again. A lucky few were reassigned and swapped places with one of the livestock herders just in time to save their lives.

There was a man named "Big Belly" (real name Topgyel) with a stout neck, short, fat arms and legs, and ears that were only hinted at on the side of his head. After he'd spent six

THE RED WIND HOWLS

months working in the fields, his neck and his limbs had become long and thin and his ears had fully materialized, making him look like a real-life hungry ghost. Eventually he collapsed, and someone came from the livestock brigade to trade places with him and take him back to his family. When they got there, however, his family refused to believe this was their Big Belly Topgyel who had been sent to the fields a few months before, and he didn't have the energy to prove who he was. His family, still dubious, decided not to kick him out, but they only let him have a little of their paltry rations and wouldn't give him any of that extra food "acquired through other means." Feeling helpless and hopeless, he sat by the stove, waiting for death. When the family all went out to work, everything fell quiet, and it was then that a little pika tiptoed in under the tent flap. The pika got nearer and nearer, until it was pattering around right in front of him. But he knew that he had neither the strength nor the speed to whip out his hand and catch it, so he dropped his guard and let it carry on. The pika, deciding that he was trustworthy, clambered affectionately up Topgyel's arm and settled in the palm of his hand. Big Belly Topgyel gently caressed the creature's soft fur, overcome with tenderness, but bit by bit those feelings became eclipsed by the pain of hunger and the fear of death. Closing his eyes, he concentrated all his remaining strength in his hand, and with one sudden, tight squeeze, he dispatched the little life as it defecated in terror.

Giddiness, apprehension, expectation, remorse: a jumble of emotions made his weak heart start to pound. In a flash, he skinned and gutted the pika with his overgrown fingernails, then put it in a mug with some water and set it on the fire.

■ 171 ■

The meat of a tiny pika is nowhere near enough to restore a grown man's strength, but it gave him as much bliss as if he had feasted on the nectar of the gods. More importantly, it gave him the strength to swear to his family that he really was their Big Belly Topgyel, and he was able to relate some things only he could have known to prove it. His family cried tears of regret as they plied him with that food "acquired through other means." Over time, his body turned from that of a hungry ghost back to that of a human being, and a few years later, he even regained his big belly.

The food "acquired through other means" was, to do away with the euphemism, food that had been stolen. Even in those miserable and terrifying days there were still some people clever and brave enough to decide they would rather fill their bellies and run the risk of getting killed than simply starve to death. They put all their abilities and brainpower into that one word, "steal," and found ways to plunder seeds from the fields, sheep and cattle from the pastures, and butter, cheese, and tsampa from the communal canteen, leaving them feeling very pleased with their exploits, which some of them even bragged about to others. Little did they know that a few years later, amid the terror and torment of the "One Strike, Three Antis" movement and the "Mass Line Education" campaign, every stolen morsel they had ever swallowed would be brought back up, along with confessions about various other "problems": anything politically suspect they had ever thought or said, if they had ever flirted with or had sexual relations with anyone other than their spouse, if their fathers had ever made smoke offerings, if their mothers had ever chanted *manis*, and so on. These movements spread

THE RED WIND HOWLS

across the grasslands like wildfire, with one person denouncing ten, and those ten denouncing a hundred more, until there was almost no one left without a "problem." Everyone, whether or not they had a "problem," was made to examine their past actions, and those with confirmed "problems" were struggled against. The people's fates were entirely dictated by the howling red wind: however fiercely it blew, that's how much their lives were turned upside down.

Lozang Gyatso had never stolen so much as a mouthful of food, even in the years of starvation, but in all the endless political movements he was always the first to be struggled against and always the target of the most savage interrogations. This was due to a number of factors. One, he used to be a monk; two, his father had been killed on the Harrowing Day; three, Dranak Geshé Lozang Palden, who had died in prison, was both his uncle and his teacher; four, Lozang Tsültrim had had it in for him ever since he "married" Tashi Lhamo, on whom Lozang Tsültrim had a huge crush; and five, Lozang Tsültrim had been made the leader of their brigade. After four consecutive days of being made to stand in struggle sessions, the howling red wind whipping all around him, everything started to look fuzzy to Lozang Gyatso, and even when the wind died down, he could still hear that horrible unsettling howl. In the end, he passed out and collapsed, and they were forced to take him home for a while.

"This is all my fault," Tashi Lhamo muttered to herself tearfully. She undid Lozang Gyatso's belt and was about to remove his boots and put him to bed, but she saw with horror that his calves had swelled to this size of his thighs. She pulled for all

THE RED WIND HOWLS

she was worth but couldn't even get one boot off, so she went to the unit leader's house to borrow the large shears he used for trimming the horse's mane and tail and with great care, cut down from the top of the boots and slid them off. Gently she massaged Lozang Gyatso's reeking feet, so dirty they looked like he had been tramping about in the mud barefoot.

Since Tashi Lhamo's parents and only brother had disappeared on the Harrowing Day, she had become an orphan. A lone elderly woman with whom she had a distant family connection had taken Tashi Lhamo in and raised her like a daughter, thinking that Tashi Lhamo could take care of her in turn when the frailty of old age set in. Before that could happen, however, the old woman died of starvation, leaving Tashi Lhamo on her own again. By this time, she had grown into a young woman with a graceful figure and a delicate complexion, and even in those difficult years when copulation was the last thing on anyone's mind, she drew the gazes and captured the hearts of many young men. Her milky skin made people think of the way the female youths from Henan had looked when they first arrived. As soon as the years of famine were over, the young men made their advances one after another, hounding her day and night, whether she was working or sleeping.

Lozang Tsültrim was one of these hounds, and he was the one Tashi Lhamo liked the absolute least. He was tall and stalwart with curly black hair and a pleasing symmetry to his face. If you didn't know him, you might not go so far as to compare him to King Gesar, but you certainly couldn't deny that he was quite the man. But ever since "aiming his spear" at the dakini, making Alak Drong drink piss, struggling against Dranak

■ 174 ■

THE RED WIND HOWLS

Geshé, and laying waste to Tsezhung Monastery, Lozang Tsültrim had been seen by the people of Tsezhung, and the Dranak
clan most of all, as a demon in the flesh. The women *really*
couldn't stand him, and they would shout for their parents any-
time he came near.

The young men all said that Tashi Lhamo was one of a kind.
Although no one had ever heard of her sleeping with a man,
she wasn't like some of the other women, who swore and cursed
at any late-night visitors and called for their parents to drive
them off. These visitors said she always spoke with them kindly
and gently, right through until dawn. Most of the men knew
Tashi Lhamo wouldn't satisfy their desires, but still they loved
to pass the long, cold nights at her tent engaged in conversation. Later, when Lozang Gyatso and Tashi Lhamo became
close, he asked if her she really did that, and why.

"Yes, it's true," she said frankly. "If I didn't have a man here
with me, then Lozang Tsültrim would come. So I just strung
them along, chatting about this and that. The poor things.
Some of them were in tattered old coats, shivering so much they
couldn't even talk." She allowed herself a chuckle, then fell back
into contemplation. "But none of the boys dared come when
Lozang Tsültrim got his big promotion. After that, he came
every night at dusk, keeping me up all night with his dirty talk.
He said 'If you don't want to, I won't force you. Forcing women
to do it is illegal. That's what the Jap devils did.' That's what
he said, but he stroked my cheek and stuck his hand in my shirt.
It was so scary, especially after it got dark. And he said, 'The
day you accept it, that's the day you'll get a lighter workload.
I'll help you get into the Communist Youth League too. Even

if you won't be my wife, you have to sleep with me at least once.' Just last month, it was, 'If you still won't give in, I'll send you over to Lozang Gyatso and put you on latrine duty, carting buckets of piss and shit.' I lost my temper then. 'Fine, put me on latrine duty, but I'll never sleep with you,' I told him. That's why he got mad and sent me over here. But then he still kept coming back every night, not letting me get a wink of sleep. 'Have you thought about it yet?' he said. 'The day you give in, that's the day you can return to the ranks of the masses and get a lighter workload.'"

"But think about it. You can't sleep at night, and you have to do this filthy, exhausting work all day. I . . . I really . . ." Lozang Gyatso's eyes moistened with tears, and he hung his head.

In the early days, people still whispered about these things on the sly: "Lozang Tsültrim might be an idiot and he might be a demon, but one thing's for sure—he's got no direction and no purpose in life. Now Lozang Gyatso, there's a man of character and conviction. He still hasn't given up his vows. I hear he swears he never will. People of such courage are rare these days." Lozang Tsültrim liked to eavesdrop, and when he overheard such words, he flew into a rage. *Back when we were monks, the teacher always praised him*, he thought. *Saying he was smart, hardworking, and honest. But me, I always got scolded. I was "hopeless." Whenever there was something good to eat, Lozang Gyatso got more, because "his studies were harder," and all the cleaning and water fetching and other chores fell to me. Now here we are, and people are still praising the bastard and talking trash about me!* A fiery tongue of jealousy shot up inside him. As soon as he had power in his hands, he went straight to Lozang Gyatso to have

THE RED WIND HOWLS

it out with him. "Our teacher always used to go on and on about how great you were, and how terrible I was. But look where we are now. You're a piece of dog shit, and I'm the branch secretary. And maybe a cadre soon. The fact that you still haven't forsaken your vows is a serious ideological problem. If you don't renounce them right away and get married, I'll have you labeled a reactionary."

"What?" said Lozang Gyatso, stunned. "We're cousins, bound by blood, and students of the same teacher. How can you say such things?"

"No, no. You're wrong. Blood relations, fellow students— those relationships don't exist anymore. Now there are only contradictions between enemy and ally. We are two people with different ideologies and different standpoints. You could also say that you're my enemy, and I am yours."

Lozang Gyatso thought of all the terrible things his cousin had done. He was a devil come to life, or at the very least, living testament to that phrase, "If a fox becomes king, his own kind suffer the most." Lozang Gyatso was worried because he knew that Lozang Tsültrim was capable of anything, and he also knew that he'd surely end up denounced if he didn't renounce his vows, but then he recalled his uncle's instructions: "Hold on to your vows as tightly as you would a yak's tail. The Buddha's light will one day shine again on the snowy mountains of Tibet." This gave him renewed courage. "Go ahead, denounce me. You can accuse me of everything under the sun, but I still won't give up my vows," he said.

"Fine, just you wait. I'll give you exactly what you're asking for," Lozang Tsültrim spat, his face flushing with anger.

▪ 177 ▪

Lozang Gyatso knew that disaster was now heading his way. Lozang Tsültrim and Rikden, the commune Party secretary, were good friends—or comrades, rather—and they shared the same ideology, the same standpoint, the same personality, even, so there was no use trying to reason with them. He had one last hope: Lhamo Drölma, his aunt and Lozang Tsültrim's mother. Like most of the women in Tsezhung, Lhamo Drölma was an honest, kindhearted person, and moreover she was often so worried about Lozang Gyatso's plight that she was moved to tears. But like most parents, she was also inclined to believe that her offspring could do no wrong, and anyone who said otherwise was bound to get on her bad side. As soon as Lozang Gyatso related his troubles with Lozang Tsültrim, her face clouded over. "So you think my boy is a devil too? I know what my son is like better than anyone. If you want to know the truth of it, he's under a lot of pressure from the higher-ups, and he's forced to do certain things he doesn't want to. When your mother died, who helped you carry her body? If it weren't for me and him, you wouldn't have had a lamp to light in her memory. And now you think he's a devil. Well, I don't know what to say." She left without giving Lozang Gyatso the chance to say a word in his defense. The two of them had no contact after that.

Trying to cultivate the land at more than eleven thousand feet above sea level brought about as much benefit and did about as much damage as trying to graze your cattle in the ocean. As a result, the great campaign to farm the grasslands came to a premature halt. Still, fifty to a hundred *mu* of oats were planted on every brigade's winter pasture to serve as fodder for the weaker animals. They first burned off the land that was to be

THE RED WIND HOWLS

cultivated, then brought in yak manure and sheep dung to fertilize it. When he came to inspect the sites, Rikden declared, "Human excrement is the very best kind of fertilizer. I don't want any nightsoil wasted; it should all be brought to the fields."

Since it would waste too much time to have everyone transporting nightsoil up to the oat fields every day, every family was made to dig a foot-and-a-half-long, foot-wide, two-foot-deep pit outside their home, in which they were ordered to do their business. Every day in winter, the sentient "beasts" capable of speech and thought—those who had been labeled as reactionaries or members of the herdlord class—had to go around the camp and gather up all the excrement from the trenches, optimistically referred to as "toilets," and take it up to the oat fields.

The winter pastures of the former Lubum camp of the Dranak clan, now known as the Unity Commune Forward Progress Production Brigade, were located between the Tsechu River and Amnye Lhari. Up above the camp, on the sun-facing slopes of the mountain, there was a black rectangular field about seventy *mu* in size. When the red wind blew in winter and spring, it whipped up dried soil and human excrement from the field, which then came in through the skylights of the tents and settled on the nomads' heads and in their bowls as they sat by the stove. It was also blown into the Tsechu, the great Mother River that nourished the people and animals of Tsezhung alike, along with the ash piles outside the nomads' houses. The river got so turbid by the afternoon that not even the livestock would drink from it, much less humans, forcing the women to trek out before dawn, the very coldest time of the day, to fetch all the family's drinking water for the day.

THE RED WIND HOWLS

Out in the fierce red wind that forced man and beast alike to keep their eyes tightly shut, Lozang Gyatso, carrying a shovel, clad in his big coat, arms in sleeves, and Tashi Lhamo, a pale green shawl wrapped around her head and covering her face, hauling a basket, were collecting the human excrement that Rikden called "the very best kind of fertilizer." Because the howling storm had long since driven their supervisors indoors, they decided to shelter from the wind and get some rest under a cliff at the foot of the mountain.

As she removed her shawl and wiped the dust from her face, Tashi Lhamo took in Lozang Gyatso's comical appearance and his pitiable expression. "The fool's mistake is an inch, the wise man's a mile," she said, shaking her head. "That sums you right up. Couldn't you have just told Lozang Tsültrim you'd find a woman and get married? Now look at you. Just when the famine's come to an end and you're starting to recover, you get sent back to this hard, horrible work, and you'll be collapsed in bed before you know it."

"It never occurred to me to say that. And even if it had, I'd've been committing the sin of dishonesty." As he spoke, Lozang Gyatso extricated himself from his long sleeves and wiped the dirt off his face.

Tashi Lhamo shook her head again. "Hey," she said suddenly, "is it true what I heard, that Lozang Tsültrim said he'd clean the slate as soon as you got married?"

"That's what he said."

"So how come you still haven't done it? A fake marriage, I mean."

THE RED WIND HOWLS

"A 'fake marriage'? I didn't realize marriages could be fake or real."

"Of course they . . ." A sudden blast of wind cut her off. Once it had passed, she gave her face a quick wipe with the shawl, then continued. "Of course they can. There are other monks out there like you, unshakable in their faith but left with no choice. They've found devout women who'll agree to a pretend marriage. I think you should find a woman and do the same, otherwise this label will just follow you around and keep making things hard for you. I've been working my whole life, and this nasty, backbreaking labor is hard enough for me, never mind someone like you who grew up in a monastery reciting scriptures. It's time you really gave this some thought."

Lozang Gyatso said nothing for three or four minutes, then finally sighed. "But who would marry a man like me with a label hanging over his head, who spends all day carting feces? I couldn't persuade anyone to marry me for real, let alone agree to a fake marriage."

Tashi Lhamo came closer. "Well, we could give it a try . . ."

Lozang Gyatso's mouth hung open in shock, making Tashi Lhamo feel instantly sheepish for her rashness. Her white cheeks colored like sunlight piercing the rosy clouds of evening and illuminating the slopes of a snow mountain. "Ah . . . I meant a fake marriage," she hastened to add. "That is, ah . . . only if you want to."

He continued to gawp at her, not saying a word. Tashi Lhamo was desperate to explain herself properly, and she made a conscious effort to calm herself down. "To tell you the truth, it wouldn't just be for your sake. I'm working my fingers to the bone every day, and the moment my head hits the pillow at night, that damned snake shows up and keeps me up all night with his cajoling and his filthy talk; then the next day I'm even more tired than before. If I had a man by my side, he couldn't bother me anymore, and I'd at least get a good night's sleep.

"Plus, if he's a man of his word, he'll let you shake off that label, so it'd be beneficial for both of us, wouldn't it? And another thing, when a man and a woman are together, they can help each other out and take care of each other. At least things wouldn't be as bad as they are right now. Ah . . . well, the main thing is you should think about it."

Lozang Gyatso considered this for some time before responding. "It's not a bad idea, really. But remember what my teacher said: 'Hold on to your vows as tightly as you would a yak's tail. The Buddha's light will one day shine again on the snowy mountains of Tibet.' Such prophecies were made by many of the great saints of old. I won't give up my vows," he said resolutely.

"I don't know how to read, and I know nothing about the sacred texts, but I've heard many times that if a woman commits the sin of making a monk break his vows, she'll spend the next life in hell riding a burning copper horse. So even if you wanted to break your vows, I still wouldn't do it. All I want is a way to escape from that devil."

"You know very well that Lozang Tsültrim can't be trusted, that he's capable of anything. He lusts over you more than any other woman, and he loathes me more than any other man. Forget about him clearing my name—if the two of us got together, he'd slap a label on your head too."

THE RED WIND HOWLS

"He already said he'll keep making me do the most disgusting, most backbreaking jobs so long as I refuse to give him what he wants. He can label me whatever he likes. How could it be any worse than this?"

"Then you should do what you think is best. But I won't break my vows."

"Sounds like you still don't believe me. Maybe you think I'm just an airheaded woman, and who can blame you? Men pursue women, not the other way around. That's the way of the world, I guess."

"No, no, that's not it."

"I'm at the end of my rope because of that snake. But since you don't believe me, I suppose I'll just have to forget about it."

"No, no, of course I believe you. Let's do it, what you suggested."

That day, the red wind suddenly decided to calm down a little, and people began to emerge from their tents in ones and twos to get some air. That air was, however, still thick with clouds of red dust that blocked out the sun.

Once they had overcome a series of roadblocks erected by Lozang Tsültrim, Lozang Gyatso and Tashi Lhamo were finally able to get their hands on a marriage certificate. At the top of the three-square-inch certificate there were two five-starred red flags, each enclosed by a golden laurel, underneath which lay an array of red lanterns and red flowers. Beneath this was a large red Chinese character, about the size of your palm, that stood for "double happiness." The middle of the page was occupied by three printed lines of Chinese characters that detailed the names and ages of the husband and wife and proclaimed, "The issuance of this certificate hereby confirms that the above-mentioned parties have of their own free will entered into matrimony in accordance with the relevant stipulations of the marriage law of the People's Republic of China." Finally, at the bottom, there was the date and an official seal. Lozang Gyatso and Tashi Lhamo were each given a copy of this piece of paper, and neither of them had a clue what the images signified or what the Chinese characters meant. They did know, however, that the pieces of paper gave them permission to live in the same house together and to sleep in the same bed. Without delay, Tashi Lhamo packed up her old tent, her clothes, her cooking implements, and her foodstuffs, loaded it all onto a single yak, and headed over to Lozang Gyatso's place wearing a comical expression never before seen on her face that seemed to indicate neither happiness nor sadness.

Amazingly, heaven seemed to take pity on this young, long-suffering pair, because there wasn't a lick of wind that day and the sun shone warmly in the bright blue sky. Such weather hadn't been seen in winter and spring since the current Alak Drong incarnation had been enthroned at Tsezhung Monastery and since the time those thousands of youths had been joined by tens of thousands of others from Tsezhung and beyond in order to turn the grasslands upside down. The nomads all pinned open their tent flaps just like they would in summer. The women, some with shirts and some without, tied the sleeves of their coats around their waists and went to fetch dung, while the children, some with boots and some without, ran about giddily and aimlessly.

THE RED WIND HOWLS

The flap of Lozang Gyatso's tent was also wide open. After the "husband and wife" had sat in motionless repose for some ten minutes, Tashi Lhamo got a fire going in the earthen cavity that Lozang Gyatso had constructed on the day he moved to the winter pastures, a pit that, were it not for the presence of fire, you would never think to call a stove. She was about to prepare lunch when they heard a commotion outside. When Lozang Gyatso rushed out to look, he saw Lozang Tsültrim marching proudly at the front of a terrible, imposing crowd, heading right toward them.

It was a familiar sight to Lozang Gyatso. It didn't worry him all that much at first; he assumed the revolutionaries were just at a loose end and had come out to enjoy the sunshine and kill some time with a struggle session. It took him completely by surprise, therefore, when the crowd marched straight past him and into the tent, then seized Tashi Lhamo and shoved her roughly out the door. They bound her hands behind her back, stuck a pointed white paper hat on her head, and forced her to bend over to her knees. Lozang Tsültrim produced a written resolution formally labeling Tashi Lhamo a reactionary, a document that had taken all of his efforts and several days of scurrying around after the commune officials to procure. In addition to countless minor infractions, the document contained three major charges that established her reactionary status: one, her parents and her older brother had been killed while taking part in the insurrection, thus she belonged to a counterrevolutionary family; two, she had colluded with and ultimately married the reactionary Lozang Gyatso; three, she

· 185 ·

THE RED WIND HOWLS

habitually disregarded the instructions of revolutionary leaders and cadres. The document concluded that it was thus the duty of the revolutionary vanguard and the broad masses of the Forward Progress Production Brigade to put her under strict surveillance and subject her to rigorous rectification.

After the document had been read out in its entirety, the revolutionaries paraded Tashi Lhamo around the camp like the autumn wind sweeping up dry grass, after which they headed toward the camp on the other side of the Tsechu. As they were crossing the frozen river, someone deliberately stepped on the trailing end of the rope that bound her hands behind her back, sending Tashi Lhamo head over heels on the hard ice and causing her to throw up from dizziness. Now that blood was gushing from her nose and her complexion had turned yellowish, the revolutionaries decided not to bother taking her to the camp across the river, and they abandoned their impromptu struggle session, leaving Tashi Lhamo where she had fallen on the ice.

Lozang Gyatso extracted a pinch of wool from the hem of his coat and used it to stem the flow of blood from Tashi Lhamo's nose, then helped her up and took her back home. He hung his head and sighed, making no inquiries about her dizziness or her aches and pains. Tashi Lhamo seemed far less affected by the whole thing. After resting for a little while, she got up and splashed some water on her face, took a fingernail-sized piece of butter from the nine-pound pat she kept stored in a sheep's stomach—enough to keep her going all winter and spring—then rubbed it into her cheeks. Looking over at Lozang Gyatso, she laughed.

THE RED WIND HOWLS

"You're laughing? I'm about to cry," he said, turning to face her.

"I'd much rather put up with struggle sessions in the daytime than be kept awake all night."

She had a point. In all the never-ending political movements, depriving people of sleep destroyed their minds and bodies much faster than any other form of torture, be it the "vulture spreading its wings" (making someone stand for hours with their arms held straight out at their sides and their head bent right down to their knees) or "roasting the meat" (interrogating someone while they stood inches from a burning hot stove, the fire and ash continuously stoked right before them). After being kept awake for five or six days straight, people became like zombies, providing the desired answer to any question they were asked and even reporting the "problems" of anyone they were suspicious of or didn't like. By comparison, there were ways to avoid the worst effects of the "vulture spreading its wings," or at least a way to avoid your hands and feet swelling too badly—namely, keeping your fingers and toes moving at all times. Of course, "roasting the meat" was a hellish ordeal, but even this was temporary, never lasting more than a morning or an afternoon. If you could withstand that, the worst you had to suffer was shedding a layer of skin from your face and chest, just like a snake.

Due to his lack of experience, Lozang Gyatso's first experiences of struggle sessions left him with feet so swollen he couldn't get his boots off. Happily, since he and Tashi Lhamo had moved in together, they were able to look after and help each other, allowing them to overcome their hardships and miseries. Even so, these hardships, miseries, and troubles continued to dog them. What bothered them far more than the filthy, exhausting labor and the torment of the struggle sessions was that Lozang Tsültrim was constantly spying on them, showing up unpredictably at all hours of the day and night. One day, he cornered Tashi Lhamo with a thinly veiled remark: "You've been married almost a year now, how come your belly hasn't got any bigger?"

The implication behind the question was immediately obvious, and Tashi Lhamo felt a momentary jolt of fear and panic. But she was a sharp woman, good at thinking on her feet. "The cattle can never breed when the grass is bad, and people can't get pregnant when life is so hard. Didn't you know that?" she said, pretending not to have caught his drift.

"That's a fair point. But I think there might be another reason."

"How about you give me a day off, then, and I can go see the doctor."

"Haha! I think it's Lozang Gyatso who needs to see the doctor."

"Well, how about you give him a day off, and . . ."

"Think about what you just said." Lozang Tsültrim was getting angry. "People can't get pregnant when life is hard? People still got pregnant in the Old Society, so are you saying the New Society is worse than the Old Society?"

"I never said that."

"Fine, it doesn't matter whether you said it or not. What concerns me is . . . um, whether or not you two have . . . ah, I mean . . . if you're a real husband and wife."

THE RED WIND HOWLS

"What are you talking about? Since when were couples 'real' or not? If there's nothing else, I'd like to get back to work now."

Tashi Lhamo's disdainful expression angered Lozang Tsültrim even more, and he came right out with it. "Let me be clear then: I still don't know whether that sly, bald old donkey has broken his vows or not."

"Hmph. In that case, why don't you come over and listen in tonight? You like to listen to everything else, don't you?" Having worked up the confidence to say this, Tashi Lhamo gave Lozang Tsültrim a cold glare and walked away.

In those days, there was absolutely no way a reactionary would dare speak to an official in such a manner. But both of them knew that Tashi Lhamo had seen him crying and begging and doing all sorts of other things considered embarrassingly shameful for a man in Tsezhung, so Lozang Tsültrim had no choice but to let her go.

Lozang Gyatso and Tashi Lhamo each slept in their coats, with another that also belonged to Lozang Gyatso laid over the top of them. From the outside of Lozang Gyatso's tattered old tent you could see everything on the inside, and from the inside you could see out, just like a sieve. As Wang Aiguo had once remarked, it would have "made a great fishing net." It was a clear moonlit night, and not long after getting into bed, Tashi Lhamo sensed there was someone outside watching them. Rolling over on top of Lozang Gyatso, she glued her lips to his and started moaning theatrically. Lozang Gyatso struggled for all he was worth, his muffled cries of distress sounding for all the world like groans of desire.

■ 189 ■

Before too long, the shadowy figure outside disappeared, and Tashi Lhamo released her hold on Lozang Gyatso.

"Are you mad, woman? We talked about this already . . ."

Tashi Lhamo clamped her hand over his mouth. "Be quiet," she hissed. "Lozang Tsültrim is watching us."

"What are you talking . . ."

"He suspects that you haven't broken your vows. Just be quiet." Draping her coat over her shoulders, Tashi Lhamo went to peek out of the tent flap. Lozang Tsültrim was scurrying about in the dark, clutching his crotch and wailing softly like an animal in heat that couldn't find a mate.

Tashi Lhamo's momentary surprise was quickly overtaken by amusement, and she put her hand over her mouth to suppress the laughter. "What is it?" whispered Lozang Gyatso, sitting up in bed.

"Come here, quick. There's a show on." She pointed at the gap in the tent flap, then started chuckling into her hand again.

"What's wrong with him?" Lozang Gyatso asked, puzzled.

"No woman will go near him, so he's very . . . ah . . . he's in a lot of discomfort. It's not something you'd know about."

"Three Jewels have mercy." Lozang Gyatso closed his eyes and clasped his palms together. "What kind of time are we living in?" he muttered, overcome by misery.

"There's nothing to be sad about. You should be happy!" Tashi Lhamo took one last look at Lozang Tsültrim, then tugged at Lozang Gyatso's sleeve, leading him back to bed. "Don't you see? He torments us during the day, but we get to torment him at night! I think he's suffering even more than we are."

THE RED WIND HOWLS

"What is all this? I never knew you were such a wicked woman. 'All sentient beings have been our mothers'—that means that in a past life he could have been your parent, and in another life you could be his. That's why we need to treat the suffering of all sentient beings as our own and cultivate compassion. Taking joy in the suffering of another living thing is a grave sin."

"Oh come on, that devil has put us through all kinds of hell, and he won't stop now. Don't you know that saying, 'If you don't repay a kindness, the good dwindle; if you don't avenge a wrong, the bad multiply'? Besides, he brought all this on himself. He deserves it."

"I won't hear it. We must have tormented him in a past life, and that's why he's tormenting us in this one, to call in his debts. For someone with an enlightened mind, the suffering we're enduring now should be seen as a kind of happiness, because however much we suffer in this life, that's how much happiness we'll find in the next, and more importantly, it will take us one step closer to buddhahood. Therefore . . ."

"Okay, okay, enough. I don't understand all that deep stuff. But tell me this: if there's such a thing as karma, how come so many bad people are living it up as officials while so many good people are getting denounced and thrown in jail to rot?"

"That's . . ."

"Ah, yes, Lozang Tsültrim asked me today why we still haven't got a child when we've been married almost a year. Of course, what he was really asking was whether or not you've broken your vows. That's why I had to do what I did just now when he came to spy on us. I'm sure you've heard what's

■ 191 ■

happening to monks and nuns in some places when they've refused to forsake their vows. How they force them." Without giving him the chance to respond, Tashi Lhamo got up and went to look out the tent flap again. Seeing no sign of Lozang Tsültrim, she got back in bed and went straight to sleep.

I wish we had a good guard dog, Lozang Gyatso thought. He was reminded of Tiger, his family's old mastiff with a head as big as a frying pan and little yellow spots above his deep-set eyes. He had a clear memory of the time his father stretched out his hand and held it up to Tiger's paw, discovering that they were more or less the same size. During the day, he slept down by the side of the tent, ignoring anyone who came by, familiar or not. But as soon as it got dark, he began circling the tent and the livestock and belting out earth-shaking barks like a brass horn, a clear message that you shouldn't come anywhere near if you wanted to live. Not even people they knew would come to their house at night, let alone jackals and wolves. But Tiger had disappeared on the Harrowing Day, and in the three years of famine that followed, almost all the thoroughbred mastiffs died out. There weren't many dogs to be found anymore, and those that remained weren't worth half of one of the old thorough-breds. They put on a menacing front with women and children, but grown men had little to fear other than the dog sneaking up from behind and nibbling the hems and sleeves of their coats. It was even worse with wolves. At the mere sight of one the dogs bolted into the tent in terror, completely forgetting about the sheep and cattle. Right now, Lozang Gyatso couldn't even get the services of a mongrel like this. He didn't know if his political status denied him the right to have a guard dog, but even if it didn't, he couldn't afford one anyway, so he had to drop the idea.

"Comrade Lozang Tsültrim, your superiors in the government want to make sure that revolutionary activists like you are taken care of not only in political terms but also in quality-of-life terms." This was something Wang Aiguo had once said to Lozang Tsültrim. "You're no spring chicken anymore. Wouldn't it be a good idea to get married and settle down?"

"Yes, yes it would!"

"Your mother's not in great health either, so if you got yourself a wife you wouldn't have to worry about things at home and you could concentrate fully on revolutionary work and serving the people. Isn't that right?"

"That's right, absolutely right."

"So, is there anyone in particular you've got your sights on?"

"Haha, ah . . . there's a couple, but, ah . . . I don't think any of those bitches like me."

"Well, we can work on their ideological standpoints. Who have you got in mind? Tell me."

"Ah . . . Tashi Lhamo, for example . . ."

"The one whose parents and brother were killed in the insurrection?"

"That's the one."

"No, no, that won't do. A revolutionary needs a revolutionary comrade-in-arms."

". . ."

"I think you and Künga Huamo are a match made in heaven."

THE RED WIND HOWLS

"Künga Huamo? That hag is my relative!"

"Relative? How close are we talking? On your father's side or your mother's?"

"My mother's, but I don't know exactly how we're related. My dad moved from elsewhere, so none of his side of the family are around here."

"Well, you're probably not that close, not within three generations at least?"

"Not within three generations, no, but around these parts, it's considered taboo for anyone with even the slightest family connection to have a relationship, and you can forget about marriage. Plus, that hag has a daughter, and no one even knows who the father is."

"Hmm, this is a traditional and outmoded way of thinking. The nation's marriage laws are clear on this point: as long as the connection isn't within three generations, it's legal. Relations on the mother's side, particularly, aren't considered a big deal."

"He's right!" Rikden chipped in at this point to lend support to Wang Aiguo's argument. "I'm a born and bred Tibetan, and where I'm from, relationships on the mother's side don't count and marriage isn't a problem."

"But around here we don't distinguish between the father's side and the mother's side—they're both taboo. Any relationship like that is considered inbreeding, and the couple would be total outcasts from society. Plus, inbred children have tails . . ."

Wang Aiguo tutted and shook his head. "That is quite simply feudalistic gibberish. I'll have you know that my wife is in fact my cousin on my mother's side, and I haven't noticed either of my kids growing tails. If you don't believe me, come to the county seat sometime—I'll pull their pants down and you can see for yourself."

Rikden said, "It seems to me that you don't appreciate Künga Huamo's feminine qualities."

Wang Aiguo said, "It seems to me that there's nothing wrong with Künga Huamo at all, apart from her skin being a bit dark and her head being a bit big. She's sturdy and tall, a proper woman of the grasslands. Don't you think that Tashi Lhamo of yours is like one of the 'youths' compared to her?"

"And what's wrong with her having an illegitimate child? That's even more commonplace for you nomads than it is for us farmers," Rikden added.

"Haha, but, secretary, you see . . . if I married Künga Huamo, my mother would have a fit, and I'd be a laughingstock in the community."

"I can work on your mother's ideological standpoint. And if anyone dares mock you . . ."

"I'll agree to any woman you can name—just not her."

Unfortunately for Lozang Tsültrim, the two county and commune leaders couldn't find a single woman who was willing to marry him, and Lozang Tsültrim certainly couldn't find one for himself. They had to drop the matter for the time being, but it couldn't remain unresolved forever.

Faced with this desperate, insurmountable situation, Lozang Tsültrim turned his mind to more optimistic fantasies: if he listened to the county and commune leaders and married Künga Huamo, then maybe he could become a state cadre, and if he

THE RED WIND HOWLS

became a state cadre, then there was the chance he could become a high official, and if he became a high official, then he'd be allowed to carry a gun, wouldn't he?

It was almost Losar. The nomads of Tsezhung gathered up the little booklets listing the small amount of cash and grain they had been allocated according to the number of work points they had accumulated, and they pocketed the cloth coupons, tea coupons, and sugar coupons that were allocated according to the size of each family. The larger families borrowed a pack animal or two from the commune and went to the county seat to buy all the grain and other things they would need for the next six months to a year, which included the twenty pounds of barley and four pounds of flour that each person was permitted per month, along with some general items for daily use. The smaller families likewise made their way to the county seat, but with two saddle bags loaded on the sides of a horse. In the afternoon, the children mounted the hills and looked out toward the county seat, chattering to each other excitedly: "My dad's coming back with sweets for me!" "My mom's coming back with a new shirt for me!" "My brother's coming back with firecrackers for me!" They waited in the thick of the howling wind, shivering.

In addition to food and clothes, the pitiful amount of paper money had to be used to buy something else, something strictly mandatory that was increasing by the year and covering every inch of space on the earth: portraits and pins of Mao Zedong. As would be the case with images of Alak Drong many years later, these portraits had to be placed on the highest, cleanest spot you could find. The nomads returning from the county seat attached the Mao pins to their hats, carried the rolled-up portraits on their backs, and stuffed their pockets with all kinds of other Mao-related paraphernalia.

The day after returning from the county seat, every family was busy making fried bread for the new year and every camp was suffused with a buttery aroma. The oblong bread sticks, about five inches long and two across, were the main dish served on New Year's Day in the nomads' homes, and when three or four of them were topped with a portrait of Mao Zedong or some Mao pins, they became New Year's gifts for friends, relatives, and neighbors. The wealthier families also presented their close relatives and friends with butter, cheese, droma, and delicious, sugary *zhün* cake.

In every home, the walls of the tent were plastered with portraits of Mao Zedong. In some, Mao was also preceded by pictures of Marx, Engels, Lenin, and Stalin—in that order. Some years later, Hua Guofeng was added to the pantheon, though he didn't last long. The only real dish they had for Losar was the heaps of fried bread, but this didn't stop the men and children from going house to house in big groups to celebrate the New Year. Those who could sing and those who couldn't all went around belting out revolutionary songs in poorly pronounced Mandarin, which, translated into Tibetan, went something like this:

Chairman Mao is like the sun;
on the ground his light is shone.
The Communist Party came and won;
now the masses have liberation!
Sailing the seas depends on the helmsman,

THE RED WIND HOWLS

Life and growth depend on the sun,
Rain and dewdrops nourish the crops,
Making revolution depends on Mao Zedong Thought!

The runny-nosed, muddy-faced children danced and sang along merrily despite not understanding the words. Since there was no turf left on the bare ground, each footfall sent up clouds of dust, sending the children into coughing fits that eventually brought their dancing to a halt.

The joys of Losar shunned those families with the stigma of a label as though they were lepers. In the Forward Progress Production Brigade, for instance, this meant families like Lozang Gyatso's. They had no portraits of Chairman Mao on their walls and no Mao pins on their chests. Not even Wang Aiguo could decide whether or not labeled people had the right to display images of the chairman, so everyone simply sidestepped the issue and ignored them. Their families stayed away just like everyone else, making Losar a cold and lonely affair for the labeled. Ever since Tashi Lhamo had moved in, however, Lozang Gyatso's home had been kept spick-and-span. The few old articles of clothing they owned were neatly folded, their small supply of grain had been stored away in pouches, and their modest amount of kitchenware was clean and organized. When work was finished for the day, Tashi Lhamo cleared away the stones the children had thrown at their tent and got a nice cozy fire going in the stove. Even Lozang Gyatso, who was of the belief that "the mortal realm is a prison of demons," couldn't help but feel a wave of warmth when he stepped into his home, making the pain fall from his face and the weariness lift from his body.

THE RED WIND HOWLS

Each production brigade was subdivided into five, six, seven, or eight units, depending on its size and the number of livestock it contained. Four or five women together composed a milking unit, within which one man was assigned to look after the livestock. In winter, each unit would construct a square cattle pen in the center of the camp using turf or rammed earth. In one corner of the pen was a roughly one-square-yard boxlike enclosure fashioned from still-moist dung that had then been allowed to freeze, and within the enclosure was enshrined a picture of Mao Zedong. Without fail, the unit assembled before the image twice a day to raise their hands in solemn salute and "seek instruction in the morning and present reports in the evening." This was preceded by the unit leader or an enthusiastic revolutionary addressing a few words to the portrait: "Chairman Mao, our Great Teacher, Great Leader, Great Commander-in-Chief, and Great Helmsman! Today we pledge to hold fast to your flawless guidance, carefully study your wise words, redouble our efforts, and get some more milk out of these yaks. Through our diligent herding efforts, we will make a great contribution to the country and the collective!" After the careful enunciation of each phrase, the others recited it, like a primary school teacher drilling first graders. In the evening, they reported back to the portrait: "Chairman Mao, our Great Teacher, Great Leader, Great Commander-in-Chief, and Great Helmsman! Today we held fast to your flawless guidance, carefully studied your wise words, and got seventeen (or seven or eight, or twenty or thirty) quarts out of those yaks. We didn't let a single animal fall into the hands of the wolves or the class enemies, thereby making a great contribution to the country and the collective." In spring, summer, and autumn, the unit leader performed this ritual before his family's own framed picture of Mao, which they brought outside every day and hung up with the tent ropes. One time, they forgot to take it back in after completing the evening report. Come morning, their old pater familias, always fond of a joke, chuckled heartily: *"Ah ho!* The chairman got left outside last night? He must have scared the hell out of the gods and demons in the valley!" Someone overheard this and reported it, and the old man was labeled and struggled against until he laughed no more. His wife lost her job as unit leader of the milking unit, after which she cried for several days, harbored a grudge against her husband for several years, then wound up divorcing him.

This sort of thing was no laughing matter in those days. The woman really couldn't be blamed for her reaction, because when you were a unit leader, you were a law unto yourself: you could boss around your underlings as you pleased, and their lives were pretty much in your hands. In winter, for example, when there were no stores of butter or cheese, the small amount of milk still available could be divided up among the members of the unit, and the unit leader decided who got what. It was also entirely up to the unit leader who got to ride the best mounts, and whether unit members were even allowed to ride one at all. Perhaps their greatest power, however, lay in the apportion of work points: when the time came at the end of the year to decide how to divvy everything up, it was the unit leader everyone looked to. If you were on their bad side, then it didn't matter if you had spent all year working your fingers to the bone: you would be left empty-handed and without the means to pay for meat, butter, cheese, wool, yak hair, hides, and all the other things a nomad needs. The cost of those essentials would have to be deducted from the following year's work points.

The labeled were at the unit leader's mercy even more than regular folk. They could be ordered around like slaves and even dealt savage beatings, which made them prized "labor machines" for the unit leaders. In the winter season, the least busy in terms of a nomad's work, Lozang Gyatso and his "wife" had to fertilize the fields in addition to performing all the tasks required of an ordinary citizen. It was a cause of relief for them that each one's unit leader happened to be a decent person and didn't let them suffer too much. Lozang Tsültrim, however, still spent his days taking out his pent-up "nightly frustrations" on Lozang Gyatso. After calling Lozang Gyatso over and making him stand to attention, the first words out of his mouth were always: "Just look at the state of you! The spitting image of a 'youth.'"

He wasn't wrong. The only clothes that seemed to fit Lozang Gyatso were the robes of a monk; when he wore anything else, it looked somehow wrong and clownish. His hair, long and matted, had become a veritable home for family upon family of lice. If he had been wearing Chinese clothes, he would indeed have looked exactly like one of the "youths" from a few years ago.

The second thing Lozang Tsültrim said was: "Have you been studying the words of Chairman Mao?"

"I've been studying Chairman Mao's words nonstop. I've even got some parts memorized."

"Let's hear it then."

"Erm . . . 'Superstitious thinking is still having a pernicious influence on the broad masses. Such thoughts are enemies in the minds of the masses.' Um, 'We must teach the masses that they have to rise up and struggle against their illiteracy, their superstition, and their unhygienic habits . . .'"

"There, you see? 'Superstition and unhygienic habits.' That means people like you. What else?"

"Erm . . . 'After the enemies armed with guns have been wiped out, unarmed enemies will still be among us. They will be sure to fight us tooth and nail, and it is imperative that we do not overlook them.'"

"There, you see? 'Unarmed enemies.' That's you." Lozang Tsültrim jabbed a sudden finger in Lozang Gyatso's face. "You—you unarmed enemy you!" Thinking of all the joys Lozang Gyatso must have enjoyed the night before while he himself was suffering, Lozang Tsültrim shook with rage, and his eyes burned red.

Three tents from where they were standing was a large black tent that had been confiscated from a wealthy family. During the time of collectivization, it had served as the communal canteen, and now it had been converted into a locally run primary school. From within came the melodious sound of students intoning their times tables, the alphabet, and other such fundamentals of knowledge: "The mighty axis that guides our work is the Communist Party of China. The theoretical foundation that governs our thinking is Marxism-Leninism." Overhearing these mellifluous recitations, Lozang Tsültrim dragged Lozang Gyatso off in the direction of the school.

THE RED WIND HOWLS

These mindless brats were more reckless, vicious, pitiless, and downright evil than even the most extreme of revolutionaries. Throwing rocks at the labeled and their homes on the way to and from school was their favorite game, which they also treated as a solemn responsibility and an opportunity for glory. They were like impeccably trained hunting dogs who pounced wherever you pointed. It was for this reason that Lozang Gyatso was now terrified. "Wh . . . what did I do wrong this time?" he stammered.

"What did you do wrong? I'll tell you what you did wrong. You're too happy. At nighttime especially . . .!" Lozang Tsültrim shoved him roughly through the door of the tent. "Heirs of the revolution!" he bellowed. "As Chairman Mao teaches us: 'After the enemies armed with guns have been wiped out, unarmed enemies will still be among us. They will be sure to fight us tooth and nail, and it is imperative that we do not overlook them.' This man Lozang Gyatso who stands before you now is precisely one of these unarmed enemies. We must struggle against him until he can no longer stand and the stink fills the air! Let us commence the struggle, comrades!"

No sooner had he said this than a snot-nosed boy raised his fist in the air and yelled, "Down with Lozang Gyatso!" The boy pounced on Lozang Gyatso and grabbed his hair, while an eight- or nine-year-old girl dashed over and clawed at his face, leaving three scarlet welts in his left cheek. An instant later, blood began to pour from the wounds, causing the little girl to recoil in shock and look down at her fingernails. A horde of children mobbed Lozang Gyatso and pinned him to the floor, some pulling hair, some punching, some kicking. After a little while, no one could see a thing through the cloud of dust that had filled the inside of the tent, and some of the children began to cry.

Classes at the school used to be taught by a man named Zhang Drakpa. After four years at the combined school in the county seat, he had come back with his empty head on his shoulders and his empty hands by his sides, nothing to show for it except the Chinese surname Zhang sitting in front of his Tibetan name. Since he was the only one in the camp who had spent any appreciable length of time at school, he was appointed as the teacher at the tent school—the locally run primary school, rather. His daily lessons consisted of dividing the children into two groups ("China" and "the enemy"), handing them some sticks, and having them "wage war" with each other. Either that or taking them to carry out struggle sessions against the labeled. Because he didn't actually teach them anything, he soon lost his teacher's post and was packed off to herd cattle.

The new teacher at the school was named Lodrö. He, like Lozang Gyatso and Lozang Tsültrim, had been a monk at Tsezhung Monastery. The sudden eruption of violence in his classroom left Lodrö stunned and speechless, but the cries and wails of the children brought him back to his senses, and he rushed over to Lozang Tsültrim to say that if they didn't stop this now, the children would start attacking each other, and then things would really get out of hand.

Lozang Tsültrim had calmed down a bit by this point, and he walked out the door without a word, a satisfied expression on his face. Lodrö waved his hands frantically and yelled at the children to stop. When the dust settled, a bloodied, battered, and groaning Lozang Gyatso was revealed, and just as Lozang Tsültrim had hoped for, he was unable to stand and the smell of blood wafted in the air. Lodrö, cradling his head, cast an angry glare over the children. "You're real heroes," he said bitterly. Some of the children hung their heads in shame, and some cried.

Lodrö's reaction brought something back to Lozang Gyatso's mind: the night after his mother died (or rather, was murdered by Rikden), when some mysterious stranger had tossed a copy of the *Sutra of Great Liberation* through his door. There was something else too. After the communal canteens were shut down, everyone was given a sheep each winter, or a yak shared among three, to serve as their allotment of meat for the winter months (in reality, it had to last through both winter and spring). These animals you had to take home and slaughter yourself. To a monk like Lozang Gyatso, who strictly abided by the codes of the Dharma, this was far worse than having to endure hunger and thirst. He had left his sheep tied up outside while he tried to figure out how he could set it free without anyone finding out. When he crept out of his tent halfway through the night, he discovered the sheep lying dead on the ground. Someone had bound its mouth and suffocated it, and there was a four-finger-wide cavity in its chest where the heart had been removed. Clearly, someone was trying to help him out of his predicament. It had been the same every year since: he left the sheep tied up outside in the afternoon, and by the next morning, someone had slaughtered it and cut out the heart. They obviously knew that Lozang Gyatso was sticking to his vows, because it continued even after he began living with Tashi Lhamo and they were allotted a sheep each. Reminded now of these incredible events, Lozang Gyatso inspected Lodrö closely, but there was nothing in that face to give any hint that he might be the mystery visitor.

Lozang Gyatso was worn out, he had lost a fair few handfuls of hair, and his face was all scratched up and bloody, but other than that he wasn't in too much pain. After the bleeding stopped and he'd had a chance to rest, he got to his own two feet and left. But when Tashi Lhamo saw the marks and the dried blood on his face, she unleashed a terrifying howl that could be heard almost across the whole camp. Even Lozang Tsültrim shuddered in fright. Worried, he went to check things out, but seeing Lozang Gyatso and his "wife" moving about in the horse and cattle pens, he relaxed. That night he went to eavesdrop again, and the sounds of the bastards enjoying their "marital bliss" drove him completely mad.

He did a round of the camp, pleading with every woman he thought he might have a shot with—the ugliest, the oldest, even the one-eyed—but none of them would sleep with him. The next morning, at the end of his rope, he slung his rifle over his shoulder, mounted his horse, and set off to find Rikden at the People's Commune with the intention of informing him that he would marry Künga Huamo and establish a revolutionary household. But Rikden wasn't there—according to the cook, he had gone to the county seat to attend a struggle session. *Well, that's all right*, Lozang Tsültrim thought, *In that case I can go to the county seat and report to Secretary Wang while I'm at it, let him know that I've renounced my traditional and outmoded ways of thinking and that I'm ready to get married to Künga Huamo. I'm sure to get on his good side that way. Maybe they'll even make me a cadre!* His raven-black stallion, strong and swift, had been chosen from among some six hundred horses belonging to the Forward Progress Production Brigade. With a light flick of the reins and a tap of the stirrups, the steed took off like lightning, leaving a cloud of red dust in its wake.

At this point in time, the slogans and big-character posters were multiplying by the day in the county seat: TO REBEL IS JUSTIFIED! STERNLY DENOUNCE CAPITALIST ROADERS WITHIN THE PARTY! DOWN WITH THE CAPITALIST ROADER CLIQUE IN THE PARTY! Yesterday's poster was always replaced by today, and whatever went up in the morning was pasted over with something else by the afternoon, leaving the baffled public doubting their own eyes. On the walls either side of the main road they had chiseled out a rosary-like string of pot lid-sized holes, each of which was filled in with whitewash and contained a Chinese character and its Tibetan equivalent printed in a red paint that reeked of petrol: NEVER FORGET CLASS STRUGGLE! FIRMLY GRASP REVOLUTION, ALWAYS INCREASE PRODUCTION! On top of these, every whitewashed house was also in the process of being covered with the sayings and slogans of Mao Zedong, likewise painted in large red characters.

Lozang Tsültrim ran into Rikden right outside the Tsezhung County Party Committee building. Rikden was clad in a green army uniform, the left breast pocket of which boasted a large badge showing Mao Zedong's face hovering over Tiananmen Square. He wore a red armband on his left bicep printed with two yellow words written in the chairman's hand: *Red Guard.* He looked, at first glance, like a force to be reckoned with, but a closer inspection would reveal a pallid and uneasy demeanor. Oblivious to this, Lozang Tsültrim struck up a jovial chat. "Aha! Just the man I've been looking for. Is Secretary Wang about?"

"Fuck Secretary Wang. Aiguo's done for." Rikden glanced around furtively and tugged at Lozang Tsültrim's sleeve to guide him to a more secluded spot, but the latter just stood there dumbfounded, unable to take a step.

"This isn't a good place to talk," Rikden hissed, pulling him off to the side and glancing around again. "Turns out Wang Aiguo is a counterrevolutionary. He's already been arrested, and there's going to be a public denunciation this afternoon in the auditorium. We were too close to him. If we're not first in line to struggle against him, suspicion will fall on us. You better get ready."

Lozang Tsültrim didn't have a clue what to prepare, so when the afternoon came around, he took a page out of Künga Huamo's book and simply walked up to Wang Aiguo and punched him in the face without so much as a word. Wang, hands tied behind his back, stumbled three steps and collapsed, blood gushing from his nose. With a single blow, Lozang Tsültrim had proclaimed his unyielding revolutionary stance to the cadres and the masses of the whole county.

The next day, when Wang Aiguo was dragged to a struggle session at the county school, he discovered that Lozang Tsültrim's solitary punch was little more than a gentle caress. At that time, aside from fighting and playing football, the students' primary task was to unleash inhuman struggle and violence against their teachers and members of the "Four Bad Categories." They treated such people as brutally as they did animals. This was the main reason that the nomads of Tsezhung refused to send their children to school for many years after, no matter how severe the political or financial penalties.

Wang Aiguo followed in the footsteps of all those people he had personally sent down the path of no return. A raft of interviews conducted some thirty years later with people from the time shed some light on the situation. The leadership of Tsezhung County had been divided into two factions: the Gansu Clique, led by Wang Aiguo, and the Shandong Clique, led by a man named Zhu Xinmin. Wang Aiguo had always held the upper hand and kept the Shandong Clique under his thumb. However, Wang belonged to the August Eighteenth group, which was, for a time, branded an illegal organization by the Party. When the order came down that August Eighteenth was to be ruthlessly suppressed, the Shandong Clique was handed its chance to get even for all those years of subjugation. So, not only was this a cutthroat political struggle, it was also the result of conflict between local factions.

Just a month or so later, the August Eighteenth group was rehabilitated and ended up with even more power than before. But by then, Wang Aiguo had already gone to a destination even more permanent than the prison camp, leaving political power over Tsezhung County entirely in the hands of Zhu Xinmin. This didn't last long: with the establishment of the Chinese People's Liberation Army Tsezhung County Command Headquarters for Grasping Revolution and Promoting Production, power passed into the hands of the military, making Zhu

THE RED WIND HOWLS

Xinmin a leader in name only. The military officer who was actually in charge was known to the people of Tsezhung as Section Head Zhao.

While the death of Wang Aiguo didn't present any obstacles to Lozang Tsültrim's marriage, his mother was another matter. Casting aside all decorum, Lhamo Drölma loudly cursed her son: "Filthy, shameless mutt! Inbreeding? You're lower than a beast! If you bring that red-faced demoness anywhere near me, I'll string myself up, I swear. If I don't, then this here belt is tied around the waist of a dog!" His mother's categorical opposition to the union put Lozang Tsültrim in an awkward position for a brief time, but Rikden's threats soon put that right. He informed her that this was a political duty, not an ordinary marriage, and whoever interfered would surely meet with a bad end, giving Lhamo Drölma no choice but to shed her tears silently and keep her mouth shut.

No one to see off the bride, no one to welcome her, no wedding presents, not so much as a *khata*: that's how Künga Huamo arrived at Lozang Tsültrim's home to begin married life. She had cut off her braids and was wearing a green liberation army cap atop her sizeable and now androgynous head, and she wore her big lambskin coat like a man, tied around the waist and hanging down to her knees. Though she wore no necklace, earrings, milking hook, or belt, she sported one accessory that no other woman in Tsezhung had ever had: a rifle. It's hard to say just how comical a sight this represented to a regular nomad woman who had spent her whole life dealing with nothing but milk, yogurt, butter, and cheese. She was extraordinarily plump, and her deep scarlet features were a rare sight even up here at eleven thousand feet above sea level. Künga Huamo was five years older than Lozang Tsültrim, and she had brought with her an eight- or nine-year old-girl, the father of whom she struggled to identify. In short, no matter how you sliced it, connecting her to the term "bride" was out of the question. After casting aside all etiquette and stuffing her face to her heart's content, she exhibited behavior even more astonishing and inappropriate for a newlywed by looking around the room, declaring their furnishings to be "in the wrong place," and promptly rearranging them to her liking. From there, she proceeded to the one chest and two sacks containing all Lozang Tsültrim and his mother's possessions, which she unpacked, inspecting each item as though she were performing an audit, before putting everything back again.

That was when Rikden showed up, clad in a dark green lambskin coat with a four-finger-wide sable hem that he'd picked up from the confiscated belongings of a wealthy family for a mere token price. He was riding a bay horse with a white stripe that ran from the tip of its muzzle to its ear, fitted with something else he'd picked up along with the coat: a special saddle quilt made from a blanket and a dark blue rug with a yellow dragon pattern. His green aluminum army canteen, filled with liquor, was stuffed in his coat, a rifle was slung over his back, and a bandoleer was fastened about his waist, at the end of which hung a pistol in a leather holster. His mount twisted its head left and right and he bounced about in the saddle as he flew through the center of the Forward Progress

Production Brigade and headed straight to Lozang Tsültrim's place. The people gaped at him in awe, as though he were some kind of god.

They wouldn't have believed it for a second if you'd told them that twenty years later this same man would be known in the Tsezhung county seat as Rikden the Youth, a pitiful character usually to be found sprawled in a drunken stupor at the main crossroads, piss stains on his pants, snot and drool on his chin, who sobered up only long enough to beg booze money from passersby so he could get plastered again. Some people would go up to him and say, "Hey, Rikden the Youth! Do you know who I am?" to which he would respond by lifting his snot- and drool-covered face, peering at them with half-closed eyes, and sticking out his hand for change. "Crawl between my legs, and these are all yours," the person might say, holding out a couple of coins.

And without a moment's hesitation, Rikden would slither back and forth through their open legs.

No doubt, such people were the ones Rikden had once subjected to the tortures of "vulture spreading its wings" or "roasting the meat." If not that, then he had persecuted one of their parents or relatives to the point of suicide.

Some said that Rikden had been relieved of his post and driven onto the streets because he was drunk all the time and didn't do any work. Some said that he was getting an allowance from the state, but his bastard of a son was taking it all, leaving him without a penny.

By that time, Lozang Gyatso had just turned forty. The lay clothes still looked somehow wrong on him—comical, even.

THE RED WIND HOWLS

But the behavior of the monks and lamas at the now rebuilt Tsezhung Monastery had profoundly shaken his previously ironclad resolve to return to monk's robes, a hope he had cherished for over twenty years. His newfound desire to spend the rest of his life with Tashi Lhamo was growing stronger and stronger, and that was where he was heading now—through the county seat, and back to her.

Buying things in the county seat no longer required a multitude of ration tickets, and there was now an ever-increasing amount and variety of clothes and foodstuffs to be had. Lozang Gyatso thought, *Tashi Lhamo wasted her youth on me and has suffered so much on my account. She doesn't even have a child of her own to show for it. Twenty-odd years now I've thought of worldly possessions as empty and shallow, and I've never bought her so much as a nice shirt. A real ass, that's what I am.* Stung with regret, he decided to stop in at the new department store that had been built at the main intersection and buy Tashi Lhamo a new top and a scarf.

As he emerged from the store, someone caught hold of his sleeve. "Hey, Lozang Gyatso! Look over there. Do you recognize that youth?"

Lozang Gyatso turned in the direction the man was pointing and saw a beggar with long, tangled gray hair holding out his hands to everyone who passed. The man looked far older than his actual age, but Lozang Gyatso knew exactly who it was. "It's Rikden, the leader from the commune, isn't it?"

"Indeed it is. The bastard who murdered your mother."

"*Ah kha*, look at the state of him!"

■ 213 ■

THE RED WIND HOWLS

"I know. You should report the bastard to the authorities. At least that way you might get a bit of cash to arrange a Dharma service for your mother."

Lozang Gyatso walked over to Rikden, took out a five yuan note, and handed it over.

"*Ah tsi ah tsi,* what are you doing? That piece of shit beat your mother to death!"

Lozang Gyatso walked off without even looking at the man, who yelled after him, "Hey! Haven't you heard that saying? If you don't repay a kindness, the good dwindle; if you don't avenge a wrong, the bad multiply?"

Exactly—repay kindness with kindness. Lozang Gyatso turned around, went back into the department store, and spent every penny he had on sweets and toiletries for Tashi Lhamo. When he came back out, the man was still there, and he blocked Lozang Gyatso's path again. "Hey—if you've got money to spare, why don't you give some to that poor creature. He's Lozang Tsültrim's son—and your nephew." He pointed to a boy with a huge head who was grinning idiotically at anyone who passed. He was wearing a tattered Mao suit, making him look just like one of the youths from back in the day, and he was digging through a pile of trash.

Lozang Gyatso stood stunned for a moment, then gathered himself and went over to the boy. When he saw him coming, the boy just grinned stupidly. Muttering repeated prayers, Lozang Gyatso grabbed his hand and took him off toward home.

Lozang Tsültrim ran over to greet Rikden and grab the horse's reins. "I didn't think you were coming!" he called out.

THE RED WIND HOWLS

"What . . . what're you talking about, eh? You're estab—stablishing a revlushionry household! I wouldn't miss it—miss it for the world!" Rikden was, unfortunately, already drunk. Even so, the fact that he had come personally to celebrate their wedding was an honor to Lozang Tsültrim. Maybe the locals would show him some more respect now—outwardly, at least. This was a cause for celebration: one Rikden was worth more than a hundred regular guests.

Rikden retrieved the canteen of liquor from his coat pocket and took a big swig, then returned it and rummaged around for something else. Quite some time went by before he managed to extract a folded-up, tattered little picture of Mao Zedong, which he handed over to Lozang Tsültrim; then he promptly passed out and stayed that way right through to the next morning. The first thing he did upon waking up was astonishing even for a heavy drinker (at least those Lozang Tsültrim had encountered): in one gulp he polished off the remainder of the booze in his bottle like a parched cow at a pond, staggered outside to take a piss, then took off without so much as a bite for breakfast.

The reality of Künga Huamo was even more horrible than Lhamo Drölma had imagined, and she became more convinced than ever that the woman was a demoness. In her mind, this was all karmic punishment for Lozang Tsültrim's despicable actions. She tearfully bemoaned her son's wretched fate to anyone she met. She was consigned to her bed after a year, and a month after that she died. Shortly before she passed, she said to her son, "Let others say what they will—Mama knows you're a good boy deep down. You know I don't have long left. There's just one thing I want you to do for me. Will you promise?"

■ 215 ■

THE RED WIND HOWLS

"Anything you want, Mother, I promise. Tell me," said Lozang Tsültrim without hesitation. He didn't expect what came next. "You need to divorce that demoness," his mother said. As soon as the words were out of her mouth she was struck by a terrible pain, and she breathed her last without giving Lozang Tsültrim the chance to respond.

Lozang Tsültrim had no intention of breaking up with Künga Huamo, besides which she was now pregnant, so he couldn't leave her even if he wanted to. It would be another few years before Lhamo Drölma's wish was realized. At that point in time, Tsezhung County had been labeled the "Dazhai of the Plateau," and everywhere you looked the grasslands were being thunderously overturned to make way for new buildings and construction projects. One such project was the "improved sheep breeding" scheme. This involved purchasing fine-wool sheep from livestock markets in Xinjiang and attempting to crossbreed them with Oula ewes native to Tsezhung, which necessitated clearing a tract of land on the cliffs for the construction of a breeding station, a sheep pen, and so on.

Künga Huamo was extraordinarily strong, and a few words of flattery would make her work with unflagging ardor, heedless of her own well-being. It was for this reason that she was assigned, along with the young men, to perform the most demanding labor up on the cliffs. One day, while everyone was breaking for lunch, Künga Huamo was still slaving away on the worksite, her face more scarlet than ever. Out of nowhere came a deafening rumble, accompanied by a cloud of red dust shooting into the air over the worksite. After two days and nights of

THE RED WIND HOWLS

nonstop digging through the rocks, they finally unearthed the crushed, pulpy mess of Künga Huamo's body.

Cadres and senior officials from the county and the commune descended on the Forward Progress Production Brigade, where a twenty-foot black banner had been strung over the door of the tent school bearing an inscription in white Chinese characters: *In Memory of Comrade Künga Huamo—Our Grief Knows No Bounds.* Directly underneath it they had erected a huge framed photograph of Künga Huamo clutching a rifle to her chest (where exactly this came from is a mystery). The nomads were required to follow the traditional funeral customs of the region: they wore their hats inside out and tied their belts in the front, and in addition they had to wear black armbands and artificial white flowers on their chests. With wails of grief, Künga Huamo's funeral commenced.

The eulogy went something like this:

Künga Huamo was a poor nomad woman who grew up in the evil Old Society, during which time her standard of living was worse than that of a stray dog. After Liberation, she heeded the call of Chairman Mao and the Party and struggled mercilessly against class enemies while devoting herself wholeheartedly to the mighty undertaking of building a New China. Her evidently invaluable contributions in this regard saw her admitted to glorious organizations including the Communist Youth League, the People's Militia, and of course the Communist Party itself. After making yet more invaluable contributions, she sacrificed her precious life for the noble cause of building the Motherland. She is a model for the poor and lower-middle nomads of the grasslands, and her death is weightier than Mount Tai. We must never forget her, and must always learn from her!

Indeed, without delay, a movement to "Learn from Comrade Künga Huamo" swept throughout Tsezhung.

When the memorial was over, they didn't take Künga Huamo's pulverized body to the charnel ground; instead, they placed her in a large coffin that was buried underground.

Despite being six years old already, the son born to Lozang Tsültrim and Künga Huamo had yet to utter a word and could only smile foolishly at anyone he saw. His head was remarkably large and his body was corpulent to match—he was, in other words, the spitting image of his mother. It was obvious to everyone that it was extremely unusual to be in possession of such a hefty body in such desperate times. Lozang Tsültrim was plunged into despair, so much so that the frequency with which he held meetings—even those to struggle against the labeled—declined drastically.

Since his marriage to Künga Huamo, Lozang Tsültrim had ceased his nightly spying sessions on Lozang Gyatso and his "wife," giving Lozang Gyatso far more leeway to recite scriptures in secret. When Tashi Lhamo had first been assigned to work with him fertilizing the oatfields, she had once wandered off with her basket, and he had taken the opportunity to chant his mantras. Because the red wind was howling as usual that day, he hadn't heard her coming back. He turned around to find her standing right there, listening to his chanting.

Terrified, he turned white as a sheet, which also sent Tashi Lhamo into a fluster. "Don't be afraid!" she said. "I swear I won't tell anyone." Lozang Gyatso didn't seem to believe her, so she continued, "Don't be afraid. Er . . . to tell the truth, I sometimes recite the *Praises to the Twenty-One Taras*." This convinced him, and he let out a long sigh of relief.

After that, Lozang Gyatso trusted Tashi Lhamo enough to let his guard down around her, and over time he even began to extol the benefits of practicing the Dharma (and the wrongs of not practicing it). Tashi Lhamo didn't really buy into it all at first—at least, the idea that a labeled woman who spent all day shoveling shit could one day rise to the status of a buddha seemed ludicrous to her. "There was once a great lama who preached the Dharma to an old woman," Tashi Lhamo said. "When the lama was finally finished, the old woman said, 'You speak of the benefits of the Dharma. Sounds as if an old woman like me can easily be liberated from samsara, let alone a lama like you. You speak of the evils of sin. Sounds as if a lama like you would struggle to attain liberation, let alone an old woman like me.' That's how all this sounds to my ears." She was making fun of him, leaving Lozang Gyatso no choice but to defend his position with quotations and references to the scriptures.

"You have a point. As the *Hevajra Tantra* says, 'All sentient beings are buddhas, but this is concealed by temporary stains. When the stains are purified, their buddha nature is revealed.'" He elaborated further, but seemingly still unsatisfied with his explanation, he continued, "The Buddha tells us that this free and well-favored human form, like a golden stupa, is difficult to come by. Imagine a yoke being tossed about on the vast ocean, constantly carried east and west by the waves, never staying in one place for a moment. At the bottom of that ocean there lives a blind turtle who only surfaces once every hundred years. How unlikely is it that the blind turtle will surface at just the right spot to put its head through the yoke? Attaining a rebirth in human form is just as rare." Thus he continued his efforts to convince Tashi Lhamo.

Once they had saved up four years' worth of pelts from the two sheep they were allocated every winter, they finally managed to make Lozang Gyatso a proper nomad's coat. Every night, Tashi Lhamo tirelessly shoveled dung into the stove to provide them with heat and light, while at the same time she worked on tanning the eight pelts, sweat dripping from her forehead. The quality of the coat couldn't compare to one made by a professional tanner and a seamstress working in tandem, but it was big and thick, and for the next two or three years at least Lozang Gyatso wouldn't have to suffer the cold. Sadly, once he had popped it on and tied the belt around his waist, he looked just as clownish as he had before—it simply did not look right on him. Tashi Lhamo smiled wryly. "I guess you were just born to wear the robes of a monk, not the skin of an animal," she said.

Lozang Gyatso knew that he looked ridiculous, but it didn't bother him a bit. "What do I need to look good for anyway? I'm not going out to find a wife. The main thing is that it's warm, and nothing could be warmer than this. My hero! I never would have had a coat like this without you. We'll start saving up the pelts again next year, then we can make one for you too." Nothing could dampen the joy he felt, but he didn't know then that as soon as he donned his coat that winter, he would be dragged off to another camp for a struggle session. By the time he came back, his brand-new coat was missing its sleeves entirely, the collar was ripped off and hanging down, and the hem, the lining, the front and back—everything was torn to shreds. He looked like a youth who had fallen into the middle of a pack of wolves. When Tashi Lhamo laid eyes on him, she cried so hard she couldn't breathe. The others in the camp were moved to tears, and even Lozang Tsültrim took pity on him. "There's nothing wrong with a good struggle session, but why did they have to rip up your clothes?" he sputtered angrily. "Those dog shits did this on purpose to get even for that beef between our camps back in the Old Society. They can't push people around like that. I'm going over there right now to get a replacement coat. This is an outrage . . ." Lozang Tsültrim stormed straight over, but when the low-ranking PLA officer in charge of the camp's work unit suggested that he was coming perilously close to protecting class enemies, he had no choice but to come back. He retrieved two sheep pelts from the Forward Progress Production Brigade's communal storehouse, gave them to Lozang Gyatso, and told him to make new sleeves for himself.

The outrage he felt gnawed at Lozang Tsültrim all night, and the next day he went right back to the other camp. "Our masses want to express their class hatred for one of your bad elements," he declared. "Hand one over right now."

"Yes, of course, but what . . . ah, well, why don't you take old Lutso."

The woman they called Lutso was so ancient that a smack on the cheek would likely send her into the next life. Moreover, her lambskin coat was so dilapidated that even the frozen and starving youths would have turned their noses up at it. "How am I supposed to get an old bag like that back to camp?" said Lozang Tsültrim. "Go find me another one."

"The other bad elements have all been sent off on secondary work assignments. They won't be back for a month or two."

Lozang Tsültrim was seething now, but he knew if he took old Lutso away he would just be making trouble for himself, plus she had no articles of clothing that could be satisfactorily shredded to appease his wrath. Once again he was forced to go back empty-handed. On the way, he thought back on how the Dranak clan had killed someone from their camp, and liberation had arrived before the matter was settled. He was increasingly convinced that their struggle session against Lozang Gyatso was a way to settle old scores and had nothing whatsoever to do with expressing class hatred. He vowed to himself as a red-blooded man that he would get back at them for this, but the opportunity never really presented itself, and gradually he forgot about it. Many years later, however, the camp responsible for cutting off Lozang Gyatso's sleeves sought out Alak Drong's services as a mediator, requesting that he settle their dispute with the Dranak clan over the murder that had been committed some half a century earlier. Alak Drong convened a meeting attended by several monks from Tsezhung Monastery and the relevant parties from the two camps, and after three days of negotiations, he delivered his verdict: the Dranak clan would pay the victims one hundred yuan in compensation and donate a copy of the *Great Treatise on the Stages of the Path to Enlightenment* to Tsezhung Monastery by way of atonement. The two parties agreed, and to express their gratitude to the mediators, each side presented Alak Drong with a hundred yuan, plus ten for each of the monks, and they also footed the hotel bill and all the meals for their three-day stay (a hundred and thirty each, for a grand total of two hundred and sixty yuan). In this way, the dispute was successfully resolved. No one, however, remembered the issue of Lozang Gyatso's torn coat and missing sleeves from the Cultural Revolution, which went entirely unmentioned.

In Tsezhung County, the fall of Wang Aiguo was trumpeted as a great victory for the political lives of the masses of all races. Meetings increased, slogans were shouted louder, marches grew bigger. But the red wind never stopped raking over the razed black earth, and for the nomadic masses, the hard labor never let up and their quality of life never improved. A few years later, by contrast, the living standards of the fine-wool rams flown in from Xinjiang, which couldn't take the summer heat or the winter cold, seemed to have reached the level of true communism. In summer and autumn, they had to be taken to the finest pastures, the ones that even the youths never managed to set foot on, and each sheep was fed on the milk of two yaks. In winter and spring, they were fed on pure grain and given free rein of the oatfields, each was nurtured with the milk of four yaks, and at night they were kept warm in their pen by a constant supply of dung burning in an iron stove. There was something else that set them apart from every other animal in the world: they themselves didn't need to follow the ewes around to see if they were ready to mate, because this task was delegated to the Oula rams, whose reproductive organs had been tightly bound to their bellies. When taking them out to pasture in the morning, the shepherds had to memorize which ewes were mounted by the emasculated Oula sheep, and in the afternoon, these ewes were placed with the fine-wool rams. Unfortunately for the latter, no sooner had they mounted the ewes than a man standing to one side known as a "technician" pulled out an artificial vagina to collect their semen so that it could be examined under a microscope and subjected to chemical analysis, only after which would it be injected directly into the womb of a ewe.

Not only did the fine-wool rams enjoy an excellent quality of life, they had an enviable political status too. Anyone who dared say a bad word about them would be subjected to criticism at an immediately convened meeting. If the offender was of "questionable status" or had any "historical impurities" themselves, then there was a good chance they would be labeled. There was an old man named Bucktooth Tamdrin who couldn't keep his mouth shut, and since his family had once produced a reincarnate lama, he was of "questionable status" by association. One time, the old shepherd saw a fine-wool ram clashing horns with an Oula ram, a contest that didn't last long before the fine-wool scampered away in defeat. The old shepherd couldn't stop himself from bursting out laughing. *"Ah ho!"* he exclaimed, clapping his hands together. "What's such a spineless little lamb doing roaming the ends of the earth?" Someone reported this choice remark, and Bucktooth Tamdrim found himself labeled a counterrevolutionary. It was much worse if any harm came to a fine-wool while it was under your watch, a crime that was treated as tantamount to murder. Looking after them was thus an extraordinarily difficult and dangerous affair.

The lambs produced by crossbreeding the fine-wool rams with the Oula ewes were weak and couldn't withstand the cold, resulting in an extremely low rate of survival. Moreover, they were small in size, their meat was unpalatable, their hides were poor quality, and their delicate wool wore down easily. Nevertheless, because they produced a lot of this wool, and because it could fetch twice as much as an Oula's wool, no one dared question the worth of these animals. Only once all the Oulas had been "upgraded" did they discover that this new breed was completely unsuited to living at more than eleven thousand feet above sea level, and the hybrids all had to be "downgraded" to Oulas again. After that, the existence of hundred-and-fifty-pound rams became nothing but a legend, a story told about the ancient past. According to the experts, this wasn't the fault of the failed crossbreeding experiment—it was due to a decline in the quality of grass.

Having seen with her own eyes how Künga Huamo, the "model for all women of the grasslands," had been crushed to a pulp, Lozang Tsültrim had been left a widower, and their idiot son had become an orphan, Tashi Lhamo found herself with little choice but to believe what Lozang Gyatso was always saying about karmic law: actions have inevitable consequences. She asked him if there was any hope of her becoming a real Dharma practitioner—with the proper teaching, that is.

Lozang Gyatso was delighted. "Of course there's hope, of course there is! 'You don't own the Dharma, you strive for it,' as they say—there's always hope if you try. But if you want to study the true Dharma, you'll have to learn to read and write first."

THE RED WIND HOWLS

"Then how about we start with that?"

"Absolutely. But we have to keep this secret. Lozang Tsül-trim can't find out."

"I don't see why it has to be a secret. There's no rule saying the labeled can't learn to read. Chairman Mao said it himself, didn't he? The masses have to rise up and struggle against their illiteracy." A mischievous smile suddenly crept over Tashi Lha-mo's face. "I can say that right to his face. 'If I don't learn to read, how can I study the works of Chairman Mao?' How would he dare say otherwise?"

"You're a cunning one, all right." A smile spread across Lozang Gyatso's face too—a rare sight indeed. "That really is a good idea. You should go tell him now. Learning to read and studying the Dharma will be no problem for someone as smart as you. Dharma practice is all about cultivating kindness and compassion, seeing the suffering of all sentient beings as your own, and being grateful to the Three Jewels for any joy in life. You must recognize the inherent faults of samsara and focus your mind on the Holy Dharma, be willing to endure innumerable hardships on its behalf, and even give your life for it with no regrets.

"Our great teacher, the Buddha Shakyamuni, underwent great suffering for each and every stanza of Dharma teaching he received. Cavities were gouged in his flesh into which one thousand oil lamps were placed; he threw his precious body into a pit of fire; he had one thousand iron nails driven into his sacred skin. As he said, 'Crossing a sea of flames and a mountain of knives, seeking the sacred Dharma until death.' Compared to all

■ 226 ■

THE RED WIND HOWLS

that, these trifling troubles of ours are nothing at all, so what's to stop us from dedicating ourselves to Dharma practice?"

In Lozang Tsültrim's opinion, it wasn't necessary for someone with a label to learn to read, but since they said it was in order to study the works of Chairman Mao, he didn't feel right making a call on the spot, so he reported the matter to Rikden. Since Rikden had never been faced with a question like this before either, he had to take it up to Zhu Xinmin, chair of the Tsezhung County Revolutionary Committee, to ask whether or not it was allowed for the labeled to learn to read.

"Of course it's allowed," Zhu Xinmin said. "It's a good thing for someone to learn to read." After giving this resolute response, he thought for a moment. "But you must ensure first that it doesn't interfere with their labor, and second that they only study materials currently used in schools."

The nomad children called the first-year Tibetan textbook they used in primary school *Ka-kha*, after the first two letters of the alphabet. The first lesson of *Ka-kha* covered the thirty consonants and the four vowels; the second, prefixes, suffixes, and secondary suffixes; and the third, how to connect them to the root letter. The fourth gave a smattering of vocabulary: sun, moon, mountain, river, worker, peasant, soldier, car, train, electric light. In lesson 5, students began to build sentences, which were either words of praise for Mao Zedong or the words of the chairman himself: "Long live the Great Leader Chairman Mao," "Never forget class struggle," "I love Beijing's Tiananmen / The sun rises above Tiananmen / The Great Leader Chairman Mao / Leads us ever forward," etc.

■ 227 ■

THE RED WIND HOWLS

Lozang Gyatso borrowed a copy of *Ka-kha* from Lodrö, his erstwhile monastic colleague and current teacher of the primary school. No sooner had he begun giving lessons to Tashi Lhamo, however, than he was sent off on a secondary work assignment. These secondary work assignments came in many forms: gathering yak and sheep dung for fuel and rhododendrons and tamarisks for kindling and selling them to work units in the county and the commune, collecting dried animal bones and selling them to the bulk purchasing station, taking pack animals loaded with grain and odds and ends back and forth between the county seat and each of the communes, etc. The most common task of all was being sent to chop down the pines and cypresses that lined the Machu, then transporting them to the county seat some 40 miles away. For their secondary work assignments, the rifle-toting members of the People's Militia had a special side hustle: hunting bears, snow leopards, wolves, and lynxes for their valuable pelts, as well as stags, musk deer, antelope, and blue sheep for their antlers, horns, and musk glands.

On this occasion, Lozang Gyatso's "secondary work assignment" consisted of chopping down trees from the banks of the Machu and bringing them back to his own brigade to construct a winter shelter for their increasingly feeble and sickly livestock. They were also instructed to build a meeting hall for the brigade, which, to do away with the euphemism, meant they were building a venue for the abuse and torture of the Four Bad Categories.

By this point, the construction frenzy in the county seat and the communes had been going on for more than twenty years, during which there had been no letup in the felling of trees

THE RED WIND HOWLS

along the Machu. Added to this were the three years when thousands upon thousands of youths cut down every tree in sight to build cabins and to use as firewood, and the hills around the river were now as bald as the head of a newly ordained monk, with the only trees now remaining up on the steepest cliffs and down in the deepest ravines. When the secondary work detachment returned to the Forward Progress Production Brigade, they looked for all the world like the youths of old, their clothes in tatters and their faces covered in scratches. Seeing their paltry haul of wood, thin as arrows and bent as bows, Lozang Tsültrim was so incensed he called a struggle session on the spot, targeting all the labeled and the members of the secondary work assignment.

As far as the Four Bad Categories were concerned, they were obliged to accept it as gospel if someone pointed east and declared it was west—arguing would simply be making a rod for their own backs. This was the case even when the person was some little child, let alone a powerful figure like Lozang Tsültrim. At the meeting, however, there was a young man of spotless status and historical background, one of the secondary assignment workers, who decided to air his displeasure, his face scrunched up in dissatisfaction and coarse snorts emanating from his nostrils. "There isn't a single tree left around the Machu. What were we supposed to do exactly?" he said.

Lozang Tsültrim had been hunting with Wang Aiguo down by the Machu on several occasions in the past, and you could certainly say there had been a "forest" in those days. Why, just a year ago he had taken the People's Militia down there on a hunt and there had been plenty of trees—he had seen them with

THE RED WIND HOWLS

his own eyes! "Hm!" he retorted confidently. "You're seriously trying to tell me there isn't enough wood around the Machu to build a few buildings? Nonsense."

"Go see for yourself if you don't believe me."

"You . . .!"

At that moment a woman burst into the room, panting heavily, her face completely white, and whispered some words into Lozang Tsültrim's ear. Lozang Tsültrim gaped at her for a moment, then leaped up and ran with her back to the center of the camp.

A crowd of seven or eight people was gathered in one of the enclosures belonging to the milking unit, their faces likewise pale and aghast. In the dried-dung altar there was a color photograph of the Great Leader Mao Zedong and his dearest comrade-in-arms, Lin Biao. But what was causing all the furor was that someone had drawn a big black X over Lin Biao's face with a piece of coal.

After gawping at the scene for another moment, Lozang Tsültrim ordered the People's Militia to prevent anyone from leaving, then set off for the commune to report the incident personally.

An investigation team comprising primarily soldiers and military officers from the county and the commune was immediately dispatched to the Forward Progress Production Brigade. Needless to say, their prime suspects were members of the Four Bad Categories, the only problem being that all of them apart from Tashi Lhamo had been summoned to the struggle session as soon they had returned from the secondary work assignment. They hadn't had time to drink a cup of tea, and

THE RED WIND HOWLS

most of them hadn't even set foot in their homes before the meeting began and the incident occurred. This left Tashi Lhamo as the sole suspect, but everyone in the milking unit unanimously testified that the venerable visage of the Great Leader Mao Zedong's dearest comrade-in-arms, Lin Biao, had been unsoiled when they sought their morning instructions. Many more testified that right afterward, she had taken a herd of cattle up the hill and hadn't returned until the People's Militia called her back. Thus the plot thickened, and the investigators were forced to consider the sinister possibility that a wolf in sheep's clothing had infiltrated the ranks of the masses.

They used every method of interrogation they could think of: the "vulture spreading its wings," "roasting the meat," sleep deprivation, and several others. Some cried, some pissed themselves, but still the case was no closer to being solved. Since the prefecture- and province-level military authorities had also taken a close interest in the incident, telephoning repeatedly to receive updates, Section Head Zhao decided to pay a personal visit to the Forward Progress Production Brigade. He carried out ruthless interrogations, making no distinction between friend and foe, leading to one person committing suicide and another going insane. The poor, besmirched countenance of the most cherished comrade-in-arms of the most beloved Great Leader impelled him to redouble his efforts, but no matter how many interrogations he conducted, there was still no break in the case.

After further analysis, Section Head Zhao concluded that the incident had to be connected to some exceptionally cunning member of the Four Bad Categories. This individual must have persuaded a family member or a close confidant to do the deed while they were off on the secondary work assignment so they would be free from suspicion. The entrusted family member or the confidant must have then forgotten all about it and only remembered when they heard the detachment was on the way back, at which time they rushed off to perform the nefarious task. As a result of this hypothesis, the members of the Four Bad Categories who had been off on secondary work duty once again became the prime suspects and the primary targets of interrogation. This latest round of questioning produced only one result, namely that two of the labeled tied ninety- or hundred-pound stones to their bellies and jumped into the Tse-chu. For a time, every man, woman, and child in Tsezhung would tremble in fear when they heard the name Forward Progress Production Brigade.

During this period, the brigades were permitted by the authorities to trade their labeled, like slave owners at a slave market. Some of the brigades were especially generous and revolutionary; they donated entire labeled households to another brigade for free. There were three people from the Forward Progress Production Brigade who had committed suicide. One was a man named Tabha. There was nothing wrong with his political status or historical background, but because he liked to engage in a bit of trade on the side, he had been labeled an "opportunistic profiteer" during the One Strike, Three Antis campaign. One year before, he had been given to the Forward Progress Production Brigade free of charge. The other two were both women from once-prosperous households. Before the

THE RED WIND HOWLS

Harrowing Day, they had owned ten thousand sheep, a thousand head of cattle, and a hundred horses, but their fathers and husbands had long since been carted off to jail, and they had nothing but the hair on their heads and the nails on their toes. Deciding that there was no hope and it would be better to end it all quickly than to carry on suffering, they had offered fervent prayers to Alak Drong before taking their own lives.

One day, when the Forward Progress Production Brigade was in the midst of all this bubbling turmoil, old Lhalha, the professional bitterness speaker with a knack for putting people to sleep, showed up. This time she hadn't come to talk about the suffering of people under the evil Old Society, but about how some people had shown a staggering lack of gratitude for the joys of the New Society by painting an X over the face of the most cherished comrade-in-arms of the most beloved Great Leader. She said that if the perpetrator of this outrageous incident was a member of the proletariat then that would be a matter for grave concern indeed, for it would demonstrate that some people were forgetting their class suffering. In her opinion, however, the vandalism hadn't been carried out by a proletarian; it was undoubtedly the work of a bourgeois reactionary—someone with a label who belonged to the Four Bad Categories.

"If . . ." she stammered, barely able to contain her rage, biting her lip, shaking her head, and beating her fist on her chest, "if I find out who this shameless mutt is . . . I'll . . . I'll . . . rip open his chest with my bare hands, I'll stick my feet into his stomach, and I'll tear every last organ from his body! But even

THE RED WIND HOWLS

that won't be enough to ease my . . . my agony. *Ah ho,* who is the old bastard?" She unleashed a protracted howl, startling the assembled crowd and causing the children to cry in fear.

"Section Head Zhao, my dear," she said, grabbing Zhao's hand, "I have a favor to ask. I want you to get to the bottom of this case as soon as you can, and when you do, I want you to let me know right away."

"Of course, of course," said Section Head Zhao, nodding his head vigorously. "Don't you worry, we're on the verge of a breakthrough." Picking up her thick whip and the tattered fur coat that had been handed down for three generations, Lhalha went on her way.

Section Head Zhao, completely out of ideas, was about to pin the whole thing on Tabha on the basis that he had "committed suicide fearing punishment for his crimes," when an earthshaking event occurred that stunned the country and the world. As it turned out, Lin Biao, the most cherished comrade-in-arms of the most beloved Great Leader, was a wolf in sheep's clothing. The treacherous bastard had rebelled against the Party, the state, and the Great Leader above all. After Chairman Mao, ever razor-sharp, had exposed his plot to seize power, Lin Biao and his family turned tail and ran. He had perished while attempting to defect to the Soviet Union when his plane crashed near the town of Öndörkhaan in Outer Mongolia.

Section Head Zhao and the team he had brought to investigate the incident at the Forward Progress Production Brigade rushed back to the county seat in a fluster. When they returned a few days later, they brought with them the "Project 571 Outline," a document that provided conclusive evidence of the Lin

THE RED WIND HOWLS

Biao Clique's attempted coup d'état and the treason he had committed against the Party, the state, and the Great Leader. They organized mass propaganda and criticism sessions, gathered up every image of Lin Biao there was, painted a big X over his face, and consigned them all to the flames. The events of the last few days were quietly forgotten about.

Not long after everyone had taken the cattle out of their pens and gone to attend the criticism sessions, the professional bitterness speaker Lhalha returned to the Forward Progress Production Brigade. She had been given a skinny, hornless, worn-out old yak to ride by the collective, and from the way it stuck out its tongue and wheezed whenever she mounted it, you would think the thing wouldn't even manage to make it half a mile. And yet the old yak had huffed and puffed its way around every camp in Tsezhung. Wherever she went, the first thing she did was take off her tattered coat, the one that had been handed down for three generations and now resembled a youth's shroud, and toss it on the ground, sending a cloud of black dust into the air. She would then dismount her yak, retrieve the coat and the whip, march into the middle of the struggle session, and toss them on the ground again, sending another cloud of dust into the air.

"*Ah ho—!*" Lhalha began by issuing a long wail. She pounded her chest repeatedly, then issued another long wail. Finally, she cried out, "Lin—Biao—you—old—bastard!"

Everything fell silent for a minute or so; then Lhalha continued. "If . . . if I . . . could get my hands on that shameless mutt Lin Biao, I'd . . . I'd . . . rip open his chest with my bare hands, I'd stick my feet into his stomach, and I'd tear every last

■ 235 ■

organ from his body! But even that wouldn't be enough to ease my . . . my agony." She bit her lip and shook her head, tears forming at the corners of her eyes. According to Lhalha, in plotting to assassinate the most beloved and esteemed protector, Chairman Mao, the ultimate goal of that old mutt Lin Biao was to revive the evil Old Society. And if the evil Old Society was revived, then many proletarians like her would get their necks stepped on by a minority of heartless, avaricious exploiters like Alak Drong. It was therefore imperative that they struggle against the Four Bad Categories and their leader Lin Biao until they couldn't stand and the stink filled the air.

Lhalha's bitterness speaking galvanized the crowd and stirred their wrath. Suddenly someone raised their fist in the air and shouted, "Down with the old mutt Lin Biao!" at which everyone else raised their fists and repeated the cry. Someone else raised their fist and shouted, "Never forget class struggle!" and again the crowd responded in kind. Slogans then resounded from every direction: "Down with the counterrevolutionary Lin Biao!," "Down with the evil Old Society!," "Long live the Great Leader Chairman Mao!"

At some point, Lozang Tsültrim yelled, "Bring out the guilty, and let the struggle begin!" Lozang Gyatso, Tashi Lhamo, and other labeled members of the community had been made to stand some one hundred paces away from where the session was being held, their heads bowed. At Lozang Tsültrim's command, the children, who were clutching wooden toy rifles of varying sizes and waiting eagerly at the edge of the meeting like hunting dogs, began savagely beating their charges and driving them forward. What ensued could best be described as a footrace among the children, the adults, and the elderly, and some of the old folks collapsed the moment they made it to the meeting site.

In an instant, the labeled were beset by a flurry of slaps, punches, and spittle-flecked curses, and the masses were finally able to vent their seething rage at the traitor Lin Biao. This went on until the red wind began to whip up. It quickly became so ferocious that people couldn't open their eyes and the struggle session had to be called off, leaving the labeled groaning and rolling about on the ground, lashed by the howling wind. The professional bitterness speaker Lhalha collected her thick whip and the tattered fur coat that had been handed down for three generations and mounted her yak. As soon as they set off, the skinny, worn-out yak stuck out its tongue and began to wheeze. Who would have thought that some ten years later the professional bitterness speaker Lhalha would be wheezing just like her old yak as she prostrated to Alak Drong and circumambulated the assembly hall? The sight would repulse Lozang Gyatso.

As the red wind howled and the country launched into a campaign to "Criticize Lin Biao and Criticize Confucius," Tashi Lhamo finished off her first-year Tibetan language textbooks. She was now at the level where she could read the *Little Red Book*, and she was still going with her studies. Lozang Gyatso felt the time had arrived for her to learn about the Dharma while she learned to read. Whenever he had time, he instructed her in the fundamentals of Dharma practice. This began with an explanation of the rarity of obtaining this precious, free, and well-favored human form; how one ought to listen when the

Dharma was being preached; and the contemplation of the Eight Leisures, the Ten Endowments, and the Six Classes of Beings. Second, he explained that although we have gained this rare human form, life is still impermanent, and the impermanence of life must be considered from the perspective of the external container that is the world; of the inner contents that are sentient beings; of saintly and noble persons; of Brahma the Creator, Vishnu the Preserver, and Shiva the Destroyer; and of the uncertain conditions of death. He further explicated this with reference to visible and tangible examples including summer flowers, winter snow, the tyrannical Lin Biao and Wang Aiguo, and the thousands upon thousands of fresh-faced youths. Third, in teaching her about the defects of samsara, he exhorted her to regularly contemplate its substanceless nature and explained the respective sufferings of the six classes of beings: hell beings, hungry ghosts, animals, humans, gods, and demigods. Fourth, he talked about the consequences of failing to renounce the ten nonvirtues and the benefits of cultivating the ten virtues in body, speech, and mind. Fifth, he explained the causal factors that lay behind the attainment of liberation, the fruits of which were the attainment of enlightenment, which was a wonderful thing. Sixth, he explained how she had to carefully choose and then rely upon her lama, and that if she did this unerringly it would lead to the faster and easier attainment of enlightenment.

"There isn't anywhere we can find you a lama right now," he concluded, "but my wise teacher said the Buddha's light will soon shine again on the snowy mountains of Tibet, and many

THE RED WIND HOWLS

other bona fide saints have made similar prophecies, so I think there'll be plenty of lamas before too long. When that day comes, you can choose a lama and devote yourself to him faithfully."

Tashi Lhamo suddenly clasped her palms to her chest. "I want you to be my lama," she said, prostrating repeatedly.

"Wha—what are you talking about? What—" Lozang Gyatso was completely thrown off balance. "How can someone like me be someone's lama? Don't joke around."

"In truth, you've been my lama for a long time now. Doesn't it say in the scriptures, 'Whosoever expounds one verse of the Dharma is a virtuous teacher'?"

"Yes it does, but that doesn't mean the two of us can be teacher and student, lama and disciple. I'm not qualified to be someone's teacher, in knowledge or character. Besides, it's nearly impossible to have a lama-disciple relationship in these circumstances. Like I told you before, if you are in the presence of your lama and he is about to rise, you must get up first. If your lama goes somewhere, you must follow. You cannot walk in front and show your back to him, you cannot follow right behind and tread on his footprints, you cannot walk to his right and assume the pride of place; you may only follow slightly behind him and to the left, proceeding with all due reverence. When your lama is at rest you must call on him; you must know his preferences inside out and provide for him, anticipating his every need. You cannot sit in your lama's seat, you cannot ride your lama's mount, you cannot fling open curtains or slam doors. When in your lama's presence you must maintain a calm,

THE RED WIND HOWLS

solemn, and respectful bearing at all times: you cannot scowl, you cannot lie, you cannot speak rashly, you cannot joke around. It's as the song goes:

> When the lama rises, stay not in your seat.
> When the lama reposes, his needs you must meet.
> Where the lama goes, follow not in front, behind, or to
>   the right.
> Ride his horse or sit on his mat, your lama you do slight.
> Slamming doors, putting on airs, scowling, lying, joking,
>   babbling—such behavior must be left behind.
> Serve your lama with the composure of the three doors—
>   body, speech, and mind.

"There are strict rules for lamas too. In times like these, it would be almost impossible to follow those rules either, and failing to follow them is a great sin that will lead to bad karma. Anyway, Dharma practice isn't all about following the scriptures to the letter—the most important thing is that you have a good heart, that you have compassion. Like the saying goes, 'A good heart, a pure path; a bad heart, an evil path. The heart is everything, so make it pure.' There was once a boatman ferrying seven passengers across a river: six monks and a messenger. When they were halfway across, the boatman said they were carrying too much weight and would sink unless someone got out. 'If anyone knows how to swim, he should go,' he said; 'if not, I'll jump, and one of you can take the oars.' But no one knew how to swim, and no one knew how to row a boat either. The messenger, thinking it would be better if just he died

▪ 240 ▪

THE RED WIND HOWLS

rather than all of them, threw himself overboard. At that very moment a rainbow appeared, it rained flowers, and the messenger made it safely to the other side, even though he couldn't swim. The messenger wasn't a Dharma practitioner, but he was saved because he had a good heart.

"The same is true the other way around. There was once a beggar lounging outside the palace gates. He was thinking how great it would be if the king lost his head and he could take his place, and soon his fantasies lulled him to sleep. The next morning, while he still lay there out like a light, the king came flying out of the gates in his carriage, and one of the wheels went right over the beggar's neck and cut his head off.

"Under normal circumstances, a virtuous teacher and virtuous companions are your guides to achieving liberation and omniscience. No history, sutra, tantra, or shastra says you can attain buddhahood without a teacher and a lama. But these are no ordinary times. There's simply no way to do things by the book and take on a lama right now, and I am most certainly not fit to be anyone's teacher, so please drop the idea." Lozang Gyatso was silent for a moment, then he sighed. "My dear uncle—now *he* was a lama."

He clasped his hands to his chest in prayer and thought of Dranak Geshé Lozang Palden. Dranak Geshé used to wake him and Lozang Tsültrim up before dawn, and they would don their robes and cloaks, yawning all the while, and shuffle off to the assembly hall. At the main door, they took off their shoes before going inside, then proceeded over the bone-chilling stone slabs in bare feet. By the time they had found their mats by the dim light of the butter lamps, their feet were frozen stiff and

THE RED WIND HOWLS

their whole bodies trembled from the cold. As the lead cantor struck up the first syllables, he was joined by several hundred monks young and old in a recitation of that same text they repeated every single day, year in, year out: the *Vajrabhairava Mantra*. The three rounds of tea they were served in the course of the recitation didn't seem intended as a way to assuage their hunger and thirst, but rather as a means to ward off the cold. The warmth of it in their bellies brought on a pleasant drowsiness, but as soon as they caught sight of the disciplinarian making his way up and down the rows scrutinizing the posture and demeanor of each and every monk, tall and broad-shouldered, decked out like some kind of ancient warrior and clutching a steel-tipped cudgel, all thoughts of sleep vanished.

By the time they got out of their morning lessons the sun was high in the sky. Back at their quarters, Dranak Geshé, his nose buried in a thick volume of scripture, wouldn't even notice when they returned. Taking care not to disturb their teacher, they ate a simple breakfast, then headed over to the vacant buildings on the east side of the courtyard, where they sat in the shade and set to memorizing their scriptures: the *Vows of Refuge*, the *Hundred Deities of Tushita*, the *Guru Puja*, the *Heart Sutra*, the *Sitatapatra Practice*, the *Praises to the Twenty-One Taras*, the *King of Aspirational Prayers of Samantabhadra*, the *King of Aspirational Prayers of Maitreya*, the *Prayer for the Beginning, Middle, and End*, the *Prayer for Rebirth in the Blissful Realm*, the *Guhyasamaja Prayer*, the *Chakrasamvara Prayer*, the *Bhairava Prayer*, the *Prayer for Rebirth in Shambhala*, the *Threefold Praise*, the *Condensed Gradual Path to Enlightenment*, the *Glory of the Three Realms*, and so on and so on. Lozang Gyatso

■ 242 ■

THE RED WIND HOWLS

could memorize eight or nine pages a day, whereas Lozang Tsültrim struggled to master three or four lines. For the first six months or so, Lozang Gyatso received praise from their teacher every day, whereas Lozang Tsültrim's palm was on the receiving end of a daily caning, sometimes causing it to swell so much he couldn't hold the texts anymore.

One time, Dranak Geshé was testing them on scriptures by having them recite passages from memory. The only words Lozang Tsültrim could muster were "Ah . . . er, la—lama, er . . . um . . ." Dranak Geshé picked up his cane. "Hold out your hand," he said.

Lozang Tsültrim scrunched his eyes closed, bit his lip, and reluctantly extended a quivering hand, the palm of which was dark blue, swollen, and still leaking pus. *"Ah ho*, my goodness, my goodness!" exclaimed Dranak Geshé, tears forming at the edges of his clear, starlike eyes. Drawing Lozang Tsültrim close, he caressed his head and muttered in his ear, "Uncle won't punish you anymore from now on. You just need to learn to try harder. Oh, dear—" He shook his head slightly, and Lozang Tsültrim began to cry. Lozang Gyatso couldn't help but tear up too.

"Don't cry, don't cry," said Dranak Geshé, wiping away Lozang Tsültrim's tears. "Teachers disciplining their disciples is just the way things are done, but it never does much good. I don't believe there's much difference between people in terms of intelligence; what matters is whether you can concentrate and work hard. I won't discipline you anymore. But 'no one owns the Dharma, it belongs to whoever works harder,' as they say. It is my hope that you will focus your efforts and apply yourself, like Lozang Gyatso."

THE RED WIND HOWLS

"Yes, Rinpoché, yes, Rinpoché!" These were the words that came out of Lozang Tsültrim's mouth, but in reality he became even lazier and more careless than before. Dranak Geshé gave up on him entirely and charged him with water fetching, food preparation, and all the other menial tasks. All his hopes were placed on Lozang Gyatso, who received the greater share of any tasty morsels that were to be had—"It's hard work, all this studying," his teacher always said. By this point, Lozang Gyatso had mastered the *Ornament of Realization* and *A Guide to the Bodhisattva's Way of Life*, as well as the doctrines of the various schools and the science of logic, and he had already started to take on disciples of his own. Meanwhile, Lozang Tsültrim spent his mornings in the shade, clutching a short rectangular scripture, the corners of which were so worn down it had become almost elliptical, and the letters of which were so greasy and smudged that you'd have a hard time reading them if you didn't know the text already. It was the *Heart Sutra*, and he loudly recited select passages again and again in an effort to commit them to memory: "There is no consciousness, no eye, no ear, no nose, no tongue, no body, no mind; no form, no sound, no smell, no taste, no touch, no phenomenon; there is no eye element, no mind element, nor even mental consciousness element." Reaching this point, he would start from the top: "no eye, no ear, no nose, no tongue . . ." One day, an old man taking a break from his circumambulations sat and listened to this performance for a while. "Wouldn't it be quicker to just say 'no head'?" he wondered aloud.

When noon approached, it was time to return to the assembly hall. There was a seemingly endless stream of services to

■ 244 ■

perform, be it chants for the deceased or healing services for the sick. The patrons were required to serve food to the monks and give each of them an offering known as their "due"; Alak Drong got three of these "dues," while other lamas received two. Such donations were the primary source of income for most monks and lamas, but Dranak Geshé Lozang Palden was of the opinion that "there was no graver sin than an unaccomplished monk accepting the 'dues' of the dead." He refused such offerings himself, and he wouldn't let his nephews accept them either. Thus, while the other monks enjoyed their fill of delicious and nutritious bounties of rice, meat, butter, and sugar provided by wealthy benefactors, Lozang Gyatso and Lozang Tsültrim could only look on and lick their lips. At Losar, monks, lamas, and above all his disciples showered Dranak Geshé with New Year's gifts of *zhün* cake, steamed bread, and sweets, yet he kept a mere fraction of it for his nephews to enjoy; the rest was all donated to monks in need. Time and time again he told them both that material possessions were the most meaningless, impermanent thing in the world, and that the highest purpose of this precious human existence was to contemplate death and impermanence, to honor the laws of karma, and to dedicate oneself to the study of the sacred Dharma.

When his teacher was dispensing such wisdom, Lozang Tsültrim clasped his palms together, bowed humbly, and uttered "Yes, Rinpoché" even more often than Lozang Gyatso, creating the impression that here was a man of great faith and proper discipline. In reality, his only merit was his relative lack of greed.

Alak Drong would remark on this many years later: "For one thing, he's got no family, and for another, he isn't greedy. Could you ask for a better steward to oversee the monastery and the lama's estate?" At that time, there was an old monk drooling over the steward's position himself. "But Lozang Tsültrim used to be . . ." he began, but Alak Drong cut him off. "There's no point talking about the past. That was then, this is now."

After the noon assembly let out, Lozang Tsültrim bounded back to his quarters and fixed lunch, and only after he'd filled his belly did those visions of the other monks' delicious rice dishes fade. Since Lozang Tsültrim was released from grammar, poetry, and recitation duties in the afternoon, he was free to go play with the other monks, but seeing Lozang Gyatso tirelessly teaching his lessons and studying his scriptures cultivated the buds of envy in his mind. Sensing this, Dranak Geshé decided to alter one of his lessons. He began with a recitation: "Attachment, anger, pride; ignorance, doubt, false views—these are the Six Root Disturbances. Enmity, wrath, gloom, envy, harm; hypocrisy, sloth, unbelief, indolence; miserliness, intoxication, excitement, deceit, dishonesty; shamelessness, indecorum, distraction; carelessness, forgetfulness, inattentiveness—these are the Twenty Subdisturbances."

After briefly explaining each of these, he singled out "envy" for special attention. "Desire, hatred, ignorance, pride, and envy are considered the Five Poisons or *kleshas*. What is meant by 'envy'? It is a state of mind wherein one looks upon someone who is wealthier, prettier, smarter, more refined, more virtuous—someone who is in some way superior or who possesses what one lacks—and finds it impossible to bear. It is harmful, as it hinders us from carrying out our necessary affairs.

THE RED WIND HOWLS

"Envy is an extremely base state of mind. It does nothing to diminish the qualities of the envied and becomes an unbearable mental burden for the envier, a burden that becomes a serious obstacle to performing one's functions. Take Lozang Tsültrim, for example. Strong, handsome, and better than Lozang Gyatso at countless things: cooking, preparing offerings, cleaning. If Lozang Gyatso were to grow envious for these reasons, it would pose no harm to Lozang Tsültrim, and on the contrary would become a form of mental suffering for Lozang Gyatso that would hamper his studies. In the same way, if Lozang Tsültrim were to be envious of Lozang Gyatso's qualities—his intelligence, his diligence, his spiritual accomplishments—it wouldn't make the slightest bit of difference to Lozang Gyatso, but Lozang Tsültrim would suffer dearly, and it would seriously impede his work and study.

"The two of you are flesh and blood, and thanks to the Three Jewels, you're even disciples of the same teacher. You ought to get along together and help each other out. For example, Lozang Gyatso, you can help Lozang Tsültrim with his studies, and Lozang Tsültrim, you can help your cousin to eat well and look after himself. If you let yourselves get jealous of each other's virtues, you'll just be creating problems for yourselves, and others will ridicule you for it too.

"Most of all, envy will take you farther and farther from the path to liberation and enlightenment and will set you on the path to rebirth in the lower realms—or even hell. Envy is a demon, and you must cast it as far from you as a stone you've wiped your rear with."

At the time, Lozang Gyatso had no idea that there was a reason for Dranak Geshé's speech, but thinking back on it now, he realized just what a virtuous man his uncle really was. To describe him as a holy man, someone with the power to see into the future, would be no exaggeration. These thoughts brought him back to the present, and he sighed. "My dear uncle—now *he* was a lama," he said again.

Tashi Lhamo had to accept that under the present circumstances, it would be extremely difficult to adhere to the rules of the lama-disciple relationship. At home, for example, they had but the one worn-out sheepskin mattress, which the two of them had to share. For the time being, she had to abandon the idea of taking Lozang Gyatso as her lama.

Before too long, however, the idea resurfaced, brought on by another of Lozang Gyatso's teachings. He was explaining to Tashi Lhamo how to develop a mind set upon supreme enlightenment. "Do not hate your enemies, do not love your kin," he began. "Treat all sentient beings equally, with no partiality or prejudice—this is known as the principle of equality. In these times, people treat their parents, friends, and relatives with favor, while despising their enemies—this is the flaw of failing to exercise proper examination and consideration. Those you see as enemies were loved ones in a past life, the ones you cherished, helped, and held dear, and those you see as kin were enemies in a past life, the ones you loathed, fought, and sought to harm. In the same way, those you now consider enemies may be reborn as your sons and daughters, so you must treat them with love and affection, and your parents and relatives in this life may be reborn as enemies, those with whom you will fight tooth and nail. In fact, we needn't look to past and future lives—in this one right here, our friends in the morning might be enemies by the afternoon, and vice versa. Just look at Mao Zedong and Lin Biao. And it's not only people—the same is true of countries, just like China and the Soviet Union. If one sees the fleeting impression of friend and foe as solid truth, as something permanent, then one is accumulating the bad karma of attachment and aversion. Why would you want to burden yourself with such a millstone and drag yourself to the lower realms? Therefore, you must treat all sentient beings as though they were your parents and children; you must be like the sages of old and look upon friend and foe with absolute equality."

Rare was the person who could grasp such esoteric teachings, Tashi Lhamo realized, and rarer still the one who put them into practice. Lozang Gyatso, however, was just such a person. No matter how much people like Lozang Tsültrim had beaten and abused him, he didn't harbor an ounce of ill will toward them; in fact, he regularly prayed to the Three Jewels on their behalf. There was even that time when Rikden, his mother's murderer, was riding his horse drunk, and Lozang Gyatso got all flustered and prayed to the Three Jewels that he wouldn't fall off. Meanwhile, Tashi Lhamo had been bending over backward to help him and look after him, but he hadn't bought her so much as a scarf by way of thanks. Didn't all this go to show he had freed himself from all attachments and animosities? If he didn't count as a holy man, who did? What good karma she had, to encounter such a saint in this life and to be blessed with the elixir of his words. If she could be his disciple, she would surely reach liberation much faster. Once again, she asked Lozang Gyatso if he would be her lama, but once again he refused, insisting that he wasn't qualified, and that they were in no rush, besides. "Is it because I'm a woman?" Tashi Lhamo asked him dejectedly.

"Of course not!" Lozang Gyatso said quickly. "In the tantras it says, 'Despise not the woman, for she is the root of all vows.' And 'The yogini accomplished in secrets possesses a human body capable of supreme enlightenment. There is no difference between the lowly bodies of male and female; if she aspires to cultivate bodhicitta, then the female body is in fact superior.'"

"What's a 'yogini accomplished in secrets'?"

"That's . . . it . . . you don't need to worry about that right now. The most important thing is that there is no difference between men and women when it comes to cultivating bodhicitta—in fact women might even be better at it. Like when we were young, and there was a genuine dakini living in the Kelden Hermitage."

"So it was true then, that she was a real dakini?"

"Of course it was true! My esteemed lama told me so himself. The dakini used to be a completely ordinary woman. She was married, in fact, but then her husband got sick and passed away. At first she was drowning in an ocean of sorrow, but soon she came to understand the meaninglessness of samsaric existence. She renounced worldly affairs, went into meditative retreat, and dedicated herself wholeheartedly to the Dharma, and thus she was able to attain nirvana in this very lifetime."

"Who was her lama?"

"Oh . . . I don't know, actually."

"I heard all these amazing stories about her when I was little. One time my mom took me to see her to pay my respects and take refuge."

"My great teacher once said the time will come again when the Buddha's light will shine on the snowy mountains of Tibet, and many other venerable saints have made such prophecies. I think that joyous day might be near at hand, and when it arrives, we can do our research and find you a proper, capable lama. As a wise and saintly master once put it, 'This degenerate age is not a time to seek spiritual liberation for others but a time to persevere with one's own practice; it is not a time to act high and mighty but to lie low in humility; it is not a time to rely on one's retinue but to rely on solitude; it is not a time to cultivate disciples but to cultivate oneself; it is not a time to be beholden to literal interpretations but to consider true meanings; it is not a time to keep company but a time to keep to oneself.' The return of the Buddha's light is nigh, and until then, we must keep a low profile and contemplate the true nature of the Dharma."

"Yes . . . yes, of course."

This was the night they moved to their summer pastures. The earthen stove in the center of their eight-square-yard tent, yet to bake dry, still issued plumes of steam. Before sunrise that morning, Lozang Gyatso and his "wife" had eaten a small allotment of tsampa made with old butter, then packed up their tent and tied it tight with the guide ropes. They assembled all their belongings—a small amount of grain, worn-out clothes, a little cooking pot, a kettle, some cups—and once packed, they happily formed a bundle of equal weight to the tent, the two of which could then be loaded on either side of the old yak loaned to them by the commune. After topping it off with a sack of dried dung, they hit the road, driving the commune's cattle herd before them. Around noon they arrived at the Forward Progress Production Brigade's summer pasture: a meadow past their winter grounds and way over on the other side of Amnye Lhari, a place where not even the pikas or the youths had set foot.

First off, Lozang Gyatso and another of the labeled pitched the tent for the primary school, then dug up the turf around it to create a ditch. Tashi Lhamo had just emerged from her unit leader's tent, where she had been helping to construct a large stove. Looking around, she caught sight of Lozang Gyatso emerging from the herd and leading over the old yak with their tent and household belongings, and she ran over to greet him. By the time they had unloaded the yak, pitched the tent, fetched water, and dug up and tamped down the earth to build the stove, it was time to corral the herd, and the "couple" parted ways to go about their own business. Lozang Gyatso herded the cattle from the milking unit into their pen, after which he had to go to the center of the camp to help the stable keeper tie up the mares. Once she had helped round up the cattle from her own unit, Tashi Lhamo and the other women set about their milking duties, the fruits of which they took to the unit leader's tent.

Once all this was done and they were back home, it was already dark. They lit the stove, made tea, and ate a little tsampa, then sat on either side of the stove and quietly entered into the conversation, or rather lesson, relayed above. No matter how busy or tired they were, they almost never missed their daily lesson.

THE RED WIND HOWLS

Tashi Lhamo's thirst for knowledge was insatiable and she wanted to keep going, but Lozang Gyatso was so tired he could barely keep his eyes open, and the two of them had to get up at four o'clock the next morning. From the cattle pen came a noisy drone, like that of a beehive, as the *shak shak* of milk hitting the pail was accompanied by the sound of the women doing their recitations: "All men must die, but the significance of a man's death varies . . ." "Comrade Norman Bethune, a member of the Communist Party of Canada . . ." This was just like ten years before, when the *shak shak* of milk hitting the pail was accompanied by different chants: "Homage to you, Tara, the swift heroine; Whose eyes are like an instant flash of lightning . . ." The funny thing was that in those days, no one was forcing them to remember those things and there was no test or anything, yet everyone memorized them quite easily. Now, whether or not you had mastered the *Little Red Book* determined whether or not you should be subjected to criticism, and it determined your number of work points at the end of the year—in other words, your livelihood depended on it. For this reason everyone strove like mad to commit Mao's essays and speeches to memory, but even the "Big Three"—"Serve the People," "In Memory of Norman Bethune," and "The Old Fool Moves the Mountains"—were a nightmare for most people to recite from beginning to end. The psychological pressure of this was an even weightier burden than their physical labor.

Fortunately for them, Lozang Gyatso and Tashi Lhamo were highly intelligent people, and all it took was three or four readthroughs to get the texts more or less down. Since they didn't have to worry about this too much, Lozang Gyatso could spend his time mentally reviewing the sutras, and Tashi Lhamo could focus on all the new terminology she was learning.

By this point in time, the daughter that Künga Huamo had brought to Lozang Tsültrim's home had grown into a young woman. She had abandoned her stepfather and her blimp-headed halfwit of a brother and gone off to get married, leaving all the heavy household duties, including looking after a mentally challenged boy, entirely in Lozang Tsültrim's hands. This meant that he no longer had time to harass the "happy couple"—or at least had far less time to harass them than before—leaving Lozang Gyatso free to spend his nights instructing Tashi Lhamo and turning her mind to the Dharma with teachings from the biographies of Shakyamuni, Milarepa, and Tsongkhapa, and tales from the *Garland of Birth Stories* and the *Sutra of the Wise and the Foolish*. However, because it had been over a decade since he had last cracked open his books, Lozang Gyatso encountered all kinds of difficulties in his lessons, on top of which Tashi Lhamo was asking more and more questions. Eventually, he decided to simply have her read the scriptures herself.

"After I've finished the midday milking tomorrow, I'm going to take the herd to the rocky valley at Amnye Lhari. I want you to bring your herd and meet me there. Look carefully to see if there are other shepherds around, and if the coast is clear, slowly head in my direction. I want to show you something."

"What is it? Scriptures?" Tashi Lhamo replied, sharp as a tack.

"How did you know?"

THE RED WIND HOWLS

"Don't you remember when the People's Militia said there were religious texts and statues hidden in the caves on Amnye Lhari? They went searching everywhere and even set fire to the *labtse* shrine on the summit. When they dug up the treasure buried beneath it, they found a gun and a pile of silver coins, which they took off to the county seat."

"Three Jewels protect us! They couldn't have got their hands on them, could they?"

". . ."

"The entrance to the cave is tiny, and it's covered by thick azalea bushes. You wouldn't know it was there unless it was right in front of you. But it's been over ten years now, so who knows? Either way, we'll go take a look tomorrow."

"Were there a lot of books there?"

"Lots of them. And there were statues and *thangkas* too."

"Did you put them there?"

"No, but I added a copy of the *Sutra of Great Liberation* to the collection. There's a strange story behind that. Someone tossed it through my door the night after my mother died, but when I went outside to look, I couldn't see anyone. That night I recited the sutra for my mother, and the next day I hid it in the cave. I think that whoever was kind enough to bring me the *Sutra of Great Liberation* and whoever slaughtered our winter sheep for us, they're one and the same person. They must know that I haven't given up my vows. Such a saint—but who could it be? Whoever it is, we've got a friend in the camp looking out for us.

"I've thought about it nonstop. This person is the very definition of a bodhisattva. They slaughtered those sheep with no

■ 255 ■

qualms about accumulating bad karma for themselves, all so that someone else wouldn't go hungry and wouldn't have to break their vows. What a wonderful thing, that such a good person still exists even in these crazy upside-down times."

Tashi Lhamo's mind was still on the scriptures. "So who hid all those books?" she asked, saying nothing about the mysterious benefactor.

"I have no idea. I only found them by accident." Lozang Gyatso's mind was entirely on the mysterious stranger. "*Eh*— who could it possibly be?"

The rainfall was decreasing year after year, and the quality of the grass declined along with it. Now, at the noontime milking, the nomad women squatted under the midday sun, and hardly had they touched the udders of the yaks and *dzos* before they ran dry. The milking was over in barely an hour and the animals were set loose, leaving Lozang Gyatso free to take his herd toward Amnye Lhari. He drove them on as quickly as he could, all the while looking over his shoulder to see if Tashi Lhamo was following.

The long-suffering "couple" were finally able to meet in peace on the remote mountainside. It looked like the winter snows still hadn't receded from the peak of Amnye Lhari, which was a glittering, frosty white. A puffy white cloud was slowly drifting south across the mountainside and a smattering of waterfalls crashed over the cliffs. The shady side of the mountain was covered in dense azalea bushes dotted with pale red blossoms, while the foothills hosted tamarisks with yellow flowers and bushes of pink rhododendrons. From afar, the mountain sometimes resembled the local protector deity of legend, the one with a silver helmet and bejeweled armor. The scene brought to mind a Chinese poem: "Jade Mountain pierces the sky / White clouds roll over the mountainside / Nectar rains on the steep slopes / A paradise of meadows all around." Here, the enchanting aroma of flowers and fresh grass filled the nostrils and the chatter of birds and bugs soothed the ears. Rabbits and marmots gamboled about while musk deer and antelope pranced to and fro. This natural paradise, which had somehow escaped unscathed, allowed the two of them to temporarily forget their horrible circumstances and bask in carefree bliss.

Lozang Gyatso found himself gazing at Tashi Lhamo. She was past thirty now, but the red wind hadn't altered her fair complexion and the hunger and hardships hadn't managed to line her brow. She still seemed like an innocent, pure young woman. Lozang Gyatso's heart started pounding and he was overcome with a sudden desire to kiss her cheek or to clutch her to his chest. He didn't know if it was because of how adorable she was or because he wanted to show his gratitude to her, but either way, that was all he felt in that moment: the urge to kiss her and embrace her as tightly as he could. He stood like a statue, staring at Tashi Lhamo. Later that night, he still couldn't get the image of her out of his mind, and he lay in bed awake, praying to the Three Jewels right through till dawn.

"What a lovely place," Tashi Lhamo exclaimed, suddenly turning to face him. Lozang Gyatso was shaken out of his daydreaming, and a prayer involuntarily escaped his lips as his face turned bright red. Tashi Lhamo, whose sensitivities were highly attuned, pretended that she hadn't noticed his unusual expression. "Shouldn't we go see if we can find those books now?" she said, looking up at the position of the sun in the sky.

"Yes, of course. But, ah . . . could we wait a minute more? It's so beautiful here. The white peaks of Amnye Lhari are probably the last clean, untouched bit of land in all of Tsezhung." Lozang Gyatso gazed wistfully at the scenery, but his line of sight quickly alighted on Tashi Lhamo once more. He said another prayer to himself in his head and rose to his feet. "Let's go."

Some twenty years later, thousands of people from all corners of the land—men and women; Chinese, Tibetan, and Muslim; nomads and farmers—descended on Amnye Lhari just like the youths of old to dig for that medicinal caterpillar fungus so prized on the Chinese market. They peeled back the soil; razed and burned the azaleas, tamarisks, rhododendrons, and all other plant life; and set to work hunting down the rabbits, marmots, musk deer, and antelope.

Caterpillar fungus. Experts, scholars, geshés—none could say for sure whether or not the little things were even alive, never mind whether or not they really could prolong life and restore youth. And yet for a period of four or five years, there was a never-ending series of thefts, muggings, beatings, and murders as factions and individuals fought to get their hands on them. The white slopes of Amnye Lhari turned red, plastic trash littered the valleys, springs and streams ran dry. Before you knew it, the land had become unlivable—for humans, animals, even the birds and bugs—and all that remained was the howling red wind.

THE RED WIND HOWLS

Lozang Gyatso found the cave with no trouble at all, but when he squeezed inside, he let out a gasp. *"Ah ho*, they're gone!" They felt a cold shiver of despair. As their eyes adjusted to the gloom, however, the ever-observant Tashi Lhamo spied a pile of dirt in the corner. She went over and carefully felt the mound, discovered that it was soft to the touch, and pulled away a handful of dirt to reveal a yellowish object. The scriptures, as it turned out, had been buried under the dust blown in by that fierce red wind a decade before. As more handfuls of dirt were removed, all the texts, *thangkas*, and mandalas appeared before their eyes, miraculously protected from the damp and mold. Lozang Gyatso and Tashi Lhamo turned to each other with delirious, beaming smiles, and they each clutched their hands to their chests in prayer, overcome by a feeling of faith. They caressed the scriptures one by one, until Lozang Gyatso extracted a text wrapped in an old piece of felt and pulled aside the cover. "Look, this is the copy of the *Sutra of Great Liberation* I recited for my mother," he said.

Palms clasped reverently, Tashi Lhamo craned her neck to look. It was a poor-quality woodblock *pecha* printed on ordinary Tibetan paper, but evidently Lozang Gyatso treasured it enormously. He held it for a long time, reluctant to put it back. "Why don't we take this one home with us first?" Tashi Lhamo suggested.

"What? How could we take it home with us? We'd be done for if anyone saw it," said Lozang Gyatso as he wrapped up the scripture. "When you have time, you can come here to read the books—but with the utmost caution. You can never take them back with you."

"I wouldn't dare come in this cave all alone, never mind sit here and read by myself."

"What's there to be afraid of? Many of the saints of old achieved spiritual enlightenment in out-of-the-way places just like this."

"But how often will I get the chance to come here? There's only a month left until we leave the summer camp. I'd be lucky if I could come here ten times before then, and I'd be lucky if each visit lasted the time it takes to drink a cup of tea. Just think about it: who ever comes to the house of a labeled person? I can't think of a single one in the time we've lived together. In my opinion, the most dangerous place is in fact the safest place of all."

"Well yes, I suppose you have a point there, actually."

"Quickly then, let's pocket a book each. Which ones do you think we should take?"

"Normally I'd say it's time for you to study the *Great Treatise on the Stages of the Path to Enlightenment*. But that one's so thick, it would be tricky to carry . . ."

"Why don't we take half of it each?"

"Yes, I . . . I suppose we could do that."

The longest and rarest of rains finally came that summer. As the melodious *shak shak* of rainfall came before dawn, the nomad women covered up in felt rain protectors, and alongside their own *shak shak* of milk hitting the pail they concentrated all their efforts on reciting the *Little Red Book*. Tsezhung was in the process of becoming a desert, and the bountiful rains revived it like a dying patient receiving that vital hit of oxygen. Many of the long since dried-up streams flowed again and the grass and flowers grew at double speed. There were other consequences to the rain, however. Dense, wet dung began to pool in all the yak, sheep, and horse pens, and as soon as you set foot in one, your boot was left behind when your leg came back up. Lozang Gyatso's ragged old tent became like a sieve, and there was barely any difference between inside and out. Their small store of tsampa got so waterlogged that it basically became a ready-to-eat soup. Lozang Gyatso later dried out his drenched fur coat in the sun and it became stiff as a plank. When he put it on, he looked even more ridiculous than usual—his sleeves stuck straight out at his sides, making him look like a newly hatched chick. A more serious problem was that the damp, cold conditions caused many of the nomads to come down with rheumatism. People far from old age now found themselves with swollen, painful joints. Tashi Lhamo was one of them. From the year she turned thirty on, her hands, feet, and hips caused her constant pain, and she could always be heard groaning softly: "*Ah yo, ah yo . . .*" Sometimes, if she squatted down for too long, she couldn't get back to her feet. *If she's like this now, what'll happen when she gets old?* Lozang Gyatso thought. *She's got no children to look after her. If she ends up all alone like this . . . what a horrible fate that would be.*

It rained for days on end until they really couldn't take it anymore. Tashi Lhamo unpacked her old tent and put it over the top of Lozang Gyatso's, hoping that would keep out a bit more of the rain. But the comments this provoked came as a surprise: "*Ah lala!* Who knew the labeled had it so good? A double-decker tent! Even the herdlords of old didn't live in such luxury."

THE RED WIND HOWLS

Overhearing this comment, Lozang Tsültrim determined this was a serious issue. He convened an immediate struggle session, and after Lozang Gyatso and Tashi Lhamo had been struggled against until they couldn't stand and the stink filled the air, he had one of their two tents confiscated.

To the masses, and to the children especially, the homes of the labeled were places to be shunned like you would shun a leper colony; but at the same time, they were places full of mystery, like ancient castles where no human had set foot for a thousand years, and no one could contain their curiosity on seeing one. The children, hearts full of fear and wonder, therefore took this opportunity of the confiscation order to explore Lozang Gyatso's tent. But when they tentatively crossed the threshold of his home, all they found was a worn-out lambskin mattress, a tattered fur coat, a small pan, an old teapot, two cracked bowls, half a sack of barley, a tiny amount of butter, cheese, and tsampa, and a very sad-looking saddle. They didn't even have a picture of Mao Zedong. Feeling let down, the children were on the verge of leaving when one of them suddenly uttered a cry. "What's this?" he murmured, furtively peeling back the felt cover from an oblong object.

"What's this?" "What's this?" all the children began shouting, drawing Lozang Tsültrim into the tent. He stood for some time, staring open-mouthed at what they had discovered.

The children were even more astounded now, their wide eyes darting back and forth between the object and Lozang Tsültrim's face. Like a cop who had just discovered a bomb with the timer ticking down to zero, Lozang Tsültrim silently ushered the children back, delicately picked up the object and its felt

THE RED WIND HOWLS

cover with both hands, and ever so slowly stepped out of the tent. Beads of sweat were pouring off his head. The people outside likewise stared wide-eyed and open-mouthed, completely forgetting whatever it was they were doing.

Lozang Gyatso and Tashi Lhamo came stumbling home at just that moment, groaning in pain. When they saw the object in Lozang Tsültrim's hands, they called out in unison: "*Ah ho! The Great Treatise!*" They forgot about their pain in that instant and their groaning ceased.

Lozang Tsültrim summoned the People's Militia and ordered them to carry out on-the-spot searches of every labeled household. This strategy reaped great rewards: a bronze statue of the Buddha, a *thangka* of Tara, and three photographs of Alak Drong. When Lozang Tsültrim went to present this haul to Section Head Zhao, the army officer in charge of all Party, political, and military affairs in Tsezhung County, the latter decided to return in person to the Forward Progress Production Brigade at the head of a work team. After he'd spent one week implementing a "high tide of mass-line education," two of the labeled committed suicide and the Forward Progress Production Brigade was heralded as a "model brigade that grasps revolution and promotes production" and a "brigade in the mold of Dazhai." With each passing day, the loudspeakers and the newspapers proclaimed with ever-increasing vehemence just how red and just how prosperous the people of the Forward Progress Production Brigade were under the leadership of Lozang Tsültrim. It got to the point that the name Forward Progress Production Brigade became synonymous with the very idea of communism itself. Word came down from on high that

■ 263 ■

the authorities in Beijing were dispatching an inspection team comprising senior Party, political, and military officials from every province to see for themselves what miracles were being worked in the Forward Progress Production Brigade, Unity Commune, Qinghai Province.

The imminent arrival of this inspection team sent cadres from the county, prefecture, and province levels alike into a panic. But as that Chinese saying goes, "There are policies at the top, and remedies at the bottom." The cadres went to all the major stores in Xining and raided their warehouses, establishing a flow of luxury goods that made their way to Tsezhung County day and night. Many of these were things most of the cadres had never laid eyes on, never mind the nomads of Tsezhung: bicycles, sewing machines, milk separators, watches, radios, pots, pans, kettles, thermoses, plates, bowls, chopsticks, Mao caps, leather shoes, candy, cookies. Furthermore, fearing that the higher-ups might not buy the whole charade if it was devoid of ethnic character, the cadres also raided the provincial ethnic song and dance troupe and the academy of arts, where they acquired the gaily colored costumes used for performances of traditional Tibetan dance, garments so light they'd leave you shivering uncontrollably even in summertime in Tsezhung, and then they had every man, woman, and child of the Forward Progress Production Brigade put them on. The old belongings and old clothes were taken from every household—except those of the Four Bad Categories, of course—and hidden at the base of a mountain. Sacks and sacks of flour, rice, and grain were taken from the cadres' and urban residents' supplies at the

THE RED WIND HOWLS

county grain and oil co-op and used to stock up all those sieve-like old tents in the Forward Progress Production Brigade. Every tent was furnished with a sewing machine, a milk separator, a radio, and all the homeware and household utensils the occupants could need. Portraits of Mao Zedong were erected. Scores of yaks and sheep were slaughtered and mountains of meat were piled high. Plates were heaped with candy, cookies, liquor, and cigarettes brought from Xining, and the people swam in veritable oceans of milk and yogurt. There was enough for dogs to eat their fill, never mind the humans. A red flag was hoisted over every tent, and a bicycle was placed outside every door.

It was autumn, which meant that smatterings of snow occasionally dusted Tsezhung County. The nomads stood at the edge of the camp shivering in their dancers' costumes, arranged into two rows and holding red paper flowers to welcome the inspection team with a "really bam bing," just like they had when welcoming the youths all those years before. Fortunately, they didn't have to wait too long before the arrival of the officials, and the air was promptly filled with a hearty chorus of really bam bings.

The senior officials of the inspection team responded in Chinese with their own cries of "Learn from the Forward Progress Production Brigade!" as they cut through the colorful greeters and made their way into the camp. The officials were surrounded on all sides by camera-wielding reporters, medicine bag-toting doctors, and notebook-clutching secretaries. The pictures snapped and the stories filed by the journalists were

■ 265 ■

reprinted in local newspapers and journals across the land, leaving readers unfamiliar with the pastoral regions of the Qinghai-Tibet Plateau rubbing their eyes in astonishment.

After a whistle-stop tour of the camp in which they briefly poked their heads into each tent and took in the straw storage enclosure and the breeding station, the officials gathered at the entrance to the tent school, which had been pitched at the center of the camp, where they convened a meeting to deliver their work report and share their experiences. Section Head Zhao, clad in a brand-new military uniform, read out the work report himself. This report was unearthed some thirty years later, and it stated the following: "The average net income of nomads in the county is three hundred and twenty yuan per annum, while the average net income of nomads in the Forward Progress Production Brigade is four hundred and thirty yuan per annum." According to the *Annals of Tsezhung County*, however, the average net income for nomads in Tsezhung that year was just eighty-nine yuan.

The members of the delegation nodded their heads in deep satisfaction, then entered the sturdy military tents that had been pitched for them the day before and kitted out with beds, burning stoves, and plates of food. The nomads, shivering incessantly from the cold, were finally able to call it a day.

The news that there was to be a film shown that night at the Forward Progress Production Brigade had already spread far and wide. Men from as far as six miles away rode their yaks to come and see, wives parked on the rump and children held in their laps. Some had as many as four or five kids piled on the yak, and they spent the whole way slipping off and clambering

THE RED WIND HOWLS

back on again. When all these folks arrived before dusk, the reporters ran around in even more of a frenzy than they had earlier that day, snapping as many pictures as they could of this curious crowd of tousle-haired, dirt-encrusted, shirtless and shoeless nomads. Section Head Zhao flew into a panic and rushed off to report to Commander Gao, the officer in charge of the provincial military district.

"This is a very thorny problem." Commander Gao stroked his chin and thought for a moment. "But I have a solution."

Commander Gao's solution was to wait until the journalists had finished their busy day of work and had fallen asleep, send in a few soldiers to remove all the film from their cameras, then blame the whole thing on members of the Forward Progress Production Brigade's Four Bad Categories.

The generator came to life with a sudden splutter, sending yaks, horses, and sheep scattering in all directions. Stray mongrels ran yelping up to the hilltops, and terrified children clutched their mothers' breasts. But when the film started, an irresistible force caused everyone to gravitate toward the center of the camp.

The first feature was a war film chronicling a battle between what the people of Tsezhung traditionally called the "White and Red Chinese," or what we would otherwise call the Guomindang and the Communist Party. By this point, the nomads had taken to calling the Guomindang "the enemy," while the good guys were all "China." These were two of the many neologisms that had been brought back from the county seat by Zhang Drakpa, the man who went to the combined school in the county seat, failed to graduate, returned home,

■ 267 ■

became the teacher of the locally run primary school, and was reduced from there to the level of an ordinary shepherd—and even that role he barely managed to perform. When he was still teaching at the tent school, Zhang habitually divided the children into two groups, assigned one the role of "the enemy" (the Guomindang) and the other the role of "China" (the Communists), then set them to fighting each other. Once, one of these battles led to one of the children's eyeballs popping out. This, in addition to his total inability to teach the kids anything whatsoever, resulted in him being fired and sent out to herd animals instead. Nevertheless, the new terms he had brought back with him spread like wildfire, and there were now a number of revolutionaries who had followed his lead and added "Li" or "Hua" or "Wang" or some other Chinese surname to their Tibetan names. There was a Li Lhamo, for example, and a Hua Sönam, and a Wang Yangmo.

Zhang Drakpa had seen the film many times and pretty much knew the plot by heart, so he took it upon himself to perform the role of translator and commentator. "Look, look!" he cried, raising his voice higher and higher, "That bastard was originally China, but he's double-crossed them and gone over to the enemy, and China knows it, but they're deliberately pretending they don't so they can keep tabs on the enemy! Look look, that's a China general! At the end he sacrifices himself to save his comrade, who's another China general. Just wait and see if you don't believe me. Oh, he just said, 'We must closely watch the traitor's every move!' Oh there there, that woman's the wife of the enemy general. She's saying that if they can't win, they'd be better off fleeing now. That one, that one! That's the

THE RED WIND HOWLS

turncoat who's spying for the enemy and passing on China's intelligence. But it's fine, China's wise to it and they know every move he makes. Ah, ah, now look! China's about to blow the enemy to smithereens. There you go, the enemy stronghold is toast, and China is on the verge of victory! Look look, now the traitor is about to flee, but . . . there, the China general sacrificed himself. *Ah ho!* Look, the traitor has finally met his end. Serves the bastard right. Now look, the enemy is surrendering. China is victorious! Haha! No one can beat China! Those enemies should have given up long ago." As his commentary came to an end, so did the movie, and a floodlight as bright as the sun was suddenly switched on.

By this point the shivering people of the Forward Progress Production Brigade were almost frozen solid in their dancers' costumes, and they were fixing envious stares on the big fur coats worn by the nomads who had come from other camps. The nomads from the other camps, on the other hand, were gazing in wonder and envy at the clean, beautiful clothes worn by their counterparts from the Forward Progress Production Brigade. Some couldn't help themselves and reached out to touch them, leaving behind greasy black fingerprints.

The second film of the night was in color, which initially delighted the audience so much that they temporarily forgot about the cold. Unfortunately, the sole effect of the film itself was to put the nomads to sleep, because all the people in it seemed to do was run around insanely on their tiptoes and jump up and down in the air while incessantly screeching at one another in high-pitched yelps that were apparently supposed to be singing. Even Zhang Drakpa, who had volunteered his

THE RED WIND HOWLS

services as translator and commentator, had fallen as silent as a cuckoo in winter. Whether this was because he didn't understand the film or because the cold had rendered him incapable of speech is unknown.

Cajoling, shaking, pushing, and pulling their sleeping children, the people who had come from other camps made their way home. When the people of the Forward Progress Production Brigade got home, they all spent the whole night by the fire, right through to dawn.

At the wrap-up meeting the next day, Section Head Zhao did as Commander Gao had instructed and made an announcement: "Under the correct guidance of the Great Leader Chairman Mao, Tsezhung County—and the Forward Progress Production Brigade in particular—have made colossal strides in both political and economic terms. However, a minority of class enemies are still trying to rise from their graves. Just last night for instance, some bad elements stole all the film from the reporters' cameras. Clearly this was part of a malicious plot, and the nefarious saboteurs were hoping to prevent the great achievements of socialist construction from being broadcast to the outside world. But they have failed utterly, and their aims will never be realized! Comrade reporters, I invite you to once again document our remarkable achievements and the joyous lives of our people with your cameras, and to spread the news far and wide, at home and abroad." The journalists got out their cameras and began clicking away, and once they had all the pictures they needed, they made themselves scarce.

Three days before, Section Head Zhao had gathered everyone from the Forward Progress Production Brigade, young and

■ 270 ■

old alike, to lay his preparations in advance. He impressed upon them with the utmost seriousness that the clothes they had borrowed were to be kept spotless and that they weren't to have so much as a bite of the food. Above all, the property of the state had to be kept in mint condition. If any item was damaged in any way, it would result in serious political consequences, or at the very least, in the offender having to compensate for the damage with half of their rations at year's end. And yet, a number of incidents had still occurred: some foolish children had eaten a piece of candy or two, a few brainless young lads had smoked the odd cigarette, and a couple of senile old codgers had soiled their dance costumes. Section Head Zhao, absolutely furious, stuck his finger in Lozang Tsültrim's face and blamed him for the whole thing. It was a matter of great relief, therefore, that Section Head Zhao ended up getting a transfer before the end of the year, and naturally no one breathed a word of this when it came time to divvy up the work points.

The moment the inspection team had departed, all the grain and the odds and ends went back whence they had come. The people of the Forward Progress Production Brigade finally managed to wrangle all the animals that had run off after being startled by the sound of the generator. The labeled awaited the struggle sessions and the beatings, but strangely, there was no investigation into the matter of the missing film, and in fact no one ever mentioned it again. There was even more reason for the people to be happy: it was announced that they could keep all the beef, mutton, yogurt, and milk that had been left in their homes. For several days afterward, everyone in the Forward Progress Production Brigade had a healthy red glow in their

THE RED WIND HOWLS

cheeks, and their bodies were visibly heartier. One night, someone poked a hefty package of boiled meat under a gap in Lozang Gyatso's tent. Lozang Gyatso decided that this must once again have been that mysterious visitor, the one who had left the copy of the *Sutra of Great Liberation* and who had slaughtered their winter lambs for them. At every struggle session he paid close attention to see if there was anyone who pulled their punches, but absolutely nobody seemed to have mercy on him on those occasions. Lozang Gyatso was absolutely baffled. "*Eh*—who could it possibly be?" he sighed. "A guardian spirit, a protector of the Dharma," Tashi Lhamo whispered in response.

"Come off it. It's obviously a person, someone who has decided to help us. They know that I still haven't broken my vows."

"But who would dare help one of the labeled? And who knows that you haven't broken your vows? Who knows that we aren't a real couple? Have you ever mentioned any of this to anyone?"

"No."

"Me neither. So how could anyone know? I think this is a reward for our faith and piety. It's a Dharma protector watching over us."

"You really think so?"

"I do."

"Ha—looks like your devotion is even deeper than mine. Or as they would say, your superstition. To tell you the truth, there's no such thing as a Dharma protector like that, one that you can see and touch."

272

"What? But what about that saying, 'The karma you cultivate now bears fruit in this life'?"

"Yes, karma and the law of cause and effect are real. But you
shouldn't put so much faith in the idea of gods and demons.
There are even some high lamas who are no different from ordinary men. Not as good as ordinary men, in fact."

"What? I . . . don't scare me."

"Come on, this is nothing to be scared of. Many of the great
saints of old said as much themselves."

"Well, no matter what, I don't think there's anyone out there
who would help us, other than a Dharma protector."

Not wanting to keep arguing with her, Lozang Gyatso
returned his thoughts to the question of the mystery benefactor. He mulled it over and over, and again landed on the primary school teacher Lodrö as a likely candidate. First, Lodrö
had attended many teachings with Dranak Geshé, so many in
fact that it wouldn't be inaccurate to call him a student of his
uncle's. That would make them disciples of the same lama, and
as the saying goes, disciples of the same lama are just like children of the same parents. Second, like most other monks, Lodrö
had long since given up his vows and returned to lay life, so killing a sheep or two would be no big deal for him. Third, Lodrö
seemed like a man with a good heart, or a down-to-earth,
upright type of guy, at least. Lozang Gyatso couldn't think of
any other possibility.

Many years later, however, when everyone was once again
clutching prayer beads and chanting their mantras, Lozang
Gyatso brought this up with Lodrö, with unexpected results.

"I can never repay the great kindness you showed me, but I will never forget it as long as I live," he said to him.

Lodrö assumed he was being sarcastic. "Hmph," he shot back irritably. "Back in those days, I don't think there was a single person in the camp who didn't give you labeleds a beating at the struggle sessions."

Lozang Gyatso then told him the whole story of the *Sutra of Great Liberation* and the slaughtering of the winter lambs. "I thought it must have been you?" he said.

"Oh my, who'd have thought such a thing could happen!" said Lodrö in amazement. "But it wasn't me. I had no idea you were sticking to your vows. It never even occurred to me to help anyone like that in those days, and even if it had, I wouldn't have had the guts. So it wasn't me, I can tell you that much. If it was, there's nothing to be afraid of now, so there'd be no harm in admitting it, would there? But I had nothing to do with it, I swear on the Three Jewels."

Lozang Gyatso sighed helplessly. "Who do you think it could have been, then?"

"It's hard to say. Whoever it was, could be they're already dead."

"No, I don't think so. We only just signed the contracts to return the animals to private ownership this year. Last year, this saint, whoever they are, still came at night and slaughtered our two lambs from the communal allotment. Since then, there have only been two deaths in the camp, and one was an old man and the other a child. So whoever they are, they must still be alive."

"Well, it wasn't me. On the Three Jewels."

THE RED WIND HOWLS

This period saw an increase in people's quality of life, an increase in their freedom, and at the same time, an increase in their avarice. One day, when Lozang Gyatso went to visit the cave on Amnye Lhari, he found that the turquoise and coral inlays on the silver mandala had been pried out and stolen. When he went back again a few days later, the entire mandala was gone. Fearing that the whole collection might soon disappear, he gathered up all the scriptures, statues, and *thangkas* and donated everything to Tsezhung Monastery, which at that time was still in the process of being rebuilt. According to a wise lama who was visiting from Labrang Monastery, one of the *thangkas* and one of the bronze statues were at least five hundred years old, and it would thus be fitting to give them pride of place as Tsezhung Monastery's primary religious artifacts. Word began to get around that Tsezhung Monastery housed two priceless antiques, and in the end, two of the monastery's own monks ran off with both the *thangka* and the statue. It was said that they were bought by a wealthy trader from Lhasa and ultimately found their way into the hands of an even wealthier Hong Kong businessman, who shelled out a hundred and fifty thousand yuan for the *thangka* and two hundred thousand for the statue.

The people of the Forward Progress Production Brigade were still hacking away at the hillsides, clearing tracts of grassland so they could erect straw storage enclosures on the bare turf. One day during the lunch break, when Lozang Tsültrim switched on the Red Lantern radio that had been given to him as a reward by his superiors, they were greeted by a stream of plaintive songs. When these were finally over, a solemn,

THE RED WIND HOWLS

grief-laden voice made an announcement: at ten minutes after midnight on the ninth of April 1976, Comrade Mao Zedong, the great Marxist and great proletarian revolutionary, Chairman of the Central Committee of the Communist Party of China, Chairman of the Central Military Commission, and Honorary Chairman of the National Committee of the Chinese People's Political Consultative Conference, had passed away in Beijing.

The color drained from Lozang Tsültrim's face and his hands trembled as he quickly turned off the radio. He looked around and saw that everyone was staring at him in shock. He turned even paler than before, and as he sat there not knowing what to do or say, someone appeared on the low ridge before him—Lhalha, the professional bitterness speaker. In contrast to her usual leisurely demeanor, she was riding a brand-new black yak, lashing it with her whip and spurring it on for all she was worth. As she approached, it also became apparent that the tattered fur coat that had been handed down for three generations, the talisman that never left her side, was nowhere to be seen. She was wearing a black armband on her left arm and a white cloth flower pinned to the left side of her chest. All of a sudden, she unleashed an ear-splitting wail, then dismounted her yak and made her way into the middle of the crowd. "*Ah ho!* Class brethren! All is lost! The sun has set!"

Some of them looked up involuntarily. The sun hadn't set at all—it was shining bright and warm in the middle of the sky.

"*Ah ho!*" Lhalha began again. "All is lost! Our most esteemed and beloved Great Leader, he . . . he . . ." It was only at this point that everyone connected Lhalha's arrival with the

THE RED WIND HOWLS

announcement that had just been made on the radio. One after another, people began to wail and pound their chests. "*Ah ho!* All is lost! The sun has set!" said some. "How could Chairman Mao be dead? Impossible. I don't believe it," said others. Eventually, everyone abandoned their shovels and their lunch and returned sniveling to the camp.

Only Lhalha and Lozang Tsültrim were left at the worksite. Lozang Tsültrim switched on the radio again and once more a barrage of plaintive songs filled the air, moving him helplessly to tears. He was struck by a feeling of abject misery and utter loneliness, worse even than when his wife, Künga Huamo, had died. Slowly he got to his feet, and accompanied by those sad songs, began heading back toward the camp.

"Hey, wait up," Lhalha called from behind. "Let's go together."

Quite why was unclear, but in that moment, Lozang Tsültrim loathed Lhalha. "Bad news comes from bad people—a phrase that was made for you! I don't want to go anywhere with you." He stumbled off in a half-run, and when he got to the camp, soldiers and cadres wearing black armbands and white flowers had already arrived from the county seat. They organized the masses of the Forward Progress Production Brigade and had them take down the white tent of the People's Militia and cut it up to make mourning flowers, and they made all the men cut strips off their fur coats to make black armbands.

The nomads had experience from Künga Huamo's funeral, so they knew just what to do: they wore their hats inside out, tied their belts in the front, then donned their black armbands and white flowers. A few days later, every brigade held its own

■ 277 ■

memorial service, and a couple of representatives were chosen from each brigade to attend the larger memorial service in the county seat, just as they had done many years earlier when welcoming the youths. In the county seat, those plaintive songs blared endlessly from the loudspeakers, many people sobbed and heaved uncontrollably, and some even fainted and had to be taken to the hospital.

As one of the nomads later told it, "On this day when absolutely everybody was in mourning, Rikden couldn't contain his happiness. He was drinking nonstop and singing his heart out. He ended up losing his job as a cadre and almost got arrested." A document consulted some years later described the incident as follows: "On the day that the masses of all races in the nation joined together in their boundless grief to mourn the passing of the Great Leader Chairman Mao, Rikden, Chairman of the Unity Commune Revolutionary Committee, got drunk and sang songs. This was a clear sign of his lack of affection for the Great Leader, which constitutes a serious political problem. Rikden is habitually inebriated and lackadaisical when it comes to grasping revolution and promoting production, which makes him a very bad influence on both cadres and the masses. It is for these reasons that after discussing the matter internally, the Tsezhung County Revolutionary Committee has decided to expel Rikden from the Party and to remove him from all his posts." This document seems to indicate that Rikden would still have been left with a monthly stipend from the state that he could use to buy booze, so he shouldn't have had to crawl through people's legs and beg. The fact that he sank to that level suggests that it was indeed true that his bastard of a son was taking all the money.

Many people were genuinely grief-stricken, as though the sun really had set and would never rise again. Thinking back on it now, out of the eight hundred million mourners in the country, no doubt the most bereaved of all was Jiang Qing, wife of the Great Leader. While she was still in the process of trying to endure the anguish and "turn her grief to strength," another piece of news so shocking it was almost unbelievable reached everyone's ears: Jiang Qing, at the head of a clique known as the Gang of Four, had long been conspiring to seize control of the Party and the state from the Great Leader, but her faction had been "crushed by the Party Central Committee under the wise leadership of Hua Guofeng."

Before the traditional forty-nine days of bereavement was even up, all signs of mourning were abandoned, and the country turned instead to celebration of this mighty victory. What had been hailed for the past ten years as the "Great Proletarian Cultural Revolution" finally "came to a successful conclusion," and at the same time, everyone began to "sing the praises of Chairman Hua." As far as the Forward Progress Production Brigade was concerned, there was some even better news: Lozang Tsültrim's authority was revoked and he was removed from his post. And there was happier news still for the "man and wife" Lozang Gyatso and Tashi Lhamo: their labels were removed once and for all.

Many people now took the opportunity to hurl rocks at Lozang Tsültrim's tent, just as the children from the tent school

THE RED WIND HOWLS

used to throw rocks at the homes of the labeled as they passed by. Some people quite unsubtly shoulder checked Lozang Tsültrim as they walked past. What Lozang Tsültrim really couldn't stand was that some of the young lads came to his house dragging iron chains, whistled at his two old mutts until they got all riled up, and as soon as the dogs came close, beat them till they whimpered pitifully or fled into the safety of the tent.

Lozang Tsültrim was seething. *If I had a gun like I used to, I'd damn sure teach those little bastards a lesson, even if it meant a stretch in prison.* But he didn't have a gun anymore; he didn't even have a knife. In fact, the tent he had now was hardly any different from the ones the labeled used to live in. He could barely get his hands on a warm scrap of clothing or a hot bite to eat. He was living more or less like the youths of old. And on top of all that, he had a huge-headed halfwit son to care for.

Gazing at his simpleton of a son, the one who grinned idiotically at anyone he saw, Lozang Tsültrim felt a wave of anger directed at Wang Aiguo, whose harebrained scheme it had been in the first place for him to marry Künga Huamo. He was even more mad at Künga Huamo for having left him and the boy all alone. He stared into the face of his son with unblinking red eyes.

"Heh heh heh . . ." The idiot boy stared back at Lozang Tsültrim, laughing a loathsome, moronic laugh.

Losing his temper, Lozang Tsültrim slapped the boy viciously, sending him reeling. The boy cried for some time, and Lozang Tsültrim joined him. At the end of his tether, he went time and again to the county seat and to the commune to file complaints with the officials there, but all they did was fob him off with empty words. They did nothing to address his hunger or his cold, and they never once dispatched anyone to the camp to give the masses a talking to. More furious than ever and completely out of options, Lozang Tsültrim burst into the county civil affairs office and made an announcement. "This boy is the descendant of a revolutionary who sacrificed her life for the people! It's up to you whether you take care of him or not. If you Tsezhung County folks aren't bothered about people gossiping, then I've got no reason to be either." Having said this, he bolted out the door without giving them the chance to reply.

In the days that followed, Lozang Tsültrim spent a lot of time away from the camp, until one day he returned with another man leading two saddled-up yaks. They loaded up his tent and his few remaining belongings onto the yaks, fetched the two old mutts, and departed. The old folks of the Forward Progress Production Brigade claimed the man who had accompanied Lozang Tsültrim was a relative on his father's side, so he must have been moving over to their camp. Whatever the case, no one saw him again until several years later, when he returned in the guise of Alak Drong's right-hand man, sporting monks' robes and directing the reconstruction of Tsezhung Monastery. At that time, he held his head tall and exuded a radiant glow, and people probably wouldn't believe you if you said this was the same Lozang Tsültrim who had been living like a youth just a few years before.

"Hey—hey! Not that one, this one!" Lozang Tsültrim's rosary swung about in the air along with his gesticulations. "For the love of the lama. These builders are as dumb as beasts." In the midst of his cursing, a jeep pulled up to the entrance of

THE RED WIND HOWLS

Tsezhung Monastery, and out stepped a woman whose figure could barely be seen beneath all her silks, whose silks could barely be seen beneath all her sable furs, and whose sables could barely be seen beneath all her jewelry: it was Alak Drong's consort. Lozang Tsültrim immediately slipped the corner of his shawl off his shoulder and held it respectfully in both hands. He ushered her inside, bowing and scraping just like he used to for Wang Aiguo all those years ago.

It appeared that Alak Drong's consort was taking an even greater interest in the affairs of Tsezhung Monastery than Alak Drong himself. After listening carefully to Lozang Tsültrim's report on the monastery's recent income and expenditures, she spun around and went right back to the county seat, offering him neither a word of praise nor one of criticism.

As Alak Drong's consort sped off into the distance, Lozang Tsültrim slowly raised his head again. "*Ah ya*, for the love of the lama . . ." he muttered, returning to his work.

Compared to a few years before, the living standards of the people of Tsezhung had improved by a factor of two, and their pride, wrath, and avarice had doubled along with it. Another thing that had doubled was the intensity of the howling red wind, while one thing that had halved was the size of the rivers and streams, the bright blue Tsechu above all.

Amid this howling red wind, the people were busy implementing a privatized contract system and divvying up the livestock, arguing until they were hoarse over the coat of an old yak or the age of a ewe. It got so bad that fathers and sons were coming at each other with weapons. Lozang Gyatso and Tashi Lhamo, however, had their noses buried in their scriptures,

■ 282 ■

THE RED WIND HOWLS

completely oblivious to the quantity or quality of their livestock. In fact, Tashi Lhamo was so absorbed in her recitations and her fasting that she plain forgot about the herding and the housework, cooking included. This meant that responsibility for all their work, domestic and otherwise, fell on Lozang Gyatso's shoulders. A burden that weighed even more heavily on him was the question of how Tashi Lhamo, childless and in poor health, would manage all alone if and when he returned to the monastery.

Tashi Lhamo wasn't concerned. "You don't need to worry about all that," she said to him. "What was it that wise old master said? 'No Dharma practitioner ever died of hunger.' Once you're back at the monastery, you mustn't worry about me at all. You need to focus all your energy on your Dharma practice. It's almost winter now. You should go stay at Akhu Gendün's place, just for now; then in the spring we can sell the yaks and sheep and build you a monk's hut."

"If we sell all the animals, how will you manage?"

"What did I just say? No Dharma practitioner ever died of hunger. You don't need to worry about me. The day you've been waiting so long for is almost here. This is something to celebrate! We should thank the Three Jewels."

Though the day that Lozang Gyatso had been waiting so long for was indeed finally upon them, the fact of it had come as a surprise to him, and a single day of solitude and reflection was all it had taken to convince him that he could never be separated from Tashi Lhamo in this life.

Lozang Gyatso was driven onward by his intense desire to be with the kind and beautiful Tashi Lhamo, to lead a whole

■ 283 ■

THE RED WIND HOWLS

and normal life with her. He was returning from the county seat, gently tugging along the halfwit boy, who was staring at him and grinning idiotically. As they were passing by the outskirts of a camp there erupted a sudden chorus of barks. In the same moment, several people emerged from one of the tents, but instead of reining in the dogs, they sicced them on the unsuspecting passersby with a shout of "Go on boy, get 'em!"

The dogs raced at them, barking savagely. Two of the pack leaped, and Lozang Gyatso received a bite to his left sleeve, while the boy got one on his right calf. The dogs circled, ready to pounce again. Lozang Gyatso stuffed his hand into his coat and rummaged around, but there was nothing he could use to fend them off. When the two dogs came at them again, Lozang Gyatso threw himself off on the idiot boy, now wailing loudly, to protect him with his body. Strangely, the dogs did nothing but give him a sniff. The owners arrived on the scene at that moment and shooed the dogs away. "It doesn't look like a youth," remarked one.

Rising to his feet, Lozang Gyatso discovered he had come to no harm, bar a palm-sized piece of leather missing from his sleeve, but the halfwit boy's calf was bleeding profusely.

"What is the meaning of this? Setting dogs loose on passersby? Just look at what you've done," cried Lozang Gyatso as he tore a four-finger-wide strip off the end of his cloth belt and used it to bind the boy's wound.

"*Ah ho!* We thought you were youths!"

"How is this a way to treat anyone, youths or not?"

"There are a lot of thieves among the youths these days, so . . ."

■ 284 ■

THE RED WIND HOWLS

Lozang Gyatso didn't want to hear it. He pulled the boy to his feet, and they shuffled off on their way. He thought back to all those years ago, when his mother gave her life for that young mother and her child. Back in those days, when the nomads didn't even have enough food for themselves, let alone enough to help the youths, countless were the times his mother had brought youths in from the cold to warm themselves by the fire, heedless of the risks of denunciation and struggle sessions. Somehow even more countless were the times his mother had shed a tear and said, "These poor children. They must have a mother and a father somewhere!" He said a silent prayer, and as he did so, a sudden violent wind whipped up all around them, so fierce they couldn't open their eyes.

Scarlet blood was flowing freely down the boy's calf and the makeshift belt binding was completely soaked through. There was nothing Lozang Gyatso could do but take him back to the county seat.

There, the doctor slapped a piece of paper in Lozang Gyatso's hand before he had even looked at the boy's wound. "Pay first," he said in Chinese.

Lozang Gyatso realized he didn't have a penny on him. "Good doctor, I don't have any money with me right now, but . . ." he said, prompting the doctor to rise to his feet and issue another curt response in Chinese. "Then there's nothing I can do," he said as he sailed out the door.

"Good doctor . . ." Lozang Gyatso persisted, following him. The exasperated doctor turned to him and snapped irritably in Tibetan. "I've seen plenty of your type before—con artists." So the doctor was a Tibetan after all.

■ 285 ■

THE RED WIND HOWLS

Feeling powerless and forlorn, Lozang Gyatso turned back to the boy and saw that there had at least been a small upturn in their fortunes because his wound had stopped bleeding. Ever so gently, he raised the simple-minded child to his feet, and the two of them went back out into the fearsome red wind, heading for home.

When they arrived on the outskirts of the Forward Progress Production Brigade, Lozang Gyatso's heart began to pound and his face turned pale. The tents of the camp were like the neatly arrayed teeth in a youth's mouth, except one of the teeth had fallen out: his own tent was nowhere to be seen, only an empty plot left behind. Forgetting all about the boy's injured leg, he seized his wrist and tugged him as fast as he could over to the remains of his home. "Tashi Lhamo packed up the tent yesterday, as soon as you'd left," said his neighbor, emerging from the tent next door. "She gave it to us, along with all the things from your home, and told us to sell the lot and pass the money on to you. She even told us to do the same with all your livestock. There's eleven yaks in total, thirty sheep, and a horse as well."

"Where did she go?"

"We asked her, but she wouldn't tell us. She didn't take anything with her except some scriptures and holy images and the like. My guess is she's gone off to become a nun."

"Kind sir, could I trouble you to get this boy something to eat? I'll be right back."

"*Ah tsi!* Isn't this Lozang Tsültrim's halfwit boy? His head's even bigger than it used to be. What are you . . ."

"Kind sir, I'll be right back." Lozang Gyatso tore heedlessly through the fierce red wind, heading in the direction of the

■ 286 ■

THE RED WIND HOWLS

Kelden Hermitage. When he arrived at the cave, he discovered Tashi Lhamo, head shaved, clad in the clothing of a nun.

"What on earth are you doing?" she asked.

"What on earth are *you* doing?"

"Didn't you go to the monastery?"

"Yes, but I couldn't sleep all night. I can't be apart from you."

"This is an obstacle to the Dharma. You must pray to your lama and the Three Jewels and get back to the monastery as quick as you can."

"No. I need to marry you for real, and the two of us can live together as a real couple."

"What? But I just became a nun, and you never lapsed in your vows."

"I never lapsed with my body, but I've already lapsed with my mind."

"It's too late now, anyway. Living in the mundane world is like child's play, but striving for the sacred Dharma is a different matter entirely. You know this much better than I do, so there's no need to discuss it. You should hurry back to the monastery."

"No."

"Don't be so stubborn. There's no use. Thanks to your teachings, I understand that there's no meaning to this samsaric existence. I am fully dedicated to the way of the sacred Dharma now, and nothing will turn me away from it, not even death."

"No!" Lozang Gyatso couldn't hold back his tears. "You gave up your beautiful, priceless, once-in-a-lifetime youth because of me. You've lost everything because of me. You've suffered every

■ 287 ■

THE RED WIND HOWLS

torment and misery in the world because of me. How can I just abandon you like that?"

Tashi Lhamo let out a lengthy sigh. "You have no idea how much I wanted to lead a normal life with you, once. Every night you went out like a light, so exhausted, and I cried myself to sleep, pressed up against your cheek thinking how wonderful it would be if you were my real husband. I found solace in fantasies, wrapped myself up in the idea that it could all be for real. But it's too late now. We're both in our forties already. And it was all thanks to you that I came to realize how valuable this precious human form is, and how I should give my whole life to the Dharma. This is why I hope that you too will go back to the monastery and continue to dedicate yourself to the sacred Dharma."

"No. Even if I'm not destined to spend my life with you as a true husband, I will spend it by your side, somewhere I can serve you. Anyway, even Lozang Tsültrim is a monk now—the monastery isn't what it used to be. I have no intention of going back there."

"Don't talk rubbish. If you don't go back, how can you practice the true Dharma? Stop being so stubborn. It's because of your stubbornness that you've suffered so much."

"I want to stay by your side."

"If you want to do what's best for me, you'll leave now. I don't want anyone by my side. Least of all you."

Lozang Gyatso was momentarily stunned. By degrees, he rose to his feet and extracted from his coat the things he had bought for Tashi Lhamo at the department store. He placed

THE RED WIND HOWLS

them in front of her, then staggered outside like a drunk and vanished into that most incessant and abhorrent of spectacles, the violent red wind.

Tashi Lhamo inspected the things that Lozang Gyatso had left behind, unable to hold back the tears. After a moment, she buried her face in her nun's shawl and wailed her heart out. With the demonic howling of the red wind outside, no one would have heard her anyway.

GPSR Authorized Representative: Easy Access System Europe, Mustamäe tee 50, 10621 Tallinn, Estonia, gpsr.requests@easproject.com

www.ingramcontent.com/pod-product-compliance
Lightning Source LLC
Jackson TN
JSHW020154040425
81962JS00001B/1